PERIPHERAL PEOPLE

A YLENDRIAN EMPIRE NOVEL

REESA HERBERTH
MICHELLE MOORE

RIPTIDE
PUBLISHING

Riptide Publishing
PO Box 6652
Hillsborough, NJ 08844
www.riptidepublishing.com

Peripheral People

Cover art: Simoné, www.dreamarian.com
Editors: Rachel Haimowitz and Carrie White
Layout: L.C. Chase, lcchase.com/design.htm

ISBN: 978-1-62649-269-1

First edition
May, 2015

Also available in ebook:
ISBN: 978-1-62649-268-4

PERIPHERAL PEOPLE

A YLENDRIAN EMPIRE NOVEL

REESA HERBERTH
MICHELLE MOORE

RIPTIDE
PUBLISHING

To Disby: Master of cue balls, comics, and inspirational caffeination.

TABLE OF
CONTENTS

CHAPTER 1

Inspector Corwin Menivie surveyed the wreckage of the victim's living room with a jaundiced eye. He had his orders, but if the Imperial Enforcement Coalition was going to call in a fly-by team for the death of every imperial counselor's maiden auntie, they were going to have to run a lot more recruits through the academy.

As he glanced through the front windows, he caught sight of the newest additions to his team, and his eyes narrowed. On second thought, maybe they should raise the standards at the academy before choosing that new crop. From what he could discern, fellow investigators (and he used that term lightly) Westley Tavera and Gavin Hale were outside sniffing the rosebushes. Tavera spotted him through the window, and the bout of waving that followed was extravagant in its enthusiasm. Like almost everything Tavera had done since their first meeting, the expansive gesture set Corwin's teeth on edge. He swallowed his annoyance and turned back to the misplaced couch and overturned knickknacks. His partner, Inspector Nika Santivan, was checking upstairs for any further signs of a struggle or break-in, and team building be damned, he wished he could find an excuse to join her.

A minute later the front door opened, hitting the wall with a loud *thump*, and Agent Westley Tavera sailed into the room, followed by his Ground, Agent Gavin Hale. Tavera hovered in the wide doorway, eyes sweeping the room before they settled on Corwin. "Someone had a wild party."

Corwin took a deep breath, his eyes firmly on the wall to the left of Tavera's head. "You are aware that a woman died here tonight, aren't you?"

"Very." Tavera turned and picked up a picture from the mantel.

"That could be evidence, Tavera."

"Wearing gloves." Tavera lifted a hand and wiggled his fingers at Corwin. "It's not actually my first crime scene, you know."

"Then treat it with the respect it deserves." He was going to regret snapping, but not enough to stop him from doing it. "A life ended here. The least you could do is act like that matters, instead of skipping around the yard smelling flowers and invading the privacy of someone's home."

"Hey, back off." Gavin's folded arms and glare were clear warnings, although his voice was even. "You want to talk about respect, try not picking a fight with a colleague in the middle of the crime scene you're so worried about."

"It's fine, Gav." Tavera set the picture down and turned to face Corwin, then began ticking off points on his fingers. "First, I've got nearly as much field experience as you do. Second, we were trying to get a look at the flower beds surrounding the house to see if anyone had been near the windows. She wouldn't have stepped on her own flowers, would she? Third, I'm not invading her privacy. She's dead, in case you hadn't noticed, and I doubt there's anyone in the room more qualified to tell you that she is absolutely *not* here anymore. She has no privacy to invade, and looking at a picture of her isn't likely to cause her unrest in whatever afterlife she may or may not have believed in." Clearly wound up, he stepped closer. "And finally, I'm a *Reader*, and that means sometimes I touch things to find out what happened to their owners. No matter how much you hate us, you can't be totally ignorant of how it all works, *Inspector*."

Corwin's blood pressure spiked with each digit, and he felt damn near rooted to the ground, inches from Tavera, the tension between them a prickling sensation on both his skin and mind. It didn't break until Tavera frowned and shrugged.

"Although apparently I'm not a very *good* Reader, because I'm having a really hard time picking up anything from this room."

Corwin stepped away under the pretense of scanning the bookshelf, grateful to defuse the moment. There were a few spots of blood, but nothing like the huge pool by the window, where she'd finally died. "It looks like the struggle, such as it was, began here. Maybe the impressions will be stronger in this area?"

He had been around enough Actives to know that hand flapping and squinty eyes were an unnecessary affectation, but he'd expected nothing less from PsyAc's most infamous Reader. Tavera's questing mind glanced off Corwin's defenses, and he pushed back without hesitation.

Tavera went stiff and silent for a moment before turning in place, gaze raking over the room. Corwin turned away and began rifling through a stack of invitations and letters on the desk with more force than the task required. Light footsteps across the carpet gave ample warning before Tavera invaded even that small corner of sanity.

"I can't get anything here." Tavera said, too close by Corwin's estimation, but there wasn't a way to gracefully escape. "It's like the entire room is full of white noise, and I can't read anything from the objects in it. I need to see the body to give you anything useful."

The same tentative brush of inquiry hit his walls, and Corwin responded with sarcasm verging on outright hostility. "Well, that will surely prove to be an invaluable addition to the case file. Thank the stars you were here to offer the insight of the Imperial Psionics Academy."

"I'm sure it will be easy to slip into your report, Inspector. 'She died of blood loss. The end.' Did I piss in your porridge this morning, or did you forget to have a wank last night?" West's expression betrayed none of the venom clinging to the quiet words. Corwin, who knew full well that he looked perpetually annoyed, almost envied someone who could convey their dislike with laughter.

"Fine. We'll go to the morgue next. Try to refrain from turning the rest of my crime scene into some poor attempt at a joke." He spun on his heel and marched toward the stairs, intent on finding Nika, and any measure of calm left to him.

West glared at Gavin's hand on his elbow as they descended the stairs into the morgue. When they reached the bottom, he moved aside so Corwin and Nika could pass. Nika stopped to give them a questioning look, but Gavin offered her the quick balm of a smile, and she headed toward the coroner's office at the back of the hallway, leaving them alone.

"West, what the hell?" Gavin's voice was quiet enough not to carry, but still demanded West's attention. "Corwin already thinks you're a screwup. Why are you swanning around a crime scene like you're an actor in a third-rate vid?"

He shrugged, his eyes drifting to the office door. "Corwin hated me for what I could do before he ever met me, so I don't give a shit what he thinks about me now."

"Well, I can see how pissing him off during a case will *totally* fix that." Gavin jerked his head in the direction of the office. "Can we go do our jobs without the dramatic flair this time?"

"Anything to make you happy, oh friend of friends. Do I get to point out that you're the one who stopped for this lovely little interlude?" West sauntered into the morgue, and got maybe five steps past the door before the blast hit him. There was nothing showy about the way he missed a step and nearly tripped over his own feet. Gavin caught him, and the familiar buffer of his Ground eased the screaming in his head, providing enough of a barrier that he could take a deep breath and shield himself against the maelstrom. He walked unerringly to the morgue drawer, and pressed his hands flat against the cold steel front.

"She couldn't get away." His eyes fluttered shut, and he let himself fall into the vision. *She tried, and she ran, but it was all inside, and there was no outside, and it kept hurting her, even when she ran, it hurt her and hurt her and the sky was made of claws, and fuck—*

He dragged himself out of it, Gavin's hand on the back of his neck an anchor as he tried to hang on to the world around him in the face of the dead woman's distress. It wasn't even her, just the psychic undertow left behind in the wake of her death, but it was so strong . . .

"Come on," Gavin was saying, over and over, and the familiar repetition helped as he fell back into himself, feeling the tears on his cheeks like raw shame, even though they weren't really his at all. "Come home, come home, it's okay."

West was down, knees up to his face as he pressed into the corner, and if he hadn't spent the last twenty years dealing with moments like this, he might have been embarrassed over the worried and slightly pitying look he was getting from Nika. The vision had clearly gone on for longer than he'd been aware of, and in the meantime Corwin, Nika, and several morgue employees had gathered around, all staring at him with varying degrees of concern. Corwin hadn't even been in the room when they'd walked through the door, so the commotion must have been enough to attract everyone's attention.

"Do you need anything?" One of the morgue employees came closer, and West did his best to push up a shield before he could see too much.

"Don't," he begged, grateful when Gavin jumped in to explain.

"Agent Tavera needs a moment to get his mental barriers in place again," Gavin said. "He'll be clear in a minute, but until then, he's going to catch anything particularly strong from the people around him. You might want to give us a little while, unless you want to be accidentally Read."

West got back to his feet, using Gavin's hand as leverage, and found his smile somewhere as he brushed off his clothing. He could flake out in a minute, but he wanted an answer now, while her pain was still fresh. Trying to play down his reaction seemed silly after the floor show he'd just given everyone, but he struggled to keep his voice even nonetheless. "So, could someone fill me in on this woman? Please?"

"She's not our case." Corwin's comment seemed mild, particularly since their last conversation had ended in him stomping off. Then again, Corwin had never made any effort to hide the fact that he resented having a psy team on his precious ship, so he was probably getting a kick out of West's apparent lack of control.

"Yes, well, she *should* be." Though West didn't remember looking up at the ceiling, he tried to force his focus away from mapping the gridwork, but only managed to switch his attention to the floor. There were four tiles under Corwin's shoes, three under Nika's, and fourteen between them. Corwin was saying something else, but West got lost halfway between Corwin's blue eyes and the matching sliver of sky visible through the window just behind his head.

"Our victim is over here." Corwin's tone implied he was repeating himself, though West had been staring at his mouth and hadn't heard him.

"Give him a minute," Gavin said again, a protective arm wrapped around West's shoulders. "If it's a strong vision, he doesn't come back right away."

"It's okay." West wiped his cheeks with the heel of his hand. "I promise. Wasn't expecting that. Show me the victim we're actually here for."

Corwin nodded slowly, eyes not leaving West for several long seconds. "Why don't you take a breather? I don't think our victim is going anywhere."

West took the unexpected reprieve, centering himself in the quiet space Gavin provided, and working to filter out the other people around them. Yes, he *could* tell the two night-shift techs were sleeping together, but it was a violation of the PsyAc ethics code to mention it. Nika was focused on the case, with a side dish of appreciation for the way Gavin looked in uniform pants, and that should have been easy enough to ignore. Better to ignore, kinder, safer, all of it, but it wasn't anything he had a choice about at the moment.

He hated that everyone wanted a piece of his head, except Gavin, and apparently Corwin. His discovery that the inspector was a null had been welcome, and one of the few things that made being around the man tolerable. It was hard to put into words, but Corwin felt nothing at all like Gavin's soft cotton-wool blankness. More like a screen before a vid started, or those blue projection walls they used for the news background. Maybe that was the difference between a null who'd trained to be a Ground and one who hadn't—who just felt like a blank spot in the world to a Reader. Corwin was a solid wall of *not-there*, and when West tried to investigate, he found himself blocked by Gavin *and* Corwin.

He realized that he'd gotten lost again when Corwin raised an eyebrow, meeting his gaze head on. "I can assure you *I* didn't kill Ms. Evanston."

"Huh?" Probably not the best rejoinder, but it was the first one that came to mind.

Corwin actually cracked a small, easily disregarded smile; if West hadn't been looking, he would've missed it. Corwin made a vague gesture between them, offering another moment of reprieve in their battle of wills. "The way you were staring. I figured either I had something on my shirt, or you thought I killed her. Neither is true, by the way."

"So you say, Inspector." West managed a grin of his own, and next to him, Gavin relaxed. "I think you're functioning as another Ground at the moment. Maybe that's what happened back at the house, too. If you'll step back, I'll see what I can get."

Corwin looked chagrined, but did as he was asked, and the fuzzed-out feeling faded. "I didn't realize that I had such an effect on you, Agent Tavera. I'll be sure to keep my distance."

There was too much to choose from, too many ways to take the words, and West wasn't up to it yet. "Just while I'm working." He wondered if he'd always find himself at a disadvantage with Corwin.

The screech of the metal drawer sliding open called his attention back to the task at hand, and he watched as the body came into view feetfirst. Though her impression was clearly less volatile, he was already bracing himself. The overwhelming feeling this time was disbelief, rather than the fear and pain that had floored him, literally, moments earlier. He leaned over, elbows resting on the edge of the table as his mouth worked over soundless words, and let the Read come to him, rather than seeking it out. He could see her as she tried to reach the comm station on the table near the window, and though his feet twitched, he was able to maintain enough control of himself not to follow her movements and flail around the lab.

"She tripped over her rug and fell on the letter opener." Attention elsewhere, his voice was monotone. "Got to the window, pulled it out, like a stopper in a wine bottle, *pop*, and then blood everywhere." Maybe it was the accidental nature of Ms. Evanston's death, or the sharp contrast between her bewildered displeasure and the frantic terror of the Read he'd stumbled into before hers, but coming up for air was easier this time. He still felt spacey, but that was the nature of the beast.

He glanced briefly at Nika and Corwin, and rubbed a hand across his eyes. "It was just an accident."

Nika confirmed his impressions with a brisk nod. "That fits with the total lack of evidence that anyone else had been in the house recently. Nothing obviously stolen, no forced entry, and Gavin was telling me that the perimeter of the house was undisturbed as well."

"Then it sounds like once the coroner has finished their report, we can file this one." Corwin's eyebrows twitched, and he inclined his head. "Good work, agents, Inspector."

Nika hid her smile quickly, but her eyes sparkled nevertheless, and Gavin looked pleased as well. West didn't really need the praise, but he wasn't going to deny that it was a nice gesture, and one he hadn't expected from Corwin. "Thanks."

Corwin went to talk to the coroner about getting the final report done, and Nika pulled out her notebook to start the reports for the case. Gavin was messing around with a squishy stress toy that had been left on the corner of a lab table.

West stopped one of the morgue employees as he came back in from the smoke break he wasn't supposed to have taken. The smell alone would have alerted West, even if the guilty cry of the man's thoughts hadn't given him away.

"Can you tell me about the woman in drawer sixteen?" He tried not to get too caught up in the memory of the first puff, the delicate burn of smoke and spice made illicit by its proximity to the hospital, as he flashed a smile he knew was falling on a totally uninterested audience. The last thing he needed was a craving he refused to satisfy; he'd tried riskier things for less enticing reasons.

"Brought in yesterday morning. Someone found her in a park nearby, dead under a bench. At first we thought it was heart failure, but her heart's fine, and she's completely healthy."

"Except for being dead."

He got an owlish blink in return for his dry remark. "Well, yeah, except for that. Basic tox screens don't show anything, so we're running a more advanced one, but she's got no identification, and nobody seems to be missing her yet. She's not top priority."

He'd been in law enforcement too long to be bothered by simple statements of procedural fact anymore. Someone would try to figure out what had left her on a slab, but she was going to fall by the wayside as more pressing cases came in. West glanced at the drawer, contemplating lowering his shields enough to try the Read again. Gavin would kill him if he didn't anchor first, and it wasn't their case, but the sense-memory of her pain tugged at him. It always cost him more *not* to use his gift, and now was no exception.

He reluctantly pushed it back, headed for Gavin, and Grounded out with a brief touch. Like a junkie's fix, it was just enough to wipe it all away again. "Hey. Want to get out of here?"

Gavin stopped his subtle surveillance of Nika long enough to give him an assessing look, and then nodded. "You bet. Where are we headed?"

"I saw a grocery store a few blocks away on the ride over, and it's my night to cook. I thought maybe I'd grab something so we could celebrate another successful case."

"I demand ice cream." Not a request, but it wasn't like he'd ever say no to such a basic dietary requirement.

"Sure you don't want to ask Nika?" He was teasing, sort of, but Gavin smacked the back of his head, and West ducked away, laughing.

"Rule Number Two. And no. We're not ready for ice cream." Gavin looked serious, as though chocolate sprinkles were something he only ate after a third date.

"Whatever, dude. You'll be settled down and raising waffle cones one of these days."

Gavin shook his head, faking an expression of pity. "It's sad to me, how weird you are. I really feel for you."

"No sprinkles for *you*." West poked the tip of Gavin's nose, his tone arch. Gavin scowled, eyes crossing, and West smiled at Nika as she came up behind him. "We're going to do a grocery run, then head back to the ship so I can make dinner. Is that okay? Did you need me for anything else?"

"Just your reports." Her gaze darted down, then back up again, obviously trying very hard not to look at the way West was touching Gavin. Or maybe she was looking at the ugly pink scar that ran the length of Gavin's forearm. Out of respect for her privacy, and a healthy dose of trepidation about possible Rule Two violations, he wrapped his fingers around Gavin's wrist, keeping the pleasant blankness between his mind and hers.

"I can do mine before I start dinner." He already knew she wasn't a stickler for immediate generation of paperwork, and he had every intention of creating a meal that would hopefully serve as a bit of a bribe. If he could soften up Nika and Corwin with food, there was a chance they'd forgive him for trying to get clearance to do another Read on the woman in the morgue.

"Sure, that's fine. Corwin will probably be happy to trade a few hours of paperwork lag for food that doesn't taste like the inside of a plastic pouch."

She glanced around for her erstwhile partner, and West noticed that some of her golden-brown hair had come loose from the clip at the back of her neck. Gavin had noticed as well, if his blatant staring counted, and West hid a smirk.

Satisfied that Corwin wasn't within earshot, Nika continued. "He has kind of a sweet tooth, if you're in the market to suck up."

"I prefer to think of it as making a friend through the application of baked goods."

"What about you? What can we bribe *you* with?" Gavin's question didn't even approach subtle. If subtle had taken out an ad on the nightly news stream announcing its intention to blow up a star, it would still have been less painfully obvious than Gavin.

"Oh, I already like you. Wait to bribe me until you've pissed me off." She raised an eyebrow at Gavin, quiet humor lurking in her expression, and West could see where maybe someone could get a little hung up on the crinkles at the corners of her eyes.

"I'll keep something suitable in reserve. For West, I mean. I plan to stay in your good graces, if I can." Gavin looked way too pleased with the smile she gave them in return, and West coughed to cover his laughter.

CHAPTER 2

It just figured that along with his passion for being annoying and his relentless need to touch people, Westley Tavera had found the time to learn how to cook. Pasta and bread was simple enough fare, but it was far beyond the meager talent Corwin had for reconstituting ready-meals, and probably outstripped Nika's repertoire of things that could be made in a slow cooker.

If forced to offer his opinion, under a no-doubt-inhumane form of torture, Corwin might have admitted it was one of the best meals he'd eaten in years. Thankfully, nobody had a gun to his head, so he settled for sneaking a second helping while Nika distracted Tavera and Gavin by recounting the time she'd had to dive into a goldfish pond to apprehend a suspect. Aside from having been unsure of where to look while her wet uniform had plastered itself to her skin, he'd been rather amused by the incident, and he cracked a smile as he stabbed another chunk of tomato. There were real vegetables on his plate, grown sometime in the past few weeks, and they hadn't had every ounce of life sucked out of them and then been shoved into a bag. It was such a nice change that he kept smiling, even when he glanced up and found Tavera watching him.

"This is really good." He didn't even sound grudging about it, and for the love of all that was holy, there should have been sunglasses issued with the beaming grin he got in return for the compliment.

"There's dessert, too," Gavin said, but it was clear from Nika's so-innocent face that she'd been telling tales. Corwin could endure a little teasing at his expense for the prospect of dessert, though.

"Cookies!" Tavera's excitement would have better served a small child or a large puppy. Corwin wondered how much effort it took to be that happy all the time, but the meal was pleasant and the company tolerable, so he didn't ask.

And Nika said he didn't pick up on social cues.

The cookies turned out to be chocolate chip, a little gooey and completely perfect, and he ate three of them without shame. Then Nika handed him a fourth, and he didn't refuse, even if he did roll his eyes a little when Tavera proposed a toast.

"To yet another successful case together," he intoned, holding up his cookie to touch the rest of theirs. Corwin tried not to imagine the germs involved as he tapped the edge of his sagging dessert to theirs, and then fumbled it into his mouth as it started to crumble. A few stray bits got caught the wrong way, and he coughed as he swallowed.

"Whoa there. You can have another."

Tavera slapped him lightly between the shoulders a few times and he froze, teeth involuntarily clenching, ready to jerk away. It had taken almost a year before Nika could touch him without a similar reaction, and even now, he preferred to be the one initiating contact. She, at least, didn't feel like a rubber mallet pounding on his brain, unlike everyone else in the 'verse. As obnoxious as Tavera was, he should've felt more like a pickax. It was a disturbing revelation when the contact came over like a pleasant caffeine buzz. Too much would make him twitch, but the first frisson was actually invigorating.

Tavera must have seen Corwin tense up, because his hand fell away quickly and he dropped back into his chair. Closest to Corwin's own, because of course he couldn't sit next to Nika or Gavin. No, of course Tavera had to sit next to Corwin. Tavera, who'd spent the meal fidgeting, playing an annoying tune with toes that never stopped tap-tap-tapping. It was undoubtedly a game to Tavera, using his abilities to dig out what would irritate the most, and because Corwin couldn't be Read, he was a challenge. A shiny new toy wrapped in psychic-proof paper that Tavera couldn't wait to tear open.

Gavin watched them, picking at a cookie that didn't deserve the treatment it was getting, but saying nothing. Nika understood that Corwin didn't enjoy being touched, at least as much as she could based on his reluctant explanations, and she was giving them a look that hovered between disapproving and concerned.

The conversation limped back to life when Gavin asked Nika what kind of vids she liked.

"Gavin likes monster vids," Tavera told her.

Gavin scowled at the disclosure, at least until Nika asked about doing a marathon some night. Having seen her collection of gory, violent bloodbaths with bad special effects, Corwin suspected she'd be thrilled to have someone to watch them with. The stars knew it wasn't going to be him.

There were still cookies left, but reaching for another seemed like it would attract attention. Better to just remove himself from the situation before Tavera pinned him in his sights again. He hadn't cooked, so he figured cleaning was his job for the evening.

Tavera stopped him when he moved toward the galley. "Before you go, I wanted to talk shop for a second. I need to ask you a favor."

Corwin sat back in his chair, waiting for the punch line.

"I don't think the woman I Read by accident this afternoon died of natural causes. I want to ask for the case, but it means you'll be stuck with it too." Either Gavin was already on board with the idea or Tavera didn't think his partner's opinion was worth considering, because he was only looking between Corwin and Nika for approval.

"She's going to be written off as an unidentified death by exposure." Corwin wasn't trying to be a bastard about it, but he was stuck on the practicalities. "I'm not saying she doesn't deserve justice if she was murdered, but you know regs require physical evidence of a crime. Nothing you said could be used to provide us with that."

"That's why I need to Read her again." Tavera was watching him, and Corwin forced himself to meet the intense gaze. "But I can't do it unless the case is mine. If I ask, Ning will let me at least go back for a second Read to see if I can find something viable, but it's your caseload too, and I wanted to clear it with both of you first."

Gavin seemed subdued, but he wasn't arguing with Tavera, and Nika looked intrigued by the idea. He really didn't have anything to lose by agreeing, and probably a decent amount of goodwill to gain. "If Ning clears you, and Nika doesn't have anything against it, I'm okay with taking on the case. Or at least with you going back for a second Read. But if you can't come up with anything solid, you know you're going to have to let it go, right?"

Tavera didn't seem the type to smirk, but the hint of arrogance in his expression hit Corwin just the same, even masked by his smile. It didn't help that the sudden trill of satisfaction under his skin resonated from Tavera, rather than the enjoyment of a good meal.

"Don't worry, I'll find something."

"Of course you will." Corwin debated with himself for a second before he gave in and stood, grabbing Tavera's plate first. "I'll clean up."

He managed to sound polite, or some variant of it that allowed him to make a dignified exit. Away from the table, away from Tavera, everything faded. Thirteen years of daily lessons on the sanctity of privacy meant that even if he was going to be stuck feeling a burst of someone's misplaced self-adoration, nobody around him would ever be forced to share his thoughts on the subject. It had been a long time since he'd needed to actively push anyone out of his mental space, and he was willing to admit, at least to himself, that the effort of hiding his abilities in plain sight wasn't helping his mood. His abilities were nobody's business but his, and if maintaining his privacy meant being a little standoffish, so be it.

It also meant he was doing the dishes because he was sulking over something that nobody could have known would bother him.

There were *pots* on the counter—they owned pots?—and it was going to take him forever to get everything loaded in the scrubber. He'd barely finished stacking all the plates to scrape them off into the garbage when Tavera hopped up onto a clear spot on the counter, feet swinging back and forth.

"I'm going to contact Ning in a few minutes."

"I'm sure Chief Inspector Ning will let me know the verdict." Corwin didn't look up from the stack of dishes; he had no intention of getting drawn into another moment of self-congratulatory gloating.

Unfortunately, Tavera seemed to have other plans. He nodded, feet smacking against the cabinetry in an irritatingly irregular pattern. *Thump thump* pause. *Thump* pause *thump thump thump* pause. *Thump* pause. After about ten seconds, Corwin cringed.

"Is there something I can do for you?" He gripped the plate in his hand tighter, then forced himself to set it down. "And where did Nika go? She could at least help me clean up."

"She and Gav went to look at his vid collection. I've talked to Nika about this a little, but it might be worth mentioning to you too."

Thump pause *thump thump*. "I would never do a Read on you unless it was required for a case, or you gave me explicit permission." *Thump thump thump* pause *thump*. "It seems like that might be an issue for you."

"Did you come by that knowledge honestly, or did you Read all the people at HQ who think I hate psys?" Corwin asked, not waiting for an answer before forging on. "And let's be candid, we both know that, ethics aside, that's not really how it works. You can't help Reading people, even when you're not trying to, can you?"

"No,' Tavera said simply, with a shrug that could have meant anything. "I do my best to keep my barriers strong, but no, you're right. In the end, I pick up things from everyone around me, all the time. It's never much, but I can't stop that, no matter how much I shield." *Tap tap thump* pause. Sweet mother of stars, now he was tapping his fingers on the metal countertop, and Corwin was going to kill him. "Not that it matters with you, since I *can't* Read you."

"Not the point," he said, though actually, that was entirely the point. "You've got no right to that knowledge. No right to invade the privacy of everyone you come into contact with, whether you mean to or not. You have an unfair advantage over every single person you've ever spoken to."

Tavera leaned forward, looming even closer, and Corwin shifted into the tight corner formed by the sink and the work surface, away from the incredulous questioning. "So that's your rub? That's why you won't work with psy teams? You think we're cheating?"

"I think you're using your gifts for the good of the people around you, and I respect that." He scraped at a bit of something that was stuck to one of the plates, channeling his annoyance into cleaning. "And I think that in your off-hours, the fact that you've honed those skills and can't turn them off is an incredible violation of the trust the public places in you."

Tavera laughed, and Corwin looked over, trying to get any sense of the man behind the ridiculous clowning. For the moment, Tavera seemed honestly amused.

"You can argue this, I'm sure, but I'm not *just* a tool, Corwin. The unfortunate thing about using real, live psychics for investigations is that you can't disarm us and shove us in a gun safe at the end of the case. As convenient as that would be, my switch is jammed at 'on' until I croak or pharm out."

"Ning says you're not on burnout watch. Is that true?"

If he hadn't been staring, he would've missed the moment when Tavera's expression completely froze before it reverted back to the ever-present smile. "You don't trust Ning's judgment on my stability?"

"I asked you." Corwin looked away briefly, then back again, more discomfited by the fleeting blankness than he wanted to admit. It didn't seem like a good sign, but then, he was probably reading more into something entirely too . . . too *feely* for him to be comfortable with it.

Tavera raised an eyebrow. "Will you believe me if I say no?"

That was the real question, wasn't it?

The smile lessened somewhat, but was still there when Tavera shrugged again, hands clasped together in his lap. Corwin was more than a little impressed that he could look thoughtful while still grinning like a child with candy. "You can request my personnel files, if you're that worried." His hands flew apart, fluttering past his stomach, his legs, before curling over the edge of the counter while he rocked forward a little to watch his bouncing feet. *Thump* pause *thump* pause *thump thump thump*. "I need a break from living planetside. It's why I requested a fly-by assignment."

Corwin snorted, covering something too close to a laugh. "Most people wouldn't call being on duty for five months a break." He didn't need to add that no one had ever accused him of having a relaxing personality.

Tavera tipped his head to the side, and the light over the sink shot gold highlights through his messy brown hair. His mouth quirked, finally, into something that wasn't a smile, his full lower lip caught between his teeth for a second.

"You're right about me not being able to turn it off. No Reader can. I'm just blessed with an overabundance of my gift, and right now, I need to be in an environment where I can control who I'm Reading. The same three people, two of whom I can't even feel, cycle after cycle . . . It's kind of comforting, since I can scan an entire building if I'm not careful." He didn't appear to be bragging, although the claim was preposterous. Most Readers could pick up a few people in range, but things went fuzzy when they couldn't deal with anyone else in their heads. There was no way in hell Tavera was that strong.

Unaware of Corwin's dismissive thoughts, Tavera forged on. "The thing is, you're the best. People might not know you personally, but they know your record, they know Inspector Corwin Menivie and his partner always get the job done. Your solve rate is incredible." He reached up to thumb an eyebrow before dragging a hand through hair that already defied gravity, and now seemed intent on disproving logic.

Despite himself, Corwin was flattered, and yes, slightly more interested. "So why, with our record, would you think that Nika and I needed the help of a psy team? Wouldn't it make more sense for you to work with a less successful team, or are you expecting to coast by on our arrests?" He managed to make it sound like the joke it was, something of an accomplishment for him.

Tavera's smile softened, eyes flicking to Corwin quickly before the laughter escaped. "Damn, you found me out, Inspector. Gavin said you'd catch on to my clever plan, but I thought I'd get more than a couple weeks out of it." The dramatic sigh as he slouched back on the counter was accompanied by a hand to his forehead. "You're far too smart for me."

"You didn't answer the question," Corwin said, more amused than annoyed at this point, but not willing to let on that he'd been charmed. It felt cheap, to be taken in by the smile and easygoing personality, like everyone else. At least Tavera was gone from the edges of his mind now. It was probably making it a lot easier to forget that he wasn't interested in being friends with the man. He finished putting the dishes in the scrubber and cast a perturbed look at Tavera's swinging feet and the cabinet they were blocking access to.

"As Gavin would tell me, use your words, Inspector. It's not like I can read your mind." The admonishment lost something when he pulled his feet up and folded his legs under him on the counter. "I asked to work with you and Nika because you're by the book, and everyone knows I'm not. It's not a problem for me, but it's not helping Gavin's reputation, and he's a lot more worried about his career than I am. I can't do anything else, but Gavin does this by choice, and he'd like to retire in a better pension bracket than our partnership currently affords him."

Corwin winced at the feet on the counter, and stooped to pull the disinfectant spray out of the cupboard. He'd wipe that part down as well, once Tavera flitted off to indulge in some sort of after-dinner activity. He turned away to spritz the other surfaces, and froze when Tavera started talking again.

"I also heard that you hated psy agents, and I really, really like messing with bigots."

"I'm *not* a bigot." Harshly said, but he was tired of the word being bandied about with his name. He knew damn well that his reticence to be near psy teams had let the idea spread among his colleagues, but it felt like a sucker punch to hear it in anything but mean-spirited whispers. Apparently he was so far removed from the everyday workings of his fellow IEC officers that nobody saw the need to stick up for him when rumors started. "I don't hate psy agents."

Tavera snorted. "So it's just me, then? You've given me nothing but dirty looks and a cold shoulder since you met me, and I doubt it's all because you're jealous of my amazing hair. You undermine every contribution I try to make to our investigations with sarcasm, if not outright hostility."

It was Corwin's turn for disbelief, and he snapped a defensive answer without looking up. "Maybe I don't appreciate being made fun of by someone I don't know. Or perhaps I don't care for someone cavorting around my crime scenes and treating the work my partner and I do as an addendum to theirs. I might not be thrilled about working with a new team, but don't pretend our lack of jovial banter is all my fault. You had a preconceived notion of how I was going to react, and you pushed to get it." He smacked the rag in his hand down on the counter with a wet *splat*, and repeated himself, more vehemently this time. "I don't have to like you to prove I don't hate psys."

"True, but it would still be nice." Corwin could almost picture the easy shrug that must have accompanied Tavera's words: the exact opposite of the tense set of his own shoulders. "You'll get something out of it too, when I mention how *keen* you are." The laughter behind him was inviting, asking him to share in whatever joke Tavera found so funny. "Not to mention all the sympathy when you tell everyone you had to work with me."

That, at least, was something he could laugh at, even if it was a bark of amusement that stuck in his throat. "I've already received cards of condolence." Trying to unbend a little, he mustered up a peace offering from the depths of his withered patience. "I have a check-in with the chief inspector in half an hour. I could mention that the team was exposed to a case that we feel could fall under IEC jurisdiction."

"That would be very nice of you." Corwin waited for the punch line, eyebrows raised, but it never came. Instead, Tavera hopped down from the counter, patting him on the shoulder with the barest of touches as he walked by. "Don't worry, I'll grow on you. You're gonna *love* me."

Corwin was pretty sure he'd settle for not wanting to kill him quite as much.

"Ning, have I done something to offend you?" Corwin asked the question with some hesitance, knowing he was crossing a line and wanting to do it as carefully as possible. "Have I not been living up to your standards? Did I somehow insult your parents?"

Chief Inspector Ning'Hala'Kahiki blinked at him, the sideways slide of eyelids over purple irises a momentary distraction. Of all of Ning's aspects, Corwin was most comfortable with their neutral guise. When Ning became Ning'Hala—or worse, Ning'Kahiki—he knew they were moving beyond professionally courteous discourse. Ning's shift into a gendered being made him nervous. Trakorans tended to adopt an aspect based on the needs of those around them, and it was too much like being Read for his taste.

"Corwin, I'm sure I have no idea what you're talking about." The slight tilt of Ning's mouth was a dead giveaway.

"Tavera. I . . . *Tavera*. He's . . ."

"Tavera. Yes, so I gathered from his personnel reports, identification, and medical records. I'm afraid I'm going to need more to go on."

Corwin tried to keep a lid on his annoyance, holding his voice steady and meeting Ning's eyes. "Completely disrespectful of my position as senior inspector. Lacking the ability to treat a crime scene like a place of work, not a playground. A bad fit for this endeavor."

The ridges above Ning's eyes rose, thin lips pursing. "Can you work with him?"

Corwin drew back in his chair, swallowing a hasty retort. "Of course I can work with him. I feel his personality and talents would be better used elsewhere, however."

A weighted silence was his only answer, and he couldn't help but feel that the longer the moment stretched, the worse his eventual repudiation was going to be. Their conversations tended to be quick and concise, largely focused on the details of a case. The few times a year he was on Rogena, they might go out to lunch, remember they were friends, to a point, beyond the specifics of the job, but it wasn't something they had the time to indulge when Corwin was in the field.

Ning shook their head. "You're holding your career back, as well as Nika's, and it's time you stopped. You're a decorated veteran with years of solid work on your record, and hers is equally impressive." This time the pause was short, but rather more pointed. "You can't be unaware of the way people talk about your avoidance of psy teams. When Agent Tavera came to me, specifically requesting the chance to work with a fly-by team, you were my immediate choice. Personality conflicts aside, Corwin, he's a fantastic agent. He and Hale have a record that rivals yours, and his selfless actions have saved the lives of his fellow officers on more than one occasion. I know he has a rather effusive demeanor, and a deplorable tendency to push people who don't care for him. I'll speak to him about respecting your boundaries, and protocol. I assume that will suffice, since you're both, in theory, adult representatives of your species." Ning blinked again, set mouth conveying an unhappiness that tinted the rest of the words. "Unless there's truth to that ugly rumor about you having a problem with Actives in the field, in which case we have an issue."

Corwin's spine felt like a flagpole as he squared his shoulders. "The personal discomfort Tavera causes me shouldn't be taken as evidence that I have an inherent dislike of all PsyAc field agents. I'm sure this is an adjustment period we'll manage to survive." Corwin swallowed around a flood of things he knew better than to share, pressing a thumb to his temple, an old gesture he'd never been able to break himself of. "I'd never considered that my preference for single-team investigations might reflect poorly upon Nika."

Ning remained quiet, and Corwin shifted topics, veering away from the politicking he'd always hoped to avoid by not actually working in a field office. "You said you'd received our reports for the Evanston case. Have you had time to read them?"

The flash of *change* across Ning's normally controlled expression was unexpected, the Trakoran equivalent of a gusty sigh. Corwin had rarely been party to a moment spent with Ning'Kahiki, and suspected the darkened, heavier set to Ning's features was an inkling of how annoyed they were.

"I've skimmed the reports. Enough to give a summary to the family before another counselor's aide calls my private line and demands answers." Features blurring again, Ning tapped something out of the vid capture's line of sight. "I suppose I should be more charitable. It wasn't a complete waste of IEC resources, since it did lead you to Agent Tavera's Read on the unidentified woman."

"What's your take on that?"

Ning's sharp focus fell on him, and it was only years of strict religious instruction that kept him from squirming in his seat. "It was within the acceptable scope of his Talent, if that's your implication. Agent Tavera is granted a certain amount of amnesty because of his psionic levels."

"That actually wasn't what I meant, but now I'll admit to curiosity. What's so special about Tavera?"

Ning's amused trill took Corwin off guard. "Minimum psionic level for a field agent is a three. Most PsyAc Actives are within the five-to-seven range. Oracles top out around twenty, but I have a very hard time imagining Agent Tavera taking well to a life of seclusion and meditation. Apparently, he shares that sentiment."

Circuitous though it was, the route Ning was taking to an answer left Corwin painfully aware that he was being felt out, his reactions cataloged by his superior officer. Smiling would be too obvious a cover, and crawling away from the conversation that was making him incredibly uncomfortable would be a disaster. He settled for waiting out the meandering. "I can't see that being his preference."

"Agent Tavera last tested out at level fifteen, but his PsyAc instructors were aware that he was purposefully blowing the test to depress his scores. He was thirteen years old at the time, and has refused to be tested ever since." Faint smile in place, Ning's brow ridges twitched again, and Corwin sensed a sort of grudging admiration to the whole affair. "As you might guess, it's relatively hard to give a pop quiz to a psychic."

"I see." And he'd be living on a ship with Tavera for the next five months. Tavera, who thought Corwin was as psychically null as any assigned Ground because he spent far too much energy making sure he was locked down tight against uninvited prying. Corwin just had to keep up the ruse for half a year, two hundred imperial days of hell, because he'd be damned if he'd let an overpowered psychic menace run him out of the only home he had left.

Setting his teeth into something that he hoped resembled a smile, he waved a careless hand in Ning's direction. "Well then, I feel better about asking you for permission to pursue the lead Agent Tavera has so generously provided us."

"Indeed." Ning's mouth twitched again, and Corwin couldn't decide if he was pleased to be included in the indulgent amusement or not.

Corwin had always believed that when there was something unpleasant to be done, it was best to get to it sooner rather than later.

When he stepped onto the bridge, Nika glanced up from the console, spinning her chair around to face him. "What's wrong?"

He took a half step back from her vehemence. "Why would you think something was wrong?"

"How long have we been partners? I recognize that whole pinched 'I need to do something disagreeable' look when I see it."

"It's not pinched; it's stoic." Her disbelieving snort made him smile, a quick quirk of the lips that he knew she'd caught when she grinned.

"Right. Now that we've established that, are you going to share what that loathsome duty might be?" She sat back and crossed her arms, the picture of tolerant patience.

He stood up straight, squaring his shoulders. "It's been brought to my attention that my actions have negatively impacted your career, and I want to apologize."

"Your actions? Corwin, you've been nothing but an asset to my career." She shook her head, obviously puzzled. "Is West yanking your chain?"

"What? No. This has nothing to do with Tavera. Well, peripherally maybe, but it's not about him." Frustrated, he forced himself to stop. It had everything to do with Tavera, actually. Without him, this conversation wouldn't have been necessary. And without Tavera, he would've unknowingly continued to restrict Nika's advancement in the IEC. Really, the only thing worse than having to do something unpleasant was being forced to acknowledge that a blight on his life might be serving a useful purpose.

Nika was leaning forward, the first signs of worry creasing her forehead. "Then would you care to explain to me how anything you've done has hurt my career?"

"My reluctance to work with psy teams."

He hadn't let himself anticipate her reaction, and struggled to not flinch under her measured stare. "I assumed you had your reasons," she finally said, voice carefully neutral.

His laugh caught in his throat, trapped by a past he couldn't share. "Thank you for your trust." He held her gaze. "I don't hate them, you know. Psy agents."

"I didn't think you did. Although West seems to put a lot of effort toward encouraging that particular emotion in people." Her laugh sounded as much exasperated as amused.

He grimaced, intent on avoiding that thread. "I want you to know that I never meant to hold you back, or limit your exposure to all areas of investigation. And it won't happen again."

Nika stood and stepped into his personal space, hands on her hips. There was a lot of him; despite being wiry, he was far too tall, and he was always reminded of their height difference at the strangest times. At her imposing best, she came close to at least *appearing* taller than him.

"I feel like I should be saying, 'And see that you don't,' or something along those lines." She wrapped her arms around him, laughing a little, but not enough to make him think she was doing so at his expense. "The apology wasn't necessary, but thank you."

He pulled away as soon as he diplomatically could, and she smiled, giving his shoulder a final pat. They might tease and argue, but she knew how difficult all the normal gestures were for him, and she'd always managed to let him know she appreciated them without pointing out his complete lack of social ability.

"You're not half-bad at that," she said, so straight-faced that she might have been doing an impression of him.

"Well. I've been practicing."

Nika rolled her eyes. "You're not as hopeless as you seem to think, you know."

He didn't bother to correct her, but smiled as she turned back to her console.

The morgue attendant eyed West uneasily, and he gave her a big, toothy grin. At least he was shielded from her pangs of guilt today.

He knew Gavin wasn't enthused about getting dragged into this particular Read again, but that was one of the difficulties of his best friend being his Ground. Gavin was frequently less than thrilled with West's plans to go digging around in the heads of murderers and other criminals, but that was the job, and Gavin always gave him a safe place to return to, no matter how close to broken he was by the time he got back.

"You ready?" He didn't really need to ask, but Gav gave him that same patient little sigh, and West liked rituals in his otherwise-chaotic existence. Gav's notebook was on the table next to them, ready to record everything he said, and there was a fresh pad of paper and a pencil in case West's vision left him enough faculty to draw something relevant. Chances weren't good, if his brief encounter yesterday was any indicator.

"Anchor, shield, investigate, get out." Gavin's directions were part of the ritual as well, though one they let slide sometimes. Gavin offered him a hand, and West tangled their fingers gratefully, fixing the familiar silence as "home" in his head before he let down a layer of the mental protections that he pretended to live behind. The woman's body was cold and stiff under his other hand, but he settled his fingers at her temple, brushing her hairline.

This time he was prepared for the rush of emotion, enough that he stumbled but managed to stay upright, Gavin's hand tying him to a tenuous reality. "There was a person . . . Human. I think a man. He gave her money, told her he wanted to help her." There wasn't anything after that, as though all the violence of her death had been unmoored from her physical body. It definitely didn't grab him like yesterday's Read, and he hadn't even been looking for it then. Today her corpse offered only a fleeting impression of someone who'd stood so the light wouldn't hit their face, a dark hat pulled low on their forehead. Money, the touch of their fingers, and nothing, nothing until the final moment when her body gave up.

"Going for more." His shields were getting in the way, so he let them go, using Gavin's close proximity as his anchor to the physical world. In he went, searching for the fear and pain he'd seen the day before.

He didn't have to look far once he'd let go of the idea that her body was the source. It was an echo of what she'd felt, at best, but it was there, and he followed the trail of her fingers, briefly clasped with the stranger's, to the first moment of terrified dreamscape as she realized that something was very, very wrong.

The crunch of gravel behind them made West flinch, and she let out a tiny whimper, lost as a hand came out of the shadows and clamped down over her mouth. It didn't do much to stifle her scream as a knife was drawn across her chest, the blade slicing through her clothes and leaving a heavily bleeding trail behind. West couldn't see who it was, but he could feel the hot line of pain as he settled fully into her experience, and then the hands were letting him go, and he was running as fast as he could, without even knowing where he was.

It was catch and release, and no matter how much he ran, he always wound up in the toxic embrace that hurt him and hurt him. The knife had torn through his hip, across his shoulders, and now made a sharp, deep slash across his stomach. Weak and dizzy, he clutched his abdomen, stumbling every few steps as fear choked the breath out of his lungs. It wasn't dark, but it wasn't light, and every time he looked up, all he could see were crooked branches covered in tiny birds . . . claws that would snatch him up if he fell. When he finally did, he kept crawling, even though the darkness was behind his own eyes now, and the gravel hurt his hands, and he knew he wasn't going to escape. It was almost a relief when the stained, muddy boots appeared in front of him, and he could finally stop. He was still afraid, so very afraid, and his sister wouldn't know that he'd wanted to come home, but couldn't find the words to explain why he'd left, and then one of the boots was over his face, dripping mud and dirt into his eyes as it slammed down—

He had to get out, and he rolled, wrenching himself from her mind too quickly, and regretting it as pounding agony filled the space between his ears. Gavin, had to find Gavin, but even that didn't make the pain recede. Warm hands on his skin while he shook and tried to talk, an arm pulling him close as he struggled to figure out what was left, or what he was, or who he could have been. Gritty tile under his hands, then cloth as he tried to push away, because it was wrong, and he'd just died, hadn't he?

"West, you're home. Follow me home."

He couldn't, though, because home was under a park bench, or a place where they didn't want him, but it might have been someone he'd failed, and he couldn't tell anymore, but they were all in his head anyway, along with the fucking *spike* someone had driven there. The pain rolled through him, bringing a familiar clench to his gut, and he found words for that, at least.

"Gonna puke." He choked it out, the burn of acid rising in his throat, and held himself together as vid clips of someone else's torture cycled past his eyes. It had been someone else. He was at least sure of that much, the closer he got to the surface.

Someone put a trash can in front of him, and he was glad he hadn't eaten much for breakfast. Except that he could remember how hungry she'd been, the twist not that different from the nausea he was fighting back now. He half expected blood on his hands where they clenched the edges of the trash can, which made him wonder how long his eyes had been open. It hurt too much to move his head, and when he was sure nothing was going to happen, he shoved the can away and slumped back against the wall. Gavin pressed a glass of water against his lower lip, tipping it up slowly so he could drink, and only a little of it spilled on his shirt.

"Hold on to me," Gavin told him, and he let himself curl into the arm around his shoulders. He knew he should have been building shields again, but he was afraid of keeping any of it inside, so he pushed away everything but the warm, safe person next to him.

"She wasn't just killed," West managed. "She was tortured." He was far from ready to share, but he needed to get at least some of it out now, before he collapsed. "He gave her money, I think she still had it when she died."

"Check it for prints, gotcha." That was Gav's business voice, the one he used to fend off the rest of the world when he knew West couldn't handle it. Competent, in charge, easy—all the things West wasn't, at least at the moment.

He could feel the rush coming, worse when he tried to lift his head. At least he'd closed his eyes, because as he'd been told on many an occasion, there was nothing creepier than him sitting there staring at nothing after he'd passed out. Well, he thought he'd closed them, but everything was black anyway, and he wasn't going to argue with the darkness.

CHAPTER 3

Corwin slid a sandwich between Nika and her notebook, making sure she got a good look at it before stepping back. Once he had her attention, he set a mug of tea next to the plate, a generous dollop of honey dissolving at the bottom. Sighing, he dropped into the seat across from her at the galley table, stretching his long legs.

"Is it my birthday? This looks almost real," she teased, taking a bite of the perfectly arranged peanut-butter-and-jelly sandwich.

"I found a recipe." He kept his expression deadpan. True, it was only a sandwich, but he'd spent an inordinate amount of time analyzing the correct proportion of peanut butter to jelly. "I figured if Tavera can learn to cook, I ought to at least learn how to work the rehydration machine properly."

"Whoa there, Corwin, keep your feet on the ground." She pushed her notebook away, flexing to ease whatever stiffness she'd developed after sitting there for hours. "Thanks. Didn't know I was so hungry."

"You looked busy." Raising his eyebrows, he reached for her notebook, and she waved her free hand at it, giving him permission to pull up her work.

"I thought maybe I could find another case like West's woman in the morgue. It can't be that common, someone dropping dead for no reason at all. The fact that she was homeless seemed like it could be calculated, like the killer chose her because nobody would look too closely." She took another swallow of tea, curling both her hands around the mug. "Gavin couldn't tell me much about the rest of the vision, just the money, but West says she was tortured. In her head. How am I supposed to track down something there's no physical evidence for?"

He snorted at the mention of Tavera's name, but it was more of a reflex. "You do what you've been doing. The hard part. I don't know if we can really narrow it down to indigent victims, but it's a starting point, if nothing else." He reached for the chips again. "Far be it from me to educate you on the finer points of law enforcement technology, but you do know that we have search processes for this kind of thing, right? You don't have to go through each file by yourself."

Nika took another bite, and he found himself watching her closely for a reaction. She laughed when he didn't look away quickly enough. "It's fine, really. I'm savoring every bite."

"I wasn't worried."

"Of course not." She wiped her fingers on the napkin before leaning back toward the notebook and pulling up another file. "So anyway, I started looking back at cases I've worked, cases where things didn't quite add up, but I went with what I had. I keep wondering how much I've missed over the years that someone like West could have caught and understood." She rubbed at her forehead, frowning. "I've never seen a case like this before. If we hadn't walked through the door with a psy team, that woman would have been written off as a freak heart attack and nobody would have thought twice about it."

He opened his mouth to snap something unpleasant and probably unfair, and then caught himself. It was better to take a minute to find the right way to say something, or if not a right way, at least a diplomatic one. Unfortunately, waiting wasn't one of his strong suits. "You could also consider that if she hadn't met someone like Tavera, she might still be alive."

"I just feel like there are so many pieces I should have found, and it's a little daunting." She sighed and powered off the notebook, pushing it aside in favor of her sandwich. "We haven't really had the chance to catch up since we got back from leave. What *did* you do with your time off? Please don't tell me you sat around in some beige IEC barracks waiting to go on our next fiver." Mild curiosity colored her words, and Corwin instantly regretted ever having opened the jar of peanut butter.

That was the problem with friendly gestures; people assumed he was offering more than a sandwich. Years of conditioning made outside interest in his life uncomfortable, and his eyes drifted back to her, wary. "I went to a gun show. My mother died. I bought some new pants." He got up, plate in hand. "Do you think there are any of those cookies left?"

"In the plastic bowl on the counter." It didn't take any sort of Talent to see the forced nonchalance in her response. When she got up, she was careful to maintain his admittedly large personal bubble as she dropped her plate into the scrubber. "And I'm sorry."

"About the pants? Me too. They looked awful. I had to return them.' It was a poor deflection at best, and he covered by offering her the bowl of cookies first. "She was old, and sick, and we hadn't spoken in years." He broke a cookie in half, and polished off the first part in one bite while glaring at a particularly offensive spot on the floor. "The pants were really bad, though. Khaki. Pleated. I looked like my grandfather."

"Well, you already look like *my* grandfather most of the time." Nika's teasing smile turned to a mock glare when he moved the cookies farther from her.

"I'll assume he was off-puttingly handsome, then." He closed his eyes as he leaned back against the cabinets, desperately wishing for some way to make a graceful exit.

"He was an inspector. Used to tell me stories about his job when I was little, and he taught me how to shoot."

"So handsome *and* talented."

Her burst of laughter startled him, and when he opened his eyes to stare at her, affronted, she laughed harder. "I'm sorry," she finally managed. "You just still catch me by surprise sometimes."

"So your grandfather inspired you to join the force?" It felt rude to be asking such personal questions, but he wasn't so much of a social misfit that he didn't realize it was what people (normal people, anyway) did.

"He helped my mom raise me. She was big on the whole communal, multigenerational family thing." Nika grinned, raking her hands through her hair. "I learned how to write a report before I learned how to tie my shoes."

"I'm shocked at the use of child labor by a respected member of the Imperial Enforcement Coalition." A faint smile tugged at the corners of his mouth, and he realized he'd become comfortable enough around Nika not to hide it.

Nika swept some crumbs off the counter. "Did your parents want you to join the IEC?"

That was at least three steps past his imaginary line in the sand, though, and he stiffened. "No, I don't think they did." He turned his back on her to get a glass. She undoubtedly meant for him to hear her sigh; he took his cue and made the effort to move on. "What about you? Did you do anything exciting while we were off?"

"I went to Caribe for a week so I could renew my diving certification." Her expression took on a sly cant when he spun around, her eyebrows rising. "Did a little beach reading."

Corwin shook his finger at her. "Oh, no. The deal was that I'd give you enough clues to figure out my pen name, and you wouldn't ever mention it once you did."

Her attempt to look innocent was halfhearted at best. "They were good, Corwin." She smiled as she put the lid back on the cookie container. "So are we closed out on the Evanston case?" Nika's sudden interest in work had to be for his benefit, and he was happy to follow her lead.

He nodded as he filled his glass with water. "Coroner's scans seem to back up what Tavera saw, so I filed the official findings this afternoon. There was no evidence that indicated anyone else had been in that room recently."

"Try not to sound so annoyed by that."

He didn't reply, but winced when voices drifted up from the gangway, and the familiar minor noises of the *Vigilance* were overshadowed by Gavin and Tavera's return to the ship.

"No. I absolutely refuse to argue the relative health merits of giving up caffeine and sugar. Sure, it might add years to my life, but they won't be years worth living."

"I'm just saying that you might sleep better if you cut back some." Gavin sounded infinitely patient. He'd need the patience of a saint to survive Tavera's migraine-inducing exuberance. Half a tenday since their first assignment, and Corwin already felt like he could cheerfully strangle the man. The fact that Gavin hadn't spoke volumes for his strength of character.

"I sleep just fine," Tavera said as they entered the galley. "It's not my fault that other people have tasty, tasty brains when I'm unconscious and vulnerable." Only supreme force of will kept Corwin from flinching away as Tavera reached out to pat his shoulder on the way by. "Don't worry, your brains are safe."

Nika laughed. "I think your brain has just been insulted. Although I feel I should point out that *I* find it quite adequate."

"I've always so hoped to have my mental prowess described in such glowing terms. Thank you, Inspector Santivan, for fulfilling my lifelong dream."

Tavera, bent over and pawing through the chiller, snickered loudly.

Nika waited until he stood before getting back to business. "Are you up for discussing what you found?"

He nodded, a piece of fruit in one hand and a canned drink in the other. Corwin tried not to stare, but it was difficult; Tavera looked drawn under the stubble and beach tan, and Corwin suspected that the way Gavin hovered within arm's reach had very little to do with an inability to keep their hands off each other in public. He was surprised and unwillingly impressed when Tavera agreed and they all went to sit at the table.

Corwin stood and edged around Gavin to the relative safety of the doorway, neatly avoiding Tavera. Nika could handle taking notes. He was a little frayed around the edges after his conversation with her, and some distance would be welcome.

The more distance between him and Tavera, the better.

West watched Corwin sidle toward the door, and propped his elbows on the table so that he could lean forward and catch Corwin's eye. "There's plenty of room, Inspector." He patted the seat next to him. "Sit right here." It was probably a mark of his oft-lamented immaturity that the dismayed expression on Corwin's face made him want to giggle.

"No, thank you, I'm fine right here." If anything, Corwin moved a little further out of the small galley.

Gavin stared at West pointedly until he shrugged, feigning innocence. He knew Gavin wouldn't fall for it, and he suspected Nika was onto him as well, so he gave up tweaking Corwin in favor of work. "Have they gotten anything off the money?"

"Not much. It's actual hard credit, not a bank card, so it's not tied to anything we can trace. There were fingerprints, but nothing that popped up a match in the system."

West didn't bother trying to hide his disappointment, fatigue returning as he nodded. "I was afraid of that. He seems too smart to make that kind of a mistake." He closed his eyes and scrubbed a hand across his face. "Whoever he is, he knows how to cover his tracks."

"You're sure it's a man?" Corwin was suddenly back in the conversation, dropping two plates on the table and shoving them at West and Gavin.

Surprised and grateful, West tore into the sandwich, mouth still half-full when he started talking again. "No, not sure, but the overwhelming feeling I had was that the victim thought her attacker was male." He shuddered, the memory of fear oddly incongruous with something as mundane as a peanut butter and jelly sandwich. "Our victim was indigent, and spent most of her nights in a park. She had a sister, so once we find an ID, I need to contact her."

"I can do that," Nika told him. "Now that it's a suspected murder investigation, they'll run her info through the system. We should have a name in a couple of hours."

"I could do it," Corwin said, turning from the scrubber with a knife still in hand.

"I'd like to be there too." Honestly, there were few places he'd less like to be, but West fought down that impulse. He could do that much for a woman whose life had ended so horribly. "She was thinking about her sister when she died. A family member deserves to know that."

Gavin continued sorting through their notes. "I know a crime scene team has already done a sweep where she was found, but West wants to do a Read there." He looked across the galley, as if daring Corwin to disagree. "It's possible her attacker will have left an impression at the scene—something that might lead us to an ID. Right now, we know there were seven instances of direct contact between attacker and victim in Agent Tavera's vision, each one violent. He's unsure of an approximate timeline because there were no indications of how much time had passed within the Read."

"Might have been a couple days," West muttered, burying his face in the crook of his arm. Gav started rubbing his head, fingers digging into his scalp in a way that melted some of the tension away. He sat up a few seconds later, an embarrassed flush rising under his skin as he batted away Gavin's hand. "I'll live, dude." He shook his head, trying to focus on his memories of the Read. "I can't give you much more than a solid guess on timing. It's just how the Read felt."

"Feelings aren't admissible in a trial, Tavera."

West bristled. "I'm well aware of that, Inspector. The only reason I'm mentioning it at all is that I'm pretty sure it will tie into the killer's methodology at some point. It wasn't something he did to her on a whim. He spread it out, kept coming back to her, and he savored it every time."

"Just pointing out procedure." Corwin was too reserved to pull off an innocent look, and it was obvious that he knew he'd been caught when he refused to meet West's eyes. "So you want to go back to the site where the body was discovered. Should I arrange for a transport to pick us up here tomorrow morning?"

As conciliatory gestures went, it wasn't much, and West rolled his eyes a little before mustering up a faint smile. "Can you make it more like afternoon? I need my beauty sleep before enjoying the scenic wonder of the Ethris municipal park system."

"We can't spare a whole week, West." Gavin *could* do innocent, fairly well in fact, and didn't bother to look repentant when West gasped in mock hurt.

"You wound me. In great and terrible ways." He climbed to his feet, picking up his plate on the way to the scrubber. "Thanks for dinner." He waggled his fingers, hiding a grin as Corwin made an impatient noise and stalked out of the room.

Gavin frowned. "I thought you were going to play nice with Inspector Menivie."

West couldn't find joy in playing up the wounded act when there was some small truth to it. "I just thanked him for the sandwich, that was it, honest. I thought about mentioning how striking his ass looks in his uniform pants, but I held off through sheer strength of will."

Nika started, and he met her suspicious expression with a guileless smile. "I'm sure he's planning on parking himself at the Nerve, researching cold cases until he falls asleep over the console." She yawned and stretched. "I, however, am not going to work till I drop. Could I interest you in a showing of something fantastically awful?"

The question was obviously aimed at Gavin, but that didn't stop West from sitting up. "Sure, what else do I have to do? Besides, if I have nightmares, I'm sure Gav will be willing to offer comfort."

Gavin deliberately turned his back on West. "I'm all over that." He slid his notebook into a case and pushed his chair in, voice conveying a level of interest that had nothing to do with shitty horror movies. "How awful are we talking? *Day of the Dog People* awful, or something more like *The Clot*?"

"I've got both. *Dog People* first, and we'll see where the evening takes us?"

"You're on."

There was no way to miss Nika's grin, short of being blind. West managed to stifle his laughter, and gave himself full marks for his decision not to sit between them on the couch.

It turned out that Nika had a pretty amazing collection of vids, just none West had any interest in watching. Horror had never been his cup of tea, not when he spent so much time trying to get it out of his head. Gav, however, jumped enthusiastically in, jotting down a list while Nika slipped off to her room to change out of her duty uniform. When she returned in pajamas printed all over with ducks drinking coffee, West stared in openmouthed jealousy.

"Those should be mine. Really."

She laughed self-consciously, and it didn't take much to pick up on her fear that Gavin would think they were too childish. She didn't seem particularly worried about West's opinion, though.

Gavin gave her a thumbs-up. "Those are the epitome of everything pajamas should be."

West stared very hard at the industrial gray upholstery of the couch, counting threads as he tried to ignore Nika's thoughts.

They settled in to watch the movie, and West endured an hour or so of the bloodcurdling screams and slobbery growling that comprised most of the dialogue, before he couldn't take it anymore. "Really? Man-eating dogs?" He groaned loudly, dropping his head against the back of his chair with a solid *thump*.

"You can go find something else to do."

It wasn't one of Gav's more subtle hints, and West shrugged, sinking lower in the chair. "Nah, it's better than nothing." He closed his eyes as the howling increased in volume.

"This is even worse than I remembered," Gavin murmured in admiration.

West looked back at the screen, trying to ignore Gavin's cheerful relish as one of the snarling dog-people was distracted from her murderous rampage by an open box of dog biscuits.

Nika groaned and buried her face in her hands, laughing. "So much worse. I forgot all about this scene."

"The fire hydrant thing from the deleted footage is worse."

"I still can't figure out why they'd bother to delete any of it to begin with. Look at what they left *in*." She gestured at the screen.

"West and I made a student film once. Black-and-white, horror, fake blood everywhere. It wasn't anywhere near as bad as this, and we *tried*."

Nika shook her head, leaning forward to pick up the remote. "That was your problem. I think half the reason this is so bad is that the director really thought he was making a great movie. It's so lovingly shot, with all the close-ups and weird panoramas."

"Are you saying we didn't lovingly shoot ours? I put my heart and soul into that film, and I hate horror." West put a hand to his forehead, miming an injured look. "I take everything very seriously, as I'm sure you've noticed."

Nika pursed her lips, the picture of sincerity. "Oh, now that would be impossible to miss. Your somber demeanor is something I've admired right from the beginning. That sad, grave face just spells seriousness."

Gavin leaned back on the couch with a heavy sigh. "You have no idea. Try having faced that moroseness for the last umpteen years. It wears on a person."

"You know, that kind of abuse can be damaging. Words hurt." West stood up, shaking a finger at Gavin as he tried for wounded dignity. "I think I'm gonna go to bed. You know, where I get no abuse." He paused for half a beat. "Or anything else, for that matter." Laughing, he ducked the pillow chucked at his head. "Night, kids. Behave yourselves." Gavin might be painfully obvious, but at least *he* knew when to make a discreet exit.

Well, as discreet as he was capable of, anyway.

It turned out that ravenous dogs and gnawed-on intestines weren't the ideal pre-bedtime viewing. Not that West dreamed about that; his nightmares were much worse. When the shadows on the walls of his cabin started crawling closer every time he blinked, he surrendered his pride and got up. He poked his head into the hallway to make sure no one else was around before shuffling into the room next door. Gavin's bed, although empty, was comfortingly familiar when he crawled in and pulled the pillow to his chest, burying his face. He was almost asleep when the door opened, but he'd been drifting on the edge for so long that he had no idea if it had been minutes or hours.

"Lights."

Gavin's voice was loud, and West groaned as the overheads brightened, and tugged the blankets higher. "Too bright. And I didn't break Rule Three." The words were thick and slow, and he blinked owlishly as he peered over the covers.

"I wasn't here to ask, so I think it's a gray area." Gavin dropped his shoes in the corner, and got a set of shorts out of his bureau. "It's fine. Just don't steal all the blankets. This ship is freezing."

"Should get some fluffy jammies like Nika." West rolled away from Gavin when the covers were pulled back.

"I thought you were the one who wanted those." Gavin flipped his pillow over, out of habit and mercy. They both knew why the pillowcase was damp, but Gavin didn't like sleeping on tears and West didn't need his pity.

Exhaustion and discomfort had scraped across West's skin, and there were places where he felt worn through. Sleeping with his best friend probably shouldn't have been a familiar thing, but it was, and the security kept his tongue loose. "She was worried you'd think they were dumb. She bought Corwin a set with cupcakes on them."

"Westley." The warning in Gavin's voice was unnecessary, probably even a bit cruel, but they both knew Readers had rules for a reason. Even if he couldn't help breaking them, he had to at least pretend that he wasn't.

"'S'not my fault. I was waking up from a dream, and she's the only person on the ship I can read. 'S'loud." The space between them in the bed was minimal, but West kept up the charade of personal space by facing the wall. "Sorry, Gav. I can go back to my room—"

"You know I don't mind. Go to sleep."

He didn't say anything else as he rolled over on his back, still decidedly separate but no longer bothering with the fiction that they weren't actually sharing the bed. His hand moved just a twitch, enough that his little finger came to rest against Gavin's.

Sighing into the reclaimed pillow, Gavin curled their fingers together, and West let his breathing even out, slowly losing the fight until he surrendered to sleep.

CHAPTER 4

As public parks went, Eustace Green wasn't the worst Corwin had ever seen. Designed and landscaped long before the push for soft edges and child-friendly play lots, it was mostly an expanse of gently rolling hills, bisected by a meandering gravel walk that wound off into the trees at either end of the open space. Exactly the sort of place he would have chosen for a romantic picnic, if he'd ever in his life intended to have one.

The bench where the body had been discovered was tucked away at the edge of the park, near the trees in the back. It was sheltered from view by a bend in the path, and he could see why someone would have chosen to sleep there. He could list just as many reasons why someone would have chosen to murder there. The area was still cordoned off by crime scene barriers, the standard warning message streaming through the air between the projection posts. Nika held her badge up to the ident scanner, and the beams shut off once her assignment to the case was confirmed.

He wasn't sure what to expect from their psychic wonder this time around. There was nothing overtly cautious in the way West stepped through the crime scene barriers, and Gavin didn't seem to be hovering any more than usual, but the tense pall over the group couldn't be denied.

Corwin paused as far from Tavera as he could and took a second with his shields, pushing out hard against the brush of thoughts that surrounded them. He met with minimal resistance, and he was careful not to expand his barriers so much that he might create static for Tavera It helped that no one was particularly happy at the moment, so his peculiar flavor of Talent didn't have much to latch on to.

Tavera looked up, head swiveling around like a groundhog coming out of its hole. His eyes were hidden behind dark glasses, and he didn't pause as he tracked past Corwin, but that didn't do much to stop Corwin's jolt of unease.

"Something wrong?" Gavin's quiet words only served to highlight the unnatural silence of the park.

"Thought I felt something. Probably just resonance from a kid." Tavera smiled and shrugged before turning to pace the perimeter.

Corwin wasn't used to feeling like the odd man out at a crime scene. When he and Nika got called in, it was usually a higher-level case, and they weren't there to stand around and wait for conclusions to be handed to them. He enjoyed the hands-on work they did, getting down to the bones of a crime. Waiting at the edges while Tavera did the full floor show was uncomfortable.

"If you clench your jaw any tighter, you're going to crack teeth." Nika wasn't even looking at him when she said it, busy clipping her badge back to her belt, but he made an effort to appear more relaxed. He offered her a patently false smile when she glanced up again.

"This is our life for the next fiver, you know. Ferrying him around so he can find all the answers while we stand here playing chaperones." He kept his voice low, but something of the sting from the past few days must have bled through.

He was surprised when she grabbed him by the arm, pulling him to the edge of the scene and dropping her voice. "Corwin, I'm telling you this as a friend, but mostly as your partner: Your attitude over this is *shit*. It's a great opportunity for us to work some really interesting cases, and okay, maybe Agent Tavera isn't your personal cup of tea, but he's doing his job just fine."

"We don't need to be here for him to do his job. It's a waste." She didn't deserve his anger, but it was there anyway, and at least she'd let him get it out before telling him how stupid it was.

"*You* are the one wasting your own time. Did you even listen to the initial report on this woman? You really think this scene got the kind of attention warranted by a murder investigation?" Her disappointment was obvious, and it would have stung more if it hadn't been richly deserved. "We get sent out as teams for a reason. It's our job, our *duty*, to find the physical evidence to back up their nonphysical Reads, and to approach the scene as some kind of pissing contest between Readers and inspectors is not only stupid, it's beneath you."

"Can you guys be angry somewhere else?" Tavera was crouched down by the bench, hands resting on his thighs, not looking particularly chagrined over his eavesdropping. Gavin had a hand on West's shoulder, and his eyebrows lifted in a silent echo of West's query.

"Sorry," Corwin and Nika said at the same time, and he hoped she knew his apology was more for her than them. Tavera shouldn't be able to feel anything from him anyway, but he could imagine that Nika's anger was as easy to Read as her joy.

"It's okay. Just, you know, kind of loud. There isn't a lot here to Read anyway, so it's making it harder to find anything."

"I'll step away for a few minutes then." Nika smiled at Tavera and Gavin, then let it fade when she turned to Corwin. "Inspector Menivie can start the physical investigation at the scene's perimeters so he doesn't interfere with your abilities."

She'd taken point on more than a few cases, and if nothing else, he owed her for not threatening him with a report to Ning. That she was right about all of it, and clearly in a better frame of mind to work with Tavera, only added to the list of reasons she'd do better as the lead in this investigation. So he nodded at her, and she nodded back. "Gentlemen."

Tavera waited for her long strides to take her well out of earshot before saying anything. "Sorry I'm making your life more difficult, Inspector." There was nothing particularly sincere about it, and Corwin hunched his shoulders, peering down hard at the grass.

"You do your job, and I'll do mine, and we'll all be happy." A few seconds later, he added grudgingly. "I'm the one being an ass, not you."

He didn't really need to look to tell that Tavera was smiling, but a quick glance confirmed it.

"Huh. Usually it's me."

"I'm sure the balance will be restored soon," Gavin said, taking his hand off his partner's shoulder and folding his arms. "We gonna do this?"

Corwin paced off the safe distance to get himself out of Tavera's range, then began walking an investigative grid, searching the ground for anything the original team might have missed. A set of grooves at the edge of the gravel path warranted taking some images with his notebook. The lawn beyond them was so beaten down there was no telling if they'd gone farther, but they looked enough like drag marks to document.

It was impossible to completely tune out Tavera and Gavin behind him, the quiet mutter of their voices loud enough to keep from being true background noise. He didn't want to get drawn into the drama, and he especially didn't want Tavera sussing him out.

He was so engrossed in trying to ignore them that it was jarring when they went silent. A quick glance revealed Tavera sitting on the bench, and he bit back an instant admonishment not to disturb the scene. If nothing else, there wasn't much of a scene to disturb; physical evidence was as thin as his patience.

Tavera looked exhausted. No . . . Tavera looked *gone*. His face went slack for a moment, then his eyes opened, milky white, and Corwin flinched without meaning to. It was creepy in a way that those horror vids of Nika's could never really hope to emulate, because they were all about the big reveal, and this was just the quiet abandonment of a human shell. He'd seen several people die over the course of his career, and this was close enough that he would have worried, if not for Gavin's focused calm.

"West, what are you seeing? Talk to me." Gavin's voice was forceful without being loud, and Corwin gave up any pretense of doing anything but watching them. Gavin had a notebook out, but wasn't writing. Both Corwin and Gavin jumped when Tavera jerked forward, voice coming in gasping bursts.

"I like it here. She's gone dark inside." Arms crossed over his stomach, Tavera laughed, slow and quiet in a way that seemed to roll on forever. "Oh, I like this, I like this, and no one cares for the sparrows, do they?"

"Westley. How did you get here?" He'd yet to hear Gavin address Tavera by his given name unless they were working, and suspected it was part of the conditioned-response training Readers and Grounds perfected for years before heading into the field. The word held a patience he couldn't imagine extending to Tavera.

"I flew like a little bird, like a little sparrow with a heart that goes *squish-squish* between the fingers." The way Tavera's fingers began to rub together turned his stomach, and the worst of it was that he could feel Tavera pushing back at his shields, could feel the utter delight that shivered through the imposed connection. He met the pressure with his own resistance, not caring for the moment that he might be called out for it.

"Flew and flew and flew like a bright little bird, filled up inside with goodness and playtime— Gavin, help me." After the soft, sibilant lilt, hearing Tavera plead in something like a normal tone was a welcome relief, though Corwin immediately felt guilty for the thought.

Gavin knelt down in front of his partner, taking both of his hands and pulling Tavera out of the ball he'd hunched into. "You're going to follow my voice back. Follow it back, now, back home, away from where you are."

"No, can't yet." Tavera's stubborn scowl was suited to a toddler, but the fact that his eyes were still rolled back in his head and his face was covered in a thin sheen of sweat betrayed the effort he was making.

"Tell me what's going on, then." Gavin seemed resigned, glancing around as if to orient himself. He was looking up—he was looking for birds, Corwin realized, and wondered how often Tavera gave a literal Read.

"She's heavy, not like a bird at all, and I don't like touching her. The touching is always the worst, people and their skin that doesn't keep anything in," Tavera sneered, hands jerking out of Gavin's. "They're all so light inside, and so heavy when you have to drag them."

Gavin's expression sharpened. "Where did you have to drag her?"

"All the way through the sky, with my claws sunk into her head." Disgusting, tittering laughter punctuated the sentence, and Tavera began to shake.

"That's enough, West. Let it go."

"I can ride it out." The tremors that twitched through his body had nothing on the one in his voice. "There could be more here, and she's like a tree inside, count the rings of failure, peel her right down to the heart."

The shift between semilucid and insane nattering was completely without warning. Gavin was reaching for Tavera when his partner lashed out, a wild punch caught in the palm of Gavin's hand before it could do any damage. Knowing Gavin was trained to deal with Tavera didn't suppress a decade of instinct, and Corwin lurched toward them to neutralize the threat before catching himself and holding back. Tavera wasn't a danger to anyone, and Corwin didn't want to be any closer than he had to be.

"West, start the countback. By one, you'd better be here, or I'm triggering your fail-safe." Gavin held on when Tavera tried to twitch away, face tight with worry. "Five. Four. Follow it back. Three. Two."

"I'm back, I'm back. Stop fucking *touching* me." The tension in Gavin drained away, and Corwin swallowed, trying not to stare. Tavera gripped the edge of the bench like the tight curl of his fingers was the only thing stopping him from shaking apart entirely, and if the way his teeth were chattering was any kind of tell, it might have been.

"C'mon, West," Gavin said, voice calm and gentle, "let's head back to the ship. We can work on the Read report there, away from the scene." It was the wrong offer to make, and it was clear that Gavin knew it. Even he winced when Tavera laughed hoarsely.

"I don't need to be spirited away so I can swoon into your arms." Tavera batted away Gavin's proffered hand and eased back on the bench. "I can swoon perfectly well in public."

Footsteps behind Corwin served as a reminder to at least pretend to be doing his job, and when Nika knelt down next to him, he was sending the pictures of the drag marks to be added to the official case file.

"I got the security feed footage from a bunch of the businesses around the park that night. It's going to take a while to analyze all of it, but it's a start." Her voice didn't betray any lingering anger, but the coolly professional clip wasn't precisely friendly, either.

Tavera must have spotted her coming back and saved enough energy to explain his Read. "He . . . I don't know if it's a he. The Read was so stripped away from any kind of physical grounding that I don't even know for sure if it came from a Human." Exhaustion was plain in every word. "The killer brought her here, though. Carried her part of the way, and then started dragging her when she got too heavy, so they must have had ground transport of some kind. Maybe a flyer or something parked close by?"

"We can look for it in the security footage, but I don't think any of the cameras had a bead on the lot here." Nika thumbed over the screen of her notebook, no doubt narrowing a search parameter for footage that might have caught movement in the green space flyer lot.

Corwin waved a hand toward the edge of the scene. "I think I found some drag marks, so we should be able to corroborate that."

"Well good. At least we'll have some admissible evidence to leave in a file that will never get closed." Cynicism sounded wrong coming from Tavera. He stumbled to his feet and headed for the perimeter. "I need a minute, Gav."

"I'll take down the beams," Nika said. She'd always been good at pushing through awkward situations with work, something Corwin had been thankful for on more than one occasion.

Gavin tucked his notebook into his jacket, giving her a quick smile. "I can help, if you'd like."

Corwin stood and brushed off the knees of his uniform pants, letting his gaze drift to Tavera's retreating form. "I'll go call a patrol flyer to pick us up." Nika and Gavin were speaking in normal voices that sounded too loud, and rather than talk over them, he wandered toward the play lot to make the call. The dispatch officer confirmed that a flyer would be there within the half hour, and he killed the connection.

Tavera sat on the other side of the play lot on a swing, the picture of morose failure as he pushed himself back and forth with one foot while staring at the ground. There was a coffee shop across the street, and a quick glance back at their respective partners confirmed that they were still dismantling the crime scene blockade. He had time to buy an apology, if he hurried.

Luck was on his side, and there was no line in the café. After a brief consideration, he decided that the odds of Tavera taking coffee black were pretty low, dumped some cream into both cups, and shoved a few packets of sugar in his pocket before jogging back across to the park.

Tavera was right where he'd left him, staring off at nothing. Corwin cleared his throat and approached slowly, coffee held out like a peace offering at first contact.

"Do you like your coffee sweetened?"

When Tavera raised his head, it took him a moment to track: a few long seconds before he blinked his strange, every-color eyes and offered up a smile that was worn around the edges. "Yeah, thanks."

He took the cup and popped the lid to dump in the packets of sugar, stilling his swaying seat.

There was nowhere else to sit, and Corwin could only imagine the tragedy of coordination that awaited him if he tried to perch on the other swing, so he stood there instead, watching Tavera gulp down far too much coffee before putting the lid back on.

"I'm sorry I wasted everyone's time. I really thought that with a Read that strong from the body, I'd be able to walk right into a solid arrest at the scene."

"There are other avenues we can explore. There's still the security footage we sent for analysis, and we can try walking the park before we go to see if you get a spike somewhere else. You said she was dragged here, so there's another scene somewhere." It was amazing how magnanimous he could be when it wasn't his failure that was holding back an investigation.

"I'm pretty sure she wasn't killed here. Anywhere near here, actually. There was no sense of any kind of tie to the park. I thought maybe she'd lived here or something, but none of the people interviewed had ever seen her before, and the Read I got from her didn't have any connection to it either."

"It didn't? I thought you said that the killer found her in the park?"

"*A* park. Not this one." Tavera paused to take another drink. "I can't prove it, and I know that's going to be useless for us, but I think this was just a dump site. Nothing happened here."

Corwin scowled back at the crime scene. "If she wasn't killed here, then what the hell did you just spend twenty minutes doing, Tavera? That seemed like an awfully clear impression from a spot where nothing of any great import happened."

Tavera met his eyes, resolute. "Imagine how much stronger it'll be when we actually find a murder scene." He lifted his coffee in salute, the small twist of his mouth almost a return to his usual smile. "Thanks for the drink, Inspector. It was a nice gesture."

"I'm good with gestures," Corwin said, but he wasn't sure if the smile he got was what he'd been trying for or not.

West's hands hurt by the time he was done in the workout room, and a couple of his knuckles were cracked open, bruises already purpling the skin around the cuts. There'd be no hiding it from Gavin, who would fuss without saying a word, but at least he was used to that. What he wasn't used to was Nika's inquisitive concern, and to avoid it for a little longer, West closed his eyes and leaned his sweaty face against the punching bag.

"If you'd rather be alone, I can work out tomorrow." Nika sounded friendly as ever, and he almost wanted to say yes, to pretend that he *couldn't* tell that the offer was genuine, but it wouldn't be her first choice. Pretend that she wasn't wishing, with more than a little guilt, that she'd stumbled upon Gavin, alone and sweaty.

That was the problem with nice people. They were so much easier to Read than everyone else, and they deserved the intrusion so much less.

"No need, I was just catching my breath. I'll be out of your way in a minute."

He didn't know what she was going to say before she said it, not really. That wasn't how it worked, most times. He had a flash of her affection, a glimpse of an older man he didn't recognize flickering across his mind as he wiped his face off with a towel.

"My granddad was one of the first inspectors to work in the field with PsyAc agents. He always spoke very highly of their work." West was surprised when she touched his arm, since most people weren't eager for even that much contact with a psy. "I know it doesn't stop when you're off the clock, and I wanted to tell you, I don't mind." She hesitated, shaking her head. "And if there's something I can do to make myself less distracting when you're trying to work, let me know."

"Thank you for not telling a 'some of my best friends are PsyAc agents' story. It ends up being really awkward for all the parties involved."

Nika gave him a startled look, obviously uncertain about how to respond, and he waited for a count of three before taking pity on her. "I'm kidding. Well, about some of it." Another few seconds of the patented Westley Tavera goofy grin, and he felt her relax. "It does end up being awkward. But in all seriousness, thank you for sharing that, and for your offer."

Crushing fatigue washed over him in a sudden wave when he moved away from the bag, and his grin fell apart as he stumbled a half step.

Nika caught his shoulder, giving it a gentle shake. "You need to ice your hands and get some rest."

"I'm fine," he muttered. It was one thing to swoon into Gav's arms—they had their *thing*, after all. But collapsing into the arms of a relatively new coworker when it was dangerously close to a true faint wasn't cool.

She snorted, an inelegant habit that she seemed fond of. "I have absolutely no psy skills and even I can tell that's a lie. Come on, I'll help you find some ice."

The arm around his shoulder was the only solid thing in a world that was starting to fade alarmingly in and out, and he swallowed hard. "Yeah, okay, maybe I'll take you up on that. It was kind of a long day."

Once in the galley, Nika pushed him into the closest chair, and immediately turned to fill a towel with ice. "Put your hands flat on the table."

"The last time I heard that, I got my knuckles smacked."

"I promise I won't unless you give me a good reason." She grinned as she draped the towel across the tops of his hands. Once it was arranged to her satisfaction, she pulled another chair out with one foot and sat down. "Any better?"

"Corwin brought me coffee today." West blinked and closed his mouth. Apparently the gesture had made more of an impression on him than he'd thought, if he'd blurted it out.

Nika took it in stride, shaking her head with a wry grin. "Corwin is . . . good with gestures."

"Funny, that's exactly what he said."

Leaning forward, she adjusted the towel. "Does it make you a little more kindly disposed, as my granddad would've said?" There was more than just idle curiosity in the question, her expression intent as she met West's eyes.

"Like I'd need to be more kindly disposed. I *adore* Corwin."

"I'm serious." She tapped him on the arm with a faint scowl. "I'm not asking you to be best friends, but it might make things run a little smoother if you didn't tease him quite so much."

He'd received almost the same lecture from Gav, though less gently hinted. "It's not really teasing . . ." Nika raised an eyebrow, and he sighed. "Right, okay, less teasing it is, then."

"Thank you."

Her smile was infectious, dazzling as it lit up her whole face. Or it might've been the fact that he was seeing two of her. He blinked hard, bringing her back into focus. "I think I'd better call it a day."

"You do look a little worse for wear. And West, for what it's worth, I'm really sorry. I know how much you wanted to solve this. Corwin spoke with the department chief before we left, and they're going to leave the case open. He also ran it by Ning, and if anything else comes in, we have permission to pick the case back up."

"But it'll never be solved, and her sister will never know what happened to her." He pulled his hands out from under the towel, pressing his palms against his eyes.

He could feel Nika wavering over her response, and was grateful when she decided on honesty. "That's probably true." She busied herself with picking up the towel, wringing it out before she dropped it in the sink. "But if not for you, there wouldn't have been *any* effort to try to find out what happened to her. You did your best. And that was a whole lot more than anyone else was going to do."

"That sucks." His reply was less than professional, especially when muttered between his fingers, but it was heartfelt.

Nika laughed, but there wasn't much humor in the sound. "True." She hesitated for a second or two. "I set a search alert. If a case comes up with similar parameters, it'll ping me. That might give us another shot at getting this."

Absurdly grateful, he gave her a tired smile. "Thank you. That's not going to get you in trouble with Corwin, is it? I don't want him to think I'm corrupting you into going behind his back."

"I'm not a probie, and I'm allowed to monitor whatever cases I find relevant to the execution of my duties as a fly-by. In any case, Corwin should know better than to worry about my loyalties." She grinned and held out her hand. "C'mon, I'll walk you to your room, and you can get some rest."

When they reached his door, he wavered again.

"Do you want— Uh, would you rather go to Gavin's room?" Nika looked equally uncomfortable.

It was incredibly tempting. Alone, the dreams would take control, but the thought of explanations, to Nika or Gavin, was too exhausting to contemplate. "This is fine. And thank you for, you know—" He hesitated for a second and then shrugged. "For everything."

His vague wave was meant to encompass Nika's understanding, sharing, and sympathy, and from her quick smile, he could tell she got it. "Anytime. Get some rest, we've got about ten hours before we start up our next case."

The door had barely closed before he collapsed on the bed, wincing as his abraded knuckles rubbed against the blankets. Curling up on his side, hands held away from his body, he resolutely closed his eyes. The dreams, when they came, were full of sickening swoops and the patter of blood in his eyes and mouth.

CHAPTER 5

West was in the middle of an expansive gesture with a piece of spice toast while explaining the finer nuances of hacky sack when Nika joined them, and Corwin lit up like she was the walking face of salvation. Even without the benefit of his Talent, West could see that his cheerful constitution surprised Nika. Not that he blamed her, given that he'd looked (and felt) like warmed-over death last night. Her loose hair fell forward, obscuring her smile as she turned her full attention to making a cup of tea.

"Ah, Inspector Santivan, there you are." There was no missing the relief in Corwin's voice when he finally got a word in edgewise. His reversion to formality with her said a great deal about the level of discomfort in the room. West mentally checked himself and shut up.

"Good morning, gentlemen. Am I late? I didn't think we were due to dock on Tosc for another two hours." Nika smiled at them over the rim of her cup, obviously aware that she was just in time to keep her partner from throttling West.

"No, no, you're not late," Corwin said rapidly. "We'll hit atmo on Tosc in a couple hours, then proceed to the crime scene in Kastner. I, uh, thought you'd be interested in hearing Agent Tavera here talk about that, uh, well, he'd probably be better at explaining it to you."

Both Corwin's hasty answer and the way he scooted over to make sure Nika would sit between them were amusing. Corwin clutched his coffee mug in a death grip, face twisted in a grimace that he undoubtedly thought counted as a smile.

West sighed, shaking a finger at Corwin and scattering crumbs. "You know, I don't think you were listening to me at *all*."

"To be fair, it looks like you caught him before he's had time to finish his first cup of coffee." Nika took the open spot at the table without making an issue of it, and he had to admire her ease with people or her protective instincts toward her partner. "So what have I missed?"

Corwin was halfway off his seat by the time she settled into hers, pausing for some silent communication with Nika that ended in a faintly guilty glance in West's direction. "I'm going to go check the comm. See if anything new came in overnight." He didn't wait for a reply before disappearing.

"Was it something I said?"

West took the pointed look from Nika with good grace. "I don't know, was it?" She sighed into her mug. "That toast looks really good. Just the sort of thing a person would want to eat before she went to talk her partner down from the heights of his discomfort."

"I'll just make you a piece, shall I?" He shoved a bite of toast into his mouth as he rose, and in a feat of gymnastic skill he'd never be able to replicate, grabbed the bread off the bottom shelf and neatly flipped a couple slices end-over-end, managing to land them on the toaster oven tray.

Nika shook her head, her mug no longer hiding her smile. "There *are* easier ways to do things, you know."

West glanced at the doorway before turning back to find her watching him. He sighed. "Somehow I don't think you're offering me cooking tips." He leaned against the counter, hip braced on the cabinet doors below. "So do you think there's really an update on the case, or was Corwin trying to escape? Because I got the distinct feeling he was trying to get away to cover for the fact that he wasn't listening to me."

"That, and the cloud of cinnamon and sugar you seemed to be raining on him when I walked in."

The toaster beeped, and he grabbed a plate with one hand and burned the other pulling the toast out. Butter first, since he hadn't put it away after making his breakfast; then he covered both slices with far too much sugar and a dusting of spice that was perfunctory at best. Satisfied with the results, he crossed the room and set the plate in front of her with a flourish not often reserved for toast.

"What can I say? I'm an enthusiastic person."

Nika patted him on the shoulder as he stepped back. "I gathered that, believe it or not."

He picked up his own breakfast again, butter slicking his fingers. "I was telling him about the last kidnapping case Gavin and I got assigned to, which is actually relevant, since that's what we're picking up when we dock."

"Well, tell me about it instead." Nika's earnest attention took a bit of the sting out of her partner's dismissal, not that there'd been much to begin with. After another quick glance at the door, he sat down, eager to fill the space between them with words, if only to drown out the exuberant curiosity of Nika's mind.

The office encompassed the entire top floor of the building, floor-to-ceiling windows making it feel like it was floating over the city. Even without the nameplate on the door, it would've been obvious that it belonged to the head of the company. Corwin moved closer to the windows, stomach dropping abruptly as he glanced down. The floor itself was glass in the meter's distance from the edge of the priceless silk rug to the windows. This story of the building extended out farther than any floors below it, an architectural detail designed to further emphasize the power of its tenant.

Next to him, Nika took a stumbling step backward, her arm brushing his. He looked up, raising an eyebrow questioningly, and she managed a nod, lips white around the edges. "It just startled me." Her voice was tight.

The victim's elderly assistant, a Mrs. Phinean, sat huddled in a chair in front of the huge executive desk. She sniffed, clutching a handkerchief in her hands. "This room has the best view of the city you'll ever find."

"It's impressive. I've never seen anything like this before." Tavera stepped around them and onto the open glass, staring down between his feet. "Kind of feels like falling off the edge of the world, doesn't it?"

Nika moved closer to the center of the room, gaze darting down and immediately back up, before she closed her eyes for a second and swallowed. "Doesn't that make you uncomfortable at all?"

"I've experienced worse."

Corwin grimaced in unwelcome sympathy. Flying and falling and blood that for all intents and purposes were real to the Reader would have to be worse than some businessman's illusory decorating trick.

Tavera leaned against the closest window, palms flat against the glass, earning a dismayed sort of squawk from Mrs. Phinean. "Young man. Excuse me, young man. Please don't touch the glass. You'll leave smudges."

Corwin made little attempt to hide his pained expression, a false smile tight across his mouth as he tried to reassure the woman. Only Tavera could manage to be annoying by merely looking out the window. "I'm sure Agent Tavera will wipe off any handprints he might leave on the glass."

"He was afraid of this, of standing here," Tavera said, almost offhandedly. "He never came close to this window until, ah, until the other day, and it wasn't willingly."

Gavin had been ghosting along behind Tavera, and looked up, expression sharpening as he reached for his notepad.

"How silly. Mr. Survey had this office designed to his specifications. Of course he wasn't frightened of anything here." The little woman stood up, outrage in every line of her body. "That's the most ridiculous thing I've ever heard."

Tavera kept going as if she hadn't spoken. "He pressed his face to the window, and the glass was cold against his skin, but it felt good because he was sweating."

There was another disbelieving sound, this one more of a low growl, and Nika quickly stepped forward to take the woman's arm. "Why don't you tell me a little more about Mr. Survey? You were the last person to see him, and your information is going to be invaluable to the investigation."

Slightly mollified, Mrs. Phinean let herself be guided back into the chair, and Corwin heaved a sigh of relief. Dealing with Tavera was difficult enough. An overwrought assistant was more fuel for a headache.

Nika pasted on her professional smile. "I know you've already spoken to the local authorities, but I'd like you to tell us everything you remember about the last time you spoke with your boss."

"Well, it was two days ago, and we were finishing up a new contract with Shea Industries." Mrs. Phinean paused significantly, obviously expecting a response. When Nika merely nodded encouragingly, she sighed and continued. "Of course, he would never trust anyone else with a client that important. It was just the two of us left in the office, and once I'd finalized the paperwork, he told me to go home."

The drawn-out silence dragged on for several seconds. Mrs. Phinean twisted her hands together, eyes suspiciously red, and Corwin rolled his own, looking away to hide it and thankful Nika was dealing with her. He could be appropriately compassionate when the need arose, but it wasn't his first instinct. "I shouldn't have left him here alone. If I'd been there—"

"It wouldn't have made any difference, and would've put you in danger too," Nika said. "The report says you didn't notice anything suspicious as you left the building."

Mrs. Phinean shook her head, blinking rapidly. "There was no one here on this floor but the two of us. Even the cleaning staff was gone. The security desk in the lobby was still manned, of course."

"Thank you, Mrs. Phinean. Why don't you go freshen up? And I'll make sure you have a way to get in touch with us if you think of anything else you feel we should know about."

The woman gave Nika a steady look, holding it together for a second before her eyes grew damp. "He's always remembered my birthday." She pressed a hand over her mouth and fled, presumably to break down in private.

"Well." Nika scrubbed a hand across her forehead. "That's what you call a devoted executive assistant."

Corwin shook his head, vaguely appalled. "Was she *crying*? How close do you think they were? Close enough for Mr. Phinean to have a motive?"

"I'm sure she did more than just bring him coffee," she said dryly. "He remembered her birthday. I don't know about you, but that's a trait that endears a person to me." Off-center, Corwin spent a frantic moment trying to recall what, if anything, he'd done for Nika's, and almost missed her imitation of him. Rolling her eyes, she looked back at her case notes. "In any case, Mr. Phinean died two years ago, so I doubt he's the jealous sort."

Still skeptical, he went back to his examination of the missing man's obsessively clean desk. Gavin was prompting Tavera, voice a low murmur set against the shuffle of papers and the otherwise quiet office.

"What about last night? What was he feeling last night?"

Tavera cracked an eye open and fixed his gaze on his partner. "Fifteen years, and you're still trying to get me to time-stamp something?"

"Fifteen years, and you still can't?" Gavin's answer made Nika grin at her notepad for a second, and Corwin quickly hid his own amusement by ducking his head to investigate another drawer in Mr. Survey's desk. Tavera made a noncommittal little huffing noise, eyes closing again before he slapped a hand against the window. Nobody bothered to voice a reminder not to smudge the glass, and Tavera walked the full length of the clear edge, obviously dropping deeper into the Read with every step.

"He sat in this corner and looked down and said never, ever again, never gonna be down there again. And he hated it." Tavera's head met the glass with a solid *thunk*, and Gavin reached out for him, only to have the friendly hand shaken off. "She reminds him of his mum, and he's left her half his money; he thinks about it when he can't forget that he's going to fall. Going to look down one day and it's going to come up and get him *splat*, but he's going to screw them all first, and he let them in, and he knew, *he knew*, so he smudged the window to make his mark."

Corwin glanced up and caught Nika looking too, eyebrows raised. They abandoned their investigations, moving closer as Tavera shook himself out of it, his hand wrapped around Gavin's wrist to Ground himself.

"Is that a literal Read? Should we actually be looking at these windows for something, or was that some kind of artistic metaphor for the windows of his soul?" Corwin directed the question at Gavin, excluding Tavera, who clearly wasn't up for speaking yet if his distant, wandering look was any indication.

"It sounds pretty literal. Usually when he has details like that, they can be interpreted pretty much as given."

"Great." The dry note was aimed at the wall of windows, the expanse suddenly shedding a whole new light on the investigation.

Nika faced the windows, eyes narrowed against the glare. "He was about your height, Gavin, so if we look at the windows that fall into that range, we eliminate half of them, if it's something he did with his hands. Any idea what we're looking *for*?"

"A curse in his breath," Tavera murmured, his finger shaking as he pointed at one window after another.

Corwin opened his mouth to snap something about the relative uselessness of superstitious mumbo jumbo, but Nika scowled and took his arm, aiming him at the far end of the room.

Tavera spoke up again, voice stronger and far more present now. "I think he wrote something on one of the windows. You know, like you do when you're a little kid." He seemed to be visibly composing himself, Gavin's arm tossed loosely over his shoulders.

"What do you—"

Corwin whirled around on his heel, cutting off Nika's question, and leaned over to blow against the pane of glass. Nothing appeared, and nothing on the next one either, but by the time he'd hit the third, Nika had started on her side of the office. He stopped long enough to give her a thin, smug smile.

"Meier." Corwin stood back, eyeing the word on the window as it began to fade. Nika was across the room in three steps, notebook out and ready. She angled it to take a picture as he bent over and let his breath steam up the glass again.

"You have impressive lung capacity, Inspector." The bland, innocent tone of Tavera's voice was a poor imitation of the real thing.

"I've always blown well." He didn't bother to look over, and the silence on Tavera's part was more satisfying than it should've been.

Nika frowned as she bent over her notebook. "Shea Industries holds a property on Meier Landing, in the shipping district."

"Program in the address, and let's go." Corwin didn't wait to see if anyone was following as he strode toward the door. With kidnappings, time counted, and since the local authorities had found no evidence of an altercation here, he had every reason to believe they might find Mr. Survey alive and relatively unscathed.

West hadn't actually planned on shoving himself into the back of the flyer, but the expression on Corwin's face when he plopped down on the seat almost made him wish he had. "Strap in for safety, Inspector." Cheerfully ignoring their animosity, West reached across to pat Corwin on the knee.

Gavin's warning glare was a veritable ocular laser. West knew he wasn't going to be yanked out of the backseat by his hair, simply because there was no gracefully professional way for Gavin to get away with it, but the finger Gavin jabbed at him before settling in the front passenger seat held an unspoken threat.

Nika's position as chauffeur seemed to catch only her by surprise, and she squinted at all of them suspiciously. "Right. I guess I'm driving, then."

"I can do it." Corwin lunged forward, hand going for the door handle.

"No, I've got it." She laughed, rolling her eyes. "No offense, but your planetside sense of direction is notoriously bad. Even with the nav system on."

"It's not my fault the system wants to tell you the turn two seconds before you have to make it." Corwin sat back with a scowl, using the opportunity to slide as far from West as possible.

In return, West yawned and stretched, left hand casually draping across the back of the seat, fingers a scant few centimeters from the inspector's ramrod-straight back. "So what makes you so good at taking directions?" he asked Nika.

Nika hit the turn signal, waiting for the light to change before pulling across the intersection. "My secret is not trying to anticipate. It keeps me from having to correct myself too often."

Still toying with the edge of Corwin's personal space, West felt his friend's narrowed eyes on him, and eased back on the invasion as Gavin spoke up. "I try to do most of the driving, no matter where we are. West's philosophy is that if his passengers have their eyes open, he's not going fast enough."

"Hey, just because I don't drive like your granny . . ."

"I should get you out on the Tazo salt flats some time. You'd love it." Nika grinned over her shoulder. "Although my granny would probably take you down. She raced cycles in her younger days."

"This sounds like a challenge, me versus Nika's grandmother. I guess you'll just have to hang on tighter, Gav."

Gavin rolled his eyes. "Yeah, right. I wouldn't climb on that death trap with you unless the alternative was my imminent demise. Even then, I'd take into consideration whether it was going to be a painful death."

West laughed, sneaking a glance at Corwin. "What about you, Inspector Menivie? Brave enough to ride with me?"

Corwin's glare would've taken down a lesser man. "I'd hardly call that brave. Self-destructive, maybe. Or misguided."

Nika maneuvered the narrow city streets at speeds her granny would doubtless appreciate. Within minutes, she pulled the flyer up tight against the curb, cutting the power before turning to look at Corwin. "Not going to join us for the race, then?"

Corwin didn't bother to reply, slamming a charge pack into his blast gun instead. "The schematics show one ground-level door on a loading dock bay, and another emergency door on each wall. Other than that, just windows, and those are second floor."

West craned his head to scan the street. The warehouse was an unremarkable two-story span of metal siding, with thick bars welded over the windows. The flat faces of the surrounding buildings provided no cover, and even sitting in the unmarked flyer, he felt exposed.

Nika interrupted his visual inspection. "If you cover the door, I think Gavin can boost me up high enough to see in one of the windows." Corwin shifted in the seat, and she held up a hand. "Unless you want West to do it, I'm the obvious choice."

"Gav, I think you've just been described as heavy, and me as scrawny and weak." West snickered, nerves crawling as he forced himself not to reach out for a Read he might not be able to grasp yet, as far away as they were. It would only be a distraction he couldn't afford, not with guns being waved all about. "I'm not sure what it says about Inspector Menivie, though."

"You might be weak, but I think Inspector Santivan was basing her decision on your partner's relative musculature, which we both lack. He can physically lift her." Corwin delivered the assessment without looking up from the notebook he was clutching in a defensive hold. "And though I'm loath to volunteer time with you, it would also make sense for Agent Hale to do the recon work, as he's much less likely to be debilitated in the middle of the street by a stray childhood trauma."

He shifted focus to the warehouse again, eyes narrowed, and West followed the line of sight, ignoring Corwin's muted insults. The tint on the flyer windows was opaque from the outside, and blocked enough light that his squinting had nothing to do with the sun streaming down between the buildings.

Corwin continued without bothering to turn around. "I've informed dispatch of our location, and told them to have a recovery team ready in case we've found the kidnappers. Agent Tavera, are you armed?"

West managed to stifle his snort, and refused to give in to the perfectly adolescent urge to show his weapon to Corwin. Subtlety wasn't his specialty, but neither was blatant alpha posturing. "I'm a field agent. I'm armed with a standard-issue blast gun, Topsail model Atom-5, and licensed to use it with deadly force if necessary."

"I wasn't debating your qualifications, Agent Tavera, I was asking if you could provide me with cover. Inspector Santivan, you take right with Agent Hale, I'll take left with Agent Tavera, and we'll convene at the back of the building."

Needling Corwin fell by the wayside as West checked his combat gear one last time. Everything seemed fine, except for the part where having it on meant someone might be shooting at him, so when Gavin caught his eyes in the rearview mirror, he nodded his readiness.

"Comm channels cleared and open?" Everyone tapped their badges, and the resulting microburst of feedback went off like an electric charge in the close confines of the car. The hair on West's arms stood up, and the shift into street-ready attentiveness echoed back at him through Nika.

"And go!"

The four of them were out in seconds, silently shutting the flyer doors before they broke off into teams and ran full out for the cover of the warehouse. West hated the distance that grew between them, the silence stretching until it broke as Gavin moved out of range. While Corwin's null status provided a similar buffering effect, he tried to avoid latching on to him as a substitute.

The front of the building offered an array of barred and boarded windows, and rusty metal patched with slightly less-worn acrylic, the shabbiness doing nothing to sell West on the structural integrity.

Corwin edged forward with his side pressed to the wall, and West followed, looking ahead of and behind them as they rounded the corner. There was no one in the alley between the warehouses, and they darted toward a forklift, ducking down behind it.

"Can you cover me if I go for the door?" Corwin whispered.

"Sure." He had barely answered before Corwin was moving again, a low, skittering crouch taking him to the door. The shielding Corwin provided faded with every step he took, and West was left with an unexpected Read from the warehouse.

He couldn't get a lock on it, but there were at least two people inside, probably more. He started to reach out for them before snapping back to the reality of the situation. If he spaced out into a Read now, Corwin would have no backup close enough to make a difference, and that was entirely against protocol.

Protocol, and corruption thereof. He could smell the corruption from here, rotting from inside the system he clung to. Was it time to bring it down? He could. A word, a file kept locked in a nanotech vault in his head—

"Tavera," Corwin hissed in his ear, the hand on his shoulder an unexpected path back to his own head. "Damn you to the ground, we need to *move.*"

Very much wanting to bat the hand away, he rose from his crouch instead, and followed the inspector down the alley. There really wasn't much choice, what with Corwin latched on to his arm and dragging him. He let go when they reached the corner, shoving West behind him and looking around the back of the building. Apparently deeming it clear of threats, he glanced at West, but didn't touch him again.

They stepped lightly, keeping noise to a minimum. When they came to the corner where they should have met Gavin and Nika, apprehension made West more alert, his hand steady around the grip of his gun.

Corwin looked at him again, and seemed to find him acceptable backup, or the only option available. Either way, Corwin made a gesture for quiet, and they both peered around the corner.

The man standing between them and Gavin was large enough to almost block their view of Gavin's gun. At first West thought that Nika was nowhere to be seen, but then he spotted her, hanging from the side of the building, one arm looped through some rusty bars on the windows. Gavin wasn't looking up, and the potential kidnapper didn't seem to know she was there.

Corwin stepped back out of sight, pulling the badge from his belt. West interrupted him before he could activate the comm, leaning forward to whisper, "Survey is in there. I Read him."

Corwin's blue eyes narrowed, suspicion and dislike clear on his face. He tapped the comm without acknowledging West's statement. "Inspector Menivie to dispatch, requesting immediate deployment of urban assault and retrieval team to hostage situation. Engagement with suspect in progress. Confirmed location of Amano Survey by Agent Tavera."

"Copy that, Inspector. UAR team is en route, approximately three minutes out."

"Keep the patrol flyers back until UAR gets here. Hostile situation in progress. Menivie out."

West's gaze flicked to the charge on his weapon and back to Corwin's face. "Let's go. That's my partner." Gavin was out in the open, and that could go bad in seconds.

They rounded the corner again, guns raised. West didn't expect to see Nika drop on the suspect like a hunting spider, her elbow catching him in the face as both went down hard, but his attention didn't waver from the threat to his partner. Gavin looked momentarily stunned, but managed to pull it together, surging forward to yank the man's gun out of reach.

Nika was already rolling the man over, a knee pinned in the middle of his back to keep him flat as he groaned and made a weak attempt to get away. "Stay down, asshole." She punctuated the order by yanking his arms up behind his back and holding his wrists together, then looked up at West and Corwin's approach.

"Corwin, can you give me a set of cuffs? I can't reach mine." She dipped her head to the side, wiping the scrape on her cheek against the sleeve of her shirt. Gavin already had his zip cuffs out, and he knelt beside Nika and the suspect to put them on. When the man opened his mouth, presumably to yell a warning, Nika shoved him between the shoulder blades, pressing his face against the dirty street. "Don't even think about it."

"We should get him back to the flyer. The UAR team will be here in minutes, and we need to coordinate the strike before anyone inside spots us." Corwin turned away without offering Nika a hand up, but after she braced a knee on the suspect's back and got easily to her feet, West guessed that she didn't often need one.

Gavin pulled the man up, keeping a hand fisted in his shirt as they made their way out of the alley. While Gavin locked their prisoner into the restraints in the backseat of the vehicle, Nika went to the trunk and started poking around through their gear, her grin barely hidden. Hovering on the edge of the action, West ran through a series of centering exercises, forcing some of the mental distraction away by reconnecting to the physical world.

"What are you so happy about?" He formed the words carefully, trying to speak to Nika rather than Read her. She picked up a riot gun and a mask from the things she'd sorted out, handing them over, and he finally caught sight of the blast packs in her other hand.

"We get to blow stuff up. Probably." Her expression radiated cheerful mayhem, and he couldn't help but return the smile. "It doesn't hurt to be prepared."

He didn't take one of the blast packs, but only because nobody in their right mind would trust him with any, and he didn't want Nika to regret her hasty actions later on. Or to lose his thumbs. He really liked his thumbs.

Gavin emerged from the flyer, and Corwin finished the update to dispatch, then joined them near the trunk and reached past him for a mask. Gavin's expression was openly admiring in a way that had less to do with how Nika filled out a flak jacket, and more to do with the explosives she handed over. "Inspector, I like how you think."

The arrival of the UAR team covered West's hastily suppressed groan, or so he thought until Corwin glanced over at him and offered the barest of commiserating grimaces. It was a moment he wasn't sure how to interpret, but they were about to blast their way into the warehouse, and he didn't have time to worry about anything else.

CHAPTER 6

Corwin carefully loaded his plate and glass into the scrubber, straightening up just in time to sidestep Nika, dressed down in her civvies and barefoot. His toes curled a little in sympathy, despite being sensibly clad in both socks and regulation boots.

"I just got a ping on my search parameters." She set her notebook on the counter, turned it to face him, and pointed at the screen. "Not a homeless person this time. A prostitute on Bodum, and if she hadn't shown up there, where everyone is registered and licensed, she probably never would have gotten any notice. There was a Reader getting field training with the team investigating the case."

He dried off his hands before leaning closer to read the report she'd pulled up. "The agent screamed and passed out? Sounds like an even bigger dog and pony show than Tavera."

"She's just a kid." Nika gave him an exasperated glare. "*And* it was her first murder investigation."

"So they were able to determine it was a murder?"

"The report on her Read sounded remarkably close to West's. That's what triggered the ping." She turned the notebook back around. "So do we have permission to follow up on it?"

It wasn't really a question, for all that Nika looked at him expectantly. The case was still open, and it didn't seem possible that Ning would let something like potential serial murders slide under the rug. Even as he nodded, he thought back to that terrifyingly empty expression on Tavera's face after the Read in the park. "I think you better ask Tavera first."

"Yeah, I will. I don't think it'll be an issue, though. He's . . ." she hesitated a second ". . . really invested in that case. And if this one *is* connected . . ."

"Let me know what he says, and then I'll let Ning know."

"Don't forget that we're supposed to meet with Mr. Survey before we leave." Corwin was pretty certain he wasn't mistaking the teasing nature of the smile that curved Nika's lips. "It's very nice of him to want to personally thank us."

"You know what? I'll let Ning know right now. I'm sure Tavera is okay with this, and the sooner we get going, the sooner he can start investigating."

There was absolutely no mistaking the teasing grin now as she shook her head. "One day you're going to have to face the fact that people like to thank you sometimes. It's not a bad thing."

He grimaced. "It's also not a necessary thing. I'm just doing my job."

"All those commendations you keep tucked away say otherwise, but who am I to criticize?"

He rarely saw the inside of Nika's cabin, but the few quick glances had shown that she wasn't as ambivalent over accepting recognition as he was. Whereas his plaques and medals and letters were all stuffed in a storage case under his bed, hers were proudly displayed in her quarters. Not that he wasn't proud of his. It was more a matter of being raised not to make a fuss about doing a job well.

"Inspector Menivie, are you hiding things in your underwear drawer?"

Tavera stood in the galley doorway, disheveled hair and loose stance making him look half-asleep.

"No." There was always the hope that if he kept it short and sweet, Tavera wouldn't want to engage him in conversation. It hadn't worked yet, but that hope was still there.

"Gav tells me that it's entirely too clichéd to keep porn in your underwear drawer, but where else would you keep it? I mean, I suppose you *could* just leave it sitting out, but then if you have unexpected visitors who don't share your interests, it might be awkward and uncomfortable for everyone involved." Tavera turned his patented innocent look on Nika. "What do you think? Hidden away or proudly displayed?"

Nika laughed, shoving him in the shoulder, and Corwin envied her the blithe, easy interaction. "I think that's none of your business."

She nodded toward the table, her face sobering. "Actually, I need to show you something. Sit down."

"Do I want to see this? Or am I in trouble?"

Corwin waited until Tavera sat down and Nika dropped into the closest chair before making an escape.

The bridge was blessedly empty, and he let himself enjoy a minute or two of silence before pulling up the IEC relay to message Ning. It didn't take long, though it was nearing the end of the chief inspector's office hours.

"Inspector. I understand congratulations are in order. I received a most complimentary message from Mr. Survey."

Years of familiarity let Corwin read the amusement in Ning's voice, and he winced. "But?"

"Oh, it was a complimentary message, very effusive in its praise." The pause seemed to drag on exceptionally long. "Equally effusive was a message from a . . ." There was yet another pause while Ning scanned through the notebook screen. "A Mrs. Brinta Phinean. I believe there were actually some tears in the recording she sent. Her praise, however, was for that lovely young lady who was so sympathetic. You, she stated, are rather a cold fish."

He'd never been in the habit of apologizing when he hadn't done anything wrong, and he wasn't happy at being made to feel like he needed to do it now. He was about to tell Ning exactly that when his thoughts were interrupted by a trill of laughter.

"I'm quite familiar with your work, you know. You've never given me any reason to doubt your professionalism. And if it provides any comfort, I find you quite engaging."

"Thank you. I appreciate your trust." Their conversation over Tavera was still at the back of his mind, so it was reassuring to know that he hadn't damaged Ning's faith in his skills.

"But I'm sure you had something on your mind when you contacted me . . ."

"The alert that Inspector Santivan had out on anything similar to the case on Ethris pinged. I wanted to clear it through you before we investigated."

Ning nodded. "I'll trust your judgment on this." The words seemed to carry more weight than was immediately explicable, and

Corwin twitched uncomfortably, waiting for the rest. "While sending an IEC fly-by team to handle what was obviously a job for local law enforcement was a questionable decision at best, tying up a team with an investigation into the death of unidentified women who may or may not have died under suspicious circumstances is worse. If this lead should prove unproductive, you will need to disengage Agent Tavera."

There it was. He scrubbed a hand across his face, trying to hide a grimace. "You realize that's like trying to get a bureaucrat on Rogena to give you a pass on filing all paperwork in triplicate?"

"Understood. Keep me informed."

He leaned back as the screen went dark, already massaging the ache in his temples. While he was the senior officer and held nominal command and final say on where they went and what they did, he didn't relish the thought of having to exercise that power if it brought him up against Tavera's single-minded focus. It was a very small ship, and he was certain that Tavera could make it a living hell given half a chance.

A rustling sound behind him was too loud to be Nika, and he grunted in annoyance before turning around.

Gavin didn't look particularly happy to see him, either. "Sorry, I didn't mean to intrude."

Corwin shrugged, not bothering to deny it.

"Nika says we're taking a case on Bodum. She was just briefing me and West on it."

"Ning's approved it, so this might be a little late, but what's your take? Does it sound like a decent enough lead?" The thing of it was, he wasn't sure how much of a true partnership they had, or if Gavin simply followed Tavera's lead. He'd seen no sense of deference in the field, but he was curious if that was different when they weren't acting out the roles they'd trained for at PsyAc.

"West thinks so."

That both answered his curiosity and piqued it all in one shot, and he made a noncommittal noise designed to buy him a few seconds to think. "How attached is he to this case? I know that Read hit him pretty hard."

The question wasn't out of line, given his responsibility to keep them all functioning as a team, but Gavin still looked troubled. "Yeah, it was one of his tougher ones, which kind of makes him more anxious to solve it."

"So he's really counting on this lead?"

"I guess you could say that," Gavin said cautiously. "Why? Do you know something about the case?"

"Nothing more than you. But I need to know what happens if this doesn't pan out."

Gavin cracked a small smile. "I know you're not a real psy fan, and that West rubs you the wrong way, but I can tell you what *won't* happen. He won't lose his shit and kill us all in our sleep, if that's what you're worried about."

It didn't take a Reader to sense that Gavin's joking tone was covering anger. "I'm not implying that at all. But a couple points: First, the two of you recently came off a bad case, and I think we all know that messes with your head." He felt a wry half smile tugging at his lips. "Second, Agent Tavera is like a dog with a bone. Once he gets his teeth into it, I suspect you could lose a finger trying to take it away. I'd rather not have that kind of discord on my— on *our* ship."

"Fair enough. Gently extricating him probably falls equally under my duties as both a Ground and a friend. If it's needed, I'll take care of it."

"Take care of what?" Tavera's voice seemed to echo off the walls.

Corwin covered a small sigh as Tavera bounced into the room, reaching out to pat Gavin's head before dropping into the chair next to him, one leg over the arm. Corwin's medical training wasn't comprehensive, but he was sure he felt an incipient aneurism building in response to the way Tavera made every room feel like it was too small.

Gavin pushed Tavera's leg off. "Ensuring that you eat your vegetables and practice proper oral hygiene."

"It sounds so dirty when you say it like that." Tavera grinned at Gavin, and Corwin suddenly felt very out of place.

"Right, then. I'm just going to go take care of some reports or something . . ."

Tavera transferred the grin to him, and he flinched under the full force of its power. "Remember, if you need any help, I have that flair with words."

"I'll be sure to come get you."

His own cabin seemed the last safe place on the ship, and he beat a hasty retreat, the tight set of his shoulders finally easing when the door closed and locked behind him. His notebook was the only thing on the desk, but that kept down distractions when he was working.

Chapter ten was almost finished. He just needed a couple of sentences to tie up the aftermath of the accident. The ferry had sunk quickly, and he wasn't quite ready to reveal just who'd survived and who might still be trapped inside. That was for chapter eleven.

In his mind, Corwin still disparagingly referred to his books as "time killers," but he enjoyed writing them, if only for the novelty value of having everything turn out the way he wanted.

He'd sworn his agent to secrecy about his identity as the author of the moderately popular adventure series. Nika knew, but he trusted her. He could imagine the kind of grief he'd get from other colleagues if it became common knowledge, and he preferred to avoid it altogether.

Opening his notebook, he settled in and prepared to get lost in the story.

Bodum was a planet largely devoted to pleasure, although nothing like the more genteel and pricier pursuits of Giverny. Bodum's specialties fell more along the lines of gambling and escorts. With the concentration of sex workers came imperial and planetary regulations, but the dead woman hadn't been licensed on the planet. Corwin kept his expression neutral as they rode up to the scene in the elevator, but he suspected this particular establishment wasn't terribly stringent about checking credentials.

He watched Tavera walk the perimeter of the hotel room, Gavin within easy reach at all times. Neither seemed to be particularly anxious to touch anything, especially after the BioTeam had reported finding over two hundred DNA samples. There was a reason he was standing in the middle of the room. The air felt heavy with despair, but there was arousal too—sex and release close enough to happiness that they lingered—and he didn't dare push out his shields while

Tavera was working. He could only imagine what Tavera was sensing from the room already.

"Excuse me . . ."

The young woman in the doorway barely came to Nika's shoulder, wispy black hair falling over the only life-size part of her: the huge eyes that immediately sought out Tavera. When he turned, she walked toward him. "I'm Enny. I'm glad you came."

Much as Corwin hated to acknowledge it, there was no use denying the unease curling in the pit of his stomach. Not one but two PsyAc agents in the room didn't bode well for him, and he considered and then discarded stepping out, unwilling to draw attention to himself.

Tavera gave her his permanently crooked grin. "You did a good report."

"You wouldn't think so, from the report done on *me*." She didn't sound exactly bitter, but there was more than amusement in her voice.

Nika shook her head. "Your report was good enough to trigger an alert for us."

"Thanks." She turned her wide, barely blinking gaze on Nika and nodded, but then turned back to Tavera. "Are you going to follow through on the investigation?"

"If it's what I think, yeah. Haven't seen the body yet, since the morgue was closed for lunch. Must be nice to work someplace where people die during business hours only." He nodded vaguely toward the room. "I'm going to try a Read here first, though. Any suggestions?"

Enny tipped her head to the side, considering. "You and Agent Hale are next to legendary, so you should be okay. Do you want me to leave, though? I don't want to be a distraction."

"You're fine. With Gav and the wonderful Inspectors Santivan and Menivie at my back, I'm virtually unstoppable." Tavera's dramatic hand wave and overblown tone rankled Corwin, although oddly enough, not as much as he would have expected.

Nika seemed to be perfecting a look of resigned tolerance. "Thanks for the vote of confidence. I'll try to live up to it."

Gavin pulled a simple plastiform chair away from the wall, and hovered close while Tavera folded himself into it, hunched so that his chin almost reached his knees.

"Do you want to sit on the bed?" Nika asked. "Might be more comfortable." The combination of Enny's choked-off gasp and Tavera's expression, lips twisted in disgust, obviously caught her by surprise. "Sorry, what did I say?"

Tavera gave an exaggerated shudder. "No need to apologize, it's not like you'd know. Beds are . . . problematic. Things happen in them, memories are left. It can get uncomfortable."

"Oh. *Oh*." Nika blushed, and Corwin felt a stab of sympathetic embarrassment that had nothing to do with his abilities. "Never even thought about that."

Tavera shrugged. "It's not like you'd ever have a reason to."

"It's not just the sex." Enny's already-soft voice was even quieter now. "That's just, well, voyeuristic. Nightmares of the people who've slept in them are worse. You can get caught in those."

"Right. So the chair it is." Nika took a couple of steps back, until she was leaning against the doorframe.

Gavin positioned himself behind Tavera, hand resting lightly on his shoulder. "Whenever you're ready."

Tavera nodded, drawing a deep breath. "Don't pull me back until I say so. I need to get something concrete on this guy. Need to stop this."

The stubborn set to Gavin's mouth seemed to indicate he'd be making the decision regardless of Tavera's wishes. "Anchor, shield, investigate, get out."

Tavera nodded before he slumped down in the chair, eyes closing as the seconds stretched long. "There was no sky here. Little bird, little bird, beating herself against the ceiling until the blood dripped like warm rain." The cruel smile on Tavera's face was so foreign that Corwin felt his breath catch. "Broken wings, bones snapping like tiny. Little. Twigs."

With a quiet sound of distress, Enny brushed past Nika and through the door. Corwin half turned, attention divided between Tavera and the young psychic, afraid someone needed to follow her. Nika shook her head, silently mouthing *Let her go*.

"Poor tiny bird. Object lessons are the hardest to bear. No one wants to learn, no one wants to see, and the crushed feathers are drifting back and forth. One breath and they float away." Tavera sat up straighter, the movement causing Gavin's hand to tighten. "He paid her, said it was for sex. It was so easy. She smiled at him. She was *glad*." He practically spit the last word out, barely contained fury edging his voice.

Corwin stretched his cramped fingers, unaware until then just how tightly he'd clenched them. Deep down, where he hadn't been comfortable admitting it, at least to anyone else, there'd been hope that this case wouldn't be connected, that it was just a random murder of an undocumented prostitute. Horrible, violent, tragic, but not the work of someone planning to do it again. Having that hope dashed meant having to think about a serial killer with both psy abilities and the means for interplanetary travel. "Damn." He shoved a hand through his hair, keeping his voice low. "We could conceivably stay a step behind this person for the next twenty years . . ."

Nika's own answer was just as quiet, imbued with a faith he didn't think himself capable of at the moment. "Or West could pick up something, and we could catch him tomorrow."

"That too." He didn't bother trying to keep the doubt out of his voice.

The low mutter of conversation pulled their attention back to the center of the room, and Corwin found himself leaning in closer, hoping to make out the words. Tavera was smiling again, that same cruel little smirk, directed at some point where the wall met the ceiling. When he spoke, the words were clear and cold.

"There's so many ways to fuck someone. I've no interest in what's been used, already broken so someone could see what was inside." His face twisted. "Couldn't find what we wanted, so we settled, didn't we?"

"What did you do to her?"

Tavera shrugged away from Gavin's hand, turning in the chair to face him. "Anything I wanted to. No one's going to stop me. No one can."

Nika started to open her mouth, but Corwin nudged her shoulder before she could speak. "You need to keep your distance, let Gavin do his job. You'd only pull Tavera out." It seemed to Corwin that to someone in as deep as Tavera was right now, her interruption would be less of a distraction and more like getting hit over the head with a steel pole.

Tavera's gaze skipped past Gavin's face and around the room, probably at random, at least until he zoned in on Nika. "I know you, know what you're thinking." There was a childish glee in his words. "I know what you're going to *do*."

"What are we going to do?" In contrast, Gavin's voice was carefully neutral, devoid of curiosity.

"What are you going to do? You're going to trail after me like little children, and when you look up, the blood and feathers and tiny bits of bone are going to fill your mouths and your eyes . . ."

They were words, just words, and there was absolutely no reason for the sudden cloying taste of iron in Corwin's mouth or the wispy bits of gray drifting across his vision. He shoved outward with his shields, feeling Nika tense beside him. He spared her a glance, saw her eyes following something that wasn't there.

"Now, West. Pull back *now*."

Tavera gave a panting gasp as he slumped to the side. When Gavin reached to steady him, he batted the helping hands away with a hoarse exclamation that sounded like terror. The movement was enough to send him to the floor with a jarring thud. This time, Gavin kept some distance between them, at the ready but not touching.

"I'm sorry." The gaze that flicked desperately around the room was truly Tavera's, shadowed with fear. "He . . . Fuck, he *used* me to do that, I'm so sorry."

Nika swallowed hard. "That was real? The . . . the feathers?"

"Real enough." Tavera rolled to the side and sat up, movements slow and awkward.

Gavin offered Tavera a hand, and Corwin couldn't help the words that spilled from his mouth, even though they weren't meant to admonish. "I could actually taste blood. That wasn't normal, was it?"

Tavera's eyes were huge, nearly all pupil as he warily accepted the proffered grip, and he held on to Gavin's arm for a moment before shaking his head.

Gavin grimaced. "No, no, that was not normal at all."

"He . . ." Tavera trailed off, the silence stretching on too long for comfort. Corwin tried not to prompt in his impatience, and Tavera finally shuddered, refocusing. "He's strong, really strong. He should never have been able to use me as a conduit. That's not good."

"So what does that mean, exactly?" Nika rubbed at her eyes, then seemed to realize what she was doing, and dropped her hands to her side with obvious effort.

Tavera collapsed back into the chair, grip white-knuckled on the plastic sides. "That not only can he get inside the heads of his victims and torture them, but he can use other psys, channel through them to create any sort of illusions he wants."

"Any psy, or just you?" Corwin asked it too sharply—not necessarily his "interrogating the criminal" tone, but close.

"That's the big question, isn't it?" Tavera's grin faded before it reached his eyes. "Am I the weak link? That's what you're asking, isn't it?"

"Yes, I am." He rubbed at the crease in his forehead, frown deepening. "He's obviously unstable. If he's able to, for lack of a better word, hijack anyone, then we potentially have a more dangerous situation on our hands than just the murder of a homeless woman and a prostitute."

"And if it's just me?" Tavera must have taken lessons from Gavin, for all the inflection in the words.

Agents were equal to inspectors. It was in all the training materials, hammered into the IEC code of interagency conduct. But he still felt like he was endangering a civilian as he said, "It gives us some degree of control over the situation. And maybe, just maybe, makes you intriguing. Maybe draws him to you."

"Uh, *no*." Gavin's voice was unnaturally loud, and Tavera was the only one who didn't jump. "You are not using him as bait for some sort of trap. No."

Tavera sighed, focus seeming to drift between them. He looked to be fighting to maintain his lucidity as he waved a negligent hand, his voice a weary drawl. "I appreciate your concern for my virtue, Gavikins, but I don't think Corwin was intending to use me as the sacrificial lamb. Were you, Inspector?"

Corwin's shoulders shifted up in an awkward shrug. "That wasn't *exactly* how I meant it."

"See, everything's fine." Tavera levered himself up out of the chair, and Corwin wondered if anyone else noticed the slight tremor in his hands when he waved them all toward the door. "I think we're done here, now. I, for one, could use some lunch."

"What about the mor—"

His question was cut off by the sharp pain in his foot, and he gave Nika a slightly offended look as she pushed past him, raising her voice over his. "That sounds great. Let's get something to eat. My turn to buy."

Gavin's grateful smile was unmistakable. "First one to the flyer gets to choose where we eat."

In the hallway, it was easy to see that Tavera knew their diversion for what it was. He shoved his hands into his pockets, a silent, narrow-eyed stare speaking volumes about how much of the good cheer was an act. Corwin trailed everyone out of the building, waiting to see if there was a dustup incoming, but by the time they hit the street, Tavera was smiling again.

CHAPTER 7

A meal and prodigious amounts of caffeine went a long way toward easing the ache behind West's eyes. Even Corwin looked less tense than usual, and West snickered, leaning in close to whisper in Nika's ear. "Gav usually carries snacks for me. Maybe you should think about that for Inspector Menivie. Look how sweet and docile he is now."

"I don't know if I'd go that far, but you could be onto something. Not that I'm interested in playing the part of Corwin's . . . well, anything. We're friends, and partners. He can carry his own snacks."

He grinned, voice teasing. "Don't worry, no one could ever mistake you for his mother. Girlfriend maybe, daughter if you pushed it, but never his mother."

She laughed very quietly. "Gee, thanks for that vote of confidence. Given that we're standing in a morgue, that makes me feel so much better. Younger."

The attendant raised his voice to be heard over the grind of the metal drawer sliding out. "No one's claimed the body, but that's hardly a surprise. When you're finished with your investigation, it'll be sent to our central facility for cremation." He stepped back, gesturing them forward. "So make sure you get any information you need."

West nodded. "Thanks, we'll let you know when we're done here." While the man didn't exactly run, he certainly didn't waste any time leaving, and it didn't take any sort of Talent to see that he'd never been around a working psy agent before and wasn't anxious to start now.

Drawing a deep breath, West stepped closer to the body, and fought down a twinge of unease. Gavin was right there, his presence a solid wall of comforting blankness, and that helped, but it couldn't cleanse him of his last Read.

There were no obvious signs of trauma on the body, but he was always surprised, even after all these years, at how much smaller death made a person appear. They had no ident but the credit chit she'd been carrying, so they had a best guess of twenty-five imperial years until a facial match came through. Laid out on a steel shelf, twisted and frozen in an expression of abject terror, she looked much younger. He carefully rested his fingers across hers, closing his eyes.

It was just a job, just a job, no matter what anyone else tried to make it into. She sold a product, and he was buying. Tapping into the well of her lingering psychic impression proved clearer than most of what he'd Read, a common side effect of a violent death. When something, some*one*, tried to sever a life, the residual was stronger, a shout where normally only a whisper was needed.

He let it play out. Kenara, the dead woman, filled his head with her last moments: anger, and fear, but there was nothing straightforward about any of it. "She screamed for him. That's what he paid her for, but she didn't know it, and she didn't want it. She wanted the money, money for hours, money for skin and a smile, but he didn't want a smile, and it says in the rules no screaming, no hurting, but he didn't follow the rules. Sh— she screamed, she did, a lot, but it didn't stop, the b-birds kept tearing at her face, her— her eyes. But there's no blood."

West rubbed at his face, pushing hard against his eyes, then held his fingers up. Not so deep into the Read that he wasn't aware of Gavin close by, Corwin and Nika just beyond him, he saw all three flinch, but then they faded away, and it was only her. "See? No blood." He stared at her hands, she stared at his, bloodless and nothing against the storm of sparrows, and then it cleared, and she stopped screaming, because this was never meant for her.

The blow from behind, like a wind made of knives, buffeted his back before knocking him down. All the pieces were jagged and broken and wrong, so wrong, everything was wrong since she'd gone, but not the same she, the bird. Not a bird, but with wings, wings made of fire, and if West could only hold on a little longer, he'd understand . . .

"West, I need you to come home now." Gavin pulled at his hands, and he wanted to shove, to stay where he was, on the edge of finding something worthwhile. He must have managed some resistance, because he won the tug-of-war, their clasped hands resting on his chest.

Gavin's voice was more insistent this time, and through his own eyes, rather than the Read, West saw him frown. "I'm going to start the countback. You need to follow."

"Doesn't want me to go. Left this pretty little bomb here, all for me, but I know the wires to cut." He wasn't meant to see beyond the murdered girl, not to the hand and heart that had guided the death, but he could keep pushing, keep following her screams and pain down the wormhole, and he'd find his way out the other side and into the head that'd pulled the strings, making the sparrows fly.

"Five, four, now, West, three—"

West's explosive flurry of movement caught Gavin by surprise, sending him stumbling backward as West slammed into him. The funny thing was, West only realized he was moving when he careened off the metal shelf, the sharp pain in his shoulder a background buzz. Nika dropped her notebook, arms outstretched to catch him, but Corwin was one step ahead of her, absorbing the full force of his panicked flight without a sound, both arms wrapped around him, pinning his hands to his side.

"You're out; you're okay now." Corwin was so close, their faces touched. "Let it go."

West bit his lip hard enough to draw blood, unable to look away as Corwin's eyes seemed to grow larger until they filled his entire field of vision, a blue-gray sky swallowing him up. "You're not there." It was all West managed before he was sliding out of Corwin's arms and toward the floor.

"What the hell was that?"

West groaned and started to roll over, both Nika's voice and concern hammering with equal intensity in his head. He swallowed hard over nausea, and wanted to beg her to stop, but settled for muttering, "I'd tell you if I had a clue."

There was a rustle of movement as Gavin knelt next to him, drawing him in with an arm around his shoulders. He leaned without meaning to, still seeing feathers and hearing their words through a filter of screams. "It should only have been her, Kenara, but it wasn't. Never done a secondary Read on another psy before, not *through* someone like this. And guess what they didn't cover at the academy?" His eyes were open, but he wasn't having much luck focusing, at least until he found Gavin's face. "He was there, hidden under her, under the feathers and the wings, and he *wanted* me to know that. He . . ." He licked his lips and tried again. "This guy, he's really strong. Gav, this is bad. I don't like it."

"You did good. It's okay."

The fingers petting his hair went a long way toward calming him, and West slumped a little lower. Solid human touch was grounding in the most basic sense, even to a non-psy, and Gavin's casual acknowledgment that he wasn't entirely present yet let him come back slowly from the precipice.

"He was inside her with me, but he was just a ghost, and so is she. This is so bad." He cracked one eye open, unsure of when he'd closed them in the first place, and peered over Gav's shoulder. "Cookies and coffee might help."

Nika laughed, her nervous relief unmistakable. "I think we can manage that, as long as I don't have to carry you all the way back to the ship. Think you can walk, swooning boy?"

"I can't help it if I have a delicate constitution," he said with grave dignity. "It's a burden I simply have to bear." He couldn't stop seeing the overlay of a rented room, feeling the blows that hadn't been real. Real enough to kill her, but not— He shook it off. "Where did Corwin go?"

"He excused himself once you let go of him. Said he was going to make sure the body wouldn't be cremated yet, and arrange for it to be transported to an IEC facility." Gavin's tone never changed, but West could tell, even in his punch-drunk state, that Corwin hadn't made a graceful exit.

Nika reached out a hand to help pull him to his feet, then hesitated, obviously thinking better of it. She glanced at Gavin, her arm falling back to her side. "Just so it's clear, I'm not carrying either of you." She did, however, hold the door for them, and once Gavin slipped a shoulder under West's arm, the three of them made a slow, awkward trip back to the flyer.

It always took him forever to get warm again, but he had work to do. Once they returned to the ship, West pulled on a shapeless old sweatshirt and pants before padding toward the galley, silent in stocking feet as he paused outside the doorway to collect himself.

"Thanks for being so quick to react," Gav said grudgingly. "West really caught me by surprise."

Corwin's muttered reply sounded equally ungracious, but West figured that was because he *regretted* being so quick. He knew Gav was motivated by guilt, though. Twenty-odd years of watching out for him, and Gav still took every failure personally. Subdued, West forced a grin as he stepped into the room. "How lucky am I, having all of you watching out for me?"

Corwin's lanky body sprawled across an entire half of the table, doubtless the reason that Nika was standing, hip leaned against the counter. Corwin glanced up, then quickly away as West slipped in next to Gav on the far side of the table.

Gavin gestured toward his open notebook. "I've typed up my observations. When you're ready, you can add your part."

"Yeah, okay." West slid into the seat next to Gavin. "Want to type while I talk?" The talking was going to be hard enough, and while typing meant he could avoid looking at anyone, it seemed like a cheat, somehow. He stared at the notebook for several seconds, feeling Nika's poorly concealed worry sliding in and out of his head. "I'm okay, really." He gave her what he hoped was a convincing nod.

She started, the guilt even more obvious on her face than in her thoughts. "Of course you are."

"Are you sure you're ready to debrief?" From the way Corwin was leaning forward, though, intent investigative face on, it was pretty clear that he wasn't anticipating a negative answer.

West shrugged, the movement sending his ratty old sweatshirt dangerously close to sliding off one shoulder. "Of course. Why wouldn't I be?" He knew his grin was faint at best, but he was too tired to care. "You think I'm worried just because there's a crazed killer out there who might be stronger than me, as unlikely as that seems? And because he obviously knows I'm investigating him, that would make me not okay?"

Nika whistled softly through pursed lips as Corwin shot up straight on the bench, obviously as surprised as her. Gavin, however, merely looked resigned.

"Say again?" Corwin loomed across the table, as if proximity would get a quicker answer.

West didn't find the movement threatening, but he still jerked back as far as the chair would allow. Corwin stopped abruptly, and sat down with obvious effort, hands on the table. His fingers twitched, but he stayed put.

"This guy *knows*?" Nika shook her head. "How?"

"I don't know." He ran both hands through his hair, likely leaving it standing up in random tufts. "He left a . . . I don't know, for lack of a better word, a marker."

"But one that any psy agent investigating would've found, right?" West gave her a bleak smile. "Enny didn't pick it up."

"Not to stroke your already considerable ego, but maybe that's because she's not as strong a Reader as you?" Gavin shrugged. "It was her first time out. It's easy to miss things."

"Much as I do love your big, strong compliments on my ego, I think it's accurate to say that while he may not have known that *I* would be the Reader called in, he knew someone was going to be, and he kindly left that little snare for them. Me. Us." West waved a hand. "Whatever." He stared at the table for several seconds, pulling his thoughts together. "As big as my ego is, it's not really overstepping to say that there isn't another Reader out of PsyAc with a Talent half as strong. I don't know for sure if this guy knows it's me. I *do* know that nobody else would have gotten that much from the Read."

Gavin's brow creased. "So is this guy stalking you through these victims, or has he somehow figured out that we're investigating them?"

"I just told you, I don't *know*. I'd need more information to hazard a guess. Even if he's picking them knowing we've flagged the file, he'd still be killing. The victims don't feel personal to me, just the challenge." He felt like he was talking in circles, being goaded into conclusions he wasn't sure were even likely, but that was just perception, and perception was a bitch when he could rarely get a handle on whose perception it actually was.

"Then we need to figure out if he knows that you're catching his clues, or if he's testing you." West could feel Corwin's intense gaze on him, and nodded as Corwin continued. "He's left these clues for a reason. Do you think he's watching somehow?"

"Couldn't tell you. He could be a Remote Reader, or he could just not care. About the only thing I'm certain of is that he's not in my head." After the last little fiasco, that'd been his main fear. He clenched his hands into fists on the table, and made a point of uncurling each finger, forcing his anxiety down with every crack of a knuckle. "We have to figure out how he knows there's a psy team on the case, and we have to figure out the connections between the victims, or at least *his* connections between them."

Gavin tapped his notebook, spinning it around to show them a picture of the girl. "She was from Ethris. What if he's daisy-chaining victims—picking someone new up wherever he dumps his last one?"

The young, smiling face was barely recognizable as the woman he'd seen just hours before in the morgue. West looked away, his last image of her overlaying the one on Gavin's screen.

"We can't be certain of that unless a victim shows up from Bodum." Nika stated firmly, and he had to agree. The theory made sense, but IEC policy was clear: evidence proved theories, not the other way around. "We should look for a port connection between Ethris and Bodum. Maybe we can track down a ship that's been screened through port authority on both planets."

"Except that Bodum doesn't require vessels staying for less than an imperial tenday to register with port authority." West sighed as he sprawled back in his chair. "It's worth looking into, but I wouldn't count on finding anything."

Gavin raised his eyebrows. "And how do you know about Bodum's docking laws?"

West grinned, a little smug, but Corwin beat him to answering, voice deceptively mild. "I'm sure Agent Tavera is familiar with all sorts of illicit docking maneuvers."

West choked over a smothered snicker. He was still trying to figure out if their relationship was strangely antagonistic flirting or just strangely antagonistic, but either way, Corwin amused him. He stretched before getting to his feet, yawning into his hand. "And on that note, I'm heading to bed. Good night." He waved, sauntering toward the corridor with the kind of deliberate sway he could only manage when he was tired or drunk, and left silence in his wake. At least until he paused at the doorway, turning his head to call over his shoulder, "If anyone wants to put into port later, just come wake me up."

Gavin groaned softly, burying his face in his hands for a second as he shook his head. "Why is this my life?"

The sound of Corwin's chair scraping across the floor was loud, and West lingered in the door. Corwin's eyes widened, meeting West's amused look with no small amount of startled chagrin, before he abruptly turned to head for the bridge. His footsteps were rapid, and West and Nika both snickered loudly enough that Gavin abandoned self-pity to glare at them. "You're not helping."

She screamed, screamed his name, screamed in his head, and then she filled him up with her anger and his body turned, the knife in his hand slashing out—

West woke when he hit the floor—a colder bedmate than Gavin, who stirred and reached across the mattress. Encountering only empty space, his partner settled back into untroubled slumber. West tried to filter the fear through a lens of reason and control, pressing the heel of his hand over the ache in his chest. When that didn't work, he gave up and untangled himself enough to get to his feet.

He was just slipping out of Gavin's room when Nika turned the corner in the hallway, coming toward him. She was dressed in a faded pink shirt and shorts that were fraying at the hem, clearly on her way back from the workout room. West faked a smile for half a second, until he couldn't keep up the illusion anymore and winced. He glanced over his shoulder at Gavin's door, noting that Nika was making a deliberate point not to. It didn't matter, since he felt her discomfort like a physical presence. Her jealousy, and the way she fought it, equal parts resignation and logic, pushed at him, and he swallowed. He wasn't sure if the intrusion on her emotions was worse than letting her believe something that wasn't true.

Nika gave him a little wave. "What are you doing up so late?"

"We're not fucking. We don't, I mean. It's not—" He pressed the flat of his hand against his eye again and groaned. "Gavin's going to kill me"

"I. Um. That's . . . good?"

Slightly frantic and still not awake, he gripped her elbow and propelled them down the corridor toward the galley, well out of earshot of Gavin's quarters. "I'm sorry, I'm sorry. Just, I haven't been able to sleep, and you're so guilty, and so *loud*—" Realizing he was still holding her arm, he let go and backed up a step. "Sorry."

"It's okay. Really, I should be apologizing to you. Or not?"

West croaked out a laugh, tension and a weird sort of relief warring in his head. "Oh, I'm going to be in so much trouble. This is a direct violation of Rule Two, just so you know. I am going to be smited— smote? Gavin is going to kick my ass."

Nika raised her eyebrows. "What the hell is Rule Two?"

"I will not interfere with Gavin's love life, even if I mean well." Supremely uncomfortable, he turned to the cabinets, locating the coffee pods and shoving one into the machine. His exaggerated search for a mug was a ploy not to have to look at her while he spoke. "And he doesn't have one. With me, I mean. He does have one, obviously, but not with me."

He shoved his mug under the pod, then pushed the button, setting it to brew before turning around very slowly. "Not that I don't love him, just, you know, we're not. I'm not his type." When the machine beeped, he grabbed his mug and sucked down half a cup of black coffee in one gulp, still unwilling to meet Nika's eyes. He wasn't kidding. Gav was seriously going to kill him when he found out about this conversation. Or maybe glare and not talk to him for a few days, which was worse.

"Do you want to be?" Nika asked carefully, and he had to give her credit, because he hadn't seen that coming.

"No. I mean, sure, when I was about thirteen, but I've since learned that being around someone all the time and having an erection isn't the same thing as having an erection *because* you're around someone." Finally looking up, he couldn't help a fond smile, or the bemusement that made him lift his mug in salute to her. "And since I'm already going to die a terrible death, I'll tell you that he's an awesome kisser. Or at least he was, when we were thirteen."

Nika ran a hand through her sweaty hair. When his smile stretched at the corners, she glared at him. "Now you're just being a jerk."

"Guilty." He hesitated for a second before reaching out to pat her arm. "I'm really sorry. I know it's a horrible violation of your privacy, and if it wasn't the middle of the night, I would've tried really hard to annoy Corwin instead."

"You know you don't have to *try* for that, right?"

"I can't just coast on my good looks and charm, or he'll think I'm not really wooing him."

He'd been trying to make her laugh, and clearly the too-serious look was working.

"I didn't realize you were wooing. Don't let his apparent lack of interest or stunning degree of contempt for your methods and professionalism put you off. I'm sure he'll be putty in your hands."

He tapped the side of his cup with a fingertip, smile softening. "All part of the fun, Inspector. One day he's going to wake up and realize that we're made for each other." He cocked his head to the side, considering. "Either that, or he really will snap and kill me." He dismissed the thought with a shrug, and thumped his mug back on the counter.

"Use your words, please." She didn't exactly snap at him, but it was sharper than normal, and he realized that he'd been staring for a lot longer than he should have. She obviously wasn't expecting him to start laughing at her, though, if her glare was any sign.

"That's Rule Five. I see you've skipped over a couple." His fingers twisted, plucking at the hem of his shirt. "I just wanted to say I think you'd be good together. That you'd be good for Gavin."

"I . . . Thanks."

"So. This is awkward." He clapped his hands together, inclining his head toward the door. "I'm just going to go pretend we never had this conversation."

"Perfect, I think I'll do the same."

"Pleasure not talking to you, Inspector Santivan." He pushed away from the counter with all the casual nonchalance expected of him, and managed to wait until he was out of sight before breaking into a trot. If nothing else, he wanted to be safely ensconced in his room cn the off chance that Gavin woke up and decided to have a midnight conversation with Nika. It was a matter of personal safety.

CHAPTER 8

West possessed a healthy distrust of mornings. Being awake and coherent before Gavin, who had no problem with being a disgustingly early riser, felt wrong. The nightmares had ramped up again after he'd returned to his own bed last night. Bad enough that he'd slunk back into Gavin's room, despite promising himself he wouldn't. Chances were his dreams had disturbed Gav's rest as much as, if not more than, they'd screwed with his. With that thought in mind, he'd made a mature decision, choosing not to plant cold feet on his best friend's bare legs and jolt Gavin awake.

Now he shuffled down the corridor to his cabin, considering the possibility of a shower and shave, but discarding the idea in favor of coffee. He was well into his third mug when Nika came around the corner and jumped back with an exaggerated double take.

"Who are you and what have you done with Westley Tavera?"

"I have no idea what you're talking about." He put as much wounded dignity into his voice as he could.

Nika pulled out a chair with one foot and dropped down, giving him a smile when he slid a mug in her direction. "Only because you're not used to being awake this early. Your brain hasn't engaged yet. And seriously, didn't we just meet here?"

It didn't seem worth the effort to fight the truth. "Be nice, or I won't make you breakfast." He rose from the table, intent on another cup of consciousness, and grabbed a package of frozen pastries to dump on a heating tray.

The warmer dinged just as Corwin stepped into the galley, eyes locked on his notebook. He glanced up at the sound, visibly blanching when he saw West, and started to turn around.

"You're *just* in time!" West cranked up the wattage on his smile, trying like hell not to throw himself at Corwin and cling, just for a respite from his spinning, exhausted head. "Sit down, I fixed you breakfast."

"I'm not hungry," Corwin mumbled, but West reached around the inspector to pull out a chair, nudging until Corwin sat down in an obvious effort to put some space between them.

There was something wrong with getting as much satisfaction as he did from tweaking Corwin. Equally disconcerting was the fact that he'd made the pastries knowing Corwin's weakness for them. Nika's warning cough made him start, guilty, and he dropped back to an acceptable distance, covering his discomfort with a mouthful of sugary goodness.

Corwin's suspicious glare was probably meant for West, but he still picked up a fork. His smile was undoubtedly meant for the pastry, but West wasn't above taking the credit. "See? Just breakfast. I wasn't out to poison you or anything."

"Your concern for my well-being is noted."

"You're welcome." Corwin hadn't actually thanked him, but he preferred to give the benefit of the doubt.

Gavin shuffled silently into the room, and West gave him a wave. "Made you breakfast." He pointed to the counter, where a bowl holding a packet of instant porridge was waiting. Gavin muttered a half-awake acknowledgment, ripped open the packet, and dumped it into the bowl with a shot of hot water from the coffee machine.

"West has been quite domestic this morning. Coffee and breakfast for everyone. *And* he was the first person up. I thought it was the end of the world." Nika's voice was far too sincere to be real, and when he looked up, her smirk was the most evil expression he'd ever seen from her.

"He makes me feel that way a lot." Gavin sighed, accepting the spoon West produced with a flourish. "So what's the plan? Do we have any leads to follow up?"

"Nothing new—"

"I'm going back for another Read—"

Nika and he both stopped, and West waved a fork in her direction. "After you."

Nika laughed, returning his salute with one of her own. "No, after you."

Corwin seemed to choke on a sip of coffee, or possibly snort into his mug, but made no other comment and didn't raise his eyes from his plate.

"I'm sorry, you're going to what?" Gavin interrupted, the stubborn set of his mouth all too familiar.

"I'm going back to the hotel today. I want to try for another Read." He spoke very slowly, enunciating each word, then sat back, eyes wide with playacted innocence.

Gavin shook his head. "No, you're not."

"Actually, I am. In about fifteen minutes." He reached across the table to dip his fork into Gavin's bowl. "So if you could eat up, that would be good."

Gavin pushed the fork away with his spoon, resulting in a solid metallic *clink*, and West grinned, deciding it was a clear invitation to a silverware duel. Striking a defensive pose, he dripped oatmeal on the table with a solid, wet *plop*.

Corwin's sigh was long-suffering and loud, and West had no qualms about using that to his advantage, tuning down the wattage of his smile to a sympathetic moue. "I'm sorry, Corwin, I certainly didn't mean to exclude you from my plans for the day. I was hoping we could have a nice, quiet dinner together, maybe watch a vid afterward. I have a wonderful collection of light romantic comedies I'm sure you'd really enjoy."

"While I certainly understand your motivation for making that offer—" Corwin stood, plate in hand, as he turned to drop it into the scrubber. "I'm afraid I'd rather enjoy something from my own collection tonight. Alone."

West swiveled around in his chair, one eyebrow raised high. "Alone? Are you sure? It's usually more enjoyable watching something romantic *with* someone romantic."

"I'm not nearly as enamored of you as you seem to be of yourself, and I'd hate to intrude, so the answer is still no." Corwin smiled blandly, refilling his coffee cup before sitting back down.

West was caught at a rare loss for words. Impressed despite himself, he focused his wide grin unerringly on Corwin. Corwin refused to look up.

"If we could just get back to the matter at hand." Gavin took a deep breath, obviously working on modulating his annoyance in front of Corwin and Nika. "I don't want you going back to the hotel. I don't want you attempting another Read that involves this guy right now."

He struggled not to be hurt, knowing full well that Gavin had his best interests at heart. It didn't make it any easier to swallow the idea that Gavin didn't think he knew when to call himself back from a case. Apparently he didn't know how to hide his hurt either, because his words came out sharp, bitter as overbrewed tea. "I don't think that's your decision to make."

"As your Ground, I think it is."

"And as a self-actualized free citizen of the Empire, I'm going to have to disagree with you." He was smiling, but he knew full well that the stubborn little line between his eyes was growing deeper. Being corrected was annoying. Being overridden in front of Corwin and Nika was embarrassing. Being reminded that Gavin couldn't trust him was worse than any of the rest.

"What do you think you're going to get out of it? He only left information he wants you to know." Gavin jammed his spoon into his bowl, not looking up.

"Right, because I'm *only* capable of Reading information that's been deliberately left for me? That's going to severely limit the usefulness of my skills."

"That's not what I said *or* implied," Gavin snapped. "Don't put words in my mouth."

"Are you sure? Because that's the impression I'm getting. That this guy is soooo much better than me that the only things I'm capable of getting are what he's left all gift wrapped." This was showing every sign of being one of their thankfully infrequent big arguments, but damned if he was going to back down when he knew he was right. Even if it did mean dredging up the time he'd been so, so wrong.

Gavin blew out a harsh breath, eyes narrowed when he looked up. "Oh for fuck's sake, that's why I'm against this. You and your damned ego, that's all this is about, isn't it? Let me make things crystal clear: I'm not going to let you put your life and mine in danger just so you can fulfill some need to prove that you don't follow the same rules as us ordinary mortals. We've played that game before, and it didn't go well."

It was the first time the Rashium incident had come up between them in anger, and the flash of guilt on Gavin's face was nothing compared to the wave of shame that rose to choke West. They'd been circling it, but he hadn't thought either of them would take the first swing. The unfairness of it hit harder than it had any reason to. It hadn't been about ego, not when all he'd meant to do was help. Except that it had. He'd wanted to do something no one else could, and in the end, that made it his fault.

"Agents."

To be honest, he'd completely forgotten about Nika and Corwin. Nika's eyes were huge, mouth open a little, and she jumped when Corwin reached around her for the cream. "Don't get involved," he warned her.

She turned to stare at Corwin, his soft rebuke loading the room with more tension. His jaw tightened, and West fixed his attention on Gavin, refusing to look at Corwin's calm detachment.

"I wasn't—"

"Yes, you were." Corwin's smug tone was everything West hated. "You were going to interrupt their little tiff and try to defuse the situation. Don't. They'll just turn on you. You had your domestic-dispute training." Corwin cradled his mug of coffee and took a small sip.

"But leave it to you to defuse it with your wonderful sense of humor, Inspector." West held on to his brittle smile, afraid it was going to shatter. He couldn't even look at Gavin anymore, but managed to turn down the venom in his denial. "I don't make my own rules," he muttered at the wall.

Corwin glanced at him and shrugged, then went back to sipping coffee.

"No, of course you don't." Gavin sounded exhausted, but West had no sympathy to spare. "You've just got this all-consuming need to be right, no matter what it costs. Stop trying to make up for a mistake nobody is blaming you for. I don't want to go through all the pointless partnership training again, and I doubt you really want to take another vacation."

West didn't give Gavin time to apologize, unsure at this point if it would even happen. His chair slammed back against the counter as he stood up, the need to escape overriding everything else, guilt and pain and betrayal a solid knot in his stomach.

He made it as far as the hall outside the galley before he had to lean against the wall, fighting to quiet the snatches of emotion from Nika, and the memories that always lurked in the shadows of his head. Unfortunately, he hadn't made it far enough, because he could still hear the conversation.

"Well, that went swimmingly," Gavin muttered.

"If it helps, I'm one hundred percent behind you, Agent." Corwin was all bland amusement.

Gavin's voice rose. "Oh, I'm sure you're very supportive. You've made your position on Actives pretty clear. This ought to be great for you, Inspector. You can watch West sink his teeth into a case that'll ruin him as an agent and destroy his career, and tell people you were right all along about his instabil—"

West swallowed hard, wanting to believe that Gavin was simply angry, that his partner hadn't lost that much faith. He didn't want to hear anymore, didn't want to hear Corwin agree, but he couldn't move.

"Before you finish that sentence, I think you should take a very deep breath, and think about how it's going to sound out loud when you tell us that you think your partner, your friend, is incapable of following proper investigative procedure and may not be safe for fieldwork." There was steel in Corwin's voice.

"Excuse me, inspectors. That was extremely unprofessional of me. It won't happen again." Gavin was obviously gritting his teeth.

"You shoving him into cryo storage? Because I can't think of another way that you're going to avoid having the rest of that fight." Corwin's easy sarcasm almost helped. The stars knew, nothing else about the man was easy.

"I should go find my partner. Excuse me."

West pushed himself away from the wall. The last thing he wanted was to face Gav right now. The doubts were there, the seeds planted, and he had to get away while he still had some shred of dignity to hide behind. To that end, the comm in the lounge was the closest place to call for transport, and he could grab his badge on the way out.

"Bodum Planetary Enforcement, please identify yourself."

"Agent Westley Tavera, Imperial Enforcement Coalition, PsyAc Field Team. I need transport from IEC vessel 041685, *Vigilance*, to active scene B-197-TN."

"Stand by, Agent." The stretch of silence made him twitch, and he had to fight to keep from constantly glancing over his shoulder. "Confirmed, Agent Tavera. Transport is on the way."

"Thank you."

CHAPTER 9

"**Y**ou blighted little bastard."

Corwin pulled up short outside the bridge, hesitating to interrupt Gavin's tantrum, especially since it didn't take a genius to figure out who the blighted bastard in question was.

Gavin had a notebook out, and was hitting the screen with a little more force than necessary.

"Bodum Planetary Enforcement, please identify yourself."

"Agent Gavin Hale, Imperial Enforcement Coalition, PsyAc Field Team. I need transport for one from IEC vessel 041685, *Vigilance*, to active scene B-197-TN."

Corwin wavered, professionalism warring with a desire to stay out of their little spat, but professionalism won out. "One minute, Agent Hale," he said, loud enough to carry over the comm channel. "Make that transport for three please, Dispatch."

Gavin spun around, expression far from welcoming, but didn't countermand the request.

"Stand by."

Gavin's scowl deepened as he waited. Corwin shrugged, willing to postpone the conversation until the call was finished.

"Agent Hale, transport has been dispatched, but we would like to remind you that not every department has the resources of the IEC. If you and your partner could manage to coordinate your transportation needs next time, it would be greatly appreciated."

"Noted, Dispatch, and my apologies."

Not that he'd ever want to be, but Corwin was particularly glad not to be in Tavera's shoes now. Gavin's anger wasn't disguised in the least, his gritted teeth and furious glare a dead giveaway. Corwin raised an eyebrow, keeping his voice deliberately neutral. "I think Inspector Santivan and I should be there with you. It's stupid to walk into a dangerous situation without full backup."

Gavin seemed to consider arguing, but common sense eventually overrode pride. He gave a short nod. "Agreed. I'll see you on the landing field in five."

Gavin had the entire ride back to the hotel to fume, and made full use of it. Corwin ignored it as best he could by staring out the flyer window, but he could see Nika shooting Gavin quick, questioning glances.

By the time they got upstairs, badged themselves through the crime scene barriers, and found Tavera pacing the confines of the room, the anger radiating off of Gavin was palpable. It was obvious that the guilty look Tavera was trying to hide wasn't going to garner him any mercy from his Ground.

Gavin held a hand up before Tavera could get a word in edgewise, head shaking. "No, dude. No. We'll do this because you seem to think we're going to get a decent lead out of it, and apparently my input as your partner no longer matters to you. But don't try to charm your way out of the consequences."

Corwin had no interest in becoming involved in their personal war, whatever the cause, so he stood in the doorway with Nika, updating the file to document their visit to the scene.

"It matters." Tavera stared at Gavin for a long, silent moment, and Gavin spent it alternately glaring back and fiddling with getting the notebook recorder set up.

"Really? Because it seems like I'm less your partner now, and more the guy who follows you around cleaning up your messes and explaining your bullshit to everyone else." Gavin didn't even bother looking up from his notebook.

"Because everything I do is a mess, right, Gav? At least you'll always be busy."

Corwin narrowed his eyes at the familiar words. Nika obviously recognized them as well, distress flashing across her face. Only Gavin seemed too angry to pick up on the fact that Tavera had overheard their conversation.

Tavera continued, voice rising. "And how nice of you to bring Inspector Menivie and Inspector Santivan along to witness me fucking up proper investigative procedure and being unsafe for fieldwork." The smile he flashed at Gavin was so wide it must have hurt. "I'm going to try a touch Read this time, see if I can find anything that he left behind without knowing it, instead of what he wants us to know." There was no missing the sneer on the last few words, although for Tavera it was actually rather subtle.

"Fine. Are we setting a time limit, a distress level, or should I just wait until you reach max load and pass out at my feet?"

"You know how I love a good swoon," Tavera snapped, slapping his open palm down against the top of the nightstand, jaw clenched.

Nika shuffled her feet on the dirty floor, obviously intending to draw attention to herself. Tavera turned to look, and she met his gaze with a small, tight smile. "If you're both done ripping each other to shreds, and ready to get some work done, Corwin and I are here to provide whatever backup you need." She waited until Tavera acknowledged her with a short nod, then took a step back. "We'll stay out of the way until then."

Tavera started pacing the perimeter of the room, trailing his fingers across the dirty walls. Gavin moved along with him, waiting and watching.

"So many people have had sex in this room that it's not even funny. When I'm done with this, remind me to bleach my hands." Tavera's face contorted, voice choked. "Oh hell, and my brain. Remind me to bleach my *brain*. People shouldn't bend that way, Gavin. But they do. They bend any way you want—over, under, you just have to get into their heads, right? Fill up their heads with sunshine so they don't notice the poison when it burn burn burns."

Corwin had already reinforced his shields against the residue in the room, but even so, Tavera's words caused an involuntary shudder. For a room frequented by sex workers, there was surprisingly little pleasure to be felt, like the place had been wiped clean of its yesterdays, as well as prints.

Gavin stepped closer and snapped a picture of Tavera's hand where it rested against the edge of the window, fingers curled over the cord for the curtains. "How does it burn?"

"Oh, so smart, so ready, but you know you're only fighting a shadow, don't you? You're up against the echo of a voice you've never even heard, and it's going to crush you." Black, bitter amusement colored Tavera's words.

"So tell me how to hear the voice. Where's the voice coming from? Who wants to speak?" Gavin didn't seem distressed, and Corwin was willing to take his cue from that.

"Too many questions." Tavera waved his free hand impatiently, voice his own, if subdued. "Trying for more."

"West."

The begging note was enough for Corwin to see that Gavin wanted Tavera to stop, and knew it didn't matter.

"He knows there's a PsyAc team assigned. He— Oh, clever, clever, but he can't hurt me that way, because I've already played that game. He wants to hurt, he wants everyone damaged, blown apart inside, he's proving a point. We always have to prove our point, don't we? Always have to be right, even if it hurts, even if it kills, because if we're not right, we're useless." Tavera's demeanor changed abruptly, his shoulders and head snapping back. "He's useless, this one, useless on the inside and the drugs don't work, the stars don't work, the sex doesn't work, nothing works, nothing, and he tried to let go. Tried to wash it all away in a kitchen, but the dishes never ended, and they found him."

The delighted little coo of Tavera's voice wasn't familiar, but Gavin's reaction, shoulders tight with tension, was. "West, tell me a different story."

Corwin's knowledge of PsyAc consisted of several briefings and one class, but he knew that the phrase, ingrained by a combination of hypnosis and training, served as a kind of soft reset and test all at once. If Tavera still had enough self-awareness to guide the Read, they could back it up and try a different thread.

Tavera jerked, forehead smacking against the window frame, and Gavin reached out, face going oddly blank.

"Don't. Don't, I'm not done telling this story yet. He wants to know the end. He wants to know the worst of me, and I'm not done telling him." Tavera hunched his shoulders, head down, voice rumbling from deep in his chest, soft and pleading.

"No, you've already told that story. Pick another, or it's time to come home." Gavin put a hand on Tavera's arm, squeezing.

Corwin tried not to let the scene affect him, though Nika seemed to be doing a better job of it. It wasn't pleasure that was building outside his shields, but it felt close enough to it to worry him. Gavin might not enjoy watching his partner falter, but whoever'd left the trap had certainly gotten their kicks finger-painting horrors on the wallpaper for Tavera to find.

"He says I have to finish. He wants to know the worst of me, and I haven't told him yet. I'm supposed to pretend that what I did doesn't matter, like nobody can see it, but they can all see. He says all I have to do is show him, and he'll let me go."

The skin on the back of Corwin's neck tightened with gooseflesh, the sense of wrongness harsh, and he found himself stepping toward Tavera without even being aware of moving. Gavin's voice brought him up short.

"You don't have to do anything." Gavin tightened his grip, tugging a surprisingly tractable Tavera away from the window a few centimeters at a time.

Tavera stopped, his eyes opening slowly, and he shook his head, tone still mournful when he spoke. "That's what he wants from all of us. For everyone to do their best worst thing, so we know he pushed until he made us do it. I'm sorry, I'm sorry, I'm sorry. The worst was that I hurt you. I'm sorry." He continued to apologize, and Gavin patted his shoulder as the vision seemed to lose its sway.

None of them were prepared for Tavera to grab the heavy glass ashtray on the table and swing it, still whimpering a litany of apologies. Gavin jumped back and managed to avoid getting hit, and the ashtray shattered when it smashed into the wall.

Corwin moved quickly enough that the shards were still rolling when he shoved past Gavin and wrapped his arms around Tavera.

"Westley, eat the cosmic egg." Gavin's voice was level and calm, for all that the words made no sense. Tavera's reaction was more surprising; he stilled instantly before crumpling in on himself, leaving Corwin to support his weight.

Gavin brushed the glass out of the way and knelt down. Seeing that Corwin didn't need her help, Nika put a hand on Gavin's shoulder, and where Corwin would have appreciated it but still flinched away out of instinct, Gavin actually seemed comforted by it. "What the hell happened?" she asked.

"He'll be okay," Gavin said tersely. "Just help me get him out of here."

Corwin slid an arm around Tavera's back, and between the two of them, they managed to hoist the unconscious man upright. The limp weight forced them to take careful, shuffling steps, broken glass crunching underfoot as they dragged Tavera out of the room and toward the stairs.

There was nowhere in the lobby to sit, the few chairs taken by a mixture of clients and workers, all of whom turned to stare as the four of them stumbled by. No doubt they'd seen far worse than someone being carted out unconscious, and that was before a dead girl showed up in one of their rooms. Corwin looked across at Gavin and jerked his head toward the door. Once outside on the street, they jostled Tavera around until they could ease him down on a bench between them.

Nika hit her comm badge. "Inspector Nika Santivan. We have immediate medical need for transport to *Vigilance* from active scene B-197-TN." She paused, obviously listening to the response through her earpiece. "Hold, and let me confirm. Do we need medical assistance?"

Gavin slipped off the bench, kneeling down to check Tavera's breathing. "No, just need to get him back to the ship."

She nodded. "No, Dispatch, no medical support needed on-site. Just transport as soon as you can spare a flyer."

It was unnerving, seeing Tavera silent and unmoving except for the rapid flickering behind his closed eyes, but Gavin seemed calm enough. That still didn't stop Corwin from asking. "So what the hell happened back there?" He held himself still, hyperaware of Tavera pressed against his side. "How did you make him collapse like that? Was that another of PsyAc's hypnotic plants?"

Gavin's glare could only be described as baleful. "Something like that."

Nika stepped smoothly between them, drawing some of Gavin's attention away. "Transport should be here within two minutes. The closest officer has a PsyAc field trainee on ride along. I'm guessing it's Enny. Is there any danger to her?"

"West is in a meditative shutdown. Enny will know what that is. Besides, we're out of the building, so she'll be fine. I don't think there's any psychic traps out here in a transport kiosk." Gavin grinned, but it looked forced.

"Okay." She bit her lip, cocking her head to the side. "What about West? Will I make it harder on him when he wakes up, being close? I know I'm not the easiest person for him to be around."

Gavin hesitated, and Corwin jumped in, knowing from his own experience how unintentionally intrusive Nika's thoughts could be. He also had the advantage of not having to worry about hurting her feelings and mucking up a burgeoning relationship. "It'll be tough if he comes to in the flyer and you're there. You and I can find our own way back to the ship."

If Gavin was startled at the bluntness, he hid it well, sitting down and putting an arm over Tavera's shoulders. "Inspector Menivie is right." While he didn't exactly grind the words out, the effort was obvious. "It would probably be easier if you weren't present. West's going to be pretty susceptible to any outside stimuli. Enny will know how to shield, so she'll be okay. And actually," he nodded toward Corwin, "it would help if you could stay with us too, since you're null."

He couldn't work up a reply for several long seconds, but finally managed to choke out. "I don't think that would be a good idea." The thought of being around a Tavera who lacked basic control made him profoundly uncomfortable.

The patrol flyer was pulling around the corner as Gavin replied. "I'm going to need help moving him, and the fact that you're null will help almost as much as having another Ground. I think he'd be better off coping with you helping than what he's dealing with right now." Gavin slid under Tavera's arm, taking the burden of his weight before standing. "Ready?"

Corwin scowled, but reached for Tavera, earning a quick, approving grin from Nika. He rolled his eyes at her. "See you back at the ship."

"It will be a little while. I need to document the changes to the scene, and set up the barriers again. I'll call you if I run into anything."

He nodded. "I'll come back immediately if you need anything." Her amused look told him that she saw right through his eagerness to get away from Tavera.

The flyer stopped, the driver sparing them a scant greeting before focusing on the traffic again. Their fellow passenger didn't need a second introduction.

"Inspector Menivie, Agent Hale—" Enny's eyes widened when she saw Tavera, and she moved quickly onto the jump seat before continuing. "Is this a post-vision blackout, or something else?"

Gavin gestured Corwin into the flyer, barely waiting for him to slide across the bench before shoving Tavera in behind him. "I had to trigger his fail-safe. The first marker the killer left wasn't the only one in the room, and this one hit Agent Tavera pretty hard."

Enny nodded, looking sympathetic and a little frightened all at once. "I've never seen anyone after triggering. How long will he be out?"

"Not that long." Gavin climbed into the flyer next to Tavera. "And I don't mean this as a slight to your skills, but if you need to go back there for some reason, you shouldn't do it without a Ground. It's not safe."

Corwin wedged himself against the window, trying to leave the PsyAc business to Enny and Gavin. Somehow that meant ending up with Tavera drooping against his shoulder and Enny's knees pressed uncomfortably close across from him. A quick glare made her straighten up, pulling away as far as she could in the close confines. Between the discomfort of Tavera's physical proximity, and being surrounded by two Readers, one of whom couldn't be relied upon not to push at the moment, Corwin found he didn't give a shit about his rumored hatred of psys. Besides, with any luck, Enny would just assume he was a rude bastard, and not a bigot.

Enny's deference to Gavin was in keeping with a trainee, though he suspected a bit of hero worship at play too. "I'm just on a two-week procedural ride along. I'm not supposed to be doing field Reads anyway, but that scene was impossible to miss."

They jumped a little, lifting up to the air zone reserved for emergency vehicles, and Tavera slumped further sideways, the safety harness the only thing keeping him out of Corwin's lap. Enny watched Tavera, her words slow and quiet.

"I'm more of a physical Empath than a real Reader. Mum tried to convince me to go into medicine, but I wanted to be a field agent." She flashed Gavin a shy smile. "I've been reading your case files for years, once they released them to the PsyAc training library. When I felt the first touch of that victim, I knew that I couldn't walk away from her, even if I was only supposed to be observing."

"Why Agent Hale, it sounds like your fame is growing by leaps and bounds." Corwin smiled, making no attempt to keep the wry amusement out of his voice. Enny was young, but she wanted to serve, and not every psy was Tavera.

Eyes closed, Gavin tipped his head back against the seat and laughed. "Following our lead probably isn't the best way to advance your career. You really should model yourself after someone with a little more mainstream credibility."

Enny sat up straighter. "I don't care about my career. I care about helping people."

"Just remember that people care about you too, and that you can't save everyone by yourself." Gavin cracked an eye open, smiling at her.

The flyer dipped then, lowering into the docking yards and grounding next to the *Vigilance*. Under cover of the confusion created in getting Tavera unloaded from the flyer, Corwin leaned toward Enny, his tone gruff. "You'll make a good agent with that attitude."

It was hard to tell if she was more pleased or startled, but she did manage a quick "Thank you, sir," her cheeks pink.

"Take care of yourself, okay?" Gavin said to her as they propped Tavera up. "And if you're not convinced of our detriment to your future by then, drop me a line when you're ready for your field team training, and we'll get you assigned to us."

"I'll, um, do that. Thanks, Agent Hale. And please tell Agent Tavera thank you, for taking my Read seriously."

"When he's done napping, I'll be sure to pass it along to him." Gavin straightened up, shoulder tucked under Tavera's arm, grunting with the effort. "You have to lay off the baking, dude." Tavera's head lolled against Gavin's shoulder, but that was the only reply.

The ramp seemed to angle upward much more steeply than it did when Corwin was only walking himself, and he found himself breathing hard when they finally reached the top. "Do you want him in your room?" he asked Gavin.

"No, just get him to his room and settled in. He'll wake up on his own soon enough, but he might be disoriented. All that shit he crams into his quarters will help."

"'S not shit. 'S my stuff." Tavera's groggy voice startled them both; Gavin almost missed a step.

Corwin considered asking if Tavera was capable of walking the rest of the way, but judging from the still-limp weight hanging heavily off his shoulder, he guessed that wasn't likely.

"Gavinator. Corwin. My favorites. Don't tell Nika." Tavera's arm around his neck tightened for a moment, head drooping again. Seconds later, he lifted a hand, peering at it, squinting against the sun before turning his head toward Gavin. "You're bleeding. Or I am. Are my fingers falling off?"

Gavin didn't answer, and when Corwin started to say something, he coughed pointedly. "Must be your fingers."

They took their strange parade into the ship and headed toward Tavera's quarters. The cacophony of *things* in the room was an assault on the eyes and, if Corwin hadn't had his shields locked down, the senses as well. A much-abused stuffed hedgehog was tangled in the bedding, and there were dishes tucked between tacky souvenirs and dirty clothes. In a disturbing way, the room was rather homey.

When they got within easy staggering distance of the bed, Gavin slid out from under Tavera while Corwin ducked away on the other side. Tavera stumbled over to sit on the edge of the mattress.

"I appreciate the concern, but I'm okay." He gave them a tired, practiced smile. "You can go, and I won't die or pass out in a puddle of my own drool or anything."

Corwin snorted disbelievingly, but he wasn't going to turn down the opportunity to escape. "I'll just go make sure Inspector Santivan is back safely."

Gavin was only partially right about the comfort of being surrounded by his stuff. It was the comfort of familiarity versus being someplace strange, except familiar didn't always mean comfortable. Luckily, Corwin looming over him, concern somehow evident even if West couldn't Read any such feeling, provided enough of a Ground that he could block out the uncomfortable. He was almost disappointed when Corwin ducked out of the room, looking like he'd received a reprieve from a death sentence.

Gavin sighed tiredly, turning toward the door as if to make sure Corwin was gone. "It pains me to say it, but he was actually a help during this whole damned cock-up."

"It wasn't a—" He cut himself off, eyes widening at the splotches on the back of Gavin's shirt. "You're bleeding. You've got cuts all over your back."

Silence was his answer, as was the fact that Gavin refused to turn around and face him. West's progression from worried to horrified only took a second, and he pushed himself off the bed, grabbing Gavin's shirtsleeve. "I did that, didn't I?"

"No. It's fine, it's just some cuts I got when I—"

"What happened, Gavin?"

Gavin shrugged, reluctance in the tight lines of his shoulders. "You found another marker. A trap. You were talking about the most awful thing you'd ever done, and then you picked up an ashtray and tried to clock me with it. It hit the wall, and I guess some of the shards must have nicked me."

"I didn't Ground out of the vision, did I?" Nausea rolled through him in one continuous wave.

"In a manner of speaking, I guess. I triggered your fail-safe."

West nodded, giving up the façade of stability and dropping back onto his bed with a solid *thump*. "You don't think Corwin heard the password, do you? I think he'd have way too much fun with it."

"Now would I give him that kind of ammunition?" Gavin patted his shoulder, mustering up a smile. "So everything's safe as can be."

In and out, in and out, deep breaths forcing down the need to vomit. "Except you're not. Because I keep drawing blood, and it doesn't seem to matter how many training exercises we go through, or how many people dig through my head to see if there's something they can fix." He got to his feet over Gavin's protests, but didn't move beyond that, swaying unsteadily. "I have to finish this case. I'll listen to you from now on, but I have to finish this."

"No you won't." Gavin's lips twisted in a rueful grin. "And besides, nobody's saying we can't finish the case."

"Once you turn in the incident report, they'll pull me from the field." He closed his eyes, wishing he could shut off his brain as easily. "And they should. I won't argue with it. I can't— Gav, if I hurt you again . . ." He swallowed hard.

"Give me a little credit for being able to keep myself safe. It was an ashtray, not a blast gun."

At five, Gavin had been a few inches taller than the rest of the kids in their class. Able to wade into the mob and stand between West and the girl trying her best to flatten him. Twenty-three years later, the very idea that West could hurt someone that important to him was like broken glass in his chest. He laughed, a bitter bark. "Not like it was a knife, right? Not like I stabbed you four times. Not like you almost bled out this time. Right? Not like I'll spend months locked up in my own head, pacing a little square of sanity, thinking I killed you."

The conversation was chasing its own tail, but Gavin wouldn't let it go. "This isn't the same case. It's not the same person. There's a difference between making a stupid mistake because you think you can save someone, and walking into a trap because you're being forced to play someone else's game."

"The difference is that I let Rashium in on purpose because I thought I could help him. This guy is smarter than me, and stronger. I'm fighting shadows. What the hell am I going to do when we actually find him?"

"Stay as far away from him as possible, and let Nika and Corwin do their jobs?" Gavin grabbed his arm, shook him. "You find what he leaves behind, and try to point them toward where he's heading. That's your part of it, and the rest is up to the people with blast guns and a sense of self-preservation."

"It's not going to be enough." He pushed his free hand through his hair, mashing it flat in defiance of the amount of styling product holding it up. "Staying back from the fight isn't the problem, it's that the fight will keep coming to me because I can't block it out. I don't think it's one that anyone else can win."

"There are other Readers, even if they don't have your psy levels. We can walk off this ship tomorrow, retire, teach at the academy, take up baking and start a pie shop. But whatever we do, we do as partners, and it's not a choice that gets made to protect me. I can finesse the incident report. You didn't cause me any direct harm." Gavin still had a grip on his arm, and shook him again. "I don't think minutes after waking up from a reboot is the time to be deciding to abandon your career to raise vegetables on Torref."

The corner of West's mouth turned up as he extricated himself from Gavin's clutches. "Yeah, fine, I'll give you that one." He turned around, kicking at a few of the discarded articles of clothing, so tired that the very effort of breathing hurt. "But later on, when you admit that I'm right, I won't rub your nose in this, I promise."

Gavin growled something unintelligible and grabbed West, wrapping an arm around his neck in more of a hug than a headlock. "You're such an asshole. But you're not a lost cause yet, okay?"

West curled his fingers around Gavin's wrist, holding them in place, but they both knew better than to think his silence was assent.

West didn't remember Gavin leaving, but it must have happened at some point, because there was a mug of coffee on the bedside table, and Gavin's face was slightly more relaxed.

Sitting up slowly, West shoved pillows behind his back. "Thank you," he said, voice catching roughly. He wrapped both hands around the warm mug and took a deep gulp. Even with all the pharmaceuticals he could draw on, caffeine was still the best thing for easing the aftereffects of a Ground out. Right now, it was helping his throat as well.

"Nika's back safely. She's pretty worried about you." Gavin grinned. "Enough that I'm a little jealous."

West coughed, feeling like he was dislodging a lung full of filth and debris, but at least his voice came clearer. "You should be. I'm obviously the better-looking half of our team." He took another swallow, using the time to try to think back. "Wait, you said Nika was back safely. Where was she? Wait. Fuck." Fingers suddenly numb, he had to grip the mug tighter. "Did I hurt her, Gav?"

"No, no, of course not. She took a different flyer back. Everything's fine, you didn't hurt anyone."

That was a stupid, useless argument that he just didn't have the energy to replay. He sighed, dropping back heavily against the pillows. "Not that I don't appreciate her concern, but she's not going to come in and express it herself, is she?"

"You're safe. I told her you were feeling a little too frail for company." Gavin shoved West's feet over and sat down on the end of the bed. "Actually, she wanted me to let you know we've got another lead. There's another body, this one on Cainet. It fits the markers, and we think we've found a connection between the dump sites."

He should be having a reaction. It felt like he should, and Gav's sharp-eyed gaze definitely implied that one was expected. The problem being, he couldn't seem to find the right response. He couldn't afford to be distracted, however vivid the impression left from the hotel room; the fact remained that the killer was still out there, doing more harm than just setting traps for Readers. How the hell was he supposed to react to that?

He jumped, startled when Gavin squeezed his shoulder. "I wanted to let you know. After our previous *discussion* . . ." Gavin's eyes narrowed, giving the word more emphasis than it deserved ". . . I wasn't going to have you planning on shirking your part of the investigation."

"I wouldn't think of it. Give me five minutes, and I'll get right on that." That was a joke. They both knew he'd be next to useless for another ten hours or so, until he'd slept off the rapidly growing headache.

"Easy there, tough guy. I think we can wait for your invaluable input. I'm going to distract Nika with my dashing wit until you're feeling more yourself." There was no mistaking the way Gavin's voice brightened over the lilt of her name.

"Right. So I should join you in a couple hours."

Gavin glared at him, but it didn't hold any real threat. "I'm hoping that would prove to be very awkward, so I think you should rest instead."

West gave Gavin's arm a careless pat. "Just ask her if she'll nurse you back to health. All the ladies love an injured man in uniform."

"How would you know?"

The edge of exhaustion was cutting into his smile, but he managed one anyway. "So I've been told."

CHAPTER 10

West jerked awake, heart pounding in an irregular beat that had more to do with extreme discomfort than fear. Apparently Gavin's wit had been *very* entertaining.

He really, really didn't need to see Nika and Gavin playing out their little bondage scenario involving bits of Nika's intimate wear, and definitely not through Nika's eyes. Besides, he had his doubts about the tensile strength of some tiny scrap of lace, and its ability to keep Gavin restrained. At least Gavin wasn't wearing them. He shuddered. *That* image dancing through his dreams was more than even a best friend could be expected to tolerate.

Nika's thoughts fizzed up into his head like bright, bouncing soap bubbles full of happy sex thoughts. West groaned, burying his face in his pillow, hoping against hope that this would be the day the miracle occurred and he could block things like this out just by putting his hands over his ears.

It wasn't, of course, and rather than risk falling back asleep and having Nika completely take over his dreams, he struggled out of bed, fighting down grouchy resentment and secondhand arousal. He didn't begrudge Gavin a share of happiness because their partnership in recent years certainly hadn't been the easiest thing to maneuver a relationship around, but that didn't mean he was thrilled about giving up sleep for sex he wasn't having himself.

West hesitated, finger resting on the call button outside Corwin's door for several seconds before he finally pressed it. He didn't get a response right away, and debated pushing it again, because he knew the inspector wasn't in the galley or the common area, or on the bridge. Unless Corwin was sneaking around through the ventilation system, or hanging off the side of the ship in a space suit, this was pretty much his last option.

"What?" West hadn't been sure exactly what Corwin would sound like tired, but the annoyance conveyed by the single word barked through the comm channel didn't seem any worse than usual.

"Can I talk to you for a few minutes? Maybe from the other side of the door?"

He didn't get an answer, just a long pause before the door slid open and Corwin stood before him, arms crossed and scowl in place. "Can we do this another time? I— I'm not feeling particularly well at the moment." It looked as though the slight stutter had caused Corwin physical pain, and West considered delaying this talk, or forgetting it altogether, but he knew better than to let himself off the hook.

"Not really. It'll just be a few minutes, I promise."

Surprisingly, Corwin nodded and moved back out of the way: apparently as close to an invitation as West was going to get. He slipped past Corwin into a room slightly larger than his own, though darker and far tidier. The covers on the bed were tossed back, crumpled and tangled, and he did his best not to touch them, opting to stand next to the desk in the corner. He couldn't pick up anything from Corwin, of course, but it wasn't always the same with objects, even those touched by a null. Corwin glanced at the bed, then waved him toward the desk chair.

"I didn't wake you, did I?"

"No." Typically short, but Corwin followed it by taking a seat on the edge of the bed and rubbing his eyes with one hand. "What do you want, Agent Tavera?"

After the recent bout of oversharing, he wanted a shag and a drink, but he didn't think Corwin was going to provide either of those. Instead, he settled for the less enjoyable but more pressing matter. "I need you to act as a secondary Ground for the duration of this case."

Corwin's hand dropped, eyes narrowed and staring hard at him. "Is Agent Hale somehow incapacitated? Were his injuries more serious than they appeared?"

West had to fight down a slightly hysterical and entirely inappropriate giggle, images of Gavin as he'd last seen him still too clear for comfort. "Not exactly."

"Then what's the problem?"

He shook his head, wishing the dead space around Corwin was as familiar to him as Gavin's. Instead of being a comfortable respite, it made him feel alone. Corwin's blocking wasn't as strong as the void Gavin created, either. He'd have to get used to it if Corwin was going to back him up in the field, but that kind of hinged on an agreement that Corwin didn't look too comfortable making.

West started slightly, realizing he hadn't actually answered. "Sorry. No, the injuries were pretty superficial. The problem isn't Gavin, it's me. The Reads I'm getting are out of control, and I'm having a hard time disengaging from them."

Corwin's denial came swiftly: a head shake and a scowl. "That's completely against procedure. If you need backup, we can contact PsyAc and have them send another field team, or an unattached Ground. If I had any interest in working as a tether for a space cadet, I would have gone through the training program."

"Space cadet?" His voice rose in pitch, and he knew it wasn't an attractive sound. "Well, I guess we're not over that little case of bigotry, are we?"

"Mother of stars, that's not what I meant." Corwin's groan was loud and heartfelt as he buried his face in his hands. "I have a headache the size of your ego—"

"And I ruined your afterglow." West sniffed, a delicate, pointed sound, and he saw Corwin's spine stiffen, even though the sharp catch of a breath was mostly covered. "You could have just said you were busy having a wa—"

"Like that would have stopped you." Corwin's face was bright red when he looked up, his tone almost conversational. "I want you to know, Tavera. I really, really dislike you."

West couldn't hold back his smile, even knowing that it was only going to make things worse. "No, you don't."

"I see what you mean about your Talent not working properly. I detest you. Your presence makes me want to find a tall building and prove that I can't fly."

"Stop it, you're going to make me blush." He waved a hand at Corwin. "Then I'll look like you."

He found the struggle to read Corwin's face and mannerisms a challenge, and one that he enjoyed. Any Reader, adept or not, lived with the constant and undeniable crutch of their gifts. Always knowing the underlying mood in the room became such habit that most Readers stopped noticing it before they ever left PsyAc. But the Corwin he saw was exactly the same Corwin that the rest of the 'verse saw: silent and stern until the all-too-rare moment when the mask cracked a little, revealing something else entirely. It was hard not to push at those cracks, except what he wanted had to be given, not taken.

"I can't help you in the field. I'm not a Ground, and if you look to me for that kind of support, it's going to get ugly. I'm not trained to guide a Read, or to pull you out of one if things go haywire." Corwin stared him down, looking deeply uncomfortable. "I know you're probably worried about Gavin. But he's a good agent, and he knows the risks involved with the job. I'm sure he's aware that some cases affect the officers working them on a deeper level, and he's willing to accommodate that."

Frustration loosened West's tongue, and before he could regret it or stop himself, he met Corwin's gaze and let out the ugly truth. "I caused the wounds today, you saw it. If he hadn't seen it coming, he'd be in the hospital right now. I trust Gavin with my life, and I don't have any issues with the way he works. I need to know that there's someone keeping him safe from *me*." The admission hurt like nothing else could, the tip of a mountain of failures that he'd honestly believed they were going to leave behind with this assignment.

Corwin started to interrupt, the vee between his eyes deepening with his frown, but West rushed on.

"You asked if I was on burnout watch. I might as well be, as much as I fucked up. The hush-hush behind my break? I tried to *kill* him. My Ground, my partner, my best friend." Once unleashed, the words spilled out in a bitter, poisonous torrent. "I would've, too; it was just sheer luck that I didn't. Someone got into my head, just like today." He caught his breath, holding down his panicked need to protect Gavin by proving his own instability. "I know that Gavin would do just about anything for me, but I can't offer him the same thing when

I'm not even aware of what I'm doing. So I'm asking you, Inspector. Please help me keep my partner safe."

His voice cracked on the last word, but it wasn't his own emotion causing it. *Nika's mind soared, her thoughts racing in time with her heartbeat as Gavin's fingers slid over her skin—*

"Oh, come *on*. Again?" He winced, forcing himself to focus on the room around him, surreptitiously pinching his arm and holding on to the bright point of pain. *His hands felt like—*

He pinched himself again for good measure, peering over at Corwin in an effort to maintain the illusion of Nika's privacy.

Corwin looked like he'd checked out for a few minutes, his glassy-eyed gaze fixed somewhere in the middle distance while he took shallow breaths through his mouth. If anything, he'd drawn in on himself even more, arms crossed over his long legs. The expression on his face niggled at West, not something he could immediately place, and he was so intent on trying to decipher it that Corwin's voice surprised him.

"You need to go. Now. Please."

"Are you okay?" He scrambled to his feet, invading Corwin's space with the best of intentions. Too close, apparently, because Corwin grabbed his arm, holding him at a distance while he pushed off the edge of the bed and propelled them toward the door. *Holding her arms, tracing over the swell of muscle, and the way he looked at her—*

Corwin's grip tightened painfully, thumb stroking over the sleeve of West's T-shirt in a motion that he only half recognized and Corwin seemed unaware of. *The awakening was a stir of dominance, the urge to press her advantage, to pin and hold and take and then he kissed her again and it wasn't a fight anymore, only wantwantwant—*

Disoriented and dizzy with Nika's lust, West was barely aware when Corwin shoved him against the wall near the door, dropping both hands on his shoulders and pinning him in place.

"Mixed signals, Corwin. If I'm going, you have to let go." He couldn't get his hands free, but he wasn't sure he would have known what to do with them even if they were. Touch? Open the door and flee? Tear at Corwin's clothes? Too many options. He didn't have the faintest clue which was the most welcome, and none of them were a good idea.

He kissed like he meant it, like she was the most important thing in his world in that second, like it was a prize and a gift, his hand cupping her cheek—

Corwin's hand left his shoulder, rough fingers curving under the line of West's jaw. It took that mirror being held up for West to finally clue in to what was going on. The tension made it seem like more of a preemptive measure than an affectionate gesture, like Corwin was holding back from a surgical strike rather than an ill-advised kiss. Of course that made sense, if the gestures, the feelings, the desire itself, weren't actually Corwin's.

"You're a Reader." He could ignore Nika for that, because the unlikeliness of it, the sheer absurdity of a man who wouldn't even *work* with a psychic turning out to *be* one, was enough of a distraction for anyone, and he'd never been particularly hard to distract.

Corwin didn't answer him. The silence was pregnant with the apparently unspeakable truth, and when Nika's thoughts intruded again, a sharp burst of vibrant contrast to the dark denial between them, Corwin winced.

"It's not what you think. It's nothing useful, just . . . I pick up most easily on joy. I can Read a person's happiest moment, or—"

"Sex." West surprised himself by not finding it terribly funny, only another piece of the puzzle. "You Read sex."

"Yes, mostly. Not really something I can use in the field." Corwin's face closed down, any trace of vulnerability hidden behind steel. "And not something I want shared. Ever. Are we clear on that? It's not open for negotiation. I won't be the punch line of anyone's jokes."

"I want to know why you hate Actives so much, if you are one. I want—"

"I want you to shut up." Corwin's hand hadn't left his cheek, and even delivered in a low growl, his words were more plea than order. "I don't work with Actives because I don't want to run the risk of someone else finding out."

"But you feel like a null. I never would have known at all, if I wasn't standing next to you while you were in a Read. How do you even *do* that?"

"It's none of your business. Go, Tavera, just go."

West started to answer, but the words died on his lips as Nika joined them again. *Soft, soft, she was going to break apart if he didn't touch her, if he did; his skin tasted of salt, she could live forever in the rolling waves of softsharpcarefulwild—*

He sagged, using the wall to hold himself up. Corwin's hand was still on his face, and he knew his pulse had jumped. There was no air in the room anymore, and no space, Corwin's leg between his, pressing the advantage of height and doing . . . absolutely nothing. West could have killed the man.

"Either let go of me, or do something about it." West pushed, not entirely without his own agenda, and he wasn't surprised to feel Corwin hard against his thigh. "Because I can help you with that." It sounded wrong, impersonal, without risk, and an offer without risk mostly wasn't worth taking someone up on. "I *want* to help you with that."

"No. I'm not going to have sex with you because Nika can't keep her hands off your partner. We can talk about this tomorrow, once they get this out of their systems. Thanks for the offer." The bitterness imbued in the last words was hard to miss.

"What if you were having sex with me because you wanted to have sex with me? I'm totally fuckable, and I bet we could both use something to take our minds off the case." He hated the coaxing tone in his voice, but it hardly mattered, since Corwin didn't seem swayed. West raised his hand, his fingers brushing the faint stubble on Corwin's jaw, and Corwin leaned into the touch, obviously without meaning to. It was all the warning he got before Corwin released him and stepped away.

"The case is the case. This is my off time, and I can think of far better ways to clear my head than fucking you. I'm not interested in giving you more material. Leave me alone."

West swore that he could actually hear Corwin's teeth grinding together, and about the only positive thing he could see was that their negotiation seemed to have drowned out Nika and Gavin.

He rarely tried for obvious sincerity. It wasn't worth wasting on most people, and not really needed with those who knew him well enough to matter. He should let it go, walk back to his own quarters, and deal with the fallout tomorrow, but it surprised him how much it hurt that Corwin thought he was only playing out some kind of opportunistic practical joke. He opened his mouth, but nothing came to him at first, and then only an unflattering honesty he wished he could have polished before sharing: "If you don't want me, that's fine, and no hard feelings. But I want you. I want under your skin, and in your head, and not so I can laugh at you." He sought out Corwin's gaze, holding it while he stepped away from the wall, farther from the door, across the invisible minefield between them. "Read me, if you want. It'll block out Nika, and then when you say no, the joke will be on me."

"No. I don't Read people like that. It's an invasion of privacy."

West snorted. "Right. Because neither one of us is currently privy to a play-by-play of someone else's most intimate moments. At least I'm *asking* you to take a spin through the playground in my head."

—sliding down, the velvet drag of skin on skin, she could still taste—

They looked at each other for maybe a second, maybe two, and Corwin was the first to crack. "So show me. Show me what you actually want."

Permission granted, West moved closer still, fully expecting only one shot at it before Corwin either thought better of a liaison, or revealed a slightly crueler streak to that subtle sense of humor. West wasn't that much shorter, just enough that he could get away with fisting a hand in the front of Corwin's uniform shirt and pulling him down for a kiss that was completely at odds with the aggression involved in getting there.

His lips parted against Corwin's, a light pressure that grew strong when he nipped Corwin's lower lip and reached out, deliberately seeking the quiet space he'd come to associate with him.

"I like you, when you're not treating me like a rookie. Even then, really."

He had no idea what Corwin could pick up on, but he felt the moment that they made contact, both in the way that Corwin deepened the kiss, and in the clean, gentle mind that opened to him, a gesture he hadn't expected at all.

"Your head is like a circus, Tavera."

He ruined the kiss, pulling away so that he could laugh until his eyes watered. Leaning against Corwin, head resting against his chest, he eventually calmed himself to an intermittent urge to snicker. When he looked up, even Corwin was smiling. A little.

The tiny quirk at the corner of Corwin's mouth was far from the most obvious profession of interest he'd ever gotten, but it was invitation enough for him. His laughter faded to a warm echo, and like always, something snapped. This time the fire between them wasn't wasted on needless barbs, and he put the extra energy into pulling at Corwin's clothes, getting hopelessly distracted when Corwin turned the tables on him and reached for the hem of his shirt.

"*Impatient.*"

"*Interested. Curious about tattoos and scars, in case I ever have to pick you out of a lineup.*"

"I have a birthmark shaped like a kind of fruit, but I won't tell you what kind, or where it is." Though he was adept enough at filtering his thoughts around other Readers, he spoke aloud to stop himself from accidentally giving anything away. The spark of arousal when he imagined Corwin finding his birthmark was harder to keep to himself, but that didn't matter as much.

"That sounds like a challenge." Their clothes were in utter disarray when Corwin slid a hand into West's hair and tugged him back in, but neither of them was actually any closer to being naked. His mild outrage over that vanished as Corwin kissed the juncture of his shoulder, lips moving up little by little until he tipped West's head to the side and left the line of his neck exposed.

He didn't disappoint, lips and teeth traveling over West's throat until West gave in and whimpered. Even that was caught, and the kiss pressed at the hollow of his throat felt more vulnerable on Corwin's part than his. Finally getting Corwin's shirt untucked, West's hands moved under it to map out the valleys and peaks, a personal survey of the landscape that only seemed to feed the new tension they were creating.

His eyes closed, and the darkness brought a kind of quiet he wasn't ready for, full of sensation and sound, and Nika's tireless enthusiasm. The walls of Corwin's mind were easy to find, and hemmed in by them, he could focus with a kind of intensity he rarely had the clarity for. The frustration of the case, Nika's bubbles of lust and joy, both faded into the background, leaving only the spaces within Corwin.

"It's so clean in here. Or are these just the public rooms? Are you hiding a kinky mental playground somewhere in here?"

A frustrated grunt brought him back from the drift. Reluctance made his eyelids heavy, but when he opened them, he couldn't find a trace of the anger he'd expected, or much else.

"You push too much. If you're not happy with what's on offer, go find a better one." Rumpled, untucked and open, mouth red and something lurking in his eyes just waiting to be bruised, Corwin was the best offer he'd had in a long time. The first person in a long time that hadn't felt like the wrong kind of disaster, the familiar kind. That was a little too much sharing for him, but there was a precipice there that he was dancing on the edge of, and he was looking for a tumble, not a fall.

"I'm a curious person. Everyone else feels like somewhere I've already been before I even know them." Corwin stepped away, and West felt his smile falter. "I won't push." Wincing, he corrected himself. "I'll try not to push."

"You're the first person I've ever met who feels a connection with people and wants to use sex to feel alone." Corwin's tone gave nothing away, hovering at the default of "possibly pissed, or maybe amused" and showing no sign of moving up or down the scale either way. Essentially, until Corwin's shirt hit the pristine floor, West had no idea if he was going to get kicked out or laid.

West balled the hem of his own shirt up, crossing his arms to pull it off, but Corwin's hand caught one of his wrists. "Don't. I like unwrapping presents."

It shouldn't have been hot, and he certainly didn't have a blushing-innocent routine in his repertoire, but something about the request was exhilarating. He just couldn't decide if it was the command itself, or the thought that he was worth discovering. In the end, it didn't matter.

They were well beyond the point of asking permission for the basics, so he didn't hesitate to undo the fly of Corwin's pants. Thankfully, the inspector hadn't bothered with shoes before coming to answer the door, and stepped easily out of the pants and underwear West pushed down.

She was hunting, seeking, there was something just out of reach, she was so close, so fucking close . . .

He didn't remember hitting his knees, but the bitterness on his tongue, the way his mouth stretched around Corwin's cock—that wasn't something he was going to lose track of. There was no holding back, no casual tease, nothing tender or even personal about the way he hollowed out his cheeks and worked his hand like a pro, but Corwin didn't seem to be protesting his lack of sentiment. West usually enjoyed this, but . . .

. . . she'd enjoyed it, before it was just a job, but now it meant not having to find her panties later. Press a knuckle behind, that'd drive a trick wild . . .

—She was going to come, and she wanted Gavin with her, in her—

The hand in his hair *hurt*, damn it, and West pulled off, breathing harder than he should have been and barely aware of anything but the animal need to finish, or have it over with. To bring someone else off and bury himself in the moment when all he'd feel was the white noise of their pleasure. Not his partner leaving him by increments because of a mistake his ego had made. Not his best friend having sex. Not the workplace memories of a dead prostitute. Just a tiny little space where the only people in his head were him and Corwin.

"I can hear you." Corwin's voice was ragged, and West suddenly felt foolish and unsteady. The painful grip on his hair loosened, and Corwin's thumb dragged over his lips. "Be here." Cautious, like it was something unfamiliar, Corwin's voice spoke in his head as well. *"Be here with me."*

It wasn't an unreasonable request, given the fact that he was still on his knees, fingers splayed across Corwin's hip, face inches away from Corwin's still-erect cock. In short, all of him was present except for what Corwin seemed to want. He huffed softly, noting the resulting tremor his warm breath caused. *"I'm never anywhere."* More feeling than words, but he couldn't untangle the million directions his mind was pulled in on a daily basis from the truth that he was never actually there for anyone except Gavin. Corwin seemed to understand, the brush of wordless acknowledgment making West wonder how much of himself he was giving up.

"I lied, you know. I don't understand you, but I don't really dislike you. Much."

Another careless touch, a fingertip tracing his cheekbone, gave West an easy way out. He laughed and ducked away. "Oh, I bet you say that to all the guys who suck your dick."

"No. Not really." Impossibly dry, the answer made him look up again, just in time to catch the flash of humor before it vanished from Corwin's face. West accepted the hand when it was offered, because the IEC hadn't exactly splurged on plush carpet for their fly-by fleet, and his knees hurt.

Wariness tried to creep in, but he refused to give it a foothold. He ditched his clothes with an efficiency born of simple, twinned ideas: he wanted to be naked when they finally landed in bed, and he didn't care about making a mess on Corwin's floor. Truth be told, he rather fancied creating a little chaos with his carelessly tossed shirt and pants.

They didn't need words to know where they were heading, so they didn't bother with them. He would have preferred it darker, but Corwin left the lights on, if dimmed somewhat. Their kissing certainly didn't suffer for it, even when the angle changed as they fell into bed.

Corwin seemed to have decided on a course of action, and ever inquisitive, West went searching for a hint. He delved into the quiet of Corwin's head, and the echo of his own pleasure, filtered through Corwin's Read, left him gasping. In concert with Corwin's own arousal, the deliberate touches that held almost everything back and the thoughts that kept almost nothing secret overwhelmed him. He dug his fingers into Corwin's biceps, tipping his head and baring his throat.

"*I won't break.*" He didn't know if it was an enticement to Corwin or a promise to himself, but he considered it a fair warning before he wrapped his legs around Corwin's waist and thrust. The friction, and the warm reverberation of it, was more than enough reason to do it again.

"*Here, stay here.*" Corwin's teeth grazed his lower lip, and West didn't care anymore whose thoughts had won out. They were both circling, all the usual shields and barriers forgotten. Corwin brushed his nipples, his mouth falling over one to deliver a gentle bite and a quick flash of tongue that didn't do much for the sting, but wrung a harsh cry and a moment of unexpected bliss out of West.

The intensity of Corwin's attention was hard to miss when it was locked on him like a weapon sight, and the only apparent goal seemed to be driving everyone else out of his head. Corwin's free hand slid between them, captured and released and caught again as they rolled their hips together. When long fingers wrapped around both of their cocks, West gave over entirely, the circuit completing and Corwin's whispers a meaningless chant.

He'd never felt so isolated, so alone while with someone, and in the end, that was what tipped him over the edge. It was just them: their minds, their thoughts, the taste of Corwin in his mouth, and nothing in the 'verse between them but sweat and their own inhibitions. He made himself a liar by pushing, because more than anything, he needed Corwin to break with him, to know what the intensity felt like from the other side.

"*Want to make you feel like nobody else. Like I do.*" From anyone else it would have been a sweet nothing, but West had the proof of it in his head, and he gave it all to Corwin. The knife-edge of control cut into him, the silence buffered by Corwin's body as he held on tight, dragging Corwin with him when that control finally broke.

He had no idea who came first, or last, or if there was going to be anything left of him when it was over. Corwin gave it a voice—a harsh, wordless cry—but that was only the outmost ripple of the crashing orgasm that shook them both. One hand fisting in the sheets, the other leaving bruises on Corwin's shoulder, West held tight.

Eventually the pleasure ebbed away, and in the aftermath, neither of them could tell who they were anymore. As someone who rarely had a choice about who he got to share his head with, he found being tangled up in Corwin's afterglow almost as good as the sex.

Corwin slid his arm under the pillow that Tavera—West—seemed to have claimed for the night, trying to spread out without making it obvious that he was used to sprawling across the whole bed because there was never anyone else in it. After an awkward moment where his arm got caught, West huffed a small laugh and rolled over, closer to him, and Corwin shifted until they were arranged to his liking, West's head on his shoulder.

"Secret cuddler?" West's teasing voice made it sound more like a guess than a statement, and maybe the sex had made him stupid, but he smiled into the dark, despite knowing West couldn't see him and was still waiting for a response.

"I prefer to think of it as strategic placement. Planning ahead for the second round." He trailed his hand across West's upper arm, mapping the bare skin with his fingertips.

"Second round, huh? You wild man, you. Better save some of that energy for tromping around Cainet." Lazy, half-asleep, West still sounded enticing, the seductive promise of his tone so much better now that Corwin knew what he was being offered. "Should I be concerned that you'll only have sex with me if Nika is molesting Gavin on the other side of the ship?"

It was funny, or meant to be, but fell short of the mark, largely because West seemed to have forgotten that that was the exact reason they were lying in bed together to begin with. Corwin might not have been a ridiculously overpowered Reader, but he could do well enough when someone was tired, and anxious, and pressed up tight against him, broadcasting his fears like a teledrama.

"You really are an asshole." Corwin's words lacked their usual rancor, sounded almost affectionate, which he supposed they might have been. "I'm not in the habit of sleeping with coworkers, but just because Nika's little liaison with your partner was a catalyst, that doesn't mean it's the only reason we're here."

West's toes were like little ice cubes, dancing over the muscle of Corwin's calf, and he felt that his quiet yelp was entirely justified.

"So you and Nika never partnered up on your off-duty hours, huh?"

He started to poke, then thought better of it and put his leg over both of West's, effectively pinning those freezing toes well away from anywhere that they could do any further damage. "She's not really my type."

"Too good-natured? Too pretty? Too pleasant in the morning?" The last one made them both shudder slightly, the movement seeming to ripple between them.

"Too undamaged," he replied unthinkingly, and then cursed himself for five kinds of fool when he realized what he'd actually said, and what it implied about West. The air was heavy between them, until West shivered again. It took him a second longer to realize West was laughing. So much for those vaunted psychic powers.

"You say the sweetest things. Don't worry, I'm all kinds of broken." Still giggling, West slid a hand down to Corwin's hip, and he took the hint and rolled over, pinning West below him.

Their kiss was long and slow, clearly a prelude to something rather than an epilogue. When they ended it, he took the opportunity to rest his forehead against West's shoulder. "I didn't mean it like that."

"Did I sound worried? I know you didn't. It's fine."

This close to someone else, words, actions, and feelings all came together for him into a symphony, carrying him along on the sweeping movements. It could be overwhelming in the best of ways, but now he felt each discordant note like a blow, and he could spot West's easy lie in the space between harmony and melody. Worse, it was easy because it wasn't a lie at all, but a secret held and believed for so long that it seemed true now.

Corwin couldn't fix it, not when West would deny feeling that way at all, but as they made use of the friction between them in an entirely different manner than their usual sniping, he indulged in a pointed thought that he knew West would pick up.

"Broken is just a place to start over from."

West's fingers twined through his and squeezed, but that was all the acknowledgment he got, and that was just fine. Knowing what West was feeling didn't mean he'd wanted to, and it certainly didn't mean he was looking to play tender ear to West's woes. He wasn't uninterested so much as unwilling to meddle in private affairs that he wouldn't have been aware of if West hadn't been distracted.

"Stop twisting yourself in knots. I'm not going to start moaning about my childhood." West's teasing tone went well with his smirk. "I seem to recall someone bragging about their blowing skills."

Corwin set his face in a scowl, at once familiar and harder to keep in place than he was expecting. "I have no idea what you're talking about. *I* remember someone telling me they were fuckable, but I can't back that up with hard evidence right now, so it's totally inadmissible in court."

"Really, Corwin? Hard evidence? *Really*?"

"Oh, shut up." Laughing, he resettled his weight over West. "Have I mentioned that I don't like you?"

"Yes, and my feelings are terribly hurt. I might never recover."

"I didn't think recovery was going to be a problem for you. You're younger than I am, unless you've already hit up the rejuve treatments. It's too bad you can't keep up with me." Corwin didn't indulge in dramatics often, but his sigh was quite theatrical. Even West looked impressed.

West's eyes narrowed, and Corwin wondered if he'd ever figure out what color they actually were, then dismissed the thought when West poked him in the chest. "I see what you're doing, but you're not going to distract me from what's really going on here. I was promised a blowjob, and I have yet to receive one."

"I'm going to toss you out the airlock while you're sleeping." Corwin's warning growl lost something when he couldn't help but laugh again as he smacked at West's grabby hands. Catching them, he pinned both down, his fingers curled loosely around West's wrists as he moved lower.

He had a reputation to uphold, after all.

CHAPTER 11

The sound of breathing registered in Corwin's sleep-fogged brain a good quarter of a second behind the realization that he was pinned to the bed by a heavy weight, and he shot upright before he'd managed to connect the two. West grumbled something unintelligible, rolling away and taking most of the covers with him as he buried his face in the pillows. Both pillows.

Memories rushed back in flashes of warm skin and sweat and pleasure that was both his and not at the same time. That, combined with the fact that his heart rate hadn't quite recovered from the adrenaline rush, meant there was no way he was going back to sleep. Sparing an aggrieved glare for West—dead to the world and snoring with a soft whuffling sound that others would probably find endearing, but that he wasn't ready to make a call on yet—he crawled out of bed and reached for his discarded clothing.

Shirt halfway over his head, he froze. The sheets smelling like West he'd expected, but the idea that his *skin* would had never crossed even the remotest part of his mind. It had been a long time since he'd spent the night in bed with someone, and he tended to shower after sex.

Standing there half-dressed wasn't doing a damn thing to quell either the twitch of panic or the more immediate twinge of arousal, though. Simple physical contact still held a little forbidden thrill for him, and it had been easy to let that get the better of him with West, who responded to it without reservation. The temple Virtue's stern admonishment that touch was meant to be shared only with bondmates and family members echoed in the back of his mind, and a hasty retreat seemed the best option, if only to give himself some breathing space. He'd never indulged in morning-after regrets, and he wasn't going to start now, but enough had happened to necessitate some distance.

The galley was empty, and he wasn't ashamed that he'd peered around the corner and checked first. It took longer to make a pot of coffee than it should've, but that was because he kept jumping and looking over his shoulder every few seconds. Once it was safely brewing, he grabbed four mugs from the cabinet and set them out, then dug around in the cooler until he found the remains of a pie West had made a couple of days ago. Not exactly a traditional breakfast food, at least for anyone but him, but it wasn't like he was going to make pancakes or some such nonsense. He'd probably end up poisoning them all.

The pie divided evenly into four slices, and he set three of the plates precisely in front of the mugs. He was seconds from making his escape with the fourth plate when a discreet cough made him drop his fork. It bounced off his plate with a cringe-inducing clatter before he could grab it.

"Sorry, I was trying not to startle you. You looked really intent." Nika stepped further into the room, peering around him. When she turned back, her eyebrows were so high they almost touched her sleep-tousled hair. "Are you fixing *breakfast*?"

He let his own raised eyebrow speak volumes. "I was getting myself something and I just set out some dishes. I'd hardly call that fixing breakfast."

She smiled and made a vague noise that didn't quite make him grit his teeth, but was dangerously close. "Well, I appreciate it anyway. Do you mind if I take mine, um, and Gavin's? I don't want to be rude . . ."

That was a first. They'd never bothered over niceties like that before. He knew his jolt of resentment made no sense, but even without being in the room, West still managed to make things different and complicated. The fact that it was really Gavin's doing only pricked his conscience a little. "Of course not, why would that bother me?" He resisted the urge to flap a hand at her, instead gripping his fork tighter.

"Thanks." She brushed past him on her way to the counter, and had both plates in her hands and was turning away when she pulled up abruptly. "Wait, are you barefoot?" The shock in her voice had to be an affectation; the sight of him sans footwear wasn't enough to cause that degree of consternation. "I've never seen your feet before."

"I'm sorry to have deprived you all these years. Are you disappointed? Expecting extra toes, perhaps? Or hooves?"

She at least had the grace to look flustered. "Sorry, I didn't mean to sound so surprised. It was just unexpected."

"Right along with my supposed meal preparation. I'm just full of mysteries this morning, aren't I?" Quiet desperation was setting in. She had that little gleam of interrogation in her eyes, and that was never a good sign, especially when it was directed at him. He stared meaningfully at her hands. "Why don't you get that pie back to Gavin, I'm sure he's ready for something to eat. Probably starving by now."

He bit his tongue as soon as that last slipped out, but it was too late. Nika's eyes widened, and then she nodded slowly, hooking a chair with one foot and sitting down. "Is this about Gavin and me? I'm really sorry if we've made you uncomfortable. I had no idea. I thought we were, if not discreet, at least not obvious. I don't see how, I mean, we weren't loud . . ."

"What? No! Mother of stars, no." Anywhere in the entire 'verse, including naked on Noska in the depths of winter, would have been preferable to the galley at that point. "I don't know anything about you and Gavin." He hoped desperately that the lie didn't show on his face. "I don't *want* to know anything about you and Gavin." That part at least was true. Too late, but true.

"Oh." In any other situation, the embarrassment on Nika's face would have evoked a twinge of visceral sympathy, but now all he could manage was relief. "Damn. Sorry, I've just made us both extremely uncomfortable then." Her smile was wan. "How about we back up and erase the last of this conversation?"

"I think that is the best suggestion I've heard so far today."

"Coming back to bed? Oh no, wait, is that pie? That's the best suggestion ever." West leaned against the door, smiling sleepily, hair sticking up in hedgehog spikes, and dressed in what were quite obviously not his own sleep pants. When he shuffled in, they slipped alarmingly low, exposing an expanse of hip before West caught the waistband and hitched them back up.

Mesmerized, Corwin swallowed hard over a dry throat, unable to lock away. The images flooding his mind, effectively blanking out everything else, were a mix of his memories and West's. Holding those hips while he mapped light brown skin with only his mouth, the laughing mental nudges from West as he got closer to the promised birthmark and then veered in a different direction, leaving West gasping and writhing, sheets clenched in his hands.

"Good morning." West's greeting was directed at them both, and Corwin remembered Nika's presence with sudden embarrassed horror. He couldn't face her, not with *those* images still dancing in his head, and turned around in time to catch West's subtle brush of fingertips across the back of his neck. He unconsciously leaned into the touch for a second before he caught himself and pulled away.

"Same to you." Nika seemed to be rather studiously involved in her pie, a grin playing at the corners of her mouth, and he flinched, wondering how much she'd seen. Or was suspecting.

West was taking way too long, bent over and rummaging in the cooler, and while the galley was undeniably tiny, there was no reason to back into Corwin before standing. "Sorry about that." There was nothing apologetic in West's eyes; only a dark, wickedly teasing expression that jolted through him faster than any touch.

Nika's fork scraping against her plate was just loud enough to pull his attention away from West. She grinned cheerfully when he looked up, and gave him a brief salute with the fork. "I'm going to take Gav his pie before I'm tempted to finish it. If you need us before the briefing, we're going to watch some vids in my quarters."

West set the juice he'd spent so much effort looking for on the counter, and then put his hands on his hips. "That's great, but you kids stay out of trouble. And keep it down in there. People on this ship have to concentrate on other things besides you, you know." He patted Corwin on the back, fingers pressing in fractionally when Corwin tried to slide away, and carried on like embarrassing them all was the goal. "Corwin and I are going to be working today, and we're trying to avoid distractions."

"I . . ." Nika shook her head, cheeks pink. She precariously stacked the remaining plate and the two coffee mugs, and backed toward the door. "I'll pass that on to Gavin and we'll do our best."

Corwin cleared his throat, trying to bring a modicum of decorum back to a conversation that he'd never imagined having with his partner. Partners. "I'll monitor the comm and autopilot. Feel free to take the whole day." He waited until after Nika was gone, then turned to West. "You just embarrassed one of the best inspectors in the IEC. Not exactly professional behavior."

West shrugged. "Gavin will make it up to her, and it seemed nicer than telling her I can see her fucking my best friend when I close my eyes." West took a drink while Corwin stared, caught between annoyance and fascination with the column of West's throat. "Oh, wait." West's eyes opened impossibly wide. "You weren't talking about Nika. You meant *you*."

"The hell I did." His vehemence did nothing to dim West's grin, and he opened his mouth to further refute the injustice of the accusation, but West suddenly crowded into his space.

"Since you're not Gav's type, I guess *I'll* have to make it up to you instead of him."

The cocky self-assuredness was still as irritating as it had been before they'd had sex. Since then, though, he'd taken a tour of West's brain, and knew now that a good bit of it was an act. West's hand closed on the front of his shirt, fingers twisting in the material as he pulled Corwin closer, bringing his attention back to the moment.

"Stop thinking so much," West muttered against his lips, a faint, fruit-tinged tickle. It wasn't quite a kiss, at least not until West nipped at his mouth with sharp teeth, catching his groan. Then it became a kiss filled with desire and frustration, a struggle that had less to do with actual power and more to do with teasing out just whose desire was greater.

He was only vaguely aware of the counter digging into his back as he was shoved against it. The thin fabric of his sleep pants hid nothing when West ground against him, his breath coming in small panting gasps.

When Corwin finally pulled back, there was a question in West's eyes, and an itch Corwin felt in his mind that made him shiver. Barriers firmly in place, he shook his head, pretending not to notice the flash of hurt. "Not—" He shook his head again, at a loss for words. Not now? Not here? Not ever again? No one answer managed to encompass the rolling wave of emotion that threatened to suck him under.

West nodded slowly, hand untangling from Corwin's shirt. "Yeah, okay." His smile lost some of its edge as he stroked small, soothing circles on the bare skin inside Corwin's elbow. "But hey, we get bonus points for being all on our own. Nothing at all from Nika."

"For now, anyway," Corwin said, voice hoarse for no reason.

"I say we take advantage of that, then. Come back to bed? The same promise from before holds. I won't push."

That wry little twist of a smile cut through his layers of confusion and uncertainty with the precision of a scalpel, all the more painful because he knew it was no affectation. He wanted to say no, to leave it as a one-off he could look back on with fondness and faint nostalgia. He wanted to say no before he got himself hurt so badly that he'd be crawling away afterward, because he didn't do things like this. He didn't let people into his head, and he never, never went hunting in theirs.

Instead, he steered them down the corridor to his quarters, West a warm, solid certainty at his side as they both broke their own rules.

Ning'Kahiki's clenched fists were visible in the vid capture, his voice sharp as a blade. "It's out of my hands. I've been denied access to the cruise line's records. Until you find something I can use to press for a warrant, there's no point in my asking again."

"And what if we can't? How many victims are we going to tally up before they matter enough to interrupt someone's luxury vacation?" Corwin couldn't suppress his anger.

Ning'Kahiki shifted to Ning'Hala so quickly that Corwin blinked to make sure his eyes were working properly. "You have all the information I can give you, Inspector Menivie. There are factors I'm not at liberty to discuss, and I'll remind you that physical evidence will be required to press charges, no matter how convincing Agent Tavera's Reads are." She unclenched her hands, lacing her long fingers together before giving Corwin a pointed look. "The IEC is not in the habit of capitulating to the demands of private companies, no matter how affluent their clientele. This isn't just an inconvenience to your team. Find me some leverage."

Ning's curt nod was the last thing he saw before the connection was closed.

He was still staring at the screen in the common room when Nika and Gavin arrived for the briefing. He didn't know if it was a better idea to pass the news on first, or focus on the details of their latest victim before getting distracted by bureaucratic nonsense they had no hope of fighting. Gavin took a seat, but West was nowhere to be found. Corwin debated waiting for him, but if West's earlier argument with Gavin was enough to divert him from the case, he wasn't going to coddle that kind of idiocy.

Either way, he left the couch to the rest of them, staking a claim on the chair at the console station. He needed distance from everyone at the moment, and sitting alone in the corner was as much as he could get. He didn't even acknowledge them until Nika said hello in a determined, cheerful tone, and then he only grunted. Nika stared openly for a moment, before catching herself. Not about to be drawn into a personal conversation, he slouched lower in his seat and tucked his chin against his chest. He knew he looked unusually disheveled. He didn't need it discussed.

Thankfully, Nika ignored his rudeness. "Cainet has a fairly rigid caste system. They get a lot of news vid coverage for that, mainly because they refuse to respond to any of the imperial, uh, let's call it *encouragement*, to adopt a more democratic societal structure. They're huge on the luxury tourism circuit, so doubtless that has something to do with it. Easier to provide any- and everything when there's a distinct underclass to provide it for you."

"So which part of the system did the victim belong to?"

"None." Corwin lifted his head to address Gavin. "The victim is originally from Tasmin, late of Bodum. He had absolutely no reason to be on Cainet, which initially raised some flags. Preliminary results say that he was killed off-world and the body was dumped. He had a card for a Bodum workers' shelter in one of his shoes, and the mineral traces retrieved from the body and clothing all had small amounts of hathwa in them. A strain known for its potency, normally sold as Bodum's Kiss."

The tight clench of Gavin's jaw relayed something, but Corwin had no idea what. Perhaps West, among his other suspect knowledge of Bodum, had developed a fondness for hathwa somewhere along the line. Maybe Gavin thought it was rude to start briefings on time. He didn't care, and he wasn't going to waste more time speculating.

Judging from the way Nika's lips pressed into a thin line, though, her questions weren't going to be dismissed, merely postponed.

"There was a psy team involved, veterans, and the report said it was like there was a wall," he continued, voice deliberately flat. "Only so much information was being filtered through, and the rest was blocked in a way that made it obvious it was *being* blocked. Like someone was playing a game with them."

"He's saving the message for me."

Hands in his pants pockets, West sauntered into the room. He paused, briefly enough that Corwin felt certain he was the only one who noticed, and then perched on the arm of the couch farthest away from Gavin.

"What makes you think that?" Nika stared pointedly at West's bare feet, which seemed to have wedged themselves underneath her. He grinned, reaching to pat her knee and then slumping down onto the cushions next to her.

"Because he knew we were going to get the case." While not exactly condescending, West's tone still managed to convey astonishment that the question needed to be asked. His gaze slid briefly toward Gavin before he clarified. "Not *me*, or even *us*, but he knew it would be the same team. He knows someone has sniffed out his trail now, and he's enjoying it."

Corwin let West's arrogance slide. "From the analysis Agent Hale has made of your Reads, and the limited profiling Inspector Santivan and I have been able to build from physical evidence, he seems more concerned with someone paying attention to the victims and the crimes. Whatever thrill he's getting from the murders themselves is likely secondary to the enjoyment of other people knowing what he's doing. Evidence at this crime scene certainly follows through on that theory." His gaze returned to the vid screen, now covered with files relating to the case. Distance could always be achieved through formality and professionalism.

"He's picking victims from a pretty definite social strata too. Are we speculating on which end of the scale he's coming from?" Gavin asked.

Nika leaned forward, tapping a file open on her notebook and sending it to the screen. "It's funny you should mention that, given the connection we managed to find between the dump sites." A logo splashed up: a wine goblet superimposed over the Ylendrian Stars. "Artron Cruises leads month-long wine cruises. Very expensive, ports of call on over twenty-five planets, and access to exclusive vintages from at least forty top vineyards and distilleries." She paused, and Corwin felt the tension in the room ratchet up a notch. "There are forty-seven private vessels signed on, as well as three luxury passenger cruisers that belong to Artron, all cleared through port control on both planets. Their last stop was Cainet."

Corwin paged through the file. "Not to jump to any conclusions, but that would seem to answer the social strata question, wouldn't it?" A rustle of clothing alerted him to West's twitching, and he glanced up in time to see Gavin looking askance. "No?"

"I— Fuck." West shrugged angrily, hands up in a warding-off gesture. "I don't *know*. He's only let me see what he wants me to see. It's like a giant shell game. I mean it makes sense, since it would take money to move around that freely, but who the hell knows."

The two other occupants of the couch shifted, and Gavin's voice, although obviously meant for West alone, still carried. "Hey, it's okay. You need to chill."

West's smile grew pinched. "Sorry, I'll have it together by the time we dock on Cainet. Anything else I should know?"

Corwin had to unclench his jaw before he could speak. "I just spoke with Ning. Per a higher authority than them, we've been denied access to Artron's files until our investigation yields physical evidence that can be used to identify a possible suspect."

Nika and Gavin both made noises of protest, but West surged upright. "How are we supposed to *find* physical evidence if we can't investigate potential leads?"

"We can't question anyone until we have reason to believe we'll be able to press charges." He hated parroting Ning when he didn't want to believe the words, but arguing over them wouldn't change the facts. "Right now, all we can do is work with what we have," He nodded toward Nika. "What do we know?"

Nika got herself under control with visible effort. "Not much information on the victim, but they've identified him as Dutchan Plen. He was involved in the conflict on Tasmin that was, what, ten years ago? The only official records for the guy show that he was in a POW camp after the uprising was stamped out. Seems to have dropped off the grid after that. The authorities on Tasmin found surveillance footage from about five days ago that they believe is him, but there's no certainty."

Another tap brought up the picture of a nondescript man squatting against the side of a building, head tucked low to his chest and a blanket around his shoulders. While not obviously panhandling, there was a tarp with money on it in front of him.

"No physical signs of trauma, at least not recent," Nika continued. "Like our first victim, his death probably would've just been written off as natural causes, except for how they found the body." She frowned, leaning forward. Two side-by-side images filled the screen. The first was a standard crime scene shot, a close-up of the body. The second was pulled back to include the background as well as the body.

"What the *hell*?"

It was like a piece of abstract art—perfect in its arrangement, horrific in content. Plen was splayed at the center of an outline of the Imperial Stars, their triskele arms curving gracefully, almost protectively around his body.

"Can you zoom in?" Nika nodded, and Corwin stood to get a closer look at the large screen mounted on the wall opposite the couch. His first impression had been correct: the entire imperial seal was made out of money—paper and coins and credit chits, overlapping and spilling in bright piles. "Plen's body was found in an open lot. How the hell was all that money still sitting there?"

Gavin glanced down at his notebook. "It's not uncommon for a body to be buried with money on Cainet." His lip curled slightly. "It's unlikely anyone would have touched it out of fear that he was of a lower caste. The belief in reincarnation and walking into the afterlife is so strong that if someone can be buried above their current station, their entire family is raised to that level on the mortal plane so they can be reborn into the proper caste."

"But what's the message? The killer clearly knew enough about Cainet to create this little art project. Nobody goes through that amount of painstaking detail without a reason." Corwin found himself pacing back and forth in front of the screen, not really staring at it . . . at least not directly. More a matter of watching out of the corner of his eye, waiting for a pattern to appear.

"Oh, he had a reason." Nika's smile held no humor. "Impatience, I'm guessing. I wonder if this was planned, or if his ego got the better of him, and he wanted to hurry the game along?"

Gavin scowled, eyes distant. "Think about the peripheral people, the ones you pass every day. You don't even see them anymore because they're distasteful, or their very existence makes you uncomfortable, or you just can't do anything to help. And then think about who his victims have been."

West shook his head doubtfully. "Yeah, but that could just be because they're easy targets."

"No, I think Gavin's right. That would explain the showboating with this last case. He made it impossible to miss." Nika didn't look particularly happy with her statement. "If he felt the need to draw our attention to this so strongly, does it mean that there were more cases, more murders that slipped through the cracks?"

West slumped down further into the couch. "We'll never know, will we? Not without access to the information we're being locked out of."

Corwin started to reach beyond his shields to offer reassurance, then pulled back sharply, realizing what he'd almost done. "It's not your fault," he said, staring at West.

"The only fault lies with whoever it is that thinks wealth is more important than a murder investigation." Nika's dark pronouncement hung heavy in the air as she powered off her notebook. Much as it bothered him to think the IEC could be so easily subverted, Corwin could only agree with her.

Corwin had not, until today, realized that Nika's command chair could spin fast enough to make him motion sick. The fact that he wasn't even sitting in it only made the discovery more nauseating, but damned if he'd be cast in the role of killjoy. Eventually, West would get dizzy enough to stop. In the meantime, his chair, at least, stayed motionless.

West's spinning continued unabated, then stopped with force and apparent purpose. West leaned forward in the chair, peering at him. "Your shield is amazing. Like right now? I can see that you're really trying not to be annoyed with me—and thanks for that—but I can't feel anything." There was a brief pause, where West seemed a lot more interested in poking at the bridge computer than speaking. He finally looked up, as serious as Corwin had ever seen him. "Is there any way you can teach me how to do that?"

"Teach you? Why?" Corwin clutched the arms of his chair, thankful for the sense of grounding they provided.

West appeared to be giving the question a great deal of thought, lower lip caught between his teeth. "If *I* can't Read you, if I couldn't even tell you were an Active, then your shielding is incredibly strong."

"True." Now that the room had stabilized, he felt safe moving. Leaning forward, he cupped a hand around West's chin, smiling faintly as he allowed himself the dangerous indulgence of touch. "But as someone who seems to go out of his way to make sure everyone within the general vicinity knows exactly how he feels, I'm not sure why you'd be interested, even if I thought I could teach it. And honestly, I'm doubtful that I can."

West's disappointment was quickly masked by the heat in his eyes as he reached for Corwin's hand. Corwin hissed, the jolt of arousal when West's tongue darted across the tip of his finger catching him by surprise. It scared him how easy it was for West to get to him. It was one thing right now, and when it was just the two of them. Stars help them both if that power carried over to when they were on the job.

"See, and now I can guess that you're thinking you'd like a good, rousing fuck in the spinny chair." West's grin was smug. "Just a guess, but I'm willing to bet it's an accurate one. I want to be able to shield like that."

Corwin clicked his tongue disapprovingly, covering for the shaky breath he wanted to take. "And you call yourself a Reader."

The pout took twenty years off of West's age. "A blowjob in the spinny chair? Blowing me in the spinny chair?" When Corwin shook his head, West sighed explosively. "See, it's that damn shielding. It's not fair. You won't teach me, you won't let me in. How'm I supposed to know what you want?"

It wasn't exactly an accusation, but it still bit into him like one. It was also the first time West had called him on his reticence, and he found himself pulling back physically as well as mentally. "The rest of the 'verse seems to manage," he said, his voice brittle.

"The rest of the 'verse knows what you want in bed?" West looked honestly puzzled.

Massaging the ache between his eyes, Corwin rolled his shoulders, suddenly tense and tired. "The rest of the 'verse manages to have satisfying relationships without digging around in each other's minds." Except that West had never asked for a relationship, only sex. Even now, he was pretty sure he was being used as a convenient distraction from West's fight with Gavin. He stood up abruptly, needing to put some distance between the two of them. He really needed distance between himself and his thoughts, but that was going to be harder to manage.

"Where are you going?" West scrambled up and made a grab for him, eyes narrowing at his awkward dodge. "Right. But did you ever think that maybe knowing how somebody feels about something can make things easier? Because right now I know you're pissed, but I have no clue why."

"It's got nothing to do with you."

"But you *are* pissed. And I'd like to know why."

The worst of it was, he didn't have to Read West to know it was sincere, and while it was easy to dismiss ridiculously overdone Agent Tavera, earnest West deserved more. But that meant dredging up a past that wasn't open for sharing.

West was more cautious about resting a hand on Corwin's arm this time, like it could be jerked back any second, and Corwin laughed quietly, reluctance giving way. "You look like you're afraid I'm going to bite you."

West nodded, and an unruly bit of hair fell across one eye, somehow escaping the liberal application of hair product that kept the rest of his head in artful disarray. "I'm trying to invade your space respectfully."

Corwin snorted and brushed the hair off West's face without thinking. "Is that what it is?" West leaned in closer with a grin, and Corwin sighed. "Maybe we can try practicing the shielding."

"Really? What made you change your mi— I mean, that would be great." He glanced at the console behind him. "Do you have to keep one hand on the nav computer at all times so we don't fall out of the sky?"

Corwin raised his eyebrows. "No, the autopilot can do that without my help. Proximity alarms are a great thing."

"I do like to be warned when someone's getting too close."

He could let the words, even taken at face value, put an ugly little spin on things, or he could twist them on his own. He hated playing these games, and he hated not knowing if he needed to even more. "You didn't seem to mind someone tailing you last night."

West looked stupidly pleased, but didn't laugh. "Why, Inspector, was that a naughty bedroom reference? And outside of your cabin, too. I'm shocked by your brazen disregard for propriety."

"Do you want to try this or not?" His impatience was more put-upon than real, but West dutifully followed him down the corridor toward his quarters, even managing to keep his smile hidden when Corwin glanced back.

"You do smug satisfaction really well, Tavera." Corwin palmed the lock, his door sliding open and letting them into a room that still smelled faintly of sex. It was probably his imagination. The scrubbers on the environmental systems were very efficient.

West looked around the room as though they hadn't just left it an hour before, curious gaze taking everything in again before he plunked down in the middle of the bed and turned that same inquisition on him. "I'm not denying the smug thing, but you should know, I do appreciative even better."

"I'll keep that in mind." He sat on the bed as well, back ramrod straight, feet firmly on the floor. West inched over closer without saying anything, until their knees bumped.

The awkward silence stretched, and the unexpected anxiety he felt had nothing to do with sex. He didn't talk about his gift, or birthright, or whatever the hell it was that gave him the ability to eavesdrop on someone else's intimacies. Like so much else, it was a topic deemed verboten by his culture, and while he'd left many of the inhibitions of his youth behind, the ones that remained were harder to get past.

Cautious, he stopped pressing out with quite so much force. West relaxed with every fraction of control Corwin released, his protections dwindling down until they were as low as they'd been the night before. West's expression was all business now, baffled and serious as he swept into the space Corwin had made in his mind.

"*It's like picking up a proximity signal. You're not there, then you get a little bit stronger with every pass, until I can see you.*"

He shrugged. "Not a bad interpretation." He began to push out again, and when West recognized what he was doing, it was actually easier. Boundaries when there was nothing to protect himself from were harder to maintain, but as soon as he had something to grapple with, some border to define and defend, he knew exactly how hard to react.

"You— How— There's no way your shielding is that good. No fucking way. Nobody can keep *everything* under wraps like that, and still be filtering what's coming in." West's fingers strayed to the back of his head, and Corwin decided that he must use so much gel as a safety measure, to keep from looking as though he'd been unable to find a comb for months. He worried at the nape of his neck, digging his fingers into the artistic mess of hair and pulling it. "Do you really not Read anything but sex?"

Corwin flinched at the question, and West saw it, but there was no changing that. "I told you, I can Read joy. Whatever is making someone happiest at a given moment. Not just sex." His voice had dropped. This wasn't a temple, and he wasn't asking for West's approval. "It's— I was raised not to speak about it. It's uncomfortable." Not even the half of it, the sick feeling that still accompanied someone else *knowing*, but he refused, as always, to give in to it. He drew a slow, steadying breath and tried to answer the question that would get this over with sooner. "I don't filter, not like PsyAc teaches. I block."

West's animated features didn't do much to hide his disappointment. "Oh. I can't do that. They tried to teach me when I first got to PsyAc, but I get distracted too easily, and it was exhausting.

The best I've ever been able to do is use the clear space a Ground provides, but I can't just hang off Gavin all the time." West waved the hand he'd untangled from his hair. "I wish I could. But the less dependent I am on Gav, the safer he'll be."

Corwin frowned, catching West's fingers and turning their hands over, tracing the lines of West's palm like touch was a vaccine against silence and he was trying to build immunity. "The kind of blocking I do isn't what PsyAc teaches. It's the difference between pulling a curtain over a window and building a wall where the window used to be."

"PsyAc has been training Actives for hundreds of years. I kind of think that if there was a way to keep me under control, they would have found it." The tone was teasing, but the words weren't, and Corwin bit down a sharp reply.

"I don't know if I can explain it, and I don't know if I'll be able to maintain a connection with you and show you at the same time."

"Yeah, hard to show me what you're doing in your head when you're busy trying to keep me out of it." West's voice had dropped, and for a fraction of a second, Corwin could Read the sadness—a starburst of resigned defeat that was gone so quickly, he questioned ever having felt it at all. Startled enough to drop West's hand, he covered for it by folding his fingers together and making an offer he wasn't sure he'd be able to follow through on. "I think that if I was locked in a Read with you, I could show you enough of the basics that you could pick it up." It meant crawling inside West's head, establishing a deeper connection than they needed to direct thoughts back and forth. It wasn't his first choice, and West seemed to be even more reluctant, visibly faking a smile.

"*If you thought it was a circus before, you're going to love the dog and pony show.*"

In the years since his temple training, the number of people Corwin had shared a mental connection with, beyond an accidental dalliance during sex, could be counted on one hand. One finger, in fact. Even being the one in control, it was still daunting to close his eyes and sink below the cheerful chaos.

West surrounded him, careful, tense, afraid, hopeful, afraid, so afraid, and it was all Corwin could do to keep himself steady enough to move beyond that into the center of it all. A low hum filled his every cell, the background buzz of someone speaking just out of earshot. He could almost identify it, if he just reached—

"Please don't. It's Nika, and I have a hard enough time keeping her on the edges."

He could see that now, and should have known better anyway. Steadying himself against the unfamiliar onslaught, he started to apologize, but before he even finished the thought, the warmth of acknowledgment had already filtered through.

"I'm going to start. Watch."

He didn't bother with anything else resembling words, instead taking a moment to clear his mind as much as he possibly could while West was sharing a corner of it. The fear that hammered in his chest belonged to both of them, two minds made for this communion, yet equally reluctant to accept more than a casual connection.

West's thoughts twisted around him, a confusion of memory and visceral emotion: fractured images that he could only weather, not understand. Just as quickly gone, their absence had more to do with West's control than anything else. *"Just show me. I'll try to keep the rest of it away from you."*

"Can you let me feel Nika again?"

Corwin's answer was her clear, uncomplicated presence blooming in his head. Going slower this time, he worked outward from West's mind as a center, his isolating bubble growing until it met Nika's mind and stopped. *"When you reach an obstacle, you use the resistance as a foundation, and build your shield with that energy."*

West's amusement tickled, the only thing that stopped the next thought from hitting him the wrong way. *"You really do spend all your time keeping people away."*

"If the alternative is letting them all in, absolutely. Do you want to try it?"

"Show me again."

He drew the shielding down and built it up again, twice more before West joined him, overshooting time and again.

Corwin had never claimed to be a good teacher, and the frustration of watching West fail at something that was second nature to him only grew with each attempt. He couldn't understand why the hell PsyAc had left anyone so dangerously open. "*Too much. Let the resistance guide you. You don't need to seek things out.*"

"*You think this is me seeking things out? I can show you all the things I'm trying* not *to look at right now.*" Beyond frustration to anger, and the next second to something else entirely. A third person joining them—Nika, because he could see Gavin's face through her eyes, feel every one of her thoughts and emotions cascading over him, living in his head. Less direct and somehow worse, every object seemed to have a story to share. His desk and chair told secrets, and his bed was riddled with long nights of sleep broken by lonely, efficient self-care.

By comparison, when their viewpoint was wrenched to West's room, everything held a patchwork of meaning, every stupid trinket imbued with a laugh or a failure, a ghost carried from place to place. West's blankets crawled with nightmares, and Corwin tried to flinch away, only to run up against something else demanding his attention, everything clawing at the edges of his awareness.

He hadn't been afraid to Read since the onslaught of his abilities in adolescence. He reached instinctively for the still corner of his mind, a temple of privacy and calm built to mirror the places of holy refuge he'd been trained in. Except that West's inescapable gravity was trying to drag him along, and suddenly he was the one overshooting boundaries. He tried to pull himself away, but West was still with him when the safety he was reaching for gave way to memory instead.

The walls of the temple training ground, plain stone, seemed as pale and unforgiving as the face of the Virtue who escorted him away from the bonding test. "Your disability makes you an unsuitable bondmate."

He protested, though he'd never argued with a temple official before. "Verdan and—"

"Not Verdan. Not anyone. You will never form a safe connection with anyone. Your bondmate would be exposed to the intimacies of others, just as you are. You could ruin them." The Virtue gave him a pitying look, probably meant to seem like kindness. "I'll make sure your privacy is respected, but I'll be withdrawing your name from the bonding pool."

Murderers were withdrawn. Violators. "I haven't done anything wrong."

"You were born that way."

Corwin clenched handfuls of bedding. It took him a few seconds to make sense of seeing the world that *was*, the world through his own eyes. As soon as he was able to find his center, he pushed for the familiar boundaries of resistance, and found West too tangled in his mind to build his walls properly.

His voice scraped his throat when he spoke. "Get out. Get out of my head. Who the fuck do you think you are, to drag another Reader into your head without permission?"

West's expression closed off, his only tell the unnaturally tight line of his mouth. "I wasn't trying to see anything you didn't want me to. I know this might be hard for you to believe, but I don't actually *enjoy* eavesdropping on the entire world. It's not as easy for me to figure out where I end and other people begin as it is for you." West smoothed a hand over the bed, staring at the plain blue spread instead of Corwin. "I shouldn't have forced you to see what it's like to live without shielding, without your walls. And I'm sorry I saw . . . that."

That. Acid churned in Corwin's gut, and humiliation ran through him like scalding water piped into his veins. He felt nineteen again, stripped of his years and calluses as he realized West had seen one of the worst moments of his life. "Sorry doesn't undo anything," he growled. "Sorry doesn't make up for pushing yourself into everyone's head."

West finally looked up, barking a laugh when their eyes met. "You think I don't know that? You . . . your Talent echoes off rainbows and kittens and sex. Mine echoes off *everything*. I've been stumbling around inside the heads of rapists and killers since I was *twelve* because it's the only thing I'm good for." His voice rose as he scrambled off the bed, putting as much distance between them as he could in the small room. "Do you not get that I don't have the fucking choice *not* to use it?"

Corwin worked his jaw a moment. "I understand you'd rather wallow in your own damage than respect the privacy of others." It wasn't fair. It probably wasn't even true. All that mattered was getting West out of his room and Corwin forgetting he'd been stupid enough to lay his secrets out like a buffet just because he was lonely.

West's aborted laughter lingered in the air between them. "Oh, Corwin, I thought you *liked* damaged, so you wouldn't have to feel like the only freak in the room." He bent over to grab his shirt from the night before, balling it up in one hand as his smirk stretched into a deceptively pleasant smile. "Unfortunately, I'm leaving now, so you're right back where you started. Thanks for the fuck, Inspector."

The door shut behind West, and Corwin found himself wishing the pneumatic sliders could be slammed. Maybe the IEC had anticipated high tempers, or maybe their fleet engineers simply liked the *whooshing* sound. The reasons didn't matter, but he would have appreciated some kind of decisive end to the conversation. The quiet retreat of West's footsteps seemed more like ellipses than a full stop, and he hated indefinite punctuation.

CHAPTER 12

When Gavin commented on Corwin's absence at the next couple of meals, Nika shrugged, unconcerned. West tried for the same level of nonchalance, but fooling Gav had never come easy, and once Gavin sent Nika out of the galley with the promise that they'd clean up dinner, he knew the game was over.

After a quick glance to ensure that Nika was out of earshot, Gavin leaned against the cooler, effectively blocking West's exit. "So what the hell is going on?"

"I'm doing dishes, since you railroaded me into it?" He accompanied his words with a bit of soapy water, flicked across the galley with his fingers.

"Ha-ha. What did Corwin do to make you unhappy? He's obviously laying low for a reason. Guilty conscience?"

West's smile felt tight. "Now Gav, I know I play at the naive ingénue, and quite well at that, but really, that's just between you and me. I'm not in the habit of letting people make me unhappy."

"Yeah, but you're not in the habit of having one-night stands with coworkers, either. Or picking fights with me." West couldn't stop his flinch, and Gavin sighed, guilt sliding across his face. "Shit. That was completely uncalled for. I'm sorry."

"Nah, it's okay." Except it wasn't, not by a long shot, and he had to swallow down anger that wasn't directed at Gavin. "I'll be fine before we get back to work tomorrow." He stared pointedly at Gavin's feet until Gavin sighed and moved out of the way. "Wake me up when we dock?"

"West, it's going to be okay. We just need to get our feet back under us."

He couldn't face Gavin and say what he needed to. "I know that, dude, but it's not going to happen until we both acknowledge that we don't trust each other as much as we should."

"I'd trust you more if I thought you were only working this case, and not Rashium's as well."

West gripped the edge of the counter so hard his fingers ached, his shoulders hunching. "A good investigator works all the angles. There's no point in living through the past if you're not going to learn your lesson."

Gavin rested a hand on his shoulder. "The lesson wasn't that you can't do anything, it's that you can't do *everything*."

The flavor of Corwin's anger was still fresh in his mind. "Oh, believe me, I'm aware." He turned quickly and wrapped Gavin in a brief hug. "Thanks."

Corwin used the downtime until they docked to polish his veneer of competence. By the time he stepped off the ship, he'd recovered enough to snap a salute at the local force liaison waiting at the end of the *Vigilance*'s gangplank.

"We'll transfer all the most recent information over to you, but I have to warn you that it's not much. A definite ident on the victim, and confirmation that the surveillance footage was of him." The officer waved them toward a flyer. "The most interesting thing is that according to the autopsy, that footage was shot approximately ten hours before time of death. And three planetary days before the body was found here."

"Coinciding perfectly with the tour." Nika's anger simmered under the surface when she met Corwin's eyes. "Though I'm sure that's not enough to ask for a warrant, either."

Gavin stepped into the fray, shooting an uncomfortable glance at the planetary enforcement officer, who seemed to be trying as hard as possible to be inconspicuous. "Ning is hardly the top of the food chain at the IEC. Let's just see what we can do with the investigation here, and take it from there."

West patted Nika on the shoulder with a crooked little grin. "Besides, one of you taking this as a personal affront is enough." She shook him off, and he stepped out of her space. Corwin didn't miss the way he kept glancing at her, and wondered if West had given Nika an outlet for her anger on purpose.

The drive to where the body had been found traversed a dizzying array of terrain: slums to solidly middle-class neighborhoods to glitzy pleasure venues and palatial estates, the lines between them blurring and shifting without warning. When they finally stopped, it was in front of a tiny, dusty hill that seemed to be a sort of no-man's-land between a collection of polyboard shacks and a mansion clearly modeled on the imperial palace.

Gavin stood on the edge of the grass while the others climbed out of the flyer. "I'm surprised all the money was still there when you found the body."

The officer looked shocked, fingers twitching at her side in a warding gesture before she caught herself. "No one would touch it. It was next to a corpse, and that makes it tainted."

"Were you able to trace any of it?"

She shook her head, and Corwin sighed. If it was like the first case, it was unlikely that West would be able to pick anything up off a Read unless it had been deliberately left. Quite honestly, he was a little leery of deliberately left things now. It hadn't gone so well last time.

Nika jogged his elbow. "I'm going to walk the perimeter, maybe check out the surrounding neighborhood." She made a face, looking between the shacks and the mansion. "Neighborhoods," she amended. "Call if you need me before I get back."

They both knew it was a polite way of removing herself and cutting down on the mental chatter during the Read, and he gave her a nod. "Be careful. I . . . I'm going to stay here, in case Gavin needs help." She looked surprised at his excuse for not joining her. He didn't even know if West still wanted his help or not, but tainted happiness spilled out from the crime scene like an oil slick, and he suspected the Read was going to be just as bad as Bodum's, if not worse.

Nika patted her weapon and badge, as close to a prayer as the IEC had ever endorsed. "You too. I'll be back in a few."

When he turned away from her, Corwin found that West was already pacing the length of the dirt strip. Torn between keeping his distance and being close enough for support, he loitered just out of touch, feeling like a voyeur. When he glanced over, he saw a hint of anger in West's eyes, quickly covered by a grim smile.

"That little art display must've filled this entire space. I wonder if he had it picked out already." West kicked at a clod of dirt, voice quiet. "I wonder how many more murders we're going to find out about now."

Gavin eyed West. "So you think Nika was right?"

"Yeah."

Gavin sighed. "Me too. She's a damn good profiler." West lifted an eyebrow, but seemed to know better than to say anything to the contrary. Nika was an excellent officer, and it didn't seem likely that Gavin, no slouch in that department himself, would be swayed by something without real merit, no matter what the state of their personal lives was. "So you want to do this thing? We might as well plan on it being a bad one."

"Give me just a second." West turned toward Corwin. "Inspector, can I speak to you privately for a moment?"

Corwin scowled, but followed West. He could feel Gavin's eyes boring into his back, and his scowl deepened. "What do you want, Tavera? We're here to work, in case you forgot."

"Shit, that completely slipped my mind!" West threw his hands up in the air. "Sorry about that. Oh, actually, though, I wanted to ask about that request I made."

Even though he'd stayed for this very reason, he'd been hoping West would realize what a terrible idea it was. "You're going to piss Gavin off, and I'm not trained."

"Much as I adore Gavin, his feelings aren't really the issue here, are they?" West's saccharine-sweet tone did nothing to hide the bite behind the words. "And we've already established that you've got valuable shielding skills. I think both those facts override your objections."

"I—"

West cut him off by simply turning away, and then kept right on going past Gavin, jerking a thumb over his shoulder. "Corwin's providing backup with Grounding."

"I'm sorry, what?" When West ignored him, Gavin spun around to face Corwin, angling away from the planetary enforcement officer.

"What in the hell is he talking about? You can't do that, you're not trained. Why the fuck would he say that?"

This wasn't an argument he intended to have. It was West's doing; West could sort out the backlash. "He's starting the Read," he said, voice clipped. "Think you can save your hurt pride for later?"

"And I will pull him right back out of it if you don't tell me why the hell I'm suddenly getting backup from an untrained, psy-phobic inspector."

Corwin shrugged, fighting to keep the annoyance out of his voice. "Do whatever you feel you need to do. I didn't ask for this, Tavera did. But I told him I'd do what I could to keep him from injuring you. Again."

Gavin bared his teeth in mockery of a smile, hands clenched at his side. "Your concern is noted. And unnecessary."

"Take it up with Tavera. We have an investigation right now." He turned away, hitting his comm badge and barking out Nika's name.

"I'm fine, Corwin. I'll check back in twenty minutes, unless you find something before then."

West ignored them both, taking a lot longer than usual to prep for the Read by pacing the edge of the rough impression left by the money. Given their last attempt, Corwin couldn't really find fault with the delay. He wasn't eager to discover what else their murderer had left behind. He also had a feeling that his effort wouldn't be appreciated should he need to step between Gavin and any projectiles.

West started swaying back and forth, enough like a dance that Corwin almost couldn't tell if it was part of a performance or an effect of the Read. The grim look on West's face seemed to indicate the latter.

Gavin pulled out a notebook, ignoring Corwin in favor of prompting West. "What do you see?"

West mouthed a few words that Corwin hoped Gavin could make out better than him. He didn't read lips well enough. Worse, he couldn't tell if it was West in control, or if it was some new spin their quarry had put on the scene.

"I see— Gavin, he's—"

West screamed, and Corwin, the local officer, and Gavin all jumped. Gavin recovered first, hand closing around West's wrist almost immediately.

"He's stacked them all up for us. Not like bricks, or cards. Bread crumbs across the galaxy, but they don't lead anywhere, and he knows it. Stacked like— like—"

The next scream went on longer, and Corwin could sympathize with the indecision on Gavin's face. Protocol said that the Read could continue, and he knew West wouldn't want to be pulled out, no matter how painful it was.

In the end, Gavin stayed still, fingers loose around West's wrist.

West finally pulled himself out of Gavin's grip to walk the perimeter of the scene, retracing the imperial mark. Eyes closed, steps hesitant, the silence just waiting to be broken again.

"The first was an accident, a theory, a test. He didn't do it right, so we'll never find that one. Burned up and flushed into the black. The second wasn't a sparrow at all, to see what would happen, and then he didn't again, not for a long time. Not until he knew how to make it matter. But it still doesn't matter, and he has a whole flock of them now, feathers in his cap."

"How many feathers does he have? How many birds?"

West wandered, walking a labyrinth that Corwin could only remember from the photos of the body, feet dragging in the dirt as he chattered. "More than he has fingers, fingers on hands he won't get dirty anymore, fingers on necks and fingers make the stars, over and over, fingers make the stars, but only the birds can see, and nobody listens to the birds when all they can hear is the money. Money talks louder than pretty birds, and it'll talk louder than the law too."

West's feet kept on with their restless dancing, the strain in his voice getting worse, a wet, thick clutch to his breathing that slurred his words. He stopped moving abruptly, falling down inside the third petal of the imperial crest, and his hands scratched over the dirt as he screamed again. When blood started dripping out of his mouth, Gavin lurched forward, but Corwin was faster.

"Stop!" Corwin barked. Gavin glared at him, but he pointed at the symbol and letters West had made in the dirt. "Be careful. He fought for that."

Gavin shook him off, reaching West as he rolled away from the gouges he'd made in the soft ground. "West, are you back?"

Corwin crouched down near them, his voice a buffer between West's low whining and Gavin's cool, professional panic. "Agent Tavera, you're done. You got what you wanted."

West looked up, and Corwin could tell that something wasn't quite there yet, West's eyes rolling back every few seconds, his voice taking on an unfamiliar whine. "It hurts. Still inside me, still here, and it hurts. I tried to show you, but you don't care."

Gavin knelt between the lines in the dirt, pulling West up until he was sitting, head lolling. The blood smeared around his mouth left damp marks on Gavin's shirt. The contact seemed enough to break him out of the Read entirely, and for a change, he didn't look to be fighting the return.

"I have to get out of the seal, okay?" It sounded so calm, so reasonable, like West wasn't spitting up blood and soaked in sweat. Gavin nodded immediately, and Corwin reached down, helping without a word, until all three of them were several meters from the redrawn seal. They all stared, West with a kind of blank fascination that finally edged into bleak humor.

Roughly scraped through the wide petals of the familiar Ylendrian heraldry, West's feet and fingers had told another story: *IEC*, written large and accusatory.

West coughed, spitting in the grass at their feet. "That's just great. You know how much I like subtle—"

That was all the warning they got before West's knees folded and he passed out.

He fucked up, he fucked up— West bolted awake with the words on his lips, and lost them a second later to the thick, garbled clog of his voice. His tongue felt huge, hot and painful in his mouth, and given that he couldn't really talk, he thought the whimper that slipped out was entirely justified.

It was easy enough to tell that he was in a hospital, if only from the bed he was lying on and the lumpy ghosts of illness it imparted to him. The room was darker than he expected, and the guilt of sleeping through the rest of the afternoon was almost enough to get him upright, struggling against a very real desire to get back to the business of napping.

The lights snapped on when he moved, and before he could stop blinking away the glare, someone shoved a cup into his hand. "Here."

Some of the ice chips had already melted, but he spooned up a couple of the larger ones, wincing when they hit his tongue.

"I can't believe I'm saying this, but don't suck." Corwin's eyebrows lifted in reply to West's unvoiced amusement. "The doctor says you're supposed to let them melt, because the cold will help reduce the swelling, and suction will hurt." He stared at West until they were both a little uncomfortable, then turned to look out the window set into the exam room door instead. "Apparently you bit through your tongue. Three times. Luckily, the tongue is one of the fastest-healing parts of the body. You'll be annoying again in a couple days."

He started to answer, and wound up choking on the ice chips instead. Coughing hurt, like someone had a hand in his mouth and was squeezing, and when he was done, he could taste blood.

"*Where's Gavin?*" He didn't bother with finesse or permission, just broadcast as loudly as he could, and felt a vindictive flash of pleasure when Corwin winced, before remembering that made him an asshole. He'd already seen what happened when he pushed at Corwin, and he preferred not to be an unwelcome voyeur to that pain and humiliation ever again. "*Sorry, but it doesn't seem like you'd be the first person volunteering to hover next to my sickbed and offer succor.*"

Corwin finally turned back to him, expression as bland as always, except for the faintest hint of a smile hiding in the shadows. "I was promised that you'd be totally silent, and I've always wanted to witness a miracle."

He could've laughed at his own expense, but he really wasn't in the mood, and their fight still stung. "*Where's Gavin?*"

"He'll be right back. He and Nika went off to—"

"*Don't want to know.*"

"As I was *saying*, they went off to secure the victim's body in a private viewing gallery in the morgue, so that you wouldn't have to come in contact with any of the other potential unpleasantness associated with a major trauma center." Corwin exhaled sharply and reached forward to snatch the cup away, stabbing the spoon into the ice chips with a viciousness not usually required for frozen water. When he put a hand on West's arm, fingers cold enough to raise goose bumps, neither of them mentioned the way West immediately relaxed.

"What did the IEC have to do with the scene? Or can you remember any of it?"

He could, if he tried very hard, but they'd obviously given him something for pain; trying very hard was making him feel like he was still on the edges of the Read, spaced out and a little dizzy. Corwin spooned another ice chip into his mouth with one hand. His other came to rest against West's open palm, and the warmth of contact brought things into focus again.

"Don't think too hard, you'll hurt yourself."

"He's mad at the IEC. He was trying to hide it when he planted the Read, but he couldn't block it all, and I got to it, even though I had to escape the traps he set."

"I didn't even know that someone *could* set a trap in a Read, before this case." Corwin's grousing was another familiar comfort. He didn't seem to notice that they were holding hands, and West wasn't going to point it out, though he wondered if that was selfish. Corwin's thumb slipped over the lines in his palm again, tracing them, and there was a touch of mercy in his calm question. "Could you tell why he's angry?"

"He lost someone he shouldn't have, and nobody was listening to him, so he keeps telling the birds." He didn't remember closing his eyes, but if he focused on the ticklish rasp of Corwin's finger across his hand, he could almost make sense of the insights he'd stolen from the crime scene. People didn't seem to understand that they weren't any less confusing once he was aware of the world around him again.

"Hey, don't zone out on me. How's your tongue?"

"Still fairly useless, but thanks for asking."

"Have some more ice."

Gavin pushed the door open a few seconds later, pausing long enough that Nika bumped into him. "I'm not even going to pretend to understand how you two get along," he said.

Corwin dropped the spoon back into the cup and thrust it toward Gavin. Gavin's gaze flicked between Corwin and West. "You know there's nothing wrong with his *hands*, right? He can still use a spoon."

West flipped Gavin off to prove the viability of his hands, and got a salute in return. He inclined his head, and all was forgiven, at least for the moment.

"So, you're not supposed to use your tongue for a while." Teasing aside, Gavin was less than collected, peering at West as though he might spot something the doctor had missed. It was his first real indication of how bad he must look, because Gavin had seen everything else a Read had ever thrown at them, and rarely shown this much worry before, at least when he was awake to see it.

He started to say something to Corwin, pushing at the edge of the bubble before remembering that he was the only person in the room who knew the inspector could hear him. By his own proclamation, Gavin and Nika both thought Corwin was a null. No matter what West thought of people who treated psy talents like they were something to be ashamed of, he wasn't going to tell someone else's secret. Instead, he pursed his lips carefully and tried gurgling out something almost intelligible. "Nika?"

She looked up from her notepad, obviously confused but listening. He gestured at her, then tapped his head, and she seemed to get it, offering him a tentative nod.

"Fuck, my mouth hurts. Can you please tell them that I can still Read the body? That is, if you're willing to talk for me."

Actively engaging with Nika left him in a bit of an echo chamber, with her voice half a step behind her thoughts, but it was faster than typing everything out on a notepad, something he wouldn't be coherent enough to do in Read space anyway.

"West says he can still do a Read on the body. I can speak for him."

He was expecting Gavin to object, but the first twitch of disapproval came from Corwin, passing like a flash of indigestion, and with about as much fanfare. The narrow press of Corwin's lips firmed for a second, and then it was gone.

Gavin's scowl was a lot more obvious, and a lot less temporary. "In my professional opinion, that's a really fucking stupid idea."

"His opinion is noted. If it makes everyone feel better, we're already in the hospital, so if I accidentally give myself a vision-induced liver transplant or something, imagine the response time."

Nika coughed, turning a little pink around the ears. "Agent Tavera says he's sure that if he requires further medical care, he'll be able to find it here, but he'd prefer to proceed with his suggested course of investigation."

"*I'm only talking through you from now on. You make everything sound so reasonable. I'm going to walk out that door in about thirty seconds so unless one of you wants to carry me, you should probably point me in the right direction.*" He paused for a second, smiling just wide enough that it didn't hurt too much. "*Actually, I think I'd prefer to be carried. In my delicate condition, I can see the potential for another injury.*"

Nika raised an eyebrow, stepping around Gavin so she could lean in and flick West's ear. "West says that he's going to need a little help getting to the room we've secured, but when he's done, he's going to buy us all dinner."

"*I take it all back. You're vicious and cruel. I can't even eat dinner.*" Swinging his legs over the side of the bed, he hopped down and felt the rush of pain medication hit him hard. It was an effort not to show it, but he managed, except for a brief moment when he wondered whether the floor was going to stop rolling under him. It was easier to cover it when he was moving, so forward momentum won out over waiting for help.

They made an odd crew shuffling down the hallway, but at least he wasn't stuck in some horrible disposable clothing. Sure, the collar of his uniform shirt was stiff with blood, but the IEC, in their infinite wisdom, had chosen black for a reason. Nobody else was going to know that he'd tried to eat his own tongue. He even managed to refrain from lifting his arms and shuffling toward people, if only because the ache in his mouth would have made it uncomfortable to demand brains.

"I can tell you're laughing, and I'm about as gifted as a rock," Nika whispered in a conspiratorial tone, and he winced, patting her arm as they all squeezed into the elevator heading down to the morgue.

"*Don't you think every hospital needs a spontaneous outbreak of walking death?*"

"I think I have that vid." She still looked amused, but neither Gavin nor Corwin seemed inclined to joke at the moment.

They hit their destination a few minutes later, and he didn't hesitate to grab Gavin's arm before they entered. To communicate with Nika, he was going to have to stay at least half-lucid.

He wasn't expecting to find Corwin's mental presence waiting for him when he finally let go of Gavin and prepared to drop into the Read, but there was no mistaking the halting contact for anyone else.

"Is there something you need me to do?"

West hid his reaction, mindful of exposing things Corwin didn't want made public. *"Can you just sort of watch me, and try to catch anything I don't pass along to Nika?"*

There were no words of affirmation, just the continued presence of Corwin's mind, but that was good enough. West rested a hand against the cold metal table, exhaling slowly, and closed his eyes.

He'd been playing by someone else's rules for so long that he almost didn't know what to do when presented with what looked like a straightforward Read. It wasn't routine, or pleasant, because the violent psychic death of another being would never be normal, but there was no sense of traps or games or yawning pits waiting to drag him in.

"He was a fighter. In the war, on the streets later, so he knew what fear felt like. This . . . He wasn't afraid. He was just angry." Nika's quiet repetition of his words was an easily ignored buzz in the background as he let himself drift deeper. He followed the perimeter of the table, fingers trailing through the trough along its edge. There was nothing filling it at the moment, but that didn't stop him from thinking about what it was designed to channel away.

He'd come to the port to see the ships pour in, a whole fleet of luxury liners descending like a shower of stars, sparkling. The chain link under his hands felt gritty with the dust they kicked up as they settled into their docking cradles, the Tasmin Jewel *close enough that he could read her markings. He turned his head to spit, a curse that couldn't be completed because he'd never return to the shining city, never find the elaborate tombs of the rich citizens who'd killed his friends. Next to him, in the direction he wasn't facing, a voice asked him, "Doesn't it make you sick, how the money still flies when the wings of the birds are clipped?"*

Dutchan glanced to the left, but all he saw was a tunnel stretching out beyond him, long and dark and full of dead comrades. They'd died face up, the gas seeping in through the ventilation system while they ate. Dutchan and the rest of his cohort had come back after a skirmish and found them sitting against the catacomb walls, some midbite, the gas dissipated . . . But he couldn't be there. It was ages past, the meds worked for him, this was a flashback, and stars help him, there was something behind him, something coming up the tunnel, and then his friends started moving again, tiny little twitches, and he couldn't think, so he ran.

West came back to the table too fast, but the Read seemed to have left less residue behind than the others he'd done for this case. When Gavin touched the corner of his mouth with a tissue and it came away red, he jerked, batting at dirty hands, the grime under his fingernails permanent, filled with ghosts—

Gavin caught West's wrist, holding firm as he twitched into his own head again, and the flush of relief, the gratitude that Gavin would always offer him a hand, made him smile. Nika looked shaken, Corwin's arm tight around her shoulders, but her voice was steady.

"I don't know if I got everything out that you were sending me. Everything important, anyway. I think I might have gotten lost in some of the details." Her gray eyes flicked down to her fingers for a second, and he wondered if she felt the same dirt under them, if Corwin's arm felt more like the tight press of a drainage tunnel.

"I'm sorry. I'm so sorry, Nika." He didn't know what else to say, after forcing it on her. She shook her head, her face closing down to a guarded sort of friendliness he supposed he deserved.

"We need to regroup." He hadn't expected Corwin to give them all the easy out, but then again, Corwin probably wanted to get as far away from him as possible. Gavin nodded, a motion West only caught out of the corner of his vision, but he was going to put a great big gold star on his calendar to mark it as the first time Gavin and Corwin had ever agreed on anything but his stupidity. He started to agree, and thought better of it when all he could manage was a soft groan.

"Tongue-tied, Agent Tavera?" Corwin blinked innocently, letting Nika slide past. Gavin snorted, moving away from them to push the body drawer back in.

"You've been saving that since I woke up, haven't you?"

Corwin tidied up the rest of their mess, and tossed their gloves in the trash, but the fractional hitch of his shoulder was enough for West. *"I'll never tell."*

CHAPTER 13

Corwin winced as Nika shifted in her chair, more focused on her notebook than the vid screen when she spoke. "The security footage isn't clear, and it's a few seconds in the stream at most, but I've been able to grab images from three different cameras that clearly show a Human carrying something the approximate size of the body that was dumped. He was good, too." Her tone wasn't admiring at all, just resigned. "His face never shows up, but there are other characteristics we can pull from it, and at least we know we're dealing with a flesh-and-blood killer. I was starting to wonder."

"He? If you haven't confirmed a facial image, how do you know the suspect is male?" Ning rarely sounded sharp, and this was no exception, but Nika still flushed and looked utterly taken aback.

Gavin stepped in for the first time since the conference had begun. "Agent Tavera has indicated through several different Reads that there's good reason to believe the person we're seeking is male, and most likely Human." Corwin had to admire the way Gavin only offered relevant information, without obviously covering for Nika's unholy case of nerves around her superiors. "As it falls under the suspect profile, rather than case evidence, we've all adapted our investigations to fall in line with his findings."

Ning nodded. "Of course, that would make sense, and be entirely within the realm of acceptable profiling." It wasn't meant to reassure Nika, because that would have called attention to her, but Corwin appreciated the way Ning always took a second to clarify things in a way that didn't expressly address more awkward underlings.

"The only lead we have at the moment is the locational ties between this wine tour and the crime scenes," Corwin said. "We need to be able to pull passenger and crew manifests and itinerary information, at the very least."

"I'm aware of that, Inspector Menivie. And you know as well as I do that I could have pushed for access to that information, argued with the extremely diverse array of legal counsel representing both the cruise line and the various private parties, and gotten absolutely nowhere with it because I didn't have any physical evidence." Ning's focus shifted toward the back of the room, where West was propped on a passenger bench in the corner, silent and a little dazed from a second dose of painkillers. Corwin's appreciation of West's silence was waning, in odd correlation to their mental contact falling off as well. "Not that your contributions haven't been significant, Agent Tavera."

West waved Ning's words off, the gesture looking as worn out as he did.

"Inspector Santivan, I've put a rush in on that footage. The analysis team should have the results by early morning, your current planetary time zone."

"Is it going to be enough to get us access to the cruise?" Nika asked, looking up just long enough to meet Ning's eyes before her nerves got the better of her. "There's not a face in that footage, Chief. I've been over it myself a dozen times, and even with deeper analysis, I don't think we're going to pull a positive ident from it."

Ning's lips thinned, mouth twisting into a faint smile. "They'll be able to pull motion prints from it, though. There's the clip from after, without the burden of the body, and it should provide a recognizable walk pattern."

Words scrawled across the bottom of the vid screen as West tapped out a quick message on his notebook: *So we're going to make them dance to our tune, now?*

Ning's smile revealed a few sharp teeth before fading back to detached professionalism. "I'll be in contact. Agents, inspectors."

The comm went dark, and Corwin busied himself with setting their system maintenance and checking the projected weather for the following day. Everyone else shuffled out, West the first to head for quarters, though it was barely evening by planetary standards.

Corwin didn't mean to overhear Nika and Gavin, but they weren't making much effort to have their conversation in a private location, and no matter what the IEC thought, ships finished largely in industrial-grade metal echoed.

"Did you want to watch a movie in my quarters?"

Gavin hesitated long enough that Corwin, if he were given to such things, might have imagined him looking shifty and uncomfortable. "West. I mean, West is injured, and I should really be with him tonight. He doesn't do well with painkillers." There was another pause, shorter this time. "I should say, he doesn't do so well with keeping himself shielded when he's had painkillers."

Corwin filed the knowledge away, for what purpose he didn't know. One pleasant evening and a disastrous day after certainly didn't indicate that he'd be in a position to use it for future blackmail.

"Gavin, it's fine. He's your partner, and he was injured. Of course you want to keep an eye on him." Somehow her sincerity and understanding never made her sound like she was trying too hard, which was what happened when he attempted the same thing. Perhaps it had something to do with the fact that she was nice to people on a regular basis, but nobody ever expected it of him.

"Thank you. Maybe tomorrow, if we get the chance?"

"That would be nice." Corwin hummed quietly to cover the sound of rustling cloth, but he didn't manage to block out Gavin's voice. "It's not just because he's injured, and it's not fair to let you think that. I've never been good at balancing things like this, and as much as he hates knowing it, he needs a Ground around sometimes. I'm going to do my best, but I can't pretend he's not going to be a part of this."

If Nika was taken aback, he couldn't tell, not skulking around the corner like he was. Well, *skulking* seemed an overstatement, since he was doing actual work, but still. She answered quickly, faster than he would have if confronted with the idea that his new relationship was an unintentional threesome. "We'll figure it out as we need to. I'm pretty flexible about most things, and I'll tell you if I have a problem."

"Fair enough. So, tomorrow?"

"Sure."

Gavin's footsteps retreated, and Corwin finished up his reports, guilt warring with the knowledge that it was a small ship, and they were all likely to be privy to things they'd rather not share. Deciding on a cup of tea, he headed toward the galley, only to find Nika there, preparing the same.

She smiled at him and held out a mug. "Heading to your quarters?"

Corwin hesitated to reply. He was ahead on his next book deadline, but that could change for a multitude of reasons, and it always served him well to keep a reserve of words against the possibility that he'd be unable to write for a few days. She didn't even look like she was asking with any personal reason behind it, just being nice. Sometimes that was worse.

"I was actually wondering if you'd like to play cards or watch a vid or something. Nothing with blood." He shook a finger at her, and she grinned back.

"I've never drawn blood over a game of hearts, I swear. That would be nice. Why don't you pick a vid from your collection, so I don't accidentally scare you?"

He turned away to fill his mug, spending a little too long sorting through the sudden plethora of tea boxes in the cupboard. "Tease me all you want, but remember that if I lose sleep, I'll be even crankier than usual."

"I don't think trying to pin that on me is very fair."

"The 'verse is an unfair place, Nika."

The painkillers weren't worth the analgesic effect, not with the nightmares they spawned. Vivid, half memory, half fears he didn't want to acknowledge, but either way, the drugs held him under in that twilight state and wouldn't let him escape. West came up flailing from the last one, a scream catching in his throat when the hands from his dream held him down, pushing him under the water again—

"West. West! Stop, it's me."

Gavin's voice finally penetrated the rushing in his ears, and he gasped, now fully awake. The sharp tang in his mouth was more than fear, and he swallowed convulsively, gagging as blood ran down the back of his throat. When he finally opened his eyes, Gavin's face, tight with worry and exhaustion, filled his entire field of vision.

"Are you actually awake?" Gavin yawned, sitting back. "Must've been pretty bad. You've been thrashing around, and I couldn't get you to wake up."

West rolled over, groping at the table next to the bed until he came up with his notebook: *Pretty awful. Think I bit my tongue. Again.*

"Shit. How bad?"

He waffled his hand back and forth, too tired for anything more coherent.

Still fully dressed and cross-legged on the far side of the bed, Gavin started to unbend. "Want me to go get you some ice? And some more pills?"

He quickly shook his head, regretting the movement when it sent his tongue slamming against his teeth like a soccer ball. *Don't want to sleep, monsters will eat my brain. Gonna get up.*

"You need to rest."

More carefully this time, he pushed the covers away and swung his legs off the side of the bed, ignoring the warmth he was leaving behind. When Gavin started to follow him, he scowled and pointed at the bed.

It looked like Gavin was going to argue for a moment, but then he shrugged and flopped down on the pillow. "Yeah, okay. But if you're not back in thirty minutes, I'm going to come looking for you. Nobody wants to trip over your collapsed body on the way to breakfast. It puts a person off their feed."

West shuffled out the door, flapping a dismissive hand over his shoulder. With no destination in mind, he found himself in the lounge, the lights coming up as he crossed in front of the sensor.

There were two mugs on the lounge table. Gav had been with him, so that meant Corwin and Nika had been hanging out together. The twinge of some muddy mixture of regret and resentment was completely unexpected. Not that he begrudged Nika downtime with her partner. Not that he was pissed that it hadn't been him. Not much, anyway.

To distract himself, he pulled up his IEC account through the Nerve, and slumped into the chair, one leg over the arm as he spun slowly in a circle. Ning's message flashed up immediately, marked with a high-priority stamp, and he caught his foot against the desk, stopping midspin, and leaned toward the console.

The video analysis team was able to capture a partial motion print from the surveillance footage. You've been granted access to Artron fleet records pertaining to their current cruise, including passenger manifests and debarkation reports. You'll need to move quickly, before the tour leaves Cainet orbital space. Keep me informed as the investigation continues.

Ning was too savvy to commit it to writing, but West wondered if the need for urgency had more to do with either a corrupt judge, or worse yet, someone at the IEC, finding an excuse to discount the motion print than an irate cruise director. Since the thought of going back to sleep only to get sucked into nightmare land made West cringe, it seemed logical to pull up the passenger and crew lists and get started. At least until he realized there were no less than a thousand happy wine sippers in the database, plus an equal number of crew members and personal staff. He dropped his head in his hands with a wordless groan.

"And here I thought you'd confine your porn watching to your own quarters."

West spun around to find Corwin propped against the doorway, and raised an eyebrow. "*I was going to offer to bring it to your quarters and share . . .*" He smirked, the words slipping out on their own, funny until he thought about the last time he'd been in Corwin's quarters, which hadn't been funny at all. It was nearly impossible to stop any bleed-over when he was on drugs, even without that level of intimacy, and he suspected that Corwin picked up on it based on the inspector's sudden grimace.

"*Because that went so well last time.*"

He debated an answer, coming up with and discarding several smart-ass replies before deciding that commenting on the obvious wouldn't really serve any purpose. To say he didn't feel a little jolt of pride at coming to such a mature decision would've been a lie. "*Ning got the permissions. I was looking at the passenger manifest.*"

"Anything?" Corwin apparently possessed the power of translocation: in the doorway one second, then leaning over him the next to peer at the screen.

The hand resting on his shoulder rather than the back of the chair was undoubtedly an oversight on Corwin's part, brought about by a consuming interest in the case. Except that Corwin's thumb was absently rubbing the tight muscle over his shoulder blade while they stared at the screen.

West hid a secret smile by looking down, knowing his face would be reflected in the Nerve screen. "*A whole lot of anything. Over a thousand passengers with money to burn on expensive wine.*"

"Damn." Corwin straightened up but didn't step away, and a complete lack of impulse control on West's part made him turn his face to press a quick kiss on Corwin's knuckles.

Corwin's eyes were wide as he jerked away. "What was that?" Catching himself, he glanced guiltily over his shoulder and dropped into West's mind. It was hard to tell if he did it out of a desire for further intimacy, or because he was afraid of being overheard, but West suspected fear. "*Why did you do . . . that?*"

There was no hiding his silent laughter. "*Sorry. Didn't know that would be the reaction I'd get.*" He paused for a second, thinking up an answer that wouldn't freak Corwin out further. "*Thank you for the hospital. The ice.*" It was his turn to feel incredibly awkward. "*For being so nice to me.*"

"*You mean I'm not always?*" Everyone had a "feel," and the flash of wry humor had come to embody Corwin, at least in West's mind. Quite a bit different from the image Corwin made sure the rest of the 'verse saw.

"*You don't do so bad for somebody who doesn't like me.*"

Corwin's snort was exceptionally loud. "*I believe what I said was that I don't understand you, but I don't really dislike you.*"

West could ignore that bent version of the truth because the weight of Corwin's remorse was folded into every word. "*I apologize for invading your privacy. And for forcing you to feel the effects of my Talent. That was a terrible thing to do. No matter what argument we were having, that wasn't okay.*"

"We don't come to people new and shiny. Part of . . . Some of what I said had nothing to do with you, and shouldn't have been part of the argument." Corwin's voice was quiet, like the words were a secret. West almost wondered why Corwin had said them aloud, before realizing that mental contact was far more intimate to Corwin than mere words.

West was willing to give him a break. Rather than acknowledge Corwin's peace offering explicitly, he waved a hand at the console. "*I was going to run an IEC scan of the passenger list and see if anyone with priors pops up.*"

Corwin nodded, pulling up an extra chair and folding into it, apparently content to watch while West handled the keyboard. They both leaned forward as the results scrolled through, so intent that Corwin didn't even flinch when their shoulders bumped.

The first report managed to trim the initial list from around two thousand to a mere two hundred thirty-four. Corwin's gusty sigh ruffled West's hair. "Damn. Run it again, and try sorting by type of crime?"

"*Better hope that shows something, or we'll be interviewing for the next five months.*"

"You're only assigned to the *Vigilance* for another four, so we'd better narrow it down. Let's start with violent charges, and go from there."

"*You don't have to waste your night on this, just because I can't sleep.*" He did his best to keep anything from bleeding over into the conversation, thankful that Corwin's affinity was for happier things. Maybe it wouldn't be quite so obvious that he was afraid of what was waiting for him in the dark.

"Work is soothing. I understand work." The pads of his fingers barely touching the console, Corwin stared at the search results with an intensity they probably didn't deserve. "*I wish you felt more like work.*"

West didn't look up, didn't respond, didn't really know how to take it, so instead he let himself get lost in the dirty little secrets of their potential suspects.

"Shalla, over ice. Preferably ice that *hasn't* melted, this time."

Corwin bared his teeth as the heir to a lucrative exotic wood fortune dropped an empty glass on the tray he was holding. He managed to stretch the expression into an obsequious smile and nod while contemplating the pleasure to be derived from arresting the snotty little bastard for possession of illicit substances. "Certainly, *gestur*." The sneer was barely smoothed out by his lowered voice.

He managed to wait until he was around the corner before tugging at the tie that rested too snugly against his throat. The five months between his departure from home and his acceptance to the IEC training academy had proved beyond a shadow of a doubt that he wasn't cut out for a job in food service. He was pleased to see he'd made the right decision.

Nika looked less annoyed, but not by much. After a quick glance up and down the hallway, he dumped the empty glass in a convenient waste bin. "Find anyone?"

She made a face. "They've allowed us to set up an interview room in one of the massage studios, and I've scheduled appointments for the first round of suspects, starting in about an hour. I can't believe Ning agreed to conduct an investigation this way." Her disgust was replaced for a moment by a sly smirk as she shot a quick look at the decidedly nonregulation uniform he was wearing. "And I can't believe how natural you look in a waiter's apron."

He was saved from having to defend Ning's choice—not something he was particularly capable of doing since he didn't agree himself—when West and Gavin rounded the corner, not quite at a run, but fast enough that his eyebrows shot up. "Catch anything on your Reading expedition, agents?"

"Probably some kind of crotch rot." West shuddered, looking more angry than disgusted. The injuries to his tongue were still only half-healed by the regeneration treatment at the hospital, his voice still curdled and thick around the pain. The silence Corwin found so unnerving was gone, but the slurred, hesitant speech wasn't quite right, either. "I swear to the stars, if one more person touches my ass without asking me, I'm going to break cover and then break fingers."

Gavin leaned against the wall behind West, arms crossed and scowling. "I know Artron hires discretionaries, but that doesn't imply automatic consent."

"Discretionaries have the right of refusal." West kept the words quiet enough not to carry down the hall, and reached back to surreptitiously rub the offended area. "After the fact hardly counts, and this tour is full of drunk assholes. I hope someone files a complaint with the Cohort."

Corwin found the idea of someone's hands on him without invitation enough to inspire a shudder. For West, who didn't have even the safety of the mental barriers Corwin lived behind, he imagined the experience went well beyond outrage and firmly into nauseating.

"Anyway, in between being groped and getting asked if Gavin and I work as a team, I managed to do a light Read on every level of the ship, and aside from some really unpleasant things about the kitchen staff, I didn't find anything worth mentioning."

"What did the kitchen staff do?" Nika looked apprehensive, which was a little amusing, given that they weren't staying for dinner.

West stuck his tongue out, then winced. "Just don't eat anything."

Nika seemed a little queasy at the thought, a sentiment he echoed, but didn't say anything else as West continued. "So nothing that left a big impression happened on the cruise ship, and until we've got evidence that links us to a suspect, we can't investigate any of the private crafts on the tour. That makes these interviews our best course of action."

Corwin bristled at the casual dismissal of traditional investigation, biting back his first retort. He *could* learn. "I'm going to resume my physical investigation until the first interview appointment."

"Corwin, West just said—"

"Excuse me, Inspector Santivan. I understand what Agent Tavera just said. Without casting any doubts on his skills, I need to remind you that part of the reason psy teams work paired with inspectors is that we're *both* supposed to investigate. The agents may very well have missed physical evidence that you and I are trained to spot."

"No, you're right. I'll keep looking." She took the correction well enough, though he hated to bring it up in front of anyone else. It was a handicap he'd created for her, a gap in her training that wouldn't have existed if not for his avoidance of psy teams, and despite the fact that he'd apologized, there was no way to fix the error without drawing her attention to it. She couldn't fall back on a psy team as her default investigative technique, assuming that her own contributions weren't just as vital.

West, of all people, took the edge off the situation. "You just don't want to think you had to put that uniform on for no reason. You're not fooling anyone."

Corwin mustered up an overblown display of dignity and a sniff that would have been more pointed if he'd meant it, smoothing a hand down the satin vest he was wearing. "I have no idea what you're talking about. Undercover work is to be expected. I'm not at all annoyed that our superior officer felt it was appropriate for us to bow and scrape to a company that seems to feel the whims of the deplorably rich are more important than the deaths of at least three people. I *relish* the idea that the best way to serve justice is to dress as a member of the serving staff, be treated like so much useful furniture, and slink around a pleasure ship so we don't upset the environment of total indulgence."

Judging from the stares of his three companions, it was possible he'd gone a bit overboard, but at least he was assured they understood. It galled beyond measure that their access to potential suspects hinged on their agreement to blend in with the staff. They were imperial law enforcement, and no one's vacation should outstrip the need for a swift end to their investigation.

"I'll be back in time for our first interview." He turned and stalked off down the hall, away from the heated indoor pool deck, where someone's wish for a drink was going unanswered at this very moment. If he were a different sort of man, he might have felt guilty over the twinge of satisfaction the thought gave him.

"Corwin. Hey." West jogged up beside him, and stopped just short of reaching out. "I don't know what your range is, but you should avoid the game rooms on the third level. Some of them are in use, and they aren't playing cards."

Corwin froze, holding back a hasty rebuke. He couldn't understand how West could throw his ordered, careful life into conflict so easily. He felt at sea, but unlike on the boats of his childhood, he couldn't get his feet under him. Not when there was no rhythm to the changes, not when the tides pushed and pulled from all sides at once. Annoyed that West had so little regard for his privacy that the middle of a public hallway seemed like a good place to bring it up, appreciative of the warning, even warmed by the concern—it was all more than he could reconcile on the fly.

"You shouldn't be wandering around without your Ground."

"You're welcome. You're also a prick." The peculiar quality of West's tone didn't lessen the sting, but he knew he didn't really deserve a softer reply.

"Thank you."

West laughed, hands scrubbing over his face in a gesture Corwin was coming to recognize as a tell that revealed West's fatigue and discomfort without disarming his protective cheer. "Have you noticed that our conversations always seem to happen sideways?"

He gave a little, enough to smile, both surprised and confused by the burst of pleasure he felt, unable to tell if it was West's or his own. "I've noticed." He nodded, forcing himself outside the comfort of professionalism. "Maybe we should try it again from the top, some time. When we're not working, I mean."

The corner of West's mouth lifted, a crooked smile so natural that Corwin could pick out the remains of it even when it faded away. "Once more with feeling, eh? Maybe." He waved a hand down the hallway behind them. "I should go get set up for the interviews. Don't shoot anyone, we'd probably get billed for it."

Corwin huffed a frustrated laugh and turned away. With his thoughts so unbalanced, perhaps he could use the tilted perspective to unearth some revelation he wouldn't have seen otherwise.

CHAPTER 14

The air in the room changed as their third suspect, Anders D'lane, sat down in the plush armchair pulled up to face them. Corwin moved to take point, arms crossed. In the periphery of his vision, he saw West take a step back and run into the table behind them. Gavin reached out to grab West's arm.

It was unfortunate that Gavin couldn't do anything for the pressure in Corwin's head. He'd been fine interviewing the previous two suspects, both of whom wanted only to expound on the flaws and biases of the imperial justice system, but this force seemed to be pushing from the inside out.

D'lane watched them in silence, fingers steepled together over his stomach. Legs crossed, one foot twitched impatiently as he raised his eyebrows at them. "My leisure time is valuable to me. Perhaps we could get to the point, if your man there is done having his little fit?"

Corwin expected West to muster up some quip, but he merely stared at D'lane with narrowed eyes. Nika spoke instead, and whatever her hesitance with their superiors, she had no such trouble with civilians.

"We're investigating a violent crime, and your name came up as a person of interest. Six years ago, you were charged with four counts of assault and abduction. Your leisure time has been taking you a lot of places recently, hasn't it?"

There was very little outward change to D'lane, but the feel of the room shifted like a harshly drawn breath, and he saw West push Gavin's hand away. D'lane smiled at Nika, and Corwin found himself thinking their suspect wasn't unattractive by any stretch of the imagination. His bright-orange eyes marked him a hybrid, obviously Trakoran, but the rest of his appearance was decidedly more Human. The genetic manipulation required to link such dissimilar physiologies was no small miracle, and priced accordingly by the one company that held the imperial patent. D'lane's parents had clearly gotten their money's worth.

"The incidents you're referring to are of no concern to the IEC anymore." As if sensing Corwin's thoughts, D'lane turned toward him. "If you found my name, you know I was not only cleared of all charges, I was also paid a handsome sum not to level suit against Agent Disby and the IEC in Imperial Court."

"We're aware of that, and this isn't about those crimes." Corwin kept his tone flat as he tapped the screen of his notebook. "In the past fifteen days, this tour has been docked in three different spaceports. At each of those ports, a body has been discovered. While your previous charges were cleared, as an imperial citizen, you must feel better knowing that all avenues are being explored when it comes to solving such mysterious coincidences."

D'lane's files existed, and that was enough to bring them up in a search, but unlike the other suspects, D'lane's were sealed, locked to a clearance level well past his own, and he suspected even past Ning's. To avoid troubling his superiors, it was possible that Corwin had neglected to send a suspect list to the central station, so no one would need to object to the interview. It wasn't a requirement per se, but given the restricted access, it might have been prudent. Essentially, he knew they shouldn't be doing this, but that didn't account for all of the unease he felt as he continued the questioning. "Specifically, did you leave the guided tour group at any time during your docked stays on Ethris, Bodum, or Cainet?"

The pressure increased again, enough that the beginnings of a headache stirred behind his eyes. He pushed back, the resistance comfortable and automatic, and glanced at his partners again.

West squinted, and for a second, Corwin considered pulling him into his barriers. This was probably the least of what West dealt with in the field, though, so he dismissed the idea just as quickly. They had jobs to do.

D'lane tapped his fingers together, shaking his head. "I'm sure my personal assistant can tell you. Ave'Esy'Pel keeps a daily diary of my activities, and can vouch for my attendance and whereabouts." He turned toward West, head tilted ever so slightly, his white-blond hair falling to brush his collar. "You're a psy, I suppose?"

Pressure poured into the room like water, and Corwin lifted a finger to his collar, tugging at knit fabric that wasn't tight. West's eyes closed in a slow-motion blink. "I'm a field agent, working under the auspices of the Imperial Psionics Academy."

"I see. And you're here because?"

"The personnel assignments and specific needs of the investigation are a confidential matter." Nika's crisp words cut through the room, a distraction from the squeeze. "And we've already spoken to Ave'Esy'Pel, who says that you were late returning to your personal yacht several times on the days you were docked in those ports."

"Yes, yes, and I can account for my whereabouts, I'm sure. If you've nothing else—"

"Why do you care if I'm a psy?" West leaned forward, cutting D'lane off without hesitation. His torso curved away from the table while his fingers locked under the edge, bracing him as he fixed D'lane in his sights.

"I don't care that you, personally, are a psy. I'm more concerned that one has been set loose on me again. I know what you're all like when you think you've found something. You dream up an answer to a problem you can't solve, then cast about for coincidence to make it true. Your fellow, Disby, created an unwinnable game for himself last time, and I haven't got the time to play in your little fantasy world again."

Corwin couldn't tell if D'lane was a trained psy, or just possessed the natural Trakoran tendency to project well, but the tension felt like it was crushing the air from the room. He winced at the bright spikes of D'lane's intrusive joy as they slipped behind his walls.

"Did you enjoy it? Destroying them?"

The momentary crack in Anders D'lane's composure might have been accidental, but it looked like bragging, like the careless honesty of someone sure it wouldn't matter. "You know the answer to that, don't you?"

The table rattled back and forth, and Corwin wasn't aware at first that he was the one shaking it. The pleasure was overwhelming, lust so thick it felt like he was the focus of it, or the source. West's voice overlaid it, tight with fury.

"I know. I know how you keep it close, like it's your favorite sweater. You slip into it, and it's like the pain welcomes you home.

You remember it when you're alone, and you get off on telling people what you'll do to them, don't you? You like the chase— No. You like the hunt. The kill. The way it feels to tear someone apart." The slurred words made West sound drunk, and vaguely, Corwin remembered that psys weren't supposed to go too far under, Read too far below the surface of a suspect's thoughts without charges being filed.

But he found it hard to care about procedure, or anything else really, when his walls were crumbling against the filthy, entrancing happiness. D'lane scrabbled at his barriers, pollution clinging to his flesh, his mind, and he couldn't fight it, not against a Trakoran's Pushing.

"I like getting under people's skin." D'lane uncrossed his legs, planting both feet on the ground as he leaned forward, eager curiosity apparent for a second as his voice dipped low, the whisper of seduction. "Do you know what that's like?"

"You liked that best, didn't you? Peeling them back while they screamed. Every one a new surprise, but none of them just like you, and that was always so disappointing. So you kept trying, kept slipping inside their bodies before you sent them tumbling out into the black."

Corwin had almost managed to compose himself when it hit again, and there was no way to push against a thrill so pervasive it felt like his own. He let go of the table without meaning to, wrapping his arms around his stomach as he fought nausea, and tried to hide his body's reaction to D'lane's memories, sex buried so deep under death and pain that there was no separating them.

D'lane's eyes widened, tongue darting out over a plump lower lip that had to have come from his Human genes. "If I were to indulge? Yes. Oh yes."

"Corwin?" Nika's whisper echoed in his ears, and he managed to shake his head. She wouldn't undermine him during an interview, but he was doing a decent job of it himself. Gavin hadn't stepped in, and that was the most disturbing part of it all. West was still with them, enough that a Ground didn't need to intervene to keep the Read within legal limits. This swill was all right under the surface, barely below D'lane's smile.

"It's not worth it if you can't tell someone, is it, Anders?"

D'lane licked his lips again, his breathing twisted into a quiet moan as he closed his eyes.

Corwin couldn't fight it back. A lifetime of keeping everything safely at bay, but this was a shuddering crush of passion. Ignoring Nika, he sank to a crouch in front of the table, legs splayed as he ducked his head to hide the flush on his cheeks. Out of the corner of his eyes, he saw West move, and managed to track on that, grasping for anything that would keep him out of the whirlpool of desecration.

D'lane sprawled back in the chair, knees spread wide and hands resting on the fine fabric of his trousers, rubbing slowly back and forth as his throat worked. West stepped in close, right between his legs, and looked down at him. D'lane's face tilted up, the blissed-out smile seemingly for West. "Want to know a secret?"

Corwin wanted anything else, actually, but West nodded, and when D'lane raised an eyebrow, West leaned over, planting both hands on the arms of the chair and caging D'lane in. "I want to know all your secrets."

"The IEC can't touch me. You tried, and you failed, and now it's all locked down for good because one of you tried to frame me. Even the presents I gave Disby." The final syllable of the unfamiliar name rose in pitch, and D'lane's body went taut for the second Corwin could stand to watch. He choked back his breakfast, turning away and trying to escape, knowing there was no way out. Twisting away from Nika's hand, her concerned voice, he curled around the shame as something disturbingly like an orgasm rolled through him. It left him on his hands and knees, out of sight so at least the rest of them couldn't watch him rattle apart in repulsive increments.

West was speaking again, something Corwin almost missed as he debated clawing his way out through the floor. "I know another secret, Anders. You'll never find her, because there's nothing in the 'verse as unnatural as you." D'lane's chair scraped across the floor, and Corwin jerked his head up in time to see West push far beyond the boundaries of personal space, face centimeters from D'lane's. "You'll always be alone in your skin."

D'lane exploded out of the chair, and West was flat on his back before any of them could react. Certainly not West, who barely got an arm up in time to deflect the hands heading for his throat, and wound up with a fist in the eye for his trouble. Gavin slid in between them, pulling D'lane off with no care for anything but defusing the fight. Nika had her sidearm out, and Corwin distantly connected her mouth moving with the orders for D'lane to hit the floor and stay there.

He could feel it all, defenseless, but with the lust gone, he could push back against the fury, hard and fast enough that his vision grayed out at the edges. He tried to get back to his feet, and everything spun around him until he slid back to the floor.

Nika had D'lane's wrists pulled up and back, and Gavin had an arm around West, who was arguing, the mulish look so familiar that Corwin could've smiled.

West shoved away from Gavin and came toward Corwin. He couldn't figure out how West was walking at all, the way the ship was rocking back and forth. The lag between motions and words was noticeable, and it took him too long to answer West's worried demands after his health. "Fine. I'm fine." It was what he meant to say, but the careworn whimper that escaped him instead couldn't possibly be mistaken for words.

"Gav—" Partners. They were partners; it was easy to see in the way West didn't even need to find words before Gavin had it figured out, kneeling next to both of them and resting a hand on West's shoulder.

He was going to be mortified by this later. He'd never conducted a more unprofessional interrogation, and he was going to lay the blame for that squarely on the unsettling influence of Agent Westley Tavera.

West, who was talking, trying to bring Corwin's focus back, *warning* him, as though anything West could possibly do would be worse than the feel of D'lane's twisted bragging lingering in the back of his head.

"Corwin, I'm going to touch you."

He didn't even know if he managed to nod, because when West's hand closed on his arm, all he could feel was instant, blank relief, the kind usually afforded by the defenses of his own mind, but endless. There was no resistance here, no boundary, just infinite white space, and it seemed like the best idea he'd ever had to succumb to its welcoming safety.

He woke to dimmed lights and the comfort of his own bed, shield firmly reinforced against the outside world. One of the benefits of temple training was the ability to use sleep to repair himself, but now it just felt isolating. Corwin rolled to the edge of the bed and found a pair of slippers waiting for him, next to his uniform boots. Sliding his icy feet into them felt like progress enough, and he drifted for the next few minutes, elbows on his knees, face cradled in his hands.

His Talent was normal on Kaleia, his home world. Easily ninety-five percent of the population had a psychic ability, a gift of their shared genetic history with the largely vanished Akeloans. There must have been other people who could feel someone else's pleasure like a drug, he was sure, though the strict privacy of Kaleian society forbade him from ever asking. The same structure meant it never would have been a problem, if only he'd been content with a life where he never touched the stars. Or anyone else, for that matter.

The chill he felt was shock, and the brooding was . . . He didn't know, really, but he suspected something like the daze West existed in after a Read: his brain knitting connections between what he knew and what he'd felt, trying to excise the leavings of a mind no longer connected to his.

"Tea." He used the word as a prod to get to his feet, pushing up off the bed and heading for his door. He didn't expect to find Nika sitting on the floor outside it, but her smile when she saw him was bright and gratifying.

"Hey, you're up. How are you?"

"In need of tea. Want some?"

She stood, and they walked the short distance to the galley in silence. When he reached for a mug and almost dropped it, she plucked it from his hand and pointed toward the table. "Sit. I know you've reached new culinary horizons, but I think tea is beyond you right now."

He couldn't argue with her. When she handed him the mug a few minutes later, it startled him enough that he jumped. "Thanks. I'm fine, really. Just not awake yet, I suppose."

"Corwin, you've had the same trauma training I have. More of it. You're in shock. You don't have anything to apologize for." Her mug steamed between her fingers, and she dipped her tea bag a few times, her silence thoughtful. "I was worried about you. Sorry I staked out your door, but I know you don't like anyone else in your quarters."

"No need to worry. Tell me about D'lane. He's being held?"

She cupped a hand over the top of the mug, and when she took it away, her fingers were wet with condensation. "Not for long, I'm sure. His counselor will probably waltz in and get him remanded to custody on his home world, but since he's already asked for representation, we can't question him again until counsel is present." Her scowl was incongruous with the natural curve of her mouth and the fine lines crinkled at the corners of her eyes. "So, you remember how I told you, immediately, that sometimes my blood sugar drops, because it could be important in the field?"

Corwin groaned, pinching the bridge of his nose. "Nika . . . I . . ."

"West explained it. That because D'lane is part Trakoran, he must have their natural ability to Push. That you must be sensitive enough that you picked up on his projections, and because you're not used to it, it made you ill." Her damp index finger circled the rim of her mug, and she watched it, rather than forcing eye contact with him. "So if that's it, then I'm sorry you were hit with that. But if it's not— If it's something that could mean your life one day—" She looked up, obviously caught between anger and concern, and somehow able to balance them both. "I've always respected your right to privacy. Sometimes well past the point where anyone else would throw their hands in the air and walk away."

He could blame West's influence again for the way his mouth limped into a smile, and for his answer to her. "I've often admired your remarkable tolerance for me."

"You're my *partner*. Also, I'm reasonably fond of you." She returned his smile before taking a sip of her largely untouched tea, but refused to let him distract her. "I'm not asking you to lay bare your every thought, but I'm telling you right now, if you've got a . . . a medical issue, then I need to be aware of it, so we can compensate for it."

A medical issue. It sounded so simple, put that way, and it nearly was. He could take the out she was offering him, and it wouldn't be any more deception than he'd already engaged in. His brain was tapped in places most people's weren't. Sometimes that caused involuntary reactions on his part. There was no shame in it, nothing worth hiding. Nothing worth lying to a friend about.

"I have a very low-level psy ability, completely controlled. Today wasn't— I've never— It won't happen again." His tea tasted strange, but maybe that was just the hasty mouthful, sucked in and scalding his tongue. Maybe it was the unhappy look he was getting from Nika, and the way it settled, her unexpected disapproval far more bitter than the leaves.

"You don't know that for sure. You don't know that you'll never find yourself in the same room with someone who can hurt you like that again."

She wasn't rejecting him out of hand. He knew that. She was rejecting him with reason, and that was worse. In the end, hers would be the report that Ning would have to believe, and he'd lose his entire world again, robbed by a fault in his genetics. He felt entitled to the frustrated anger in his answer. "So I should just pack it in to a desk job, on the off chance that we'll ever run into another projector who happens to hit my very limited trigger points?"

Nika glared him down over the rim of her mug. "Don't be stupid. I'm saying you should have had a backup plan in place on the off chance it ever happened at all."

"I don't think PsyAc is going to assign me a Ground on those terms." The steam rose from his mug and hit his face, damp warmth clinging across his upper lip and the bridge of his nose. Her utter dismissal of his fears was more comforting than discussing them would have been, though it left him floundering to offer an explanation. "My Talent leans toward a very small area of emotion, and it's never been a problem before. I don't anticipate that it ever will be again. You don't have to worry about me compromising another interview."

Normally, she didn't touch him unless he initiated the contact, usually via some awkward hug at the beginning or end of a fiver. Needless to say, he wasn't expecting her to reach across the table and smack him upside the head, and he gaped at her, unable to come up with a rebuke.

"You're a fucking idiot, Corwin. By not telling me, you took away my ability to protect my partner. You didn't even give me the option. Do you know how I would have felt, if he'd come at you instead of

West? Could you have kept him away from your gun? I'm a damn good officer, and I thought— I thought our partnership meant you trusted me with your life. I certainly trust you with mine. Privacy is fine, but you don't have the right to cripple me when it comes to covering you in the field." She banged her mug down on the table and stood abruptly, the chair toppling over behind her. For a brief, confusing moment, he nearly flinched away from her anger.

"I was scared for you, when I could have helped. I was scared for you, when I could have assessed the situation and removed you from it. I was scared for you, because you didn't tell me something that I *never* would have used against you, in any way."

"You don't have to worry about me."

"You don't get to make that decision for me, you complete asshole! Telling me I don't have to worry about you is about as useful as telling me it doesn't matter if you get shot. It's a stupid thing to say, and you're not a stupid man. I'm your partner. I have earned the right to care about you. And more than that, I've *proven* that I'm capable, and willing to protect you. Either you respect that bond between us and start telling me the things I need to know to keep you alive out there, or you find someone willing to live at arm's length."

If he'd been in her shoes, he wasn't sure he would have stopped there. The worst part was, he *did* trust her in every possible way. He'd never doubted her abilities, her skill, her dedication and courage. So that left him, again, with another fire to put out, another relic of the way he'd been raised unearthed. "I don't—*didn't*—think that once you knew, you'd still feel safe around me. It doesn't have anything to do with my trust in you." His gaze had drifted down into his cup, but he looked up to finish his apology. "I keep running into walls I didn't know I'd built. I'm sorry."

She held his gaze a moment longer, challenging. "Will it happen again? Is there another D'lane out there waiting for you? And do you have any other secrets that will prevent me from doing my job?"

"Not that I'm aware of, but we can always revisit the topic."

She didn't smile at his weak attempt at a joke, but she picked up her mug without throwing it at him, and he'd take that instead. "Were you injured? Is that even what I should call it? Do you need to talk to someone about what happened? Me, or an IEC headcase?"

"Nika, I would rather yank out my own fingernails with my teeth. I'm honestly fine. I'm not Tavera. I mean, I don't see specifics. It was just a fluke, not something that's going to haunt my dreams for years. But if I did need to talk to someone, I'd talk to you. I swear."

She raised her eyebrows at him. "Don't make me have this conversation with you again. Are we clear?"

"Like glass." The table wasn't that wide, and he leaned across it, grabbing her arm and squeezing it before letting go. "Thank you for putting up with my shit."

Finally her smile returned, dim but familiar. "You can buy my coffee next time. We'll call it even. I'm going to leave before I hit you again. Go back to bed."

She went, and he didn't smart off to her. Getting up seemed like a lot of effort, and he still had tea left. It wasn't the ideal drink for drowning his sorrows, but he could make do.

"Inspector Menivie. Fancy meeting you here." West strolled into the kitchen while Corwin was still nursing his tea, and he didn't bother trying to contain his sigh. He was too tired to spar, too unraveled to try to figure out what West wanted from him.

"So, Anders D'lane is a sick fuck. But I think you know that. I *know* you know that. In the spirit of team morale, I'm here to offer you a conciliatory blowjob. Except my mouth still hurts, so you'll have to cash in those points some other way." West's patter was so fast it verged on manic, as though an interruption was imminent and getting it all cut at once would make the idea more palatable.

Corwin choked on his tea, glaring at West before he grabbed a napkin to wipe it up. "Blowjobs for the soul?"

"Whatever works for you."

"Thanks, but I'll pass. I think we agreed it didn't go well last time, and I'd rather take a nap than a pity fuck."

West grinned at him over one shoulder, bending over to right the chair Nika had toppled, and putting a little wiggle in his hips. "I'm good with naps, too."

Corwin stood and headed toward the sink, empty mug in hand, and West ghosted up beside him, completely ignoring everything they'd just discussed. Corwin shuddered as warm breath curled over his neck, pliant lips hitting the spot between his hair and the collar of his shirt. His mug shattered when it hit the sink, shards rattling, and West grabbed his hands to stop him before he could pick them up.

West's smiles haunted his face, even when they couldn't be found, and Corwin could see their remains even now. West's eyes were wide, his voice quiet and firm. "I think you need to come with me for a few minutes. I'll clean that up for you later."

His own room seemed like a good idea, even with West tagging along, intruding, and he nodded, glancing at their joined hands. West let go, even moving out of his personal space, and Corwin tried to draw a breath as he started down the hall. When his door slid shut, he found himself braced for prying, but West let the silence linger for long enough that he finally broke it himself. "I'm fine."

"You'd know better than me, I guess. I actually just wanted to take advantage of the typical urge for life-affirming sex. It's even better than angry sex. And trust me, people have a lot of angry sex with me." Without being invited to, West dropped into Corwin's desk chair, arms hanging over the sides like limp rags. Corwin sat uneasily on the edge of his bed, and decided it was high time to buy a second chair for the room.

"So if we've established that I'm fine, and I'm not planning to have *any* kind of sex with you, why are you still here?"

Loose and relaxed in his stolen chair, West shrugged. After a second, he brought his arms up and laid them across his stomach, plucking at the elbows of his shirt. "Really, I think it's a good excuse to talk about myself. I know it's hard to believe, with me being so fantastically well-adjusted and all, but there used to be a time when the stuff I saw really messed me up." He forestalled Corwin's interruption by holding up a hand. "When I was twelve, one of the instructors at the academy was pulled in on a really weird missing child case. The abductor left a piece of evidence two weeks after she'd been taken, a stuffed animal he'd stolen from her room the same night he'd kidnapped her. So they brought it to PsyAc in a null case to keep it away from the students. My teacher had it locked in his office, two rooms away from us, but I Read it anyway. She'd been holding it when he . . . Well. You can guess, I'm sure."

Corwin's chest felt tight with an anxiety he refused to acknowledge, and it translated into an impatient sigh. "I'm not a child. I'm aware that bad people do bad things."

West blew out a breath, visibly frustrated, which was actually something to behold, but somehow he managed to still sound patient and level. "You know the boundaries of your own mind like nobody else. Maybe it's easy for you to know the difference between what you feel, and what they felt. I certainly hope so."

Corwin shifted, the edge of the mattress digging into the backs of his thighs, his gaze and words directed at his hands. "I don't know what you're talking around."

Silence reigned for so long that he wondered if West had gone to sleep, and made the mistake of looking up to find out. West was staring right at him, eyes painted nearly gold by the reflection of the room's low lights. "I'm talking about wanting, and not being sure if *you* want, or if you're caught up in what *they* wanted. D'lane feels isolated. Cut off from the rest of the 'verse because of his hybrid physiology, and sure that he can't be happy until he finds someone who understands that."

Anger stirred within him, and he found himself clenching one hand into a fist, rubbing the other over the knobs of his knuckles. If West wanted to be an outlet for it, what was wrong with that? "And you presume that inside, I'm the same as him? That I wouldn't be able to tell the difference between right and wrong?"

"I think you're alone. I think you feel removed from those around you, though it may be by choice. I think back there, in the kitchen, you looked scared."

West's easy posture never changed. Open. Vulnerable, if Corwin wanted to lash out. Infuriating, because it looked like West didn't even have the courtesy to sit up straight while ticking off all the ways in which he'd been found deficient.

"I think I've been in plenty of situations, plenty of beds, because I was desperate to make sure *I* still understood normal, after getting bowled over by something that was anything but."

Here West's honesty ran aground, a confession broken open and stranded, because Corwin wanted no part in empathizing with it. He forced himself to stretch his fingers, extending them one by one. He didn't want to hurt people, and what West was offering—a proving ground of sorts, a chance to see deeper into his own mind than he could take himself—wasn't safe for either of them with the way he felt. Of course, the point being that he didn't really know *how* he felt, or if it was D'lane in his head. "I appreciate what you think you're doing, but I'm not you." His hands still looked the same, thank the stars, rubbed smooth from the familiar grip of his gun. He pushed at the palm of his left hand with the thumb of his right, worrying along the deep crease, and had a split-second image of a throat opening under his touch. "And I don't want to find out if I'm him."

"You're not." It was instant, West's denial an unfaltering absolute.

Corwin propped his elbows on his thighs and buried his face in his hands, knitting his fingers through the hair at his temples. "What do you want from me, West? I'm too tired for this."

"I want to make sure that you never wonder if you're a second away from crossing the line into someone else's sickness. I want you to know that it wasn't you. It'll never be you."

The chair creaked when West stood, shuffling the short distance between them before Corwin could find the will to look up. West's hand hovered over his head for a moment, the static tingle creating an imagined prickle on his scalp. Fingers carded through his hair, and he made himself sit still, breathing deeply enough that he felt a little dizzy. "You can't possibly know, if I'm not even sure."

West snorted, a sound he was growing distressingly used to. "Don't be stupid, Inspector. I know everything. Just ask me."

He couldn't even laugh. "I've been investigating killers for over a decade. He wasn't the worst, and he won't be the last to get off on it. It's the first time I've felt anything like that, and I have to consider the possibility that I might be tricking myself. Sure, maybe I picked up on some of his projections, but what if I just filled in the blanks? I could feel their deaths in my hands, and it felt like sex."

"Because you were Reading *him*." West's fingers, in his hair, tangled with his own and squeezed hard. "I swear to the sky, I'm not trying to get back into your bed, but I'm here if you need help drawing those lines."

Corwin's brief smile surprised him, if only because it felt real instead of forced. "So you're therapy now too? Or are you a giant psychic eraser?"

"Well, I wouldn't say *giant*, but I've never had any complaints." West took a step back, hands shoved into his pockets. "I'm not saying my cock has magical healing powers. It's just that the boring part of make-up sex is the making up. And you shouldn't be alone, because I don't think you *will* be, at least not in your head."

"And if I really don't want to sleep with you?"

West shrugged, dead serious in a way that startled him more than the rest of their conversation. "Then don't. Spend the night building a wall between us, as long as you put D'lane on my side of it. And do yourself the favor of being with someone who gives a shit about you the next time you *do* want to sleep with someone. Personal experience indicates that casual partners don't appreciate it when you have a panic attack instead of an orgasm."

If he had any claim to better judgment, he'd clearly forfeited it when it came to West. He was good alone, self-contained and content, for the most part. If he'd *felt* alone now, if he'd only been keeping his own head together, he might have managed that better judgment.

Instead, he reached out and grabbed West's wrist, pushing the sleeve of the uniform shirt up with his thumb and brushing the skin on the inside of West's wrist. "So what if I lose it?"

West didn't ask him what he meant, and he was almost glad. He wasn't sure he knew.

"Then I think we can figure the rest out."

Corwin tugged him closer, and West did one better, leaning over and kissing him at an angle that should have been awkward. He opened his mouth, tongue darting across West's lips, and for a crazy second, he thought the world had tilted in reaction to the kiss.

Instead, he found himself flat on his back, peering up at West, who stood by the edge of the bed wearing a low-key version of that familiar manic grin. "Figured the rest out yet, Tavera?"

"Working on it. Pants first. Pants are a barrier to true understanding."

"I don't want you to understand me, I just want you to fuck me." Lifting his hips, he shoved his pants and underwear down. Saying it like that was worth it for the way West's reaction rolled over him. A tiny, startled laugh, and a near-instant flush to his golden skin, his eyelids dipping closed for a second.

"You're taking all the mystery out of it, Corwin. To be clear: I'm okay with that."

He didn't waste any time in stripping. Corwin followed suit, tugging his shirt over his head and tossing it toward the end of the bed. He settled back on his elbows, staring at West. "If something happens—"

West smacked his leg, sharp enough to sting. "If you want to stop, we'll stop. If I want to stop, we'll stop. If you defy all expectation and actually turn out to be a violent psychosexual killer, well, I'm a trained law enforcement professional—stop laughing—and I will have access to your vulnerable, squishy bits. Now shut up and point me toward the lube."

Corwin closed his eyes and fell back on the bed, smirking even though he couldn't see West's reaction. "I object to your choice of descriptors, and there's something in the storage compartment in the headboard. Your psychic prowess has really failed you."

He felt the first touch of West's mind as a tentative question. It took everything he had to respond. *"Don't go looking. This is harder."*

Corwin could feel the affront, and then all he could feel was West's shockingly cold hand, cupping him. "I can fix that."

"Which?"

"Nothing to fix in here, just things to get rid of."

It disturbed him that he was hard already, that he didn't know if it was West's hand, or West's mind, or the chaotic unrest of D'lane's crimes and the pleasure he'd taken in them. West kissed him again, trailing down the tense column of his neck, biting his shoulder just enough to sting. Corwin's short nails left faint pink lines behind as he scratched over West's bare arms, down along the sharp ridge of collarbone. He rolled West to the side, but the second his perspective changed, he got lost in the feel of control, and he froze.

"Trust me. Just trust me, and I'll see you through." West urged him back without pushing, soft touches against his skin, pressing him

down into the mattress and keeping him there with a single finger in the dip between his pectorals. *"Show me what you want, right now, and we'll figure out how to get you what you need."*

"I don't need to be catered to." Snappish words that couldn't have been further from the truth, but West only shrugged at him.

"I want to make you happy. It'll make me happy. I'm really thinking of my own needs, I swear. I plan to be very selfish."

Corwin couldn't hide the way his arousal burned fresh when West settled over him again, warm and heavy. Stretched out against him and rocking, just serving to remind him of how their skin felt together. His arms seemed leaden when he reached up this time, only to have his hands caught and pushed away.

"Will you trust me?"

Clever West, to ask with his mind behind it, shades of meaning and explanation that nobody's voice could ever convey.

"I'll try." It was the easy way out, answering aloud, less a lie and more a cheat, which he knew was just the socially acceptable form of falsehood. Trying meant he didn't have to accomplish it.

"Then no touching. And no talking out loud."

"Just lie back and think of the Empire?"

"Think of anything that works for you, but remember, no touching, and no talking." West's eyebrows waggled, and again there were layers of meaning to the shared thoughts. Hands moving smoothly over his chest, warm golden-brown skin leaving trails of sensation behind; West's mind was like spice, unexpectedly spilling heat across his landscape.

His nipples peaked under West's thumbs, rough calluses adding a muted rasp, and he held himself back just in time, transferring the boldness he'd intended to share with touch into a slightly more tentative distraction: He sent an image that had crept through his dozing mind on a regular basis. Nothing explicit, just the skin at the sweet spot behind West's jaw, prickled with stubble. In his memory, his thought, there was a dawn glow to everything—West's early morning beard, and his own hand as he stroked the relaxed line of West's shoulder and neck. It made him wonder if he should change his light programming to reflect a sunrise.

"You were doing so well, until you started thinking about the environmental controls." West leaned down, capturing his mouth in another kiss, and he forgot about everything but the lights behind his eyes for a few minutes. With starbursts in his head, and tangled like this, he couldn't tell if it was the friction of West's cock against his that made him groan and push up to meet it, or the echo of the sound, the feeling, the pleasure of making someone else feel good.

West pulled back again, changing position enough to allow his hand to slip under Corwin's ass, and the first finger sliding inside was so deliberate, so focused, that Corwin had to take a deep breath and ride out the unexpected single-mindedness of it.

He didn't care who West had been with before, and he certainly had prior experience of his own, but just for a moment, he was sentimental enough to want something of West that nobody else had. Something that made them a match. It was a dangerous path to take, West's skin changing in his mind's eye, smoother, opening under his knife—

"No. That's not you. This is you."

Corwin had never been fed a memory of himself, but he took it like medicine now. His hands seen through West's eyes were strong and welcomed, wanted. Afraid to touch, because breaking the rules led to places he couldn't safely travel, he crafted a caress in his mind instead, the whisper of warm breath across freckles on West's shoulders, counted down each knob of West's spine.

As West pushed another finger inside him, Corwin took years of deliberate, precise observation and translated it to the filthiest thoughts he'd ever shared.

"Can you— Are you— Now?"

The incoherence of West's thoughts shattered his focus, and left him staring at the ceiling of his room. Lost in the drowsy world between their minds and their bodies, he closed his eyes again, needing to be fully present somewhere.

"Yeah. Keep me here." He barely knew what he meant, but apparently West did, as he settled between Corwin's legs. The next press into his body was blunt, wider, skin against skin as he lost the thread of what he wanted West to feel, and barely managed to hold on to what they both actually did.

The goal almost never changed, the mechanics only rarely, but it was new enough between them that there were still surprises to be found in the trappings. West's forceful thrusts drove him down into the mattress as a litany of unvarnished thoughts filled his head.

"You really are a tight-ass. Just bend your leg, put it over my shoulder, fuck. Love the way you look when you're out of it."

Hearing himself described, and the flash of seeing himself through West's eyes, should've been embarrassing, would have been if he wasn't too awash in sensation to care.

It lasted longer than he would've guessed, maybe because he couldn't gather his thoughts enough to pay West back in kind, or maybe because West had planned it that way all along. The pinpoint clarity of orgasm began in West's mind, shivering along the connection they'd created. He clung to their link as a way to breathe, though every bit of air in his lungs felt electrified, every nerve seeming to spark. He couldn't escape it, couldn't do anything but let it roll through them both—seconds, minutes, ages too long and too much—until it wrested a sound from him that he hadn't known he was capable of making.

This was pleasure, this shared moment of overwhelming sensation. This was what he'd been tuned to, made for, if he wanted to take it that far. What he'd left his own planet to be able to seek. D'lane's pleasure might have been just as real, but he could burn it away with this, and he lost himself to the light they'd made between them.

He only returned to his own head when West came back to bed, and it was the shock of realizing he hadn't noticed the leaving that brought him around. The warm cloth on his skin seemed bent on eroding his desire to stay awake, and after a moment, he found the energy to reach for West's hand and tug him close. "You'll stay?"

"If that's a question, yes. If it's an order, we need to talk about how you can't wear your bossy pants when you're naked."

"It was a question. A request, even." They'd made an utter wreck of his bedding, but there was enough space that it wouldn't matter.

"Well, I suppose." West looked rueful, scratching his unruly hair. "I'm kind of worn out from the past few days, though. I don't know—"

"I'm not asking you to stay for another round, Tavera. Or, not *just* for another round. I can't even promise I'm going to be awake by the time you get into bed again."

West smirked, dropped the cloth on the floor, and flung himself back onto the mattress, hard enough to bounce Corwin a little. "Are you still awake?"

"No." He swatted the lights off, trying for his best grumble, and failing utterly when West planted his head firmly in the middle of his chest and did a remarkable impression of a tentacle creature.

Corwin let several drowsy seconds tick by before he unwound himself enough to bury his fingers in West's hair, earning a muffled sigh of appreciation. He'd never believed in predestination, but he was willing to give some credence to the idea that everyone was sketched out a certain way, smudged by the hands they passed through, shaded by experience. Trust made someone into an artist, gave them permission to redraw, burnish, change the lines and the light. He might've joked that West was an eraser, but in the second before he spoke, he swore he could almost dust the charcoal off his skin.

"Thank you."

"Mmm. Sleep well, Corwin."

CHAPTER 15

Gavin looked around the empty room they were sitting in, then dropped his voice so only West could hear him. "Correct me if I'm wrong, but didn't the message we got from Ning *less than two hours ago* explicitly state that we weren't to have further contact with D'lane? Because I swear I remember reading that his settlement with the IEC after the whole 'planted evidence' thing meant nobody from the coalition was allowed to question him about those crimes, or anything relating to them. Followed by a threat to take the cost of any further legal action out of our salaries."

West stretched his arms out in front of him, cracking his knuckles. "Nope. I think that was the gist of it. You did forget the part where even if we find physical evidence that ties him to any new investigation, we're not allowed to officially charge him until it's been verified by an independent laboratory."

"Right. So explain to me again how this is legal? I'm still not clear on why D'lane's requested counsel, but wants to talk to us without them there. Or at all." Gavin's raised eyebrows only emphasized his skeptical tone.

West shrugged, looking through the glass into the interrogation room. "I haven't got a clue, Gav. Nika and Corwin both said it's technically legal, though anything we hear will probably be inadmissible if it comes to trial. We're not talking to *him*. He's talking to *us*, which I guess is the kind of technicality that keeps the planets in orbit." He scratched the stubble he hadn't had time to shave, scowling even though D'lane couldn't see him through the one-way window.

Gavin nudged his shoulder, peering through the polyglass filmed over with fingerprints and age. "I've still got a bad feeling that Ning is going to have our asses over this when word gets back."

West let his partner ramble. Sometimes Gav needed to work through his nerves verbally. At this point in the game, he didn't give a shit about anything but pinning D'lane, and if that meant pissing off Ning, the fallout would be worth it. "Let's just go talk to him before he changes his mind."

D'lane smiled as the attending planetary officer keyed the interrogation room door open. "Gentlemen, how nice of you to join me. I wasn't sure if you'd be up to it, after our last visit." He made a show of staring beyond West. "But where's your friend, the officer who became so . . . ill?"

D'lane was Pushing outward, shoving at the edges of West's mind, but this time the images weren't of some nameless victim. Since D'lane had never physically touched Corwin, the vision of blood sliding down his hand, dripping from limp fingers, was obviously a projection. Shaking free of it was harder than it should've been.

Some of his tension must have transmitted itself to Gavin, who rested a hand on his shoulder and squeezed. "Agent Tavera and I are much more patient. To a certain point, anyway. Don't waste our time, D'lane. You called us here. What do you want?"

"And here I thought you'd be grateful for another chance to interview me. I'm willing to let you ask anything you want, nothing held back." D'lane's smile slid away. "And since you've prevented me from continuing with my tour, I find I'm bored. I'd hoped you'd be entertainment of some sort."

West snorted. "And you'll just answer anything we ask, no matter how incriminating?" Except that West suspected he would. Confidence oozed off the man like a slug's trail, with not even a hint of fear. Either D'lane knew something they didn't, and all of this was just a game, or he was even more insane than they'd pegged him for. Neither were comfortable options.

"Sarcasm is the cheapest form of humor, Agent." D'lane stretched out, legs casually crossed at the ankle. "I am a very busy man. If you don't want to take advantage of this situation, I have other things I can be doing. My counsel will be here within the hour, and I expect I'll be returning to my cruise then."

"Did you commit these murders?" Gavin asked, voice tight with anger.

"Now that's a wasted question. You know you'll need to be more specific." D'lane shook his head in mock sorrow, and West swallowed, repulsed by the extended fiction of Corwin that D'lane was still Pushing. "And really, I'm disappointed. I was expecting something a bit more original." Despite the attack on an IEC official, D'lane's political power had bought him a restraint-free detention. D'lane seemed to be showing that off with a careful examination of the fingernails West was seeing just as clearly in his mind. In his head, they were covered in blood, drawing pictures over Corwin's skin. It wasn't D'lane's blood. The taste of D'lane's game lingered in his throat, and he was startled when D'lane sighed. "I'm bored now."

Prison disposables were notoriously ill fitting, even for someone with enough money to buy the manufacturing company several times over. D'lane's were no exception, the neckline of the shirt draping loosely as he shifted in his chair. When he tugged the material impatiently back in place, West felt his mouth go dry.

"What the *fuck*?" West stepped forward in horrified fascination, stopped only when Gavin yanked him back.

A tattoo covered the top of D'lane's shoulder and continued down his arm until it disappeared into the shirt. Black feathers tipped in white and blood red, an impression of a beak and claws in the stylized swirls. It wasn't a bird so much as it was the *idea* of one: a raptor every bit as dark and violent as D'lane himself, and it didn't take much in the way of ability to Read his pride in the reaction it caused.

West forced himself to disengage, falling back mentally and physically. "Nice art."

D'lane smirked. "Impressive, isn't it? I designed it myself." He pulled the arm of his shirt lower and turned in the seat. "I rather think it resembles me. Powerful. Untouchable."

"Don't kid yourself." Gavin thrummed with barely withheld fury. "People like you always end up getting too cocky and fucking up. You won't be any different."

"But that's where you're wrong. I don't fuck up. And there's a distinct difference between cocky and self-assured. You and I both know that you can't touch me. Not you, not your psychic freak here, not your overly susceptible colleague." The slow smile spreading across D'lane's face was filthy and wrong. "Not the pretty little inspector."

Gavin lunged, almost pulling them both over as West tried to yank him back. As it was, they were entirely too close to D'lane, given the lack of restraints and the obvious dismissal of any repercussions. He gave Gavin a brief shake, earning a narrow-eyed glare in return. Once he was sure of Gavin's attention, he let go, pulling Gav's presence around him like a security blanket as he reached *out* . . .

The high-pitched shriek sent him stumbling backward, hands over his ears. On and on, the sound clawed at his brain until it was the only thing left in the 'verse.

"West, come home, *now*." Gavin's voice was a low hiss, but enough to break the aural hold.

He blinked, eyes blurry, as D'lane's face swam into view. The self-satisfied smile made him want to wipe it off with his fists. Or a blast gun.

D'lane laughed. "I'm disappointed. You have a rather inflated notion of yourself, Tavera. I'd hoped for more . . . substance." He waved a hand dismissively. "But you're no better than Disby, and not nearly as interesting. I'm done with this interview."

"But I'm not." West found the edge of D'lane's filth and pushed back, hard. He kept up his offense as D'lane's smile thinned, doing his best to echo Corwin's lesson. "When was the last time you killed someone?"

D'lane's brittle smile shattered into something unrecognizable. "When was the last time *you* killed someone?"

West had plenty of experience with Pushers, but never one who'd worked so hard to find a crack in his defenses. D'lane was a crush of deep water, and the pressure gave West the perfect resistance to build his bubble. D'lane's face began to twitch as West raised his eyebrow. "I'm stronger than you, and I can do this all day. Now answer my question—when was the last time you killed someone?"

"You say 'last' with such finality. I'm afraid I can't answer such an ambiguous question."

Gavin grabbed West's shoulder when he took a step forward. "Let it go. He's just getting off on bragging."

West wasn't stupid enough to think that antagonizing D'lane any further would gain them anything. He swallowed down his anger. "We certainly appreciate your time. It's been very informative. You might want to make sure your counsel is on a nice fat retainer, because you're going to need it."

D'lane didn't bother with an answer, but West could feel the amused stare follow them out of the interrogation room. He managed to wait until they were out of sight before slumping against the wall.

"You okay?"

He nodded tiredly. "Yeah. No. No, fuck, not at all. How are we going to take him down? He's practically admitted he's still killing, and there's no way we can charge him for it."

"Let's just get back to the ship and fill in Nika and Corwin. If we're lucky, maybe Ning will have something new to go on." Gavin slung an arm around his shoulder, steering him toward the main lobby. "There's too many pieces for the IEC to just brush it off this time."

"You have a lot more faith in our superiors than I do."

Years of experience condensed into a few intimate moments allowed West to see that Corwin's annoyed expression hid worry and a tender heart. Or more likely, just annoyance. West tried and failed to hide a smirk.

The crease between Corwin's eyes deepened. "Ning is waiting for us."

"So maybe this wasn't one of those times where asking for forgiveness is better than asking for permission?" Nobody returned his grin, and he sighed. "Right. Guess we better go face the music."

"At least tell me you got something out of the interview, if we're all going to be demoted to desk jobs somewhere." Nika radiated nervous energy, and he took a step sideways, trying to get out of the immediate broadcast area. Dealing with the return of his own foreboding was bad enough.

"Yeah, we got something. It's D'lane." West spared Corwin a grateful glance as he ghosted up between them in his casually accidental way, cutting down some of Nika's noise.

"How do you know?" Corwin asked in a tone usually reserved for interrogation. West raised an eyebrow, and Corwin sighed with obvious effort. "What happened to make you sure?"

"He has a tattoo. A bird, a hawk or something. Like the birds from my Reads, but not. More like the kind of bird that would chase the ones in my Reads." It sounded so anticlimactic stated like that, and he winced, not sure how to convey the horror he'd felt.

Gavin was nodding. "It's too much of a coincidence to actually *be* a coincidence. I think he's the one."

"Then I suggest we tell Ning immediately." Corwin nodded sharply. "Since all we have is a simple assault charge now, the sooner we get an arrest warrant for murder, the less likely it is his lawyers will have him out the door and back on his cruise."

They gathered around the Nerve, looking more like a group of guilty children than law enforcement professionals, and West tried to stifle a nervous cough as Ning's face appeared.

"Correct me if I'm wrong, but during our last communication, did I not say that you were to have no further contact with Mr. D'lane?"

"Yes, but—"

"I'm still speaking, Agent Tavera. Did you find some degree of ambiguity in the statement 'No further contact under any circumstances'?"

Yes, Ning was their superior officer, and yes, they'd been warned away before D'lane had invited them for a chat. That didn't mean he had to be happy about a dressing-down over it, when someone was trying to block their access to the most viable suspect they had. "No, no ambiguity." He managed to keep the sullen argument out of his voice, and could only hope he wasn't flushing with it.

"Good. Please ensure that there is no official report filed on this indiscretion. Mr. D'lane's counsel has already recorded a harassment grievance, and we don't need to hand them more ammunition for the case. I will attempt damage control from this end, but I'll be honest: I can't guarantee that you won't be pulled off of this case and reassigned. I'll be in touch after—"

"Wait." Annoyance flitted across Ning's face at Corwin's interruption, but he pushed on. "Agent Tavera has additional information to report concerning D'lane."

Caught completely off guard, West drew a deep breath, mustering his thoughts. "During each of the Reads, the one consistent impression has been of birds. D'lane has a tattoo that matches the images I've seen."

His confidence shriveled under Ning's impassive gaze, and suddenly the damn tattoo seemed like a weak connection at best.

"And you believe this is sufficient evidence to charge Mr. D'lane with murder?"

Corwin nodded. "We believe it's enough to warrant our continuing to investigate him as a suspect."

"And I believe that every one of you is aware of IEC policy concerning psy evidence and the fact that it must be backed up with physical evidence. Am I correct?" Ning waited for Corwin to nod, the movement jerky. "Then I will reiterate what I said before. No official report is to be filed. I will be in touch after I speak with my superiors."

The screen went blank. Several seconds of awkward silence followed before West sighed gustily. "Well. That was pleasant. I'd be worried about how much trouble we're in, except that I'm more worried about D'lane walking away free."

Nika looked to have been taking lessons from Corwin, her fierce scowl a close tie to his. "How can it not be enough?"

"Maybe IEC only sees him as being guilty of bad body art choices," West said, trying for a joke, lame as it was.

"So we have to take a different tack, one that doesn't involve D'lane directly." Corwin sat down in one of the chairs in front of the Nerve. "Work the less obvious angles."

Corwin as the shining little beacon of hope was seriously messing with West's outlook on life. "What less obvious angles would those be?"

"Don't sulk, Tavera, it's not attractive."

Just to be contrary, he let his expression slip from self-pitying outrage to petulance, and directed it toward Corwin.

Nika tried to hide a grin with her hand, while Gavin made no such attempt at subtlety. "But he does it so well. Don't make him give up his gifts."

"Perhaps we could get back to the matter at hand." Corwin went on without any sign that he was in on the joke, pulling up the keyboard. "D'lane gave us a name—the agent who handled the initial case. I'm thinking it might be worth tracking him down and seeing what he has to say."

"Do you think we can find anything if he's left the IEC?" Nika leaned over Corwin's shoulder to look at the screen, and Corwin didn't move away. Privilege of partnership, West could only suppose.

The more time he spent with Nika, the less she intruded, like he was building up a callus over her thoughts. When he brushed against her side as they all leaned over the Nerve terminal, rather than calling up Disby's file on the display like sensible people, he barely shivered. The focus they were all sharing at the moment probably helped.

"He pharmed out."

Gavin's voice was flat, and that was worse than anything Nika could throw at him, if only because Gav knew about West's little foray into the world of pharmaceuticals. They'd spoken about it once. There'd been alcohol of some kind involved in the conversation, and then a vague mention of an entire year lost to drugs and silence. Gavin didn't judge him for his youthful indiscretions, but West almost wished he would, just so he could explain that he'd been lonely, confused, and utterly terrified of his own power. Instead, Gavin's monotone made the topic remote yet again, and they'd pretend, as always, that it was just something other psys did. The ones who couldn't hack it.

"He pharmed out right after the D'lane investigation, and the files on his discharge are locked." Corwin was drawn down tight too, a fortress against him, and he wondered how much of his anxiety was bleeding out. He made a conscious effort to tamp down on it, and reached over to put a hand on Gavin's arm for a second, letting it drop when he was clear again.

Gavin frowned, probably at the information they didn't have access to. "What about his Ground? Are they still working in the field?"

"His Ground, Anajin Tsan, was killed about a month before Disby pharmed out. It coincides with the dates of the D'lane investigation, but she's not listed as killed in action." Corwin scrubbed at his face. "And that file is, of course, locked."

"So Disby's Ground was killed, D'lane got away with a string of murders, and somehow nobody's allowed to touch him anymore. Sounds like maybe Agent Disby could have some unfinished business with D'lane. Maybe the kind that makes him sympathetic enough to talk to us, once we mention we're in the same boat."

They all leaned back as one, and West hid a smile. Nothing like getting in trouble to pull a team together, apparently. There was no need to ruin the moment by pointing out that Nika and Corwin weren't really *in* any trouble, at least not yet. Corwin's fingers tapped the keys absently, drumming on the console. West was a little surprised when the tapping seemed to echo in his head, followed by Corwin's voice.

"*You are very bad for my career.*" A search spilled across the screen: pinpoint traces of Disby's life and times.

Rather than reply, he flicked the back of Corwin's head, gentle enough not to sting, relishing the moment when he realized he was going to get away with it. They all stared at the scrolling text, following Christeven Disby down the trail left behind after the IEC cut loose one of their strongest field agents.

CHAPTER 16

Corwin sat back, rubbing his tired eyes. "Nothing after Accelinna. That's three imperial months of a cold trail."

According to all current records, Disby was leading a quiet life below the IEC radar, and while that wasn't unusual for an agent who'd pharmed out, it could mean a lot of things: suicide, a disappearance into the virtually untraceable underbelly of the Empire, or treatment in a facility where medical records were locked. All of which would involve a much deeper level of investigation.

"We've got the in-depth searches set up to run on their own. I say we take a break." Nika yawned and stretched. "Maybe get something to eat before we get cranky."

"I resemble that remark, Inspector Santivan."

For all that West's usual manic grin was firmly in place, Corwin had an annoying little tickle playing at the edge of his awareness that said something was off. More off than usual, anyway. "Tavera and I can handle putting a meal together. You and Gavin keep resetting the search parameters. We'll get a hit sooner or later."

Nika raised a skeptical eyebrow, but nodded. "Just don't poison us, okay?"

"Never fear, Inspector, I used to work in a restaurant with a very low incidence of customer hospitalizations. I'll make sure the meal is not only free of harmful bacteria, but nutritionally balanced." West didn't sound any different, either, but that didn't mean much, given his propensity for acting.

Gavin was still bent over Nika's shoulder at the Nerve, but Corwin saw the way his shoulders bunched for a second at West's words. Interesting.

He followed West into the kitchen, standing out of the way while West opened cabinets and began pulling things off the shelves. Spices and standard-issue pantry staples were soon joined by fresh vegetables and two knives. After giving him an assessing look, West handed over a knife, cutting sheet, and two dark purple-green lumps he assumed were peppers. "Try to keep the chunks uniform and the seeds to a minimum, okay?"

Out of his element and determined not to look it, he gripped the knife and went to work, letting West's tuneless humming wash over him as he tried his best to figure out how he was supposed to keep the seeds out of the tiny pile of cut vegetables when the inside seemed to be largely composed of them.

After a minute or so, West looked over and snickered. "Cooking really isn't your thing, is it? Haven't you ever chopped up a pepper before?"

"It's fine. This one's just extra seedy, I think." Corwin gripped the knife defensively when West covered his hand, their fingers linked around it before he finally admitted defeat. West took the remaining pepper and sliced it in half, pulling out the seeded core with the tip of the knife and tossing it in the trash.

"When did you have time to become a chef?"

He wasn't expecting the pressure from West to ratchet up, nor to feel it as anything other than an intrusion on his shields. That he could Read West's distress was a baffling breach in the defense system he'd thought he'd perfected.

"I quit school for a while. Moved to Brecken, on Holman, and got a job as a dishwasher, then a prep cook in this shitty little diner. It was kind of fun, while it lasted." West stepped away, leaving him the knife and cutting sheet and going back to work over the pot on the cooktop.

He'd never wanted to learn to cook, preferring takeout and ready-meals when he was younger, and rarely having the chance for anything else now. But in the spirit of making a meal together, he offered a tentative overture. "I came almost straight from my family kitchen to the IEC, so I never had much need to cook. I worked as a waiter for a few weeks, but that was a disaster I'll never repeat."

"Look at us. Sharing. It's almost like we're friends." West meant to tease, but the wary way he hedged the words in his mind didn't lend much humor to the situation. Of course, if Corwin hadn't been spying, that extra layer would have remained below the surface.

It took him a second to pull back from his desire to snap. West wasn't trying to mock him for sharing personal details, and however unethical it was, he could tell that West's cheerful persona was only to save face. A smile no matter the cost. "Almost. Is this okay?" He nodded toward his pitifully small pile of vegetables.

West glanced at the peppers and smiled. "Very precise, Inspector. Toss them in the bowl there. What do you feel your chances are against some eggplant?"

"I've completed several advanced hand-to-hand combat certifications. Do your worst." It was possible that he overplayed the determined grip on his knife, but it got a laugh.

Whatever West had in the pot, it smelled exotic and warm. He scattered in dried spices seemingly on a whim, and kept stirring until the whole kitchen was perfumed. When Corwin was done chopping the long, thin eggplants into rounds, West swept them away and into the pot to join the rest of the vegetables swimming in the orange sauce.

"I pharmed out right before I graduated from field training. I got up one morning and thought, 'This is what I'm going to feel for the rest of my life,' and I completely freaked out. I'm surprised I remembered to book a shuttle before I hit atmo." West stared into the pot, spoon making slow circles. "I registered for my psy-suppressants on Holman, and spent a year trying to do absolutely anything but be myself."

Corwin did the obvious thing, and dropped the dirty knives and cutting mat in the scrubber. Agents took time away from the field, but few of them touched the psy-suppressant pharmaceuticals until they were so burned out they were teetering on the brink of collapse, or ready to retire. More often than not, the two coincided. For some, there was no reason to deaden their abilities when they weren't being exposed to crime scenes on a daily basis. With his shields, he'd never need the drugs, but some agents, after using their Talents for years, couldn't shut down enough to live a normal life.

"You think it'll give you an in with Disby, if he doesn't want to talk to us?"

West glanced up from the pot, sideways, and grinned at him. "You're my favorite, Corwin. I don't know if it'll give us anything. I'm more worried that they'll have hit him like they did me, and he'll be a zombie with no short-term memory."

"So they didn't work for you? Supposedly the new cocktails are easier to adjust to."

"Not planning on trying it again, but I'll take your word for it. This needs salt." West stepped around him, all heat and emotion and inconsistency. Before he could think better of it, Corwin caught his shoulder and gave it an awkward squeeze. It earned him a smile he couldn't read as West reached behind him for the salt and turned back to the cooktop. "They didn't work well for me. It was back before they pulled Pezazuria from the cocktail, so even though my Talent was working in overdrive, I just didn't give a shit. About anything, actually. I got really depressed, felt like I was reacting to everything half a second too late, and the whole time I was still living in everyone else's head. I was just too out of it to care." He dipped a spare spoon into the pot, and licked it clean with a contemplative expression. "I did have a lot of really ill-advised sex with strangers, so it wasn't a total wash."

"Oh, well, as long as you got something out of it." The corner of his mouth twitched, a facial tic he was going to have to see someone about if it kept up.

Their dinner began to bubble, and West turned down the heat before pointing to the second pot on the counter, and the bag of rice next to it. "First knuckle rice, second knuckle water, if you please."

"I'm not putting my fingers in our food. That's disgusting."

West sighed. "Just wash them first. You have bigger hands than me, and I never make enough."

"This is an extremely suspect way to measure rations, Tavera. I don't approve." Nevertheless, he did as he was told, setting the pot on the stove and giving it a wary look.

"*Anyway*, my point with the confessional here was that we shouldn't pin our hopes on Disby. Even if we can find him, even if he's willing to talk to us, there's no guarantee he's going to be able to. If he was messed up when he left PsyAc, he's probably not any better on the suppressants."

Not exactly what Corwin wanted to hear, but then again, there was no way of knowing for sure until they found Disby. "Something obviously happened between him and his partner and D'lane. If we can just get another piece of evidence on D'lane, something that can't be covered up . . ."

"That's a big if." West reached around him to turn down the heat under the rice. "Be damn nice to have that proof for Ning, though."

Corwin didn't bother to hide his smirk. "You're not fooling anyone. You're just still stinging from that setdown."

"Well, yeah." The raised eyebrow was in contrast to West's mild tone. "Neither of us likes losing our spot as Ning's golden boy. I was counting on you to make me look good in comparison."

The shared smile was as warm as the heat coming off the cooktop. "Looks like we both had the same plan."

Familiarity only led to even more uncomfortable sharing, so he really shouldn't have been surprised when West showed up at his quarters as he was undressing for the evening. If nothing else, the man had uncanny timing. He sighed, forgoing a shirt in the hopes of sending West away before Gavin or Nika noticed him loitering in the hallway. His schedule had been thrown off for a couple of nights, what with having to bare his soul and all, and it had him on edge. Westley Tavera had him wishing he knew where the edge was anymore so he could avoid it.

"What?" he snapped.

West's deliberate up and down look was followed by a slow smirk. "Well good evening, Inspector." West effectively derailed his scathing reply by pushing past him into the room, stepping toward his desk. Corwin sprang into motion, slamming the power off on his notebook.

"There's really no shame in looking at porn in your off-duty hours. And I promise not to tell anyone."

"I wasn't—" With an exasperated groan, he folded his arms like it would stifle the urge to touch West. "What do you want, Tavera?" He didn't know when the tight formality of last names had started to feel strange in his mouth.

"Well, now I really want to see what you're hiding on your notebook." Hands behind his back, West shook his head. "I mean, seriously. You know me well enough now to realize that I can't let things like that go." Corwin silently raised an eyebrow, and West sighed. "Okay, okay, so maybe I was hoping for a shag."

Having been privy to West's bouts of lust, he felt fairly comfortable concluding that wasn't the case now. "Try again."

"You're a hard man, Inspector Menivie, just not in the way I was hoping tonight. However, I'm not above bribery." He held out a plate with the air of someone offering up a selection from the empress's treasury. "Cookies. Straight to you from the oven, no stops in between, no sharing with anyone else."

Corwin wavered, torn between accepting the cookies and knowing that if he did, West would have achieved yet another small victory in the battle to erode what was left of his common sense. Sensing weakness, West moved in for the kill, grabbing a cookie and waving it under his nose. Cookies weren't going to help him make his deadline, though, and they were a poor substitute for boundaries.

"It's chocolate," West said, breaking off a piece. "Your favorite."

It was an elaborate game of some sort—everything with West was—and he hated that level of ambiguity. West's emotions pushed at his shields, but he was damned if he was going to let them down enough to pick out just what those emotions were.

"I'll ask you again, what do you want?"

West took a deep breath, staring down at the cookies, his expression unreadable. "Gav is with Nika. They're getting nowhere on the searches, so there's no point in me skipping a sleep cycle to help. I'm just . . ." The small smile seemed more grimace. "I'm due for some nightmares. I guess I really didn't want to be alone." He shrugged, setting the small plate on the desk. "So there you have it, the soft underbelly of the famous and indestructible Westley Tavera, exposed. Feel free to start ripping."

"Hardly indestructible. I think we've firmly established that we both have our unfortunate weaknesses." Apparently West was one of his, the stars help him for the grief that was bound to bring raining down. Sighing, he reached for a cookie. "I'm writing a book."

West's smile actually reached his eyes this time. "Thank you."

"And before you ask, no, you can't read it. Only my editor gets that privilege. You can wait until publication, just like everyone else."

"Are you famous?" The question seemed honest enough, that insatiable curiosity back on West's face.

He rolled his eyes. "Oh, definitely. I only work here to kill time between releases. It keeps me from getting bored."

"I don't think I believe you."

"Don't make me regret telling you, Tavera. No, correction. Don't make me regret it more than I already do. Sit down and shut up." When West dropped down on the bed in an untidy sprawl, Corwin groaned. Obviously he needed to think through his orders before he gave them, because West looked completely at home. At home in the only place Corwin thought of as his, like the space had bent just for West, conforming to wishes he'd long since stopped making.

The silence stretched on for several seconds while he stared at the floor and tried to feel out the lies he was willing to tell himself. Finally looking up, he caught West drooping. It shouldn't have made a difference, seeing someone else unguarded, but it stilled something in him. West wanted to trust him, and Corwin wanted to trust himself enough to appreciate that. "So do you want to watch a vid or something?"

West's eyes popped open, and he half sat up with a startled grunt. "Huh, what?" He scrubbed at his face, yawning. "Sorry. I guess I dozed off."

"I said, 'Do you want to watch a vid?' In the lounge."

"Not really." West smiled sleepily. "Kind of comfortable here." He grabbed one of Corwin's pillows, tucking it under his head. "Don't let me interrupt your work, though. I promise I'll be quiet."

There was no way he would be able to write with West in the room. It seemed equally unlikely that West would be able to keep silent for longer than three seconds. He yanked his desk chair out, feeling cornered and annoyed. At least the annoyance was familiar. The sensation of somehow being manipulated by emotions he didn't want to feel? That was completely foreign.

A soft snore interrupted his thoughts, and he glanced toward the bed. *His* bed. West's face was buried in a pillow, nothing visible but tufts of hair in their usual gravity-defying disarray. He shook his head and sighed, powering on his notebook.

Two chapters and several hours later, Corwin stretched, wincing as his back cracked. Obviously West wasn't the distraction he'd feared; he hadn't been this productive in ages, and while he was cold and stiff and would be exhausted come morning, the sense of a job well done was undeniable.

He saved his work before he set the notebook to charge, stretched again, and glanced back toward the bed. West hadn't moved. Corwin opened his mouth, scowled, and closed it. He could wake up his unwelcome bedmate and doubtless get stuck in some long, rambling conversation that would only exasperate him, or he could take the coward's way out and go sleep in the lounge.

"Come t'bed. No expectations."

He jumped, looking up in time to catch West's drowsy grin. "It *is* my bed."

"Yeah." West rolled toward the edge, patting the spot he'd vacated. "'S good that there's room for two people."

Perching awkwardly on the edge of the mattress, Corwin dropped his head into his hands. Nobody had warmed up his side of the bed for him since Natane, and for a second, he gritted his teeth against everything that came with those stray thoughts. The loneliness, the failure, the litany of mistakes he couldn't correct. He hesitated at the edge of West's personal space, reaching out with his hand first, and West burrowed closer to him.

"Who's Natane?" His voice blurred with sleep; there was a pause, and West went still against him. "'M sorry, I wander when I'm tired."

West shouldn't have gotten anything, whether trying to or not, and he pushed back without thinking. Luckily, West didn't seem to mind, sighing softly and curling closer. "'S nice. You're nice."

"I'm no such thing." And then, because West hadn't taken, only asked, because maybe it meant he'd changed a little, could offer something of himself without someone prying it out of him with a crowbar, Corwin dropped his mouth to West's hair and murmured an answer. "She was my lover. Betrothed. It didn't work out."

West huffed quietly, possibly a laugh. "Because it turns out you like cock?"

Corwin rolled his eyes, even though West wasn't looking. "No, because I'm a 'recalcitrant asshole' who lacks a concept of basic emotion."

West, to his credit, didn't try to soothe away the hurt that wasn't, anymore. They were just words now, even mostly true ones. "That's impressive. I think I could actually hear the quotation marks."

It was his turn to snort a laugh. "She had an amazing vocabulary. Met her at a writers' workshop."

"Women. Never my area."

"And what a shame, when they all must find you so appealing what with that irresistible air of befuddlement and those big, soulful eyes." He wanted to call the words back before he'd even finished saying them, but had to settle for collapsing back on the second pillow, eyes screwed shut.

"Really?" He felt the bed tip, could feel West staring down at him. "You think I'm irresistible?"

"I didn't say that."

"Not in so many words."

West's soft rumble of laughter rolled over him, and he gave up, opening his eyes. "I think I like you better when you're asleep." The warm hand cupping his face was completely unexpected, and if he hadn't already been flat on his back, he might've jerked away.

West smiled, fingers leaving a trail of heat before he rolled over, face tucked between Corwin's shoulder and the pillow. "For what it's worth, the feeling's mutual," he muttered, breath tickling the hair at the base of Corwin's neck. "Except that I like you better awake."

"Corwin?"

He jerked awake, eliciting a protesting grunt from West, who rolled over and curled deeper into the blankets.

"Corwin, it's Nika. Sorry to disturb you, but I need you to see something."

He slapped at the comm privacy lock on the table next to the bed. "Is everything okay?" She didn't sound worried, but she also wasn't in the habit of disturbing him in his quarters. He scrubbed at his face, trying to fully wake up.

"There's a message from Agent Disby. It just came over the secure channel."

West, suddenly wide-eyed and alert, scrambled upright. "What did he say?"

If Nika was surprised at hearing West's voice in his room, she hid it remarkably well. "Actually, the message is addressed to you."

"Shit. We'll be right there."

West had shown up fully dressed and stayed that way; he didn't wait for Corwin to find a shirt, and was halfway out the door before Corwin could get the damn thing over his head. Forgoing socks in the name of speed, he was only two steps behind when West jogged into the lounge.

Nika and Gavin looked up from the Nerve as West shoved his way between them and into a chair. "It pinged about twenty minutes ago," Nika said. "I didn't think you'd want to wait until morning to see it."

West nodded distractedly, already typing in some elaborate password string. "No, it's okay, you weren't interrupting anything. I was already asleep."

Corwin was fairly certain his expression was as pained as Gavin's, the difference being that a flush showed up better on his face. Nika chortled, glancing over at him and then doing a double take, grin widening. When he scowled in response, she flicked a finger toward her own shirt and then gave his a deliberate stare. It was, of course, on inside out.

Oblivious to the silent conversation, West finally sat back, muttering to himself. "It's the secured account the IEC assigned me. Wasn't sure it was even still active. I never need anything that encrypted, so I just have it set to send a notification to my PsyAc account." His voice was as tense as the line of his shoulders. "I'll put it up on the display."

Disby had used some sort of a stylus, the message appearing in handwritten script rather than typed. The letters were cramped.

I have information about our common interest. Corve, 70 hours, sector 4-3 Krio.

"How does he know? None of the feelers came back." Nika shook her head. "And even if they had, nothing would show except that we were looking for him. I had it coded so it didn't link to the case."

West spun the chair back and forth, thumping Gavin's knee several times before Corwin reached out and grabbed his shoulder, getting a startled look in return. "Right. Well, somewhere there was an IEC link, if only because he was able to access this account." West stared at the screen for several more seconds. "My guess would be he still has contacts."

The fact that he'd reached the same conclusion didn't make Corwin any more comfortable with it. "Which shouldn't be happening with an ex-agent who pharmed out. It's a substantial security breach."

"Maybe he pulled himself back together?" Gavin sounded doubtful.

West shrugged. "Maybe he has friends who still trust him."

Corwin winced, then realized he was the only one who could feel the faint bitterness rolling off of West. "We can hypothesize for the next seventy hours, but I think maybe a better use of our time would be deciding if we're going to meet him."

"Of course we are." West spun the chair again, coming to rest facing him. "Why wouldn't we?"

Nika jumped in first. "We're kind of unwelcome on Corve, in case you've forgotten your imperial history. This could be some sort of a trap, and if it is, we probably won't walk away."

"Why would he bother contacting us unless he wanted our help? Or to offer us his help with D'lane?" West looked honestly puzzled.

"Who knows?" Nika shrugged, eyebrows drawing down. "It's a little too coincidental for comfort."

They'd all been taught to be suspicious of coincidences, with the unofficial IEC policy being that there was no such thing. On the other hand, there wasn't a better place to disappear if Disby had run afoul of both imperial law enforcement and a member of the powerful and moneyed ranks. Neither would be likely to go searching for someone on Corve. Corwin opened his mouth to voice these thoughts, but Gavin beat him to it.

"If he pissed off D'lane as much as I suspect he did, money and influence aren't likely to get to Disby there. Nobody knows anybody on Corve, and anybody stupid enough to test the theory loses their money or their life."

The chair jumped under his hand, a prime example of the frenetic twitches West seemed to develop during idle moments.

Corwin nodded. "It's out of IEC reach as well." He paused, weighing his next words. "We need to meet him. And we knew we weren't going to be able to do it in an official capacity. For all that Corve isn't high on my list of planets to visit, this could work to our advantage."

"Bonus: we won't have to dress up as waiters," West chimed in, prodding the navigation system to life. "And we'll get to stay armed." Nika looked far from convinced, and West reached over to pat her arm. "Just think, if anyone grabs your ass, you can shoot him this time."

"I do love unnecessary displays of firepower. Get out of my chair. You're screwing up my nav system." She shooed West away from the console and slid into the seat, fingers poised over the keyboard.

Corwin shared a grim smile with her. They both knew that with Corve being off-limits to IEC officials, they were crossing a line they shouldn't even have been close to.

CHAPTER 17

Docking on Corve in a ship lacking any official registration appeared to be the norm. West didn't realize he'd been holding his breath until Nika landed the rented shuttle with a gentle bump, and he exhaled loudly.

She gave him an exaggeratedly offended huff. "So little faith in my piloting."

"Not at all. More worried about the place you were piloting us *to*. But here we are, and right on schedule." He made a face. "As long as we don't get lost finding the address. The city looks like a damned rat's nest."

"We're taking a flyer. I don't want to be out on the street any more than I have to." She stood up and stretched, her fingertips brushing the low ceiling. "Less chance of getting shot in the back."

He hadn't thought about it that way, and Nika didn't seem the type to be unnecessarily paranoid. "You think that's an issue?"

For all her pragmatic cheer, sometimes it was easy to see how Nika's grandfather had influenced her view of the job. She didn't exactly sneer, but he could pick up the scorn in her voice without needing to Read her. "Yeah. People talk about Corve being some sort of haven for felonious chivalry, but it's a single city riding a cursed planet like a tick. The people on Corve aren't here because they value some kind of precolonization independence. They're here because it's a place to hide, and if we get made as imp law enforcement, they aren't going to wait for us to turn around before they shoot."

He trailed after her as she left the tiny bridge, moving a little slower in the heavier gravity of Corve, though at least it gave him time to adjust to Nika's vaguely menacing appearance. While the IEC uniform was black and drably professional, Nika in black civvies looked intimidating. Dangerous. And obviously well armed. There was nothing subtle about the unfamiliar blast gun at her hip, and probably nothing legal either. The shuttle had come fully equipped.

Corwin's appearance was equally as startling, and West found himself staring openly, probably openmouthed as well. Corwin's grim expression was nothing new, but the tightly fitted pants clung to the curve of his ass in an extremely distracting way, not helped at all by the equally snug short-sleeved shirt. He'd seen Corwin without any shirt at all, and it had nothing on this.

When Corwin glanced up, West smiled. Brushing a hand against Corwin's bare arm, he sent an entirely inappropriate thought, smile widening as faint color spread across Corwin's face. He focused on the flash of heated interest from Corwin, using it to block out Nika's musings on the possible effects of heavy grav on her various sexual gymnastics with Gavin. At least Gav only projected his normal fluffy blankness, but then again, there was no mistaking the covert glances directed at Nika.

Corwin coughed loudly, interrupting the palpable sexual tension in the hall. "Okay, so the plan is we take a flyer to the address. West and I go in, and Nika, you and Gavin cover us from the outside. Everyone clear?"

"Yeah, about that," Gavin said. "I've thought it over, and no, I'm not clear, or happy, or willing to back down on this. I'm West's Ground, we're trained to work as a team, and I'm not going to stand around outside when he's heading into a potentially hostile situation involving a known psy." Gavin didn't look stubborn or angry, but West could hear the death knell of Corwin's plans right there.

"I'm not doing a Read—"

"You're never *not* doing a Read," Gavin snapped in a tone far too even not to be forced, bringing it down to the two of them even though there were four team members to consider. "I know what you're doing, cutting me out like this, and it's stupid. We'll talk about it later, but right now, you need to accept that I'm coming in with you."

"I can handle it." Corwin's response was a little too heated, and West watched him swallow and take a mental step back. "If we spook Disby by showing up as an assault force, I'm going to remember this conversation. We need information on D'lane, and Disby's our best option."

"We're all professionals, we've got each other's backs, blah, blah, blah. Can we get going before we miss the appointment window and he refuses to answer the door out of spite?" West didn't wait for an answer, feeling rather than seeing the other three fall in behind him.

It was a tight squeeze in the flyer, and he found himself squashed next to the door, bare arm jammed against Corwin's shoulder. While there was physical contact, Corwin was locked down tight, shields firmly in place. Nika was likewise all business now, focus turned inward.

Sector 4 was a commercial district in the heart of the city, Krio a narrow little street of what looked to be shops, most of their windows carefully blacked out. Pedestrian traffic spilled off the sidewalks and into the street, forcing the flyer to a walking pace. The driver cursed loudly and constantly in a language West didn't recognize.

Their designated address looked no different from any other on the block, and Gavin paid the driver as the rest of them climbed out. The crowd broke and flowed around them like a stream around a rock, and he found himself forced closer to Corwin. The tension radiating off of the inspector seemed more than could be accounted for by the job, and he made a mental note to ask Corwin how he felt about claustrophobia at some point.

Corwin was already raising a hand to rap on the door, and West moved forward to get a better look. First impressions were everything, and Disby had called for him, after all.

As soon as Corwin made contact with the door, he jumped back with an exclamation, hand cradled against his chest. "What the *hell*?" There was a series of clicks, and then a buzzer sounded far off within the building.

Nika and Gavin held to the rear guard, glancing in their direction but mainly keeping an eye on the street. West pressed forward, trying to get a better look. "What happened?"

Corwin held out his hand. Over the knuckle on his first finger was a neat little circle of raw skin, a few millimeters in diameter, blood sluggishly welling up from the center.

West's stare traveled from Corwin's hand to the door. There was nothing unusual about the surface, at least nothing he could see, but as he leaned closer, a keypad slid open on the wall next to the door.

A message flashed once, then again—*Identity verified*—before the screen went blank, keypad clicking closed again.

"You have no idea how uncomfortable it makes me that someone on Corve now has a sample of my DNA," Corwin muttered, wiping blood off on his pants.

"I think I'm more worried about how he had something to match it against." West had to force himself to not jump backward as a louder series of clicks started up, right on the other side of the door this time. A low, grinding rumble finished off the sequence, and the door slid open.

Corwin's smile was grim. "Looks like you'll be able to ask him yourself."

It helped to know that Nika and Gavin were right behind him, in direct conflict with his own stupid plan to keep Gavin away, but he still couldn't tamp down the prickle of nerves as the three of them stepped inside after Corwin. The door, of course, immediately ground closed, leaving them in darkness.

"I'm pretty sure we saw this vid, Gav. I don't recall it ending well for anyone." The room seemed to swallow up his voice, leaving him with the impression of more space than should be possible, given the parameters of the stores on either side.

No answer from anyone, but there was a sharp *snick*, and then a band of light from the scope on Corwin's blaster illuminated the floor in front of them. For a millisecond, he regretted his own choice of weaponry, before remembering his inherent discomfort with guns that could take down small buildings. Easier to just fall in behind Corwin with careful, shuffling steps. Gavin and Nika closed up behind, loosely fanned out and covering the exit if they needed to make one in a hurry.

When four banks of oversized spotlights flashed on, West was left blinking, half-blinded by the white arcs. He barely managed to keep from running into Corwin, who'd stopped, blaster up and leveled at something or someone. The afterimage was seared into his eyes, and he blinked again, trying to clear it.

"Christeven Disby." It was a statement rather than a question, Corwin's voice emotionless.

"Stop where you are, and give me something to prove you're really Agent Tavera."

Though West was still seeing corkscrew glowworms, he followed the challenging voice past the edge of the light. Apparently Corwin, despite the blast gun trained on their host, wasn't the one Disby was worried about.

"I'm guessing you don't want my IEC credentials," West said with dry amusement. Corwin stepped halfway in front of him, and while the gesture was oddly touching, he found it more than a little annoying. He needed backup, not protection, and Corwin was cutting down his ability to pick up clues from the feel of the room.

"I was thinking something we'd both know was real."

It was pretty common at PsyAc to develop an impression to share with other psys, something that identified a person on the psychic level, like a calling card. West knew it was what Disby wanted, but couldn't figure out how it was going to work if he'd pharmed out. "Kinda paranoid, aren't you?"

Corwin was too professional to snap at him right that second, but the narrowed eyes indicated it was a possibility later. At least until Disby laughed and came forward. Average height, average build, and now that West could see better, sandy-brown hair, cropped short and spiked haphazardly. The glasses were something of a surprise, thin black frames lending Disby's hazel eyes a disarmingly distant look. Most people had their vision corrected medically, rather than bothering with lenses.

"More than a little, but not without reason. And you still haven't shared." Even softened by the glasses, there was no missing Disby's sharp look.

West pushed past Corwin, careful not to block anyone's shot in case Disby wasn't as calm as he looked. He was reckless, not stupid. Even the little touch it took to unfold the impression for Disby left him feeling exposed to the stifled remains of power harnessed by the psy blockers. The memory of being crippled, his strongest sense disconnected by the drugs, was a hard one to shake, overpowering anything he might have picked up from Disby.

"It's not so bad." Disby's voice was a vocalized shrug, disaffected yet somehow heavy with the lie they both knew he was telling. Disby was guessing at his discomfort, but that didn't mean the guess was wrong. "I still have some of it. Enough to keep my head on straight.

Enough to walk through your bright green field and pick a flower or two." When Disby smiled, he looked younger, and West let himself relax a little after hearing the description of his impression.

"So where does that leave us? You know he's Westley Tavera, but for all we know, you're a friend of D'lane's, and this is a setup." Gavin stepped up next to him, careful not to come in direct contact and disrupt the feelers West had out. Disby watched them together for a second before looking away, then back just as quickly.

"Anders D'lane murdered my Ground. Call me his friend again, and have a nice trip back to your shuttle." Disby ignored Gavin's quiet apology and reached for West, without regard for anything resembling personal space. West could count the gold flecks in Disby's eyes, and there was no way anybody would get a blast gun shot off in time to stop anything. He hoped it wasn't an option they'd need.

Disby's power wasn't strong when it came, the indelicate touch of someone who didn't have full control, but West could see Disby in every corner of the impression, a store filled with bright covers and flickering ads for superheroes he'd wanted to be as a kid. The disenchantment of it ached like nothing ever did once you'd stopped believing the first time.

"He's Disby." The confirmation settled all of them; Nika lowered her weapon, and Corwin's movement shadowed hers a second later. Gavin nodded, offering a hand to Disby, who took it without hesitation.

West folded his arms, fingers playing a chord he barely remembered from childhood piano practice on his sleeve. "Why did you contact us? Obviously you've got more than we do on D'lane, but we don't have access to your investigation reports."

Disby unzipped a notebook pocket on a pair of standard-issue IEC uniform pants that had seen a few years of use. "You might not have official access, but I've got everything I ever collected on D'lane right here. Sixteen bodies, before they decided maybe an agent should look into it. Sixteen victims who didn't matter to anyone, and those are just the ones we found when he got bold enough to start leaving their corpses in the gutter like trash. Anaj and I found another seven missing that we could link to cities he'd visited, but he told us he just sent them spinning out into the black."

Spikes and falls were the only stable part of what he could Read off Disby, the rest either lost to the drugs or so heavy it pulled at him more than Corve's grav. Fleeting, cutaway images of corpses he didn't recognize, each one cleaner in their own way than the last, each missing something new, until the pattern began to solidify. At some point, finding out if they were compatible with whatever fantasy D'lane harbored had changed to unmaking them to find out why they weren't.

Gavin's hand brushed his, light enough to disengage him a little without blowing away the Read entirely. "Glad you're not going to do a Read, buddy."

He snorted, focusing on Disby, who was watching them with a look that could easily pass for longing in the right light. Gavin let go, and Nika held out her notepad. "Are you willing to give us copies?"

Disby's shoulders slumped, his gaze drifting away before he nodded at Nika. "It'll be useless to you as far as official investigation evidence, but it's the only way you'll ever see the kind of evil D'lane got away with."

Got away, flew right through the storm and away, and the anger was swift and hard enough that West bit his lip and grabbed for Gavin's hand, just as Corwin caught his elbow on the other side. Disby didn't seem to notice, or didn't care, and West added another mark against the suppressants, because he couldn't imagine doing that to someone accidentally and not even being aware of it. Except he'd forced the full measure of his Talent on Corwin, deliberately, and without the excuse of drugs. It felt like parents arguing after the kids went to bed: voices in another room, raised loud enough to hear for a second as moderation was forgotten in the heat of the moment.

It would never be instinct, but he focused enough to push back, inch by inch, until he met the electrified remains of Disby's Talent. "You said he killed your Ground, but there's no way he would have walked. You don't kill an officer and buy your way out of it, no matter how much money you've got."

The boundaries were more clearly defined when Disby pushed back, fury like a rising tide that swelled clean and endless against the barrier he'd created between them. He wanted to know what Disby had seen, what had sent a powerful, solid agent so far over the edge that cutting out part of his brain was a better option than dealing with it.

Escaping the combined Grounding effects of Corwin and Gavin was easier said than done, but curling along the edge of that wave left him drifting close to a real Read, shields to the contrary. He'd never felt protected from what he saw before, but this was watching it through someone else's eyes instead of feeling the pain as his own. He kind of suspected that wasn't the point of Corwin's technique, but he was on the hunt right now, and it didn't matter. Whatever got the job done.

"We'd already been pulled off the case. We were about to be suspended, and one of our inspector liaisons was in the preliminary stages of a court martial and discharge." Disby's defeat colored the statement.

The distance between them seemed smaller, but he wasn't sure if Disby had been the one to close it. Nika was already scouring the files, her easily Read thoughts built around a history he'd already seen in glassy eyes and cold flesh. The wary trust Gavin and Corwin seemed to have settled on probably had more to do with Disby's status as a former agent, but West couldn't sort out anyone's head well enough to tell anymore. Except for Disby's, and he was tumbling down . . .

Later, when there wasn't quite so much noise in his head, when the air in the alley didn't stick in his throat, full of fetid promise. When the blast gun in his hand wasn't ten shades of illegal, and he wasn't planning to kill their futures and D'lane besides. Later, when the door didn't open under her hands, when he didn't follow her into a room that glittered with the prospect of pain, sharp and shiny as the tray of instruments on the counter . . .

No, he'd built a wall there with Corwin's tricks, and he didn't have to follow them into that room if he could figure out where his pushing met Disby's. West took a hard, fast breath, and managed to pick up on Disby's voice, rather than the bitterly familiar sensation that someone he cared about was going to die over a choice he'd made.

"He was there. He knew we'd come, and there was a girl with him. Anaj waited until she could get between them, and the girl ran. D'lane grabbed Anaj, and I tried to shoot, but I couldn't—"

Couldn't pull the trigger, couldn't hear or see or be sure of not hitting his partner, couldn't get away from the ugly smothering filth of D'lane's pleasure. Couldn't scream as D'lane pinned him against the wall with a thought and silenced his desire to cry for help. He couldn't. He didn't want to. That was the beauty of D'lane's Pushing, from the inside out. He didn't want to fight anymore, he just wanted to listen to D'lane. But he couldn't do that either, because she was—

"She was screaming. Anaj. She didn't react to pain, but he made her scream. She begged him to stop hurting her, but he kept cutting her open, peeling her back, and I couldn't save her."

The wall West had tried to mend was a farce of engineering, nothing but a thin film between the raw emotion Disby was bleeding out over the room, but he clung to it, pushing back to the edge again. Riding that edge, memory flooded West in a slow, queasy roll. When he'd been trapped within his own head, nobody had been able to come for him. He knew what it felt like to have someone turn your own mind against you. He knew how it remade you into something less, and how much easier it was to accept the diminishment than to trust yourself again. Gavin had screamed too—yelled really, roared with pain when the knife tore into flesh.

Tiny parts of her. Her fingertips, her elbows, an ear, and a toe. Her smile, wide, wider than he'd ever seen it, ear to ear, and her ragged voice giving out at last as the old-fashioned scalpel dragged a careful line around her face, light against her scalp, and he knew what D'lane was going to do before his fingers ever sunk into her hair, found the edge of her skin and started to unmask her.

Corwin bumped his elbow, and West only stopped himself from lashing out because it was taking so much effort to breathe. He jerked away from the contact, away from Gavin's measured steps, and fell into Disby's hypnotic recitation again.

"She begged me to kill her. It was the last thing she ever said, and I still hear it every time I close my eyes. He wouldn't let me close my eyes. I just watched all of it."

Like it was someone else, like he hadn't hurt her, failed her, like there wasn't blood on his hands. He just watched as D'lane smiled and walked away, until the compulsion finally faded and he found the will to crawl across the polycrete floor on his hands and knees and gather her up like a broken bird. It was only the two of them when help arrived and found him covered in her life, with nothing to prove D'lane had ever been there at all. He watched as the case was purchased, sealed tight, and locked away, her death nothing more than proof that they'd broken every reg in the 'verse trying to catch D'lane.

Nika, out of all of them, looked to be faring best. Gavin was worried about him, and Corwin was probably pushing as hard as possible to keep Disby out, but Nika had her game face on. The analytical way she processed the violence, breaking it down into puzzle pieces that didn't fit into any profile they'd worked, was a fascinating study in sublimation and logic in the face of discord.

"Those victims are a completely different methodology than our case." Grim and tight around the mouth, Corwin looked up from the notebook Nika was holding, directly at Disby, without a glance spared for West. West was okay with that, unsure about even the possibility of a connection with anyone right now.

"It's him. He's pulling from the same pool of victims because he knows he can get away with it. The ones nobody sees." The desperation in Disby's voice wasn't good—the mark of a man who could tell his options were running out, but was bound and determined to make a point. Nika was closest, and he grabbed her arm. "He bought his way out of it. You can't let him walk away again."

Gavin stepped toward her, and she shot him a warning look before twisting her arm out of Disby's grasp. Her voice was cool when she replied. "If we can make a sound case against him, we will. Inspector Menivie and I have a clear arrest record, and the sense not to create evidence when we can't find it. Even D'lane would have a hard time making a formal murder inquiry disappear a second time."

When the floor tilted, West was able to right himself before anyone else noticed. The fluttering zing along his nerves was probably nothing more than Disby's memory of pain through the lens of his Read, but it wasn't pleasant, and he found himself pulling away, trying to disengage. Disby was everywhere, sticky along his skin and in his head, and it didn't seem so crazy that he could taste blood in the back of his throat. Giving up on subtlety, he made a quiet noise, attracting Gavin's attention. "More help for me, less pissing off your girlfriend, who doesn't need your help."

He was going to regret saying that out loud. He deserved to. Gavin put a hand around his shoulders, fingers cool as they snuck under his hair, and firm when they pressed against the trigger point and sent a shuddering breath rushing from his lungs. The forced relaxation would help later, but the buffer helped now.

He missed part of the conversation while he was twitching between awareness and Read space, but he wasn't so out of it that he couldn't catch up. Corwin and Nika's vehement denial helped the context quite a bit.

"Absolutely not. Your help is appreciated, and we'll certainly keep you apprised of events as much as we're able, but there's no way we can include you in the ongoing investigation." Corwin's head shook, the gray hair sprinkled through the dark catching the spotlights, and West twisted his fingers together, remembering the coarseness of it prickling like pins.

He was still wandering, and Gavin should have been enough to block out anything Disby was broadcasting, so the anger over the injustice of it all must have been his own. He slumped out of Gavin's reach, rolling his shoulders to banish the ghost of an arm slung over him. Whatever ugly things he might be brewing behind his lips stayed there, locked away. Disby didn't seem as concerned.

"He killed my partner. He tortured both of us. He walked away! You don't think I'm owed some fucking closure?" He spit the words at Corwin, who didn't react.

Nika had to be as angry over it as any of them, but she made it sound sensible, controlled. "You're owed the justice of the Ylendrian Empire, but you'll never get it if we don't build an airtight case that D'lane can't escape, no matter how much money and power he has to throw at it. Your direct involvement, even this meeting, if it were discovered, would kill any shot at that."

West didn't expect Disby to back down, but he did, and took his latent psychic tantrum with him, narrowed to a memory instead. *Commanding. She'd been commanding, and fearless until he'd taught her fear. Until D'lane had taught her fear.*

Fear, it turned out, had a taste like damp basements, blood, and the dirt under someone's fingernails when they scrabbled for purchase on the floor as a monster cut them apart like a beast at a slaughterhouse. It echoed through his head more than his throat, but what caught him off guard was the uncertainty. Below the taste and behind the face of a woman he'd never known, the Read left him confused about who was to blame. Then again, he knew guilt like that, and didn't doubt that anyone peeking into his head would see much the same.

"We'll find a way to make this stick. You just have to give us some time." He didn't know why he was making promises about a case, something he never did. Maybe because Disby was right, and he wanted to provide that closure.

Disby laughed, broken and rusty. "Time is pretty much all I've got to give, anymore. I'll wait for you to contact me, but don't expect me to let this go." That he wasn't capable of doing so was patently obvious.

"We'll be in contact." Corwin tapped the corner of the notebook, shutting it off. "We need to get back to the ship. Ning wants us ready for a conference in five hours, and we're supposed to present our full investigation. We're going to need more than some files we're not supposed to have and the word of an ex-agent if we expect to keep this case."

Corwin didn't wait around to see the look on Disby's face, but West saw it, and he couldn't tell if the curl of Disby's lip was for Ning, the IEC in general, or Corwin's particular brand of bedside manner. When the other three headed back toward the door, Disby caught his arm, and he pushed down the shudder that ran through him.

"I know Menivie by reputation. Don't let his prejudice make you doubt your Talent. This case needs a psy who can hold out against D'lane. I don't know if it's the Trakoran genetics, or if D'lane's just a natural Pusher, but he's stronger than anyone believes."

West smirked, everything feeling distant but incredibly loud. "Easier said than done, but I'll do my best. With D'lane, I mean. And Corwin doesn't hate psys." It might have been stretching the truth, but he was at least relatively certain that Corwin didn't hate *him*, so that was a start.

"Don't let D'lane win."

The order waved like a red flag, because justice wasn't about winning. Disby didn't want justice, and West had known that before Nika had ever said anything. Disby wanted revenge, and for the open wound of loss to be cauterized.

He couldn't decide which option was fair, and without that piece of knowledge, he was left swinging between Disby's very real pain and the fact that the IEC wasn't in the business of vengeance.

CHAPTER 18

"I'm ready to be done with Corve," Nika said as she slid the rented blaster off her shoulder, and West couldn't have agreed with her more. "Definitely before Ning's conference. I don't think our comm channel can be traced here, but I'd really rather not take that chance. Best to be on the *Vigilance* before then."

Corwin nodded, stepping around her. "Good point. I'll meet you on the bridge in five; I want to change first. We can go over Disby's files then too."

West debated following Corwin, but the stiff back warned him off. It was probably just as well; he needed to clear the last of Disby's mental residue out of his head, especially since most of it tied in too closely to D'lane for comfort, and he didn't want that bleeding over to Corwin.

As if catching his unease, Corwin paused, turning to him. "We've got his files. What were your impressions from the Read?" His lips curled in a grim smile. "It was clear that he's out for revenge, but was there more than that?"

West was silent for several seconds, weighing his words. Apparently too long, if the three sets of eyes suddenly trained on him were any sign. "I don't know," he finally said. That moment of confusion he'd felt during the Read had been so fleeting, a ghost of an impression, and too tainted by his own guilt to be sure one way or another. "I don't think so."

Nika seemed to accept his words at face value, but Corwin's eyes narrowed. Gavin was likewise silent, but the tension radiating from him was unmistakable.

Corwin finally nodded. "Right. See you on the bridge."

Gavin grabbed West's arm as Corwin disappeared down the corridor. "We need to talk."

Conversations that started that way tended to end badly. "Do I get to know what about before I decide?"

Gavin didn't bother to answer, dragging him along to the tiny common area of their borrowed ship. "What the hell was with that Read? Besides the fact that we agreed you weren't going to do one."

The rush of irritation caught him by surprise, more so when he couldn't sort out how much was left over from Disby and how much he could claim as his own. He forced himself to take a deep breath before he answered. "Plans change. It needed to be done."

"Yeah, right. And if I hadn't been there to pull your ass back, would it have *needed* to be done?" Anger warred with hurt in Gavin's face, and won out. "Because you were pretty intent on keeping me out."

"I wasn't—"

"Shut up." West flinched a little when Gavin snapped. "I'm not done. I don't care what your relationship with Corwin is. Fuck him, fight with him. I. Don't. Care. But I'm your Ground and he's *not*, and that means I'm there when you do a Read."

Stunned into silence, West could only watch as Gavin fought to get himself under control.

"And before you start thinking this is some sort of jealousy issue, it's not."

He nodded, the movement jerky. "I didn't think it was."

"Good." Gavin dropped into a chair, massaging his temples. "Now can we talk about what's really going on? About how Disby and Anaj are not you and I? You need to . . . you need to let the guilt go. You don't have to protect me because you're not going to hurt me."

West's smile felt odd on his lips, twisted and stiff at the same time. "I managed a damn good job of it before."

"And you keep dwelling on that and letting it taint your Reads. Fucking stars, West, you couldn't even distinguish what was real and what wasn't with Disby."

"I never said that."

"'I don't know'? 'I don't think so'?" Gavin repeated mockingly. "Funny, that sounds a little suspect to me."

West took a deliberate step backward, hands clenched at his side. "If you feel like you can't trust my Reads anymore . . ."

"You mean just like you can't trust yourself anymore?"

"And you don't think I've got every reason in the 'verse to feel that way?" Anger bubbled up again in a thick, queasy roll. "I know how Disby feels. We're a lot alike, me and him."

Gavin scowled. "That's bullshit. You're nothing alike."

Making Gavin understand—making anyone other than Disby understand—loomed as an impossible task. "You know the only difference between us? He actually got his Ground killed. I've only *almost* killed you. Sure, a couple of times, but it's the thought that counts, right? You might remember the most recent occasion. Where I attempted to smash in your skull with a heavy object?" Gavin's face, slack and bloody, appeared unbidden in his mind, and once there, it was impossible to dismiss.

"Neither of those were your fault. You didn't mean to. Someone else was pulling the strings."

West faked a grin. "And you've just made my argument for me. Disby didn't mean for it to happen, either. But you know why he's the better person? D'lane forced himself past Disby's defenses, kept him from protecting his Ground. I *let* Rashium in behind mine. Deliberately. Knowing he was unstable, in full realization of how dangerous he could be. Was," he corrected himself, barely flinching—something he felt a hint of pride over. Months of therapy, and he could now admit that he'd killed someone in the line of duty. His headcase would have been proud.

When Gavin tried to speak, West talked louder, faster. "Do you see why I can't trust myself anymore? I'm the strongest Reader PsyAc has ever seen, and D'lane hijacked me. I can't deal with the thought of getting you killed if it happens again. At the risk of sounding melodramatic, if you think Disby ended up in bad shape, he'd be the completely sane, rational one in comparison."

"Ah, so it comes down to emotional blackmail now." Gavin was smiling, but West had no trouble seeing the coiled fury behind it. "I hate to burst your bubble, but this doesn't get to be just about you, even if you *are* the famous Westley Tavera. Not when it's about *us*. We're a team, you and me. Hell, at this point I think it would be fair to say you, me, Nika, and Corwin are a team. In which case, flaking out isn't affecting just you. It's fucking with all of us."

"You think I don't know that? And really, screw the team; you're my *family*." His voice rose alarmingly, and he forced himself to take a breath, swallowing over the lump in his throat. "I made the mistake of underestimating Rashium's abilities, and look where it got us. I thought I could help him, that he was some lost, untrained kid, but I ended up stabbing you four times, and it was just pure dumb luck that it was your arm and not your heart. Know what else I got out of that experience?" He held up his hand, ticking off on his fingers, shaking with the force of his emotions. "A big old helping of guilt over almost killing the person I loved and trusted most. Ten weeks in a self-induced catatonic state, trapped and replaying that incident over and over again. Recurring nightmares where I succeed, and there's nobody left in the entire 'verse who'll be home for me. Coming back to a career where everyone I meet is wondering if I'm on burnout watch, and me wondering if I should be. And what's really scary? D'lane is obviously more powerful than Rashium ever dreamt of being, and he's leaving traps and—"

"Tavera." Corwin's voice, sharp and overly loud, was so unexpected that West actually stumbled when he spun around. "We need to debrief. Now." In contrast to his first bark, these words were calm, Corwin's face an emotionless mask.

"How long have you been here?" West demanded hoarsely. Whatever they were, his disagreements with Gavin had nothing to do with Corwin, and he spent too much of his life trying to find a little privacy to appreciate being eavesdropped on.

Corwin nodded toward the door. "Nika's waiting on the bridge. If we squeeze, there's enough room for all of us. We can see if there's anything we can use in Disby's files." Something akin to guilt flashed across his face. "And determine how much of it, if any, we can safely reveal to Ning."

West didn't think Corwin meant it as a distraction, but it worked, at least for Gavin. "I didn't think we were going to reveal any of it. You know, since none of it was obtained legally."

"I suppose that further emphasizes the need for discussion then, doesn't it?"

It was so subtle while it was happening that it took West a second or two to realize he was being herded away from Gavin and toward the door. When he started to balk, Corwin grabbed his upper arm. "*You need to walk away from this before you both say something you're really going to regret.*"

"*It's all the fucking truth.*" Corwin winced under the force of his anger, and too late, West tried to pull back. If he wanted to ensure that Corwin never let him beyond his walls again, he was on the right path.

"*Maybe. Doesn't mean you have to share it.*"

West shrugged forcefully enough that he almost dislodged Corwin's hand. "*Coming from the man who believes in complete repression.*"

Corwin actually laughed, a low rumble that pulled an unwilling grin from West and an apprehensive stare from Gavin.

Corwin didn't so much march them down the short hallway as sandwich himself between West and Gavin, and Nika glanced over her shoulder when they crowded onto a bridge that had never been meant to hold four people. "We're clear of Corve and less than two hours out from the transfer station." She leaned back with a groan, arms stretched above her head. "I swear I'll never complain about the lack of comforts on IEC ships again."

Gavin propped himself against the arm of her chair. "So we should be safely back on the *Vigilance* before we have to contact Ning?"

"Definitely. And I've rigged the console to display Disby's files." She made a face. "It's at least a little bigger than looking at them on a notebook."

West had already seen the bodies through Disby's eyes, so watching the files scroll through only further emphasized D'lane's descent into something more horrific than just murder. As the last case played out, Corwin shifted next to him, an uneasy tremor he only noticed because they were pressed so close. They weren't touching, but that didn't stop him from Reading the disquiet rolling off Corwin.

"I still say the victims are a completely different methodology." Gavin leaned around Nika to tap the screen. "The most obvious difference is the symbolism, especially with Dutchan Plen. D'lane's priors are the work of someone who tortured and murdered because he got off on it. Now we're looking at someone who's making a statement."

Corwin turned, but had to pull up short when West blocked his way. Nika spun her chair around to face them, stepping on Gavin's foot in the process. "The circumstances are different now, though," she said. "He got away with the previous murders, so maybe he needed a new challenge. And it's pretty obvious D'lane is far from sane, so anticipating his actions is chancy at best."

"That's not it." Unable to pace, Corwin settled for scowling. "When we interviewed him, he was still focusing on the . . ." Corwin swallowed visibly, and West almost winced in sympathy. "The whole sexual connection. That might play into the case on Bodum, but it certainly didn't seem that way. The only sexual aspect of that victim was her choice of career. The scene itself was devoid of anything indicative of a sexual ritual, and she hadn't been assaulted. West's Read made it seem like the killer was actually disgusted by the overt sexuality of the victim's profession. And it doesn't play into the other victims at all, unless we missed something huge."

"Maybe not, but what about Plen? It was definitely a jab at the IEC, and that *does* sound like something D'lane would pull. He's conceited enough to throw it in our faces."

That earned Nika a nod. "Good point. Bring that up in the briefing with Ning." Corwin turned toward West. "I know we can't reference it directly, but did you pick up anything from Disby that we can use? The fact that D'lane killed his Ground and the IEC still let him walk . . ."

He'd been content to just let the conversation flow around him, allowing the images from the files to merge with the impressions from Disby, but Corwin's voice called him back to the moment. Changing gears that fast had always been an effort, though at least the current company wasn't scattering his attention in a hundred different directions. It was the only excuse West could come up with for saying something he didn't intend to share.

"I don't know. I'm just not sure what I can trust from the Read. Disby is carrying a lot of guilt over her death, but I can't vouch for the accuracy of that impression in good faith." He ran a hand through his hair, wishing he could take the words back, knowing Gavin would call him on his admission of doubt later, but it was the truth. That moment of uncertainty he'd picked up could've been anything, or nothing but grief over a lost partner.

Corwin's gaze was sharp, but his voice stayed neutral. "Keep in mind that you were Reading someone who's pharmed out. It makes sense that it could provide a contradictory set of impressions."

There hadn't been anything contradictory about it, but he wasn't going to argue the point, not when it offered a way out of the conversation. "That was probably it."

"So we've got the IEC connection with Plen." Nika absently tapped the arm of her chair. "Is there anything at all that relates the cases on Ethris and Bodum to the original series of murders?"

"What about the fact that he terrorized both female victims? It's a reach, but causing fear can be a form of sexual gratification for some people." Gavin had been noticeably silent until that point, and West carefully avoided his gaze.

"It's the best connection we've got right now, and it's not out of the question. If he couldn't find himself inside them physically . . ." Corwin paused as if considering his words, and West was fairly certain he was the only one who noticed the catch in his breath. "Maybe he thought he could do it mentally, that he could Push them out."

Nika nodded. "Makes sense to me. We've got *something* to present to Ning, at least." They all fell silent, the solitude of thought just about the only privacy the ship had to offer. West nearly jumped when Nika stood. "I'm going to see if there's anything edible in the galley. I don't know about anyone else, but I could use coffee and something that falls solely into the sugar and fat category." She made a face. "Unfortunately, I'm guessing there's nothing but ready-meals."

"I knew we should've paid for the upgrade to the next model shuttle. We might've gotten cookies," he grumbled, mostly because the distraction allowed him to ignore everything else.

West made himself presentable for the meeting, and wound up perched on the arm of the couch in the lounge. It left him close enough to Gavin that it wouldn't be immediately obvious he was trying to avoid him, but far enough away that he didn't have to meet Gavin's eyes. Ning was no fool, and advertising that he and his Ground were at odds didn't seem like the smartest move at the moment.

Corwin had a spot at the console, and glanced at the rest of them when the comm pinged. "Ready?"

"Ready as we'll ever be." Nika sat up a little straighter, face grim.

"Inspectors, agents." Ning's voice gave away nothing.

Nervousness wasn't an emotion West dealt with often, but after the setdown from their last encounter, he felt entitled to a little discomfort. Covering it by shoving a cookie in his mouth probably wasn't the most professional approach, especially when Ning's gaze turned in his direction.

"Agent Tavera. Have you been staying on the correct side of the law?"

There was a smile to go with the words, but that didn't stop West from choking on a suddenly dry mouth. The coughing fit at least covered Nika's quiet attempt to hide a strained chuckle, and kept Ning's eyes on him so Corwin's smirk went unnoticed. "Like you even need to ask." He stared at Ning with no attempt to look innocent, knowing he could never pull it off, and dusted a few crumbs off his shirt.

The noncommittal hum didn't give much indication of Ning's disbelief, suspended or not. "That's good to know. Especially since you've kept both Investigative Services and Citizens Outreach busy. I have to say, I don't think any of you are particularly popular with those departments right now." Ning looked down briefly to tap on the keyboard. "I've just forwarded all the reports, but I want to go over the main points with you directly. Just so there are no misunderstandings."

Corwin's fingers twitched, and West knew the inspector wanted to access the reports immediately, but managed to keep from doing it while their superior officer was still lecturing them.

"First, you're still on the case." Ning held up a hand, forestalling any comments. "But we need to discuss a petition filed by D'lane's attorneys. He's claiming the Read that was done is nonadmissible because of procedural irregularities."

"I followed all of the IEC protocols. I know my job." West wasn't used to defending his methods to Ning. His behavior, his lax grasp of uniform codes, but not his work.

"Did I mention your name, Agent Tavera?"

"No, but—"

"If you'll let me continue." The reprimand was unmistakable. "D'lane is claiming that Inspector Menivie interfered, that he was Reading as well, and because of that, any information gleaned from Agent Tavera's Read must be disregarded." An unblinking stare pinned Corwin in place. "Is this true, Inspector?"

Dead silence greeted the question. Corwin was rigid in his chair, Gavin openmouthed, but it was Nika's reaction that surprised West. More precisely, it was her lack of a reaction that surprised him. Lips pressed together, her eyes never left Corwin.

Corwin's shoulders hunched. "I—"

"He had nothing to do with it, Ning." While he'd never experienced it firsthand, West was familiar enough with the idea of someone's life flashing before their eyes. What he wasn't expecting was for *Corwin's* life, or at least some future version of it, to tap-dance through his head. He couldn't imagine Corwin giving anyone access to the intensely private space created by those shields.

"Oh?" Ning blinked slowly. "So what did happen during the Read, then?"

"I'm sure you're aware of D'lane's Trakoran heritage. He's a Pusher. An incredibly strong one. I'm guessing he left that out of his complaint." He waited for Ning's nod before continuing. "During the investigation, we discovered that Corwin is a low-level receiver. Not enough that he even realized what it was before, just that he's uncomfortable around psys. He didn't stand a chance when faced with D'lane." Impossible to guess if Corwin would thank him for this interference or not, and he couldn't chance looking over to gauge his reaction.

"Were you planning on sharing this information, Inspector Menivie?" Stated mildly enough, but there was no doubt what answer was expected.

"It was going to be in my report. I apologize if it has in any way compromised the investigation."

"At the moment, it's unimportant," Ning said, voice grim. "D'lane's counsel has proven to be quite effective. While you are to remain on the case, he can't be held, and shouldn't be considered a prime suspect."

"No!" West made it to his feet with no memory of standing up. "You can't do that, we have too much evidence on him. You can't let him walk."

"I'm not *letting* him do anything."

"Sorry." He paced the lounge, too angry and restless to sit back down.

"And unfortunately, all your evidence at this time is circumstantial, except for the assault charge. Which, thanks to his counselors, was dismissed. The motion prints were not a conclusive match for D'lane. Tying the tour to the murders opens it up to over a thousand other potential suspects."

"Except that those thousand people don't have a string of mutilation murders connected with them," Nika interrupted, ever the voice of calm professionalism.

"Inspector Santivan, I'm not going to speculate on how you might have come into the possession of information in a sealed case file."

To her credit, Nika didn't flinch. "He admitted it himself, during the interview we conducted. Without coercion on our part. And in great detail."

"Be that as it may." Ning's voice held no small measure of censure. "That case was closed, and he was cleared of all charges. As such, D'lane cannot be treated any differently than anyone else on the tour. To that end, his counselors have negotiated an agreement with the IEC, and the case against him has been dropped. And it will remain so, unless evidence comes to light that directly implicates their client."

There were a hundred harsh words peppering West's mouth, and he knew he wasn't safe opening it. If he did, he was going to say something not only unprofessional, but incriminating as well.

"Respectfully, Chief Inspector, what exactly would that evidence *be*?" Nika's tone didn't actually scream "respectful."

No longer having Ning's steely-eyed glare directed at him let West finally unclench his jaw.

"Incontrovertible proof that Anders D'lane committed at least one of the crimes in your active case file. Nothing from before, nothing circumstantial, no psy evidence that can't be followed up with something corporeal. He's got counselors so slick they leave grease stains behind, and his parents have bought him out of everything up to and including murder. I need physical evidence: biological if possible, but visual will do."

Gavin beat him to the incredulous demand. "He isn't committing physical crimes. How are we supposed to find physical evidence of a murder that takes place in the victim's head?"

"Agent Hale, if I knew that, I'd have D'lane behind a polyshield so fast his counsel wouldn't even have time to oil their smiles."

"No offense, Chief, but that's hardly comforting." West pulled a face, disgust and indignation fighting for equal airtime. "And neither are those images."

"None taken. And I do understand the position this puts you in." Ning's smile was grim. "However, I continue to have the utmost faith in your abilities as a team. If there's a way to obtain the evidence needed to put D'lane away, I know you'll get it."

"And if we don't obtain it?" Nika sounded like the words were being dragged out of her, back almost painfully straight, hands clenched in her lap.

"As I said, I continue to have the utmost faith in your abilities as a team. Contact me as soon as you have anything to report." The screen went black for a second, before the ubiquitous IEC emblem returned.

West started to kick at the leg of the couch before remembering he was barefoot, and settled for scowling at it instead, almost missing Nika's impassioned protest.

"Faith in our abilities doesn't count for much when we've effectively had our hands tied. What the hell do we do now, when D'lane's bought his way out *again*?"

"Unless you were planning on confronting him and beating a confession out of him, not much has changed. We investigate the crimes, and let the evidence lead us to the suspect, not the other way around." Corwin frowned at her, at all of them really, though Gavin was nodding, however reluctantly.

She shook her head, cheeks flushed. "That's not the point, and you know it," she snapped.

Corwin shrugged. "The point is that none of us can afford to stop believing in the justice of the system we work within, or we'll wind up as lost as Disby. I, for one, have dreams of retiring somewhere I can garden without worrying about who I'll unearth, so Corve is right out for me."

Nika forced a smile, but it only made her looked strained. Corwin, unconsciously or not, managed to emulate her.

"You made a joke." West leaned forward and ruffled Corwin's hair, earning a withering glare in return. It was worth it, just to break the awkward moment. "Just so you know, *I* appreciated it."

If Corwin recognized his intent, there was no indication, his tone dry as ever. "I can't tell you how much that eases my mind."

CHAPTER 19

As it turned out, the time they could spend reviewing the murder files and trying to shatter their preconceptions to find something new in the wreckage was only about six hours, or roughly eight trips each to the coffeemaker. Despite the liters of coffee and sugar West had consumed, Corwin watched him sink lower with every case they reviewed, occasionally falling into the soft, almost toneless voice he usually reserved for the trancelike state of recall.

"I'm not saying there's nothing here, I'm just saying we're not finding it. And we're not going to tonight." Nika glanced at the time on her notebook and made a face. "This morning, I guess. We need sleep and clear heads."

Their agreement was silent. Gavin rose and gathered everyone's coffee cups to dump in the scrubber, while Corwin marked what little progress they'd made in the file notes and locked down the system. He missed whatever quiet conversation West and Gavin had, but it ended with Gavin and Nika leaving together, and West staring at the empty screen for a minute before getting up and heading toward the door.

Corwin caught West's elbow, squeezing when West glanced at him. "Did you want to come back to mine?"

West didn't answer at first, then shrugged. "You don't have to take me on nights Gavin won't, Corwin. I'm a big boy, I can tuck myself in."

Frustration boiled close to the surface, but looking at West, he could see it there too. They didn't tread lightly with one another, but he found it in himself to go gently. "It's the same thing eating at both of us." He cupped the hard bump of West's elbow in his hand and blew out a sharp breath. "You can believe whatever works for you, but I'm asking because I want to, not because it's what you need."

West laughed, head dropping, but the tone of everything was so far off that Corwin couldn't tell if it was real or not. He cautiously reached out to brush the flavor of it with his mind, and found it not nearly as bitter as he'd been expecting.

"We should coordinate these awkward moments where we're trying to care about each other." West slid his arm free, then surprised Corwin by meshing their fingers together.

"Keeps us on our toes. I can barely coordinate my outfits, so I think you're asking the impossible." It was nice, the new, grudging familiarity of meaningless banter. Something he hadn't had in a long time, and hadn't been smart enough to miss.

"You wear a uniform, Corwin. A black uniform. Even your underwear is black." West smirked, looking down for a second. "At least the pairs I've seen. Have you got a secret stash of rainbow thongs, Inspector?" West's free hand settled on his belt, fiddling with the buckle.

Corwin didn't swat West away, despite the fact that they were standing in the middle of the very public bridge. "I'm a man of mystery."

"I love a good mystery. Let's go hunt for clues in your pants."

Corwin groaned in protest, but didn't hesitate to follow West down the hallway.

They busied themselves with getting ready for bed, awkwardly taking turns in his small washroom. When Corwin returned from brushing his teeth, he found West sitting on the corner of the bed, staring off into space. He still didn't feel right about the easy contact, but it was tempting to ignore his misgivings when faced with someone who welcomed the casual link between their minds like it was natural.

"*You're quiet.*"

"*Mark the date and time.*" West rolled back into the bed, flopping over on top of the covers. "So? Let's solve the mystery."

Corwin pulled down the waist of his sleep pants on one side, and West sighed. "Black again? I feel so cheated."

"Not liking the answer once you've found it doesn't make it any less true." He checked the lock on his gun case before putting it away inside the top drawer of his desk. "I think these are more charcoal gray at this point, anyway. I've washed them a lot."

It was strange to have someone else in his space, so obvious against the backdrop of his carefully tended privacy, and so at odds with everything he'd thought made him happy. Order, routine, silence. Now he realized they were rocks in his pockets lately, dragging him below the surface, when he hadn't even known he was drowning.

"This case— If we can't solve it, what's that going to mean to you?" It wasn't what he wanted to ask, not when he was afraid of the answer, but his way with words only extended to characters knowing the right thing to say. West frowned at him, and even more than the words now, he fumbled through the emotion, filtering too much of what he meant. He finally gave up and cut it off entirely, pushing up hasty walls before he could subject West to any more of his confusion.

"I'm a professional. Sometimes cases get away from me, and I move on to the next one. I'm not going to fall apart if I don't get to cart D'lane off to a supermax on Rogena." West sat up, all the easiness between them fading as his casual sprawl contracted into a more defensive pose.

"That's not what I meant." Corwin scrubbed a hand over his face, newly washed and warm with embarrassment. He didn't particularly want to share just how bad off he was, but the divide between what he felt and what he said seemed to be full of nothing but the wrong words. "Tavera. West . . ."

"Will you ask for a new assignment somewhere?"

"You mean, when this fiver is over, am I taking my toys and going home?"

It meant something to Corwin that West met him halfway, when it would have been easier to keep words out of it entirely. He kept his nod short, wishing West could manage a straight answer. He didn't need much, just a confirmation that this was convenient and fun, and nothing messier.

West reached for him, but he kept himself rigidly locked down. The flash of puzzlement on West's face wasn't enough to make him rethink it. He felt the buzz against his shields lessen, exchanged for a firm resistance as West pushed back.

"I'm tired."

"That's not an answer. You're right, though, it's late—"

"I'm tired, Corwin. I'm tired of living out of everyone else's head. There's nowhere in the 'verse that's felt better to me than this ship. So if you're asking me to leave, I'm going to need a better reason than you not wanting to fuck me forever." West gave him a significant look, but not the time to actually say something that would only muck things up. "And if you're asking because it wouldn't be the worst thing ever if I did stay, then maybe you could stop acting like I'm just waiting to make you the punch line of a really long joke."

Their breathing was the only sound while Corwin fought the paralytic effects of exhaustion and experience, both of them pinning him in place when he thought about moving forward. Why he'd started this conversation now, he'd never be able to guess. "I was hoping you'd stay. I didn't want to influence your choice, if you were thinking about asking for a reassignment."

West's unbalanced smile didn't make Corwin feel like he was being mocked, and he didn't know when that had changed. "Because I'm so tractable, normally." Even the gentle teasing faded, and earnest West was as unsettling as he remembered. "Nobody *wants* to get hurt, and you said yourself, we don't come to people new and shiny. But I think we could do this, you know? We could be okay together, if we want to try. We just have to be willing to dust ourselves off a little and pretend we don't know how stupid it is to believe we can make it work."

Everything seemed easy for West, and somewhere along the line, that had stopped being infuriating, become fascinating instead. West danced whether there was a devil at his heels or not, and without meaning to, Corwin had started learning the steps.

"*I don't love you, West.*" They were the wrong words, said the right way, and he could almost hear the music queuing up.

The wrong words, but West smiled anyway, bright teeth, eyes framed by laugh lines, entire face alight with humor that invited him to be part of the joke. "*I don't love you either.*"

Behind the words was the same echo he'd infused his thoughts with. *Yet.* Yet, and all the possibilities it held. All the future they could see, beyond regrets collected like souvenirs and the thousand ways they could break each other on any given day.

Yet. It felt new, and Corwin thought if he could make it that far, beyond the yet, he—*they*—just might reach those possibilities.

Careless, he left his clothing in the middle of the floor, crawled across the bed, and pushed West back.

West waggled his eyebrows, ridiculous as always. "What about now?"

"Absolutely not. I'm thinking a points redemption system would be the best way to go." As he spoke, he assessed his plan of attack, finally deciding on a direct breach of defenses and slipping his hand into West's underwear.

"Naturally, I'll be starting off with a lead, having gently removed your head from your ass. Oh *hell*, keep doing that." West squirmed under him, laughing and half-begging.

Corwin smirked, deliberately licking his lips. "Give me a minute, and I'll earn enough to bring it back up to a tie."

"I'll be the judge of—" West's voice caught somewhere in the middle of another laugh. "You win."

Busy sliding down West's body, he didn't respond, but he didn't really care about winning. Not anymore.

A third and fourth time reviewing the case files turned up nothing new. The fifth and sixth were equally fruitless, and frustration was ruining a good deal of the afterglow from the night before. West reached for his mug with one hand, propping his chin on the other. The coffee had long since gone cold, and while he did manage to resist the urge to spit it back, he couldn't stop the small sound of disgust.

Gavin looked up, eyes as red-rimmed and tired as West's felt. "What?"

"Sorry." He grimaced. "Coffee went all gross on me. I didn't spit it everywhere though, so I get bonus points for that, right?"

"Oh, definitely." Gavin snickered. "In fact, I think I'll put you in for a commendation. I'm sure Ning will approve it."

West pushed back from the table and stood up. "And you'll be the first person I take out to dinner on my huge bonus. Before Corwin, even. Just don't tell him, or he'll be jealous. He *does* put out more than you do."

"Rule Number Two, West," Gavin muttered, face buried in his hands. "Please don't share."

"But weren't you the one who said you didn't care who I was fucking? Also, Rule Number Two clearly dictates my actions relating to *your* love life, not mine. I'm free to share all the minute details of my illicit docking maneuvers." It wasn't really meant as a jab, and he felt a stab of guilt when Gavin winced.

"Yeah, about that. I'm sorry. It all got a little out of hand."

West nodded. "I'm sorry too. But hey, if I can't trust you to call me on my shit, who can I trust?" He laughed, leaning over to punch Gavin in the arm. The shakiness between them had been growing since the Rashium incident, but they could fight without destroying each other if they were careful.

"The person you're fucking?" Gavin said, completely deadpan.

"Careful, Gavikins, you're about to break your own rules." Still snickering, he dumped his mug in the sink, and bent to reach in the cooler. His notebook pinged as he straightened back up, juice in hand. "Damn, you're fast. That must be my commendation already."

The call was encrypted, forwarded through his IEC account, and before he even opened it, he was certain it was Disby.

"Why did you let D'lane walk?" Disby's voice was a low growl of anger. There was no visual feed, and the screen displayed only the IEC logo.

He glanced quickly at Gavin, who raised an eyebrow and shrugged. "We didn't let him walk. The decision was out of our hands."

"You could've done something!"

Gavin leaned toward the notebook. "Disby, you were an agent, you know how these things work."

"Oh, I know, all right. Power and money let you get away with murder. I just thought you were better than that. That you had more integrity."

"It's got nothing to do with integrity and everything to do with evidence." The words felt heavy in his mouth, like the lie carried physical weight.

"You don't believe that any more than I do."

The fact that he didn't wasn't helping. There was evidence. Just not evidence they were being allowed to use. "The previous cases are closed and locked, you know that. They're forcing us to come up with something new. Something that can't be challenged."

"Physical evidence," Disby said, voice flat.

"It's the only thing that's indisputable."

He couldn't Read Disby from voice only, but there was no mistaking the slipping sanity as it rose to a near scream. "The physical evidence of Anaj's body spread all over a fucking floor wasn't enough for them? What more do they want from me?"

Gavin's mouth tightened. "It's not about you. It was never about you."

For several long seconds there was only the sound of muffled breathing on the other end of the connection. "No, of course it's not."

West couldn't be sure he was the only one hearing the false calm in the words, but he didn't want to ask while Disby was within hearing. "We're doing everything we can. We want him locked away as much as you do."

"No. No, I don't think you do." The link went dead.

"Shit." West blew out a long sigh, killing the comm panel on his notebook. "That went well." He fumbled for his chair and sat down.

"Spectacularly. Think we should call Nika and Corwin in and let them know?"

He nodded, running a finger through the condensation on his glass before meeting Gavin's gaze. "It wasn't as easy to tell from this particular interaction, but something . . . something was off on that last Read. I don't want to start that fight over again, but that was what prompted my, uh, let's call it ambiguity."

"Something off besides him being certifiably insane?" Gavin snorted. "I'd think that would be enough to give you that 'something off' feeling."

"No, more than that. We've dealt with our share of crazy before. This was different." Putting it into words was proving harder than he'd expected. "Things were skewed. Disby's *feelings* were skewed. There was guilt over his partner's death—not that I don't understand guilt over failing your Ground."

Gavin started to protest or offer an excuse or something else that would derail the conversation, but West shook his head, grateful for their trust when Gavin immediately stopped.

"This was a different sort of guilt. Or a stronger guilt. Or something." He threw up his hands in frustration. "I don't know. It just didn't feel right. It felt like a story he was telling, not something he lived."

"Okay. So we take that into account when weighing any information we get from him or from the Read."

It was as simple as that, and he couldn't decide if he felt more relieved or more stupid for ever doubting that Gavin would get it. "Thanks for not thinking I'm Reading crap into this because of my own fairly large guilt complex."

"Of course not. You're too experienced to influence a Read with your own feelings. Doesn't mean you can't doubt your abilities when you're interpreting it later." Gavin rolled his eyes, but his sheepish, shifty look was an obvious nod toward an apology. "Idiot. How long have we been friends? Trust me, I know when you're reading crap." He snickered. "I've seen your underwear drawer."

"What can I say? Commifee tentacle porn is an acquired taste."

Gavin massaged his forehead, eyes closed. "Seriously? You had to say that? We need a new rule. Number Fifty-eight. No describing, mentioning, or even thinking about porn when in each other's company. *Especially* Commifee tentacle porn. Starting now."

Corwin stepped around the corner into the galley, a horrified expression on his face, and West laughed until he doubled over. "Sorry," he finally wheezed. "Bad time to make an appearance."

To his credit, Corwin recovered quickly, horror replaced by a casual shrug. "I have no idea what you're talking about, Tavera."

For some reason, it made him laugh harder, hands clutching his sides, and it took twinned looks of vague disgust before he snorted and snuffled his way to a stop. "I really wish you two wouldn't stare at me like that. It makes me feel like you're teaming up, and I can't have that."

"Never fear, you're the only glue holding us together." Corwin took as wide a berth as possible around the table, reaching for a coffee mug. "So I take it you've been going over files again. Anything new?"

"Just a call from Disby."

Corwin spun around to pin him with a stare. "What did he want?"

"He knows about D'lane." He slid his chair over, waiting for Corwin to sit down before continuing. "He's a little . . . upset."

"Screw that." Gavin scowled at no one in particular, finger tapping absently on the table. "The question we haven't asked yet is *how* he knew about D'lane. And almost as soon as we did. I guess it could be somebody who knows D'lane in some capacity, but you'd think he'd keep his people paid well enough to not talk. And if Disby still has a contact at the IEC, that person is leaking highly classified information. I can't imagine anyone being willing to take that risk for him."

Corwin nodded slowly. "Good point. Losing their job would be the least of the repercussions."

"Just because you don't like him, Gav, doesn't mean he doesn't have friends." Again that double stare down. "Okay, okay." He held up his hands in surrender. "So it would be a supremely stupid thing to do. But what else could it be?"

"No, I'm sure you're right. It just puts us in a bad position. Ning needs to know there's a potential leak. But if we reveal that, we have to reveal how we know." Gavin sighed. "While you two hold favored-agent status, I'd probably get my ass handed to me."

West reached across the table to pat Gavin's hand. "At least it's a nice ass. Maybe you can gift wrap it for Nika."

Gavin flipped him off.

CHAPTER 20

Personal tradition dictated that as soon as Corwin had turned a final manuscript in to his editor, he indulged in an extremely hot shower and something sweet. Preferably with frosting. He wasn't sure whether he was relieved or not that West was planetside finishing up a report and wouldn't be able to join him for either of those things. The tentative agreement to consider their odd relationship worth pursuing still sat uneasy on occasion. Sometimes he just wanted a few minutes where everything he was dealing with made sense.

He was reaching for the shower panel when a message notification pinged from behind him. He hesitated a second or two and groaned, turning to grab a towel to wrap around his waist. No time to find a shirt, but even fly-by officers were allowed off-duty hours, and whoever it was could damn well deal with calling him during his clearly marked break from duty.

"Inspector Menivie." Ning's eyebrows rose disconcertingly high. "Have I caught you at an inconvenient time?"

Mentally cursing his inability to use the ignore function on his notebook, and Ning's use of a private line, Corwin shook his head. "Not at all. I was informed that it's Shirtless Seventhday, and felt I should participate. In the spirit of team morale, obviously." Steadfastly keeping his eyes on the screen, he adjusted the towel in what he hoped was a covert way. "What can I do for you?"

He'd never seen Ning do a double take, but then again, he'd never made a joke about shipwide nudity before, either. Ever, as it happened. Ning's poise faltered, but they forged on. "I wanted to contact you personally to discuss the psy case." The long pause that followed was uncomfortable, and he found himself wincing preemptively. "It's been two weeks with no further evidence. I'm sorry, but I'm going to have to pull it as your primary case and start assigning you more in-depth investigations elsewhere. I can't justify my best team waiting for something to happen."

"It's not like we've been sitting around drinking coffee, doing nothing." He sounded more defensive than he meant to. "We've just closed out our current case on Oppor, successfully, I might add." From defensive to petty. It kept getting better. "West is finishing up the paperwork right now."

Ning nodded. "I know that. I'm not questioning your work; I'm saying you're too valuable to be wasted on cases that can be closed out in a couple days, or left in a hurry if you need to rush back to your primary investigation. This one's going to have to be put aside now. I gave you all the time I could, but IEC rules dictate that it no longer qualifies for a primary case status. If the case heats up again, you'll be allowed to pursue it, but I can't promise you'll be on an assignment you can drop as easily as these last few."

Further protest would be a waste of effort, he knew that, so he grasped at the other point. "So why tell me now, and not everyone together?"

"Because you're the undisputed voice of reason?"

"That's nice, but I get the feeling there's more to it than that. Just a guess, based on how you phrased that as a question."

"As we discussed before, Agent Tavera is . . . very invested in this case." Ning's smile held wry humor. "Disengaging may be difficult for him, and I feel that you're the best person to help him with that."

The hot flush hit his cheeks and spread down his neck with alarming speed. Somehow, suspecting that Ning knew about their personal affairs made him feel more naked than actually *being* naked. "Why not Agent Hale? He's Tavera's Ground."

"Agent Hale is a valuable asset, and intensely loyal to his partner. I'm sure he'll be able to assist as well. I just don't think it will be his first instinct."

Staring down at the floor rather than at the screen, he forced himself to unclench his jaw, and nodded stiffly. "I'll let everyone know as soon as they're back, then."

"Thank you. And Corwin? You did everything you could, all of you. There's no shame in this." Ning waited until he looked up before continuing. "I'm proud of you."

Once the screen went black, he groaned and ran a distracted hand through his hair. Ning seemed to believe it was just West who had been caught up in the case, but they'd all become invested, individually and as a team. Letting go was going to be an effort all the way around.

Any desire to celebrate had been thoroughly squashed, and Corwin got dressed and then called for a pickup from the local field office. Apparently he'd passed Nika and Gavin during the drive, though, because only West was left, and waiting for his transport back to the *Vigilance*.

"So are we going to celebrate somehow? Dinner that's actually been prepared by a chef, some crazy, uninhibited sex afterward?"

The fact that West saw fit to ask in an overly loud voice, accompanied by a ridiculous leer, just outside of an IEC building didn't bother him as much as it might have in the past—a sure sign he'd been beaten down and lost all sense of propriety.

His quelling look had no effect on West's manic smile. "If you feel that strongly about it, we can skip the dinner part and just go for the sex."

Corwin opened the door to the waiting flyer before replying. "Tavera, what are you talking about?"

"Your book. Aren't we going to have a celebration?" West crowded in closer than necessary, then patted him on the knee. "My treat."

"Oh for the love of . . ." Conscious of the driver, he kept his voice low. "How do you even know that? Have you been reading messages over my shoulder again?"

West at least had the grace to look vaguely guilty. "Not really? I just noticed you suddenly weren't spending as much time hunched over your keyboard. I was going to plan a surprise gala, but then I remembered that surprises make you testy. So I'm asking instead." When he didn't reply, West raised an eyebrow. "You *do* celebrate, right? Do something special, out of the ordinary? Impetuous, even?"

"No."

"Right, then this is perfect. We'll start a new tradition today. Fancy dinner that doesn't involve reconstituted anything, and then sex in the lounge. And then maybe the galley. Anything for you," he finished, magnanimously waving a hand. "You name it."

"I'm going to return to the *Vigilance*, finish up and submit my report for this case, and make it an early night." Trying to stop West when he was on a roll could only be compared to stopping a planetary orbit, and was about as successful, but he felt like he had to at least make a token effort.

"An early night it is, then. Who needs a fancy meal?" West settled back in the seat with a smirk.

When the flyer pulled up, Nika was standing at the bottom of the ramp, tension radiating off her body. Corwin wasted no time getting out, West on his heels.

"There's been another murder." As far as greetings went, it lacked something. She waited until they fell into step with her before continuing. "Notification came across ten minutes ago. It wouldn't even have pinged us except for the DNA evidence. Human/Trakoran hybrid."

"Stupid. We've got him this time." The vicious glee in West's voice was so out of character that Corwin found himself staring.

"We don't have him until we actually put on the restraints." Corwin's reminder was only partially aimed at West. He'd felt a traitorous moment of victory too, and not just because he was now saved from having to share Ning's message about being off the case.

West shrugged. "It's only a matter of time. This is the physical evidence we needed." He turned to Nika. "What happened?"

"It was on Lassiter. Another woman this time, and the profile matches D'lane's previous crimes. Physical mutilation this time."

"Serial killers refine their methods. They don't revert." Corwin shook his head.

"What if it's not just his methods that changed, it's his thrill? This case has been dark for weeks. What if we've somehow missed a victim?" Nika spoke slowly, as though she was testing the theory as she went. "If his focus is on recognition, rather than the kill itself, maybe this is a . . . a display. Like he's courting our attention."

Corwin caught the thread she'd left dangling. "Ning contacted me earlier to tell me the case was being reclassified as a secondary invest.gation. What if there *is* a leak, and it's not just Disby who knows about it?"

"D'lane could be the one getting the information, and passing it on to Disby," West suggested. "He told us on the cruise ship—his last two victims were for Disby."

They all picked up their pace, hustling into the ship and down the corridor to the common room.

Gavin was seated at the Nerve, and swung around as they came in. "I've got the full report now. They're holding the body until we get there for a Read." He hesitated for several seconds, hands over the console. "I've already scanned the report. This case was . . . bad. The field officer who filed it seemed overwhelmed."

"Maybe it's a nice peaceful city, and this is their first murder." West didn't sound particularly hopeful as he moved to stand next to Gavin. Lassiter wasn't a small, single-colony planet. There was a field office there, fully staffed and home to an entire investigative branch of the IEC.

The report started with images taken at the crime scene. The backcrop of sunny skies and improbably bright flowers made the scene surreal. It wasn't until Corwin stepped forward to look closer that he realized the flowers were crimson because of the blood. He had to squint to see that the crumpled red rag in the center of the picture was actually a body. Distance obscured the worst of it. The next photo, however, provided excruciating detail.

West drew a ragged breath, which was closely followed by a cut-off gasp from Nika. The fact that Corwin was able to keep his own reaction silent was more luck than anything. They were all exper.enced officers, but some things all the training in the 'verse couldn't prepare you for.

"A couple of kids walking to school found the body." Gavin's voice was thick with anger.

"That's . . . fuck, that's exactly like what he did to Disby's Ground, to Anaj." West spun around; two or three stumbling steps brought him up against Corwin. He instinctively reached out a hand to steady him, but West jerked away. "How long till we get there?" He looked beyond Corwin to Gavin.

"Ten hours, give or take."

"Right. I'll be in my quarters until then." West didn't wait for a response, shoulders hunched as he brushed past.

Gavin half stood as if to follow West, then eased back into the chair when Corwin started toward the hallway. His tired sigh was almost covered by West's loud, retreating footsteps as they echoed through the ship, and he waved a hand at Corwin. "Fine, you go."

West hadn't made it far, slumping against the wall in the last fork of the main corridor. "We've got to put D'lane away. This can't keep happening." He didn't look up, but Corwin didn't need eye contact to see the same exhaustion Gavin had displayed only moments before.

Empty promises would be only that, and he was all too aware of his shortcomings in the area of comforting words. Instead, he reached out, resting his hand on the nape of West's neck. *"Come to my quarters."*

West stiffened but didn't pull away. *"I'm sorry the party fell through. Don't feel much up to it right now, though. Kinda tired."*

"I'm okay with you lying there being quiet. And not reading over my shoulder."

"Ah, so that's how you want it." West grinned crookedly. *"I promise I'll just lie there and think of the empress."*

He rolled his eyes, using the hand on West's neck to propel them down the corridor. *"I refuse to pander to your royalty kink, just so you know."*

"You should probably consider that before you play knight in shining armor, next time."

The IEC field office on Lassiter was a large one, with permanent Kidnapping and Recovery, Financial, and Fraud units. It also served as the headquarters for the Biotechnological Crimes group, thanks to the presence of Slipstream Labs in Prita. As fly-bys, it wasn't usual for them to be dropping in. Corwin and Nika looked a little out of their element, but he and Gavin had spent several years attached to the Major Crimes unit on Naavil, and he was used to the hustle of a large group of inspectors, all of whom wanted their results yesterday.

West stuck close to Gavin, and didn't feel too guilty about using Corwin as another buffer. Between the two of them, they let him have a fresh mind for the Read on this body, not cluttered by the cobwebs of a dozen other crimes. He hoped like hell that this was all coming to an end now. That this Read, combined with the DNA evidence, would be enough to link all the crimes, lock D'lane away, and prevent any more murders. West owed that closure to the families of the victims he'd already touched.

They found the station manager, who scanned their badges without looking up from the scrolling Nerve screen on her desk. "You the imperial liaisons they brought in for the Slipstream Genetics break in?"

"Nope, here about the mutilated corpse they found in the green space." West leaned over just a little, trying to catch some of the Slipstream information before she whisked it away and left him sneaking a peek at the IEC logo. "Why would they bring in fly-bys for a theft?"

She glanced up finally, just to shrug. "Slipstream holds the imperial patent on Trakoran genetic manipulation; it would never be *just* a theft. And it's their third major security breach in a year and a half. The first two were supposedly some forger who dropped off the grid and came up smelling like an imperial pardon. They're a little jumpy down Prita way."

"Pardoned doesn't mean reformed." Corwin sounded typically droll on the subject. She raised her eyebrows in acknowledgment, then handed their badges back and waved them up to the fourth floor.

Ning had arranged their access, and it was easy to see the chief inspector's hand in the private room they were shown into. A proper Reading room, the likes of which he hadn't had access to since before the Evanston case, and it was so blessedly quiet inside that he almost backed out, afraid he'd destroy the psychic cleanliness with his own unsettled mind. Next to him, Corwin stopped short, and West felt the connection between them for a second before Corwin realized there wasn't much to push against in a room lined with barrier metals and cleared of psychic residue after each interview. The technician who wheeled the body in didn't linger, but that wasn't so odd; most stations with clean Read rooms instructed personnel to spend as little time in them as possible. That was the story he was telling himself, anyway. The alternative was to acknowledge that most cadavers didn't require a gurney with slop sides.

Gavin made a noise when they rolled the sheet back, and West would have too, if he hadn't lost his tongue. Except he hadn't, that was her, and while the Read room was good for his focus, it was hell on his perception. Gavin caught him without being asked, freeing him to breathe again for a second or two before he really went under.

Nika's voice was even and tight. "The killer removed her tongue, her right ear, her left thumb—"

"And her heart. He cut out her heart and held it up, to see if it was the same as his." West heard his voice like an echo, like someone else speaking in the quiet room, and Gavin, who had a strong stomach, made a soft gagging noise. Ignoring it, West approached the gurney and reached for what was left of her hand. Her nails were split and bloody; she'd fought, before she couldn't anymore.

"He told her to come with him, and she did. He told her to lie down on the ground, in the dew, and she did, but she tried to crawl away. Hooked her fingers in the cracks and begged, but he couldn't have her telling, so he made her quiet." The table rattled under his weight as he leaned closer, shaking fingers tracing the edge of where her face should have been. "I have to go."

He sank down, down, then up again, and felt breath on the back of his neck as the hissed orders wormed their way into his brain. He didn't want the arm around his chest, and he knew he was screaming, until the voice in his head told him he didn't want to. The voice told him he wanted to come along, be a good little sparrow and brush wings with his death.

He couldn't break away, but he screamed again, screamed and tried to crawl away from the pain that enveloped him as he was cut away, bit by bit. The voice wasn't as strong when the pain came, and he fought, even if it only meant that his knees scraped raw on the gravel and his fingernails tore as he tried to remember that he didn't want to die.

Except he knew that what he wanted didn't matter, and then he didn't have a tongue to form the words to beg, to ask why. Blood filled his mouth, and he cast a fervent prayer to the stars he knew must still be above him somewhere, hoping he'd drown in it before anything else could happen. And then the stars came home in his chest, all of them at once, a cold fire that tore and spread, numbing him until he almost didn't care that his last breath wasn't even his. The cold, cold stars bit into his skin, where his ear should have been, and then it was over.

West shuddered and turned his face into the wall, pressing his nose against the dull-white polyboard and moving his mouth over sobs that had no sound. He didn't have time to warn anyone when the bile rose in his throat, but Gavin knew anyway, and all he had to do was turn his head to vomit into the waiting trash can. It burned away the taste of blood, but the pressure in his head only got worse. When he was done, he staggered to his feet, his sore fingers sliding for purchase over the slick wall, his steps not quite his own.

Gavin helped him to the door, blank and not enough, though it wasn't any fault of theirs. There was no getting away from this one, and he could only be glad that Gavin would know that, and do what needed to be done.

"Do you need to fail-safe?" Gavin's voice next to his ear was soft, familiar, and if he could have torn his eyes away from the ceiling tiles, he would have. Gavin had never looked at him with pity, not once since the day they'd met on the playground, and he liked to see that lack, to remind himself that he didn't need it. But the ceiling tiles were the same, and that mattered, somehow.

"The sky was the same, Gav. The sky was the same, and she was a bird to him, and he made her a cage out of his words. It was him, I know it was him, and he did it to make sure we knew." The IEC must have bought the tiles by the warehouse load, stacked neatly and waiting to be changed out once they broke or stained. He wasn't sure which he was, right now. There was another Reader waiting to take his place, some kid carved out of the same block of resistant foam, riddled with cracks that couldn't be seen until you stared.

"Blink, dude. Or at least close your eyes."

He made himself follow the order, even though the last thing he wanted was to give in to someone else's demands. The Read room and its trapped horror were fading, but the spun-out dysphoria wouldn't let go. He had to get away from it, had to run, but Gavin's arms were locked around his chest, holding him still in a quiet corner of the hallway.

"Let go of me. Please, please let go." She hadn't had the voice to beg, so he did, but Gavin held on, and West looked back up at the ceiling, trying to find the crack he could escape through, the piece of sky he needed to fly away.

"Can't let go unless you're lucid, and I know you're not. You'll run, and you'll get scared when I chase you down. You need to breathe, West, and focus on finding your way back."

"The tiles are the same everywhere. The tiles were the same in my head when I went away with Rashium. Ten by ten, every day. Ten by ten, until I didn't think there was anything outside that room, and I was sure you were dead. But the fucking tile was always the same."

"Then look at me. Or look at Corwin's ass, if that's what gets you home, but you need to be here with us, not lost in the ceiling."

Corwin was with them, West could tell without seeing him, but he was locked away tight behind his safe walls, and West didn't want him to come out.

He had to look one way or the other, though, had to see the reaction. He wouldn't reach out, though, too afraid Corwin would answer him out of some sense of obligation, but he looked, his eyes watering as he tore them away from the tiles.

Corwin and Nika were talking quietly by the door of the Read room, and Corwin was doing a poor job of hiding his cautious glances in their direction. West locked eyes with him, and the blue was comforting: cool, clear, and nothing like the ceiling. There was the sky, and he was safe now.

Safe, and incredibly glad that Corwin couldn't tell what he was thinking at the moment, because there were limits to the sentimental twaddle a man could be expected to endure. He was pretty sure "*I found myself in your eyes*" crossed most of them.

"See? Corwin's ass. Worked like a charm." Gavin's discreet murmur didn't carry, just loud enough to get a shaky laugh out of him.

He slid free of Gavin's hold with a grimace as the taste in his mouth finally registered. "I need to go wash my mouth out." Glancing at the door, he took a deep breath. "And I'm done in there."

Gavin nodded, the hand on his shoulder brief but welcome. "I'll get the body returned and start Grounding the room. Are you sure you're okay for a little while?"

He wanted to snap, because a Read like that always left him with an edge, but Gavin didn't deserve it, and West had enough of a handle on himself not to be an ass for a few seconds. "I'm okay. You know how it goes."

Gavin's grim smile, like his own careful nonchalance, was a study in control. "Yeah. I know."

West fled to the bathroom, brushing past Nika's tempered worry but not stopping to say anything. A few minutes with his hands cupping the running water, his face buried in them to cool down, and he felt nearly calm enough to deal with the 'verse. Maybe not Corwin, though, who stepped silently through the door to lean against the wall behind him, arms folded.

"If you stay, I'm going to say something horrible, because that's how I am after a Read. And you'll say something horrible back, because I piss you off by breathing most days, and we'll wonder why the hell—"

"Oh, for the love of the stars, shut up." It wasn't a large bathroom, and Corwin didn't have to move far to press a warm hand against the nape of West's neck. His fingers barely brushed the ends of West's hair, going still after a few seconds. "I thought you'd feel better about yelling at me than Gavin."

He closed his eyes, just so he wouldn't be distracted by the color of Corwin's. He was careful to smile when he replied. "That's really sweet of you, and also pretty fucked up."

"I think that encapsulates our relationship thus far." Corwin didn't bother to deny it, fingers curving around the back of West's head and squeezing gently. "Nika and I contacted Ning. Between your Read and the bio evidence collected from the body, the chief thinks we'll have our arrest warrant in a few hours. Could be quicker, but Ning didn't want to garner any extra attention by rushing it through."

West opened his eyes, casting a quizzical look at Corwin. "When did you have time for all that?"

"Nika stepped out during part of the Read. She thought she might distract you, and it served us better to get the ball rolling as soon as you gave us something to connect to the DNA evidence." Hand dropping, Corwin took a turn looking skeptical. "You were under for nearly an hour."

Losing time during a Read wasn't unheard of, but it didn't happen to him often, and never when the trauma was so fresh, the pain so obvious and exacting. He lost time when the body was weeks or years old, or when all he had to pull from was a scrap of feeling left behind as some inanimate object bore witness. He hadn't had to dig for this Read at all, and as repellent as it was, there was nothing complicated about what had happened. He started to say something about it to Corwin, but held his tongue. What did it matter that his mind had needed a few extra minutes to steel itself against a gruesome murder? He shrugged instead, collar damp against his neck. "Glad to see you inspectors know how to multitask. I'm more of a unitasker, myself."

"Now, that's not true at all. You can annoy me and flirt with me at the same time." Anyone else would have made some broad gesture to underscore the joke, tossed an arm over his shoulders or grinned. He was growing fond of looking for the more subtle twitch at the corner of Corwin's mouth, like smiling was some childhood habit he had been broken of but couldn't shake entirely.

"I must be learning from your fine example." The taste of bile wasn't quite out of his mouth, but there was nothing else he could do about it for now, so he nodded toward the door. "If we're in here any longer, Gavin's going to accuse you of inappropriate workplace behavior. And if we hurry, we can grab takeout before the warrant comes through. I like my justice on a full stomach."

Corwin held the door for him, and even though West rolled his eyes, he brushed past him, pausing halfway out. "Thanks."

"You're doing your job, Agent Tavera. As a member of your team, I consider it my duty to make sure you're in top shape."

He didn't bother to look for the twitch this time, but he knew it was there anyway.

CHAPTER 21

"This would be easier if he was still booked on that wine tour." Nika shifted in her chair, settling back and running through a short set of stretches to ease the crick Corwin assumed she'd put in her neck from hunching over the console. While it was a lovely neck, insofar as he'd ever considered it, right now he was studiously not looking at it, or the bright-red bruise just below her ear. She hooked her fingers together and thrust her arms out in front of her. "Do you think he's gotten wind of the warrant somehow and made a run for the black?"

"I certainly wouldn't discount the possibility. It seems like he's had inside information during the entire investigation, and I can't imagine that's changed. But he'll have to get fuel and food somewhere. Even if it takes weeks, we've got his accounts monitored now, so as soon as we see activity, we can light up the closest field office." It was the long way around to admitting that he hadn't found anything either. They sat in silence for another few minutes, both the work and the quiet easy between them. Eventually he had to stretch too, and he turned his chair toward her. "Break?"

She nodded, locking down her system before she rose. Even though the break had been his idea, he lingered for a moment, reluctant to give up the time alone with her, and feeling foolish for it. She smiled at him, letting her hair loose from the tight regulation knot she normally kept it in. It fell to cover the bruise.

"Are we on break now?"

He raised an eyebrow at her. "We seem to be."

"I wouldn't want to bring up your personal life while we're on official IEC time, is all." Her nose wrinkled a little, and he huffed quietly, pretending offense he didn't really feel. "I just wanted to tell you that I'm glad you've been so happy lately."

"Have I?" He gave her a look that could probably pass for startled.

"It's news to you that you've been happy?"

"I didn't know I'd been unhappy before." He hadn't meant to have a conversation about his moods, but she didn't seem likely to give up on it, and he wasn't having it in the kitchen, where West and Gavin were likely to pop in at any moment.

"Not unhappy. But I think . . . Just not as happy as you've seemed lately. I'm sorry, this is overstepping your comfort zone, isn't it? I'm just pleased for you." She shrugged, drifting into the uncomfortable expression she only wore when he'd made it clear that she'd committed some grievous invasion of his privacy.

"No. No, I appreciate it. I—"

He was saved from further awkwardness by West, of all people, who would never have spared him if given the choice. "Going to hazard a guess that the lack of cheering and confetti means you haven't found D'lane."

Nika shook her head. "Nothing. If we don't catch up to him soon, the warrant's going to be released." The frustration was back in her voice. "And if we lose out to a bounty hunter, I'm really going to feel cheated."

Corwin's lip curled. "Not on my watch. No bounty hunter is picking up my case." For all that they provided a useful service, the intense dislike and vague distrust he felt for bounty hunters was shared by most of his IEC brethren.

"I got picked up by bounty hunters once."

Corwin raised an eyebrow. "You had an outstanding imperial warrant?"

West didn't smile so much as leer, and Corwin's incredulous stare turned into an eye roll. "No. I got *picked up* by bounty hunters once. It was awesome. Quite . . . memorable."

Nika snickered. "Do tell."

"No," Corwin cut her off. "Do not encourage him. He's insufferable enough as it is." He wasn't jealous of the sparks of remembered sex that flared off West, not really. It was just that they were working. And he was willing to keep telling himself that until he believed it.

"That wasn't what I heard that night. Indefatigable maybe, but not insufferable." The wicked grin was all for him. "But anyway, back to work. You both need to come see this. Gav and I were going to post our reports to the D'lane file, and we found a flag on it. Roggen Harrow, one of the inspectors who worked the case the first time."

"With Disby." Nika's tone made it a statement, not a question. "Gavin was wondering how he'd been getting information from an active IEC case. You think Harrow has been filling Disby in?"

Between Nika's curiosity and his cynicism, Corwin figured they covered more ground than most. It wasn't always the case that their opinions overlapped, but this time there was no doubt they were on the same page. He followed Nika and West down the corridor to the common room as West continued. "Seems like someone's been feeding D'lane details, too. And if he had an insider *helping* him make files disappear, maybe there was a reason none of the charges from the first case ever stuck."

West brought up the information flag, and Harrow's deep-set eyes and grim expression glared out at them from the contact link. "Shall we call him and find out whose side he's on?" His finger hovered over the screen of the notebook, ready to send the request.

Corwin glanced at Harrow's information again, trying to equate planetary time on Liget with imperial standard.

"He should be in the office." West smirked at him. "Your eyes were about to cross, and I looked up his contact hours before I came to find you."

"In that case, fire at will." Corwin sat down as well, expecting West to shift over, and tried not to twitch when it didn't happen. The long delay between the call and Harrow's answer didn't help matters. West slouching forward only amplified the buzz against his shields and the quiet friction of their clothing. He was about to move when Harrow's face appeared, voice a half second off until the feed settled out.

"Inspector Harrow. Who the hell are you?" Harrow's desk job was clear by the outfit he wore, the sleeves of his white dress shirt rolled up and not a stitch of the IEC field blacks to be seen. His hair stuck up on one side, like he'd had a hand tangled in it at some point. He didn't look thrilled to receive a call from a fly-by team an hour before going off duty.

"Senior Inspector Corwin Menivie, and my partner . . . s, Inspector Nika Santivan, and Agents Westley Tavera and Gavin Hale.

We're working a case and saw that you'd flagged our file. I'm hoping you've got information about the location of Anders D'lane."

Harrow's eyes had narrowed as soon as Corwin had introduced West and Gavin, but the anger at the mention of D'lane surprised all of them. West actually jumped a little when Harrow leaned in closer to the vid capture. "Don't say another word." He stood so quickly it was almost dizzying, and they all heard an office door slam, and the slap of a palm against a lock plate. The light in the room dimmed, probably smoke glass going into effect, and Harrow didn't look any happier when he sat down again. "I don't know how you got my name from a sealed file, but if you press me on this, I will have your fucking badges pulled for harassment." He turned the force of his glare on Corwin, pointing. "And I don't give a shit that you outrank me, so don't try to push me that way."

"You're the one who flagged our *open* case. I fail to see how following up on that constitutes harassment."

Next to him, West's lips pressed tightly together, holding in a laugh, though he ignored it as Harrow's scowl deepened.

"I don't know what glitch flagged me on your case, but let me be perfectly clear. I don't want anything to do with it. My ex-partner got drummed out of the IEC over that fucking debacle, and I'll count myself lucky if I make senior inspector before I retire. Maybe my name is floating around because of a previous association, but I've got no interest whatsoever in anything to do with Anders D'lane."

Corwin glanced at Nika, who raised her eyebrows in acknowledgment, before West spoke up from his other side.

"Okay, so if not for D'lane, are you monitoring information about this case for Christeven Disby?"

He could've shot West, but the regs were very clear on how many "accidental discharges" could be aimed at a coworker before he had to have a psych eval.

If Roggen Harrow had been mad before, he was furious now, and his voice dropped several decibels as he leaned forward, hand flat on the desk in front of him. "Fuck you, space cadet. If there's any kind of justice, he's crawled off and died somewhere." Harrow's mouth twisted over the slur, and West's hands clenched into fists. "Actually, if there was any kind of justice, the IEC would have learned from their mistakes and put the lot of you down like animals."

Gavin pushed in over West's shoulder, though he would have been in view of the vid capture without moving. "That kind of discriminatory bullshit—" He bit off his words when West touched his arm. It was a strange reversal to see the normally unflappable agent so angry.

West broke the tense silence. "So that's a no, then? No cozy lunch dates planned, where you talk about the old days and pass someone classified information?"

Harrow seemed to get that he'd crossed a line, and reined in his reply, either for the sake of professionalism or out of fear that it would come back to bite him in the ass. "No."

"Why did you flag the file, if you don't want to keep tabs on the case?" Quiet, patient—none of the things West actually was—but he had to admit it played well, trying to finesse Harrow into admitting something of use.

"I didn't flag the damn file. Get IS to pull my account activity and run it against registered terminals. Hell, I'll do it myself if someone is using my credentials. I don't care; I've got nothing to hide." As it so often did, anger gave way to something more like desperation, and Corwin could see why one side of Harrow's hair stuck up when his fingers sank into it and pulled. "You can waste your time hounding me over some computer error, but it's not going to get you anywhere because I wouldn't touch that case if someone promised me the stars. He cost me *two* partners, and my entire career. I'll never do fieldwork again."

There wasn't a lot to like in what they'd seen, but West seemed determined to carry on as though Harrow hadn't just said psys were vermin who needed to be exterminated. "For what it's worth, we've got him. D'lane's going down."

Harrow's gaze sharpened, and he finally sat back a little. "Good luck with that. D'lane's the least of your worries."

None of them were expecting it when Harrow killed the stream and left them looking at nothing.

While D'lane had dropped off the luxury tour, he hadn't dropped out of the luxury lifestyle. Vimto was a close second to Giverny in its population of the wealthy and famous, and the only surprising thing was that the field office had found him as quickly as it had. After all, Vimto and Corve shared the same set of rules: nobody on either planet ever saw anyone, unless they didn't mind being seen in return.

The IEC station reflected the planet's pretentiousness. The front lobby, with its leather chairs and thick carpeting, looked more like a country club than a police station, and Nika paused in the arched front doorway, leaning closer to whisper to West. "Can you imagine dragging a suspect in here? If they got dirt, or stars help us, blood, on the floor, someone would have a heart attack."

He snickered, trying to keep his laughter quiet. "Maybe they only have civilized crime, and everyone wipes their feet before they come in."

"If you two are finished?" Corwin's quelling glare stopped Nika's laugh, but not her grin.

"Did you wipe *your* feet, Inspector Menivie?" West asked, not bothering to hide his smile. "Don't want to get kicked out."

Euphoria enveloped him, despite the disturbing interview with Harrow. This was the end game, and while every crime solved provided a sense of accomplishment, this one went beyond the simple satisfaction of a job well done. He knew he'd placed more importance on finishing this than the rest of them, knew he had no logical reason for it. Hell, he even knew better than to hope they'd make anything stick this time. But putting D'lane away meant justice for Disby and Anaj, and in some dark, barely acknowledged part of his mind, meant his own lingering doubts and guilt over hurting Gav stood a chance of being exorcised. It wasn't right or proper to be so invested, to be happy over anything related to a string of horrific murders, but in the hidden corner he kept for himself, he didn't have to pretend.

"May I help you?" Even the standard IEC uniform looked better here. The front desk officer could have stepped off the runway of a fashion show, shirt crisply tailored and clinging in all the right places.

"Prisoner transfer." Corwin passed his badge under the scanner, and stepped back so the rest of them could run theirs as well.

"Thank you, inspectors, agents." The woman ran a finger down her screen. "Ah, Inspector Menivie, must be a busy week for you."

"I'm sorry?"

She nodded. "This is your second transfer this week. We don't usually have this much contact with fly-by teams."

The sickening swoop of fear felt like being a bird caught in a gust of wind. He suspected his face mirrored the shock on both Nika's and Gavin's. Corwin had gone still.

"I wasn't here this week," Corwin said, slowly and carefully. "And I have never picked up a transfer prisoner from Vimto."

Rather than arguing, she turned the screen around to face them. "This is your ident scan. And it clearly shows that you picked up Anders D'lane two days ago for transport to Rogena for trial."

"Fuck. Fuck, fuck, fuck." West didn't remember stepping close enough to grab Corwin's arm.

"That wasn't me."

The desk officer's eyes widened, but she recovered quickly, hitting her comm badge. "I need Director Tane at the front desk immediately."

The director's office was easily as luxurious as the lobby. West pulled out one of the chairs grouped around a conference table made of some exotic wood, knee bumping the intricately carved leg as he sat down. Rubbing absently at the tender spot, he turned to find Corwin pacing behind them.

At the head of the table, Director Tane steepled his fingers. "We had no reason to doubt the authenticity of Inspector Menivie's identification."

"We're not questioning that, sir," Nika said. "Our only concern now is locating D'lane."

"But *I* need to question how someone was able to use your badge to enter a secured facility and leave with a murder suspect. This is a huge security breach, and it needs to be reported immediately to Rogena." Tane pulled his notebook closer, grim faced. "If the system has been hacked . . ." He trailed off.

Corwin pivoted at the end of the table and rested his hands on the back of an empty chair. "If it's been hacked, if someone out there has access to sufficient amounts of DNA needed to create badges, the system will need to go into a fail-safe mode. It's your job to report the leak, and find out if it's tied to the failure of your video surveillance equipment to record who walked out of here with our suspect. Ours is to find D'lane. And whoever took him."

"Thank you for informing me of my duties, *Inspector*."

"Someone hired by his family," West interrupted, hoping to derail the conversation and save Corwin's job. The shrug he gave when Tane turned a scowl in his direction couldn't have looked more nonplussed, or been more fake. "Who else would have the money and the power to pull off something like this? More importantly, who else would want to?"

"While I can understand you jumping to that conclusion, Agent Tavera, I'd thank you to keep it in this room," Tane snapped, with the air of a man who knew something was about to come down on him like a shuttle with a dead flight system. "The D'lane name is respected here on Vimto, and I am not willing to have the entire family dragged through the mud because of one mistake."

Corwin smiled thinly. "Never fear, Director, the family has proven themselves more than capable of ruining their own reputations. Nothing Agent Tavera could say or do is going to affect that one way or the other."

The intercom buzzed before Tane could reply, and given the particular shade of maroon coloring the director's face, West had to think that it was excellent timing. With everything else going on, having the man drop dead at their feet from an aneurism wasn't going to look good on anyone's record.

"Director, I was told you needed to see me." The man in the doorway was young, face damp with sweat, uniform jacket over his arm rather than on. "I got back as quickly as I could."

Tane pointed at Corwin, dispensing with any pleasantries. "Do you recognize this man?"

"No, sir. Should I?"

"You released a prisoner to him two days ago. Anders D'lane, being held on a murder charge."

The kid's face paled, and West felt a twinge of sympathy. Apparently Director Tane was as much of a dick to underlings as he was to fellow IEC officers. "I released D'lane to an Inspector Menivie." To the young officer's credit, the statement didn't squeak too much.

"Except that *this* is Inspector Menivie. Which leaves us with the question of exactly who you turned an accused murderer over to."

"I—"

"It's not your fault." Corwin's interruption earned an ugly glare from Tane. "This person had an exact replica of my badge. You wouldn't have had any reason to suspect a problem. Can you please give us a description of the man who picked up Anders D'lane two days ago?"

West managed to suppress his desire to cheer, but made a mental note to devise some sort of a suitable reward later. Apparently Corwin was becoming more comfortable with the rescuing hero role, and that deserved encouragement.

"About his height," the officer nodded toward West. "Glasses, short hair, lightish brown, no distinguishing facial features. Standard-issue uniform."

"Shit." Gavin shared a glance with him, eyes wide. "We need to get back to the ship."

Corwin was a step ahead of them, voice frosted with propriety. "Thank you, Director Tane. We're done here. We can continue our investigation on board the *Vigilance*. I'm sure you'll need to contact Rogena."

West followed the jerk of Corwin's chin toward the door without thinking much about it, only wondering once he reached the hall when Corwin had developed such an utter disregard for the chain of command. Much as he wanted to take credit, he wasn't sure it would prove helpful during their inevitable court martial hearings.

West leaned over Nika's shoulder as she hunched forward in her chair, shoving a hand through her hair. "Okay, I've got the alert set with the port authorities for Disby and D'lane. If they're not already off-world—well, or dead—this should make sure they stay planetside."

"I'd be comforted by that except for the fact that Disby bypassed IEC security protocols with apparent ease. The port authority won't be much of a challenge in comparison." Corwin's expression, grim since leaving the Vimto office, finally cracked, revealing resignation. "At this point, they're long since in the black. They had too much of a jump on us."

West groaned. "Way to help morale. Didn't your mother ever tell you that if you don't have something nice to say, you shouldn't say anything at all?"

"I believe crushing out joy like an errant ember was more her style."

"Ah." West made no attempt to hide his smirk. "So you come by it naturally. Good to know." He was halfway through the list of businesses adjacent to the station with surveillance capabilities when the priority alert rang through on all their notebooks at once.

"Well, it's about damn time. Put it on the screen," Corwin said.

DNA material obtained from the crime scene identified by case number L-6TR7-004 does not match that of D'lane, Anders. Repeat, there is no confirmed DNA match between suspect and material collected at the crime scene.

West was fairly certain someone had mysteriously sucked all the oxygen from the room. It was the only thing that could account for the rush of dizziness.

Verify receipt of this notification, y/n flashed across the screen, and he forced his numb fingers to move, beating Corwin by a second. *Yyyyyyyyyyyyy* scrolled, and he blinked, lifting his hand.

"That's not—"

"It can't—"

Nika's words collided with his, and they both fell silent, his own breathing overly loud to his ears.

"That was not at all what I expected to happen."

West let a slightly off-kilter laugh bubble up at Corwin's words. "That has to be the understatement of the year. Seriously? Not what you *expected*?" The laughter died as suddenly as it started, and he swallowed hard. "Sorry, not funny."

Nika recovered first, pulling up the report attached to the message. "Okay, this just doesn't seem possible," she said without looking up. "The discrepancy is so damn close that I'm surprised they even caught it. It had to have been bumped up to a whole extra level of scrutiny beyond what any normal investigation would entail, which would explain why it took so long." She scowled, rubbing at her forehead. "I don't even recognize the test they ran."

"Do you think D'lane managed to switch out the results somehow?"

Nika glanced up at Corwin and shook her head. "I doubt it. There's a database for all Human/Trakoran hybrids, and that's what provided that first match. I guess there could've been some degradation of the sample, maybe it was mishandled or something, but this is still close enough to be a clone."

"Any way it could've been modified?"

She shook her head again, and West sighed. He hadn't really thought so. "They considered that as well. There's no way D'lane could have left modified DNA at the scene, unless the evidence was planted. If he even wanted to mislead us, which I don't think he would. It's an ego thing. He'd want us to know it was him, that he didn't care about getting caught. In the previous cases that Disby and his team investigated, there was no DNA evidence. It's why the charges fell apart and D'lane walked—Harrow's partner tried to fabricate physical evidence."

There was no refuting that. Equally impossible to get past was the fact that the only reason Disby would have snatched D'lane was revenge, and while he understood the motive, he couldn't condone it.

They all must have been half-expecting the next message alert. He saw only resignation on Corwin's face, and neither Nika nor Gavin reacted outside of nearly identical winces. Since no one else moved, he tapped the Accept button on his notebook. "Why hello again, Chief Inspector."

"It's not often I speak to the crew on a fly-by as much as I seem to be speaking to you. I don't find that I'm particularly enjoying the opportunity."

Corwin sighed. "You've seen the DNA report."

Ning nodded shortly. "I have. And I'm questioning, as I'm sure you are, the likelihood of two people with that particular combination of genetic material turning out to be murderers. It's not odds that I would ever bet on."

"So you think it's D'lane?" There was no denying the rush of hope.

"That's not what I said. I'm merely noting that if I were a gambler, those aren't odds that I would find acceptable."

Corwin suddenly straightened up. "Slipstream Labs." It wasn't a shout, but it was close. "Their genetics division had a break-in, the field office thought we were there for that."

"Slipstream? As in, holds the exclusive patent on Human/Trakoran gene splicing, and is directly responsible for the continuation of the Ylendrian imperial line?" Ning swung away from the screen for almost a full minute, then turned back with a decidedly grim smile. "Interestingly enough, that break-in involved their fertility lab. It seems that Anders D'lane had thirteen identical siblings, all frozen. He has twelve now."

West gnawed at his lower lip, eyes closed. The pieces were there, hidden in a swirling cloud of black feathers, and if he could just get a clear look, they would fall into a recognizable pattern . . .

But Ning interrupted him. "So that's one answer. Unfortunately, it only creates more questions. Did D'lane leave false DNA evidence at the crime scene? If so, why? And was he also able to obtain genetic material from you, Inspector Menivie, and replicate your badge?"

"As far as I'm aware, I was conceived without laboratory assistance." The words were joking, but Corwin's voice was tight with tension, enough that West turned to look, suddenly uneasy.

Ning fixed a disconcertingly intense stare on Corwin. "Is there some other way he would have been able to obtain it? And before you answer that, I'm going to remind you of my expectations from officers. Full disclosure, no exceptions."

From where he sat, he saw Corwin swallow, and suddenly one piece of the puzzle dropped into place, incredibly obvious now.

"It wasn't D'lane," Corwin said, voice steady. "It was Christeven Disby."

"As in former agent Disby?"

"Yes. I contacted Disby after finding out about his connection to D'lane, and arranged to meet him. During that meeting, he got a sample of my DNA."

Nika moved to stand next to her partner before he had finished speaking. "It was a team decision. Corwin didn't make it on his own, despite him trying to take the blame."

"I'm sure there's quite enough blame to go around, Inspector Santivan. However, he *is* the senior officer, and as such, I hold him to a higher standard of behavior than has been demonstrated. I'm deeply disappointed in all of you." Ning's lips thinned. "While you may not have directly violated any orders, you've gone against procedure, knowing full well I wouldn't condone your actions. And now we're all going to pay for those decisions."

"Santivan, stand down." Corwin's steady gaze never left Ning's. "As senior officer, I accept full responsibility. I'm ready to tender my resignation."

"The fuck you will!" West surged to his feet, ignoring Corwin's glare.

Ning jabbed a finger at him. "Be quiet." Once West slumped back into his chair, the finger zoned in on Corwin. "And *you*. Don't you think you've been enough of an idiot? I don't need martyrdom, I need the case solved. This little . . . revelation stays between us for now. D'lane needs to be found. I'm assuming your theory is that Disby has him, and if that's the case, his life isn't going to be worth much, assuming he's not dead already."

Corwin nodded. "That's our take on it. And as long as we're sharing career-ending revelations, you should know that Disby has access to the IEC database. We think he may have hacked the log-in of his former colleague. He's getting information as fast as we are, if not faster."

"I would like to pretend I didn't hear that." Ning's thin-lipped smile showed far too many teeth, an unsettling Trakoran trait. "But that would make me an idiot as well. I'll deal with things at this end. Find D'lane. Find Disby. I expect to hear back from you within the next thirty hours." Ning leveled a pointed look at each of them. "Don't disappoint me again."

CHAPTER  22

West found he enjoyed undercover work, right up to the point where it made him feel bad. Active agents weren't generally permitted on undercover operations. The ethics involved in Reading suspects while waiting for them to incriminate themselves were hinky at best. He didn't like the lying involved, or the potential accusations of entrapment, but he was better than most at using what he picked up by accident to play his part, adapting his behavior to inspire confidence.

He felt a little crippled without that fallback, but vidlink wasn't equipped with a handy channel for Empaths, and Disby would have suspected him of Reading anyway. If the call went through at all.

"Here goes nothing," he muttered, gesturing for Nika to be ready, and sent the request through to the last address Disby had used to contact him. He wasn't using his IEC comm credentials, and he hoped that would convince Disby to answer. Nika nodded, dropping her eyes to the console. Stationed safely out of the narrow vid-capture field, she was completely silent, and he didn't realize he'd been mimicking her until Disby's feed flickered to life.

"Agent Tavera? I wasn't expecting to hear from you again." The implication that they'd abandoned the case was there, but Disby's voice was otherwise mild.

"I didn't want to leave things as they were. You . . . you deserve to know what's going on." The hesitation was something he'd practiced— just enough to imply that he was acting on his own, possibly against the wishes of the rest of the team. He couldn't tell from Disby's expression if it was working or not. "We got D'lane. He's in custody on Vimto."

Disby's head lowered, face hidden by fingers squeezed tightly together, and West tried not to flinch. If there was any chance D'lane wasn't with Disby, what he was doing was unforgivable.

"He'll finally pay for what he did." Something about the singular force of the words struck him as odd, but when Disby glanced up again, there seemed to be more sanity there than the day they'd met. "When you get to him . . . make him say it. Make him say, 'I killed Anajin Tsan.' I need someone else to know what he did." Disby turned his head, voice soft. "I can't fail her again."

West was very conscious of Nika in the room when he spoke, and hoped she'd write it off as him playing Disby, rather than sharing anything real. "That's why I wanted to tell you. I know what it's like to carry that guilt around. To feel like you weren't good enough to keep your partner safe." He didn't even realize he'd looked away until he flicked his gaze back to the screen and found Disby watching him.

"You can never get out from under it. It's a weight that pushes you down a little more every day, and nothing touches it." In contrast to the words themselves, Disby's voice held no emotion. "I thought I'd be okay once the drugs started working, but nothing works. I think it's just made everything worse. All I can hear anymore is her begging. Everyone looks like her, for a second, and then all I can see is blood."

As close as West had come to losing himself, he had no illusions about his own triggers. Thinking he'd lost Gavin had pushed him over the edge. Rashium Sidustra might have chased him around his own head, but once the threat was gone, it was fear of his own actions that had kept him pacing that room. He wasn't sure he could make himself say the words, now that they were caught in his throat. "You can't use what happened as an excuse to lock yourself away."

Disby shook his head, face eerily serene. "Everyone would be better off, I assure you. If I wanted a pep talk about rejoining the world as a productive citizen, I could make an appointment with one of the headcases at the clinic. They come free with the pills, you know."

West almost smiled, except for the directionless anger that burned through him. It was a mistake to glance at Nika, silent, hidden, and watching him with the same careful expression he'd seen her adopt around Corwin. She didn't think any of this was for Disby's benefit, but he could Read her easily enough to tell that she'd never call him on it. He turned his attention back to Disby, hoping the lapse had looked like a man struggling to find the right words, rather than one struggling not to let them go in front of a coworker.

What he said next was something he should have said to Gavin, an apology and understanding that was long overdue. Instead, he leaned forward, as though proximity to the vid screen would help the words sink in with Disby. "The 'verse can do just fine without either of us, probably. If you hide from it forever, from what you did, from how you think you failed her, you'll never face the consequences. And that's what we owe them. Face the music. Realize that the injury was theirs. Hers. The cost was theirs. Refusing to come out of your own pain turns it into something that's about you, and that's nothing but selfish bullshit. We hurt people we love. But the hurt was theirs to heal from, and keeping it for ourselves doesn't make it better for them."

"I can't make it better for her, Tavera. She's dead." The edge to Disby's voice could have been anything, and he hated that he didn't know for sure. His best guess, and the most far-fetched, was revelation.

"Then when this is over, maybe you need to let her *be* dead. Stop forcing her to haunt you."

Disby didn't answer, fingers tapping against each other in a complex pattern he couldn't follow.

West was a lot of things, including willfully ignorant when it came to knowing when to leave off. Gavin was used to it, Corwin guarded against it, and Nika pushed back. Disby's hands tangled and untangled more rapidly than ever, and then Disby pushed back too.

"If you really understood, you'd know that I'm the ghost, not her. What haunts me is the IEC letting the death of a good agent go unpunished because she believed that justice was something the Empire owed everyone. Anders D'lane looking me in the face and telling me he killed dozens of people, and then walking out the door because he had so much money that their lives didn't matter." Disby's voice rose, and West flinched back, almost able to imagine what the outburst would feel like. "I've tried to show them ever since, but nobody listens. Nobody cares." Disby's whisper-whine as it fell again sounded familiar, but he didn't know why. "Everyone knows ghosts linger because of unfinished business. I'm just waiting to finish mine." This time it was Disby who looked off to the side of the camera. "All the birds are coming home to roost."

West shuddered inwardly at the echo of his Reads. "Should I contact you again?"

Disby turned his face back toward the screen, shaking his head. "No. There's no need. I've got everything I need to lay the ghost to rest. Good-bye, Agent Tavera."

"Disby." West didn't need to Read him to know the words were a confession of one kind or another, but he couldn't tell which. "Disby!" He leaned in closer, as though he could have some effect on the world on the other side of the screen. "Don't do anything."

Disby shrugged, a smile that seemed out of place blooming on his lips, then fading a second later. "I'm not going to do anything. I'm crazy, not stupid. There's no revenge in killing myself."

"Is there enough revenge in watching D'lane go to prison?" It was too close to admitting it was all a ruse, that he knew Disby had D'lane, and Disby gave him a second look, mouth going flat.

"No. But you should have known that all along."

For the second time this week, he was left staring at a blank screen, and it took Nika's gentle touch on his shoulder before he remembered to move.

"That was good. I've got a pinpoint lock on the signal, and I was able to follow it back through the relay points to his ship. He's only an hour away, and he doesn't seem to be moving. Corwin's alerted planetary forces in the area, but Disby's in the drift between Kasra and Dallon. Neither of them has a space force, and the closest field office is the outpost on Station 39. A full cycle out."

West scrubbed a hand over his face. "Well, that's just a perfect clusterfuck, isn't it?"

"Are you okay?"

She hadn't taken her hand away from his shoulder, and truth be told, he was actually glad. At this point, he was used to her presence, enough that between his own shields and the technique Corwin had taught him, she was more of a touchstone than a constant source of guilt and accidental emotions. As his hands dropped from his face, he brushed her fingers.

"Yeah." He couldn't feel Corwin nearby, but he lowered his voice anyway. "Just worried that if we don't find D'lane alive, Corwin's career is going to take a hit." He made a face, his laughter bitter. "I think if I was a better person, I'd just be worried that we won't find D'lane alive. And I don't know what to do about Disby."

"Probably." She snorted, sliding her hand away, but pausing to pat the top of his head. "But I have to admit that I leave it to Corwin to draw a lot of the lines for 'upright and moral.' It may be my job to find D'lane if Disby's kidnapped him, but that doesn't change the fact that he's a violent criminal who bought his freedom. I've got half a mind to make sure he hits me when we find him, just so we can charge him with something as concrete as assaulting an officer."

He stood, but it only gave the unease a chance to travel down his spine. "In space, no one can hear you plotting entrapment, Inspector."

In the common area, Corwin and Gavin were spread out, using the giant monitor there to pull up star charts, wrangle communications, and reset the nav system to follow the surveillance lock Nika had managed to pin to Disby's ident beacon.

Gavin glanced over as West rounded the coffee table and sat down next to him. Their eyes met for a second, before he looked at the screen instead. They'd been watching the conversation, of course. Down in the bottom corner, an empty black window hovered, and West made a face.

Gavin's arm settled over his shoulders, and he leaned into the contact. "I know you don't believe me yet, but we're good, dude. I promise."

"I kind of have to believe you, don't I? You're my partner." He inclined his head toward the dead window, fingers folding together in a careful temple of digits. "This isn't going to be pretty."

Gavin's look of disgust was answer enough, but that didn't mean it was the only one. "All of it's a mess. D'lane's a Pusher; Disby's taking the psy-suppressants, but his Talent mysteriously still works; and you're going to walk into it. I don't like it."

"Got your gun?"

Gavin nodded, patting the standard-issue IEC Mattox blaster, the motion ending their not-quite hug. Without looking, without reaching for it at all, he felt Corwin relax, and tried to hide a truly inappropriate smile. Corwin wasn't jealous, just worried that they were still fighting, and about to head into a crime in progress.

Gavin caught the stifled smile, but misinterpreted the reason. "I swear to the stars, West, if you make one joke about the size of my gun,

I'll let slip that you're the one who taught Ning's kids how to forge the chief's signature."

West rose from the couch, his eyes following Corwin as the inspector tried to coordinate the help of all the people who were going to arrive too late to do any good. He turned back to Gavin, but couldn't manage a smile. "I was just thinking maybe a second gun couldn't hurt."

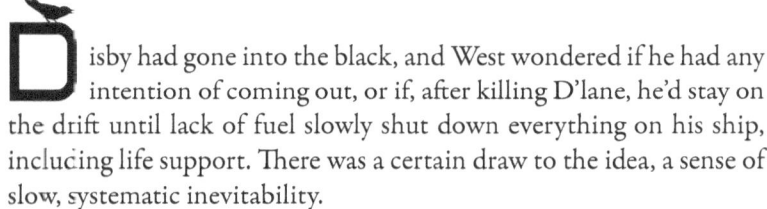

CHAPTER 23

Disby had gone into the black, and West wondered if he had any intention of coming out, or if, after killing D'lane, he'd stay on the drift until lack of fuel slowly shut down everything on his ship, including life support. There was a certain draw to the idea, a sense of slow, systematic inevitability.

"There it is." Nika's terse voice interrupted his morbid musings.

The ship was on the small side, an older-model pleasure yacht Disby hadn't bothered to register to a home port, and with any luck, it would have only the standard accoutrements. Even if it was armed, the *Vigilance* could take it in a firefight, but that wouldn't be the first choice.

"He's almost completely powered down. If we hadn't gotten that trace, chances are we could have flown right past and never even noticed him." Corwin sounded affronted by the thought. "Scans show no obvious weaponry and two life forms." He gestured at the data field. "Either he's got someone else on board with him, or D'lane's still alive."

"That just means the ship itself isn't armed. He's ex-IEC and scans don't pick up blasters." Gavin studied the scan results, frowning. "He could be armed to the teeth with hand-to-hand weapons."

"Not to mention his brain," West muttered.

Corwin ignored him. "We'll take the same safeguards we would in any hostage situation."

"Including an awareness that we're dealing with an already powerful psy who by rights shouldn't be able to access his Talent anymore, but instead is using it in ways I've never even seen." West might be the only one of them not carrying a gun into this fight, but he knew too well that the mind was a weapon, and an Active's mind, trained up by PsyAc, was more destructive than a blaster if it needed to be. His team walked in, his team walked out. There was no other acceptable option, and he refused to have his words discounted.

Apparently he'd sounded sharper than he intended, because Corwin half turned to give him a considering look. "Thank you. Point taken. I still wish you'd carry a gun."

Gavin was the one to shut that idea down. "I'm his gun, in a situation like this. There's the potential for out-and-out psionic battle, and if that's a known factor, Actives don't go in armed with a physical weapon that could be turned back on them."

"It just doesn't seem right to take a brain to a gunfight."

West shrugged, using the motion to hide the nervous roll of his shoulders. "It's better than taking a gun to a brain fight, trust me."

The low thrum of the tractor net powering on sent vibrations through his feet, straight to his head, and he pressed the heels of his hands against his eyes, trying to clear his mind. Walking in with even the smallest degree of fear or apprehension would be stupid. If Disby didn't capitalize on it, D'lane would.

Corwin bumped up against West. *"You okay?"*

He caught himself, but not before nodding. *"Yeah. I'd feel better if I had a stronger grasp of your blocking skills, though. Don't know what we're walking into."*

"Not my fault you're too soft to devote ten years to intense religious training." The flash of wry humor that personified Corwin in his mind provided more reassurance than any words ever could.

"Okay, we're good." Nika was all calm competence as she stood up. "Docking tunnel's secured at the other end so we don't get any surprises. Shall we?"

West's body armor, light and unobtrusive as technology could make it, still had him sweating by the time they reached the end of the tunnel, and he shifted uncomfortably while Nika keyed in the release code for the door. The rush of air exchange as the hatch slid open was a welcome, if short-lived, relief.

The hold had been used for food storage, at least when the ship still served as a toy of the rich, oversized coolers lining three of the four walls. He gave them an uneasy glance as they stepped off the tunnel and onto the deck, weapons drawn. It wasn't that he really thought D'lane was in one of them, just that the possibility existed.

Soft lighting came up as they slipped into the empty corridor, illuminating five or so meters ahead of them and switching off as they passed. The first doorway led to a fully equipped galley, nearly twice the size of the one on the *Vigilance*. The only sign of life was a teetering stack of dirty dishes on the table. Personal quarters next—four in all, stripped of furnishings, no evidence that they had been occupied in the recent past. So far there weren't any surprises, no architecture that differed from the schematic Corwin had pulled up for them to study.

"They're in the viewing lounge." The fear that his certainty came from some connection with Disby made his stomach roll. That path led only to madness, and he'd managed that quite well on his own.

Corwin nodded silently, and West felt a flash of gratitude at being believed without question. In a less dangerous situation, gloating might have ensued. Now he just wanted this over with. Gavin stayed a step ahead of him, weapon drawn and all business.

The lounge bled into the black, the black bled into the lounge, and stepping into the room felt like falling into the stars. Tearing his eyes away from the gently curving windows with their unobstructed view was harder than it should have been, even when he knew Disby was there.

Disby and D'lane could have been chatting like old friends, sitting across from each other, but Disby's eyes were closed, and he wasn't saying a word. D'lane was more than making up for it, a quiet litany unbroken by their arrival:

"I killed Anajin Tsan. I killed Anajin Tsan. I killed Anajin Tsan." The confession didn't change at all in tone, and D'lane's eyes were fixed on Disby, unseeing and dry.

There was no one home in D'lane's gaze, but West hadn't expected that there would be. Disby, hands folded together, was seated in a casual slump on the other couch, every bit as gone. That didn't stop West from pulling up Corwin's blocking technique.

"So how do we do this? What are we even required to do?" Nika approached first, Corwin behind her, noticeably uncomfortable. West couldn't tell if it was Disby or D'lane projecting, but with Corwin's particular slant on Reads, he could only imagine how discomfiting it would be, feeling the joy of someone else's torture.

Gavin's mouth was tight over rules he didn't want to abide by, so West spared him having to say them out loud.

"PsyAc policy says that as a trained Active, my ethical duty is to the victim of a crime. In situations where another Active has engaged a victim like this, I have to try to save the victim."

"So you'll just wander into D'lane's head, tell Disby his brain is under arrest, and pull D'lane—" Corwin glanced at the wreck on the couch, still in the midst of his endless declaration of guilt. "Pull whatever's left of D'lane out? That sounds like a great plan."

Gavin snorted, but West quelled it with a pointed stare, Gavin's jaw tightening before he looked away.

"It's not an abstract plan, Corwin. It's my duty as a field agent. And the longer I argue with you, the less likely I am to find anything in there to rescue." He grabbed Gavin and led the way to one of the couches, taking a careful seat next to D'lane, but he didn't let go, holding tight to home and remembering what he'd need to seek out later.

"Time limit, or check-in?" Gavin engaged the safety on his blast gun before holstering it.

"Neither."

"No. I won't do that. You've got half an hour, and then I pull your ass out, no matter what's going on."

West looked at D'lane, who couldn't stop talking, then across the shallow, sunken entertaining area to Disby's unaffected face. "I don't know what I'm going to find in there. I need to pull Disby out, if I can. He has to be held accountable." He made eye contact with Gavin. "And I can't leave someone locked inside themselves."

"He's a killer. You don't owe him anything."

"So's D'lane. My duty is to victims. To all the people D'lane hurt, *and* the people Disby hurt. Can you tell me Disby's life hasn't been irrevocably changed by violence someone else caused?" He squeezed Gavin's arm, harder than he needed to as his fingers encountered the scars there. "This is what I *do*."

Gavin's sigh was abrupt: resignation in the form of breath. "And I stand here and remember that you're not my best friend, you're my partner, and this is what *I* do. Just be careful. Don't get lost."

Corwin, farthest away behind Gavin and Nika, scowled at him. He closed his eyes, Corwin's frustration the last thing he saw before he let go of Gavin's arm and fell back into the couch, downdowndown into the cracks between the cushions. Into the litany of D'lane's words, and out the other side, into a sky made of claws that ripped him apart bit by tiny bit.

He was on his hands and knees in the sharp gravel when he came back to himself, or at least when he managed to pull enough of "himself" together to constitute his own separate consciousness. The gravel was disturbed, he was disturbed, and he wanted to hunch down, make himself a tiny thing to hide from the claws and the sky and the memory of how this went.

He knew the path, and most of the blood on the gravel wasn't his. The birdsong, a faint scattering of noise in the distance, seemed incongruous with the darkened sky. Drawing a deep and totally unnecessary breath, West forced himself to take a step down the trail, following the blood and the tracks of someone else's uneven travels. The trees overhead seemed to stretch forever, and he tried not to look too closely at the places where the branches were hands, flexing and grasping in the wind he was sure must be someone else's breathing.

He was going to have to find his way out of the forest when this was all said and done, and he wasn't sure the path would look the same coming the other way. He stopped walking, and the birds seemed louder for a second as he tried to memorize his surroundings—loud enough to distract him. Birds would eat any crumbs, but he could leave something else, something birds wouldn't want. Sliding a hand into his pocket, he pulled out his favorite mug, *Best Psychic in the 'Verse* branded across the front, and set it down gently in the middle of the path. He walked around it a couple times, getting the feel for it, remembering how it rested in his hand. When he was sure he could recognize it on the way back, he left it behind and kept walking, hoping that if he didn't look, the birds wouldn't notice it was there.

Each step felt heavy, but the sensation of being watched wasn't strong, and this time there was no one chasing him. It was easy to see the places where people had fought before he'd gotten here, the ground kicked up and smeared with blood that shouldn't have been so bright red. It was the only color in the landscape at all, spilling like scarlet paint across the rocks as he moved past.

There was grass ahead, dry and dead, but a change from the gravel and trees at any rate. Something hopped among the stalks—tiny dark shapes arrowing back and forth, their sounds too close to words for West's comfort. Beyond them was a door jutting out of the ground, and as much as he didn't want to walk through the grass and the birds to get there, he went anyway.

He reached out to touch the lock plate, not expecting it to open and surprised when it did. The birds stopped making noise behind him, and he flinched through the door as their wings beat at his back, shoving it closed behind him to get away. The force sent it tipping back, and it fell, shattering into shards of honeyed glass that struck little scratches in his clothes and skin, leaving him trapped in a room with no way back.

It went against everything Corwin believed to stand helplessly by while a team member faced any sort of danger alone. He tried to tell himself that his feelings would be the same if it were Nika, or even Gavin, but the truth was that if it were either of them, he could simply shoot someone. If that didn't solve the problem outright, at least it would help.

West's voice was a quiet mumble, Gavin's an occasional counterpoint, but he left it as background noise, keeping all his attention on Disby, and peripherally, D'lane. He didn't intend to shoot either of them, but he had no intention of being caught by surprise, either. Across the lounge, Nika mirrored him, blaster trained and at the ready.

Except for the slow rise and fall of Disby's chest and the jerky movement of his eyes beneath the lids, he remained still and silent. D'lane, however, appeared more agitated now, low guttural sounds obscuring his words as tremors rolled through his body. Corwin couldn't feel anything from either of them, which made D'lane's repetitious confession even more disconcerting.

"I killed Anajin Tsan." D'lane's head rolled against the back of the couch, voice rising and falling in no discernible pattern. "I killed Anajin Tsan. I killed Anajin Tsan. I killed Anajin Tsan."

There was no way to block the broken confession, and it played over and over and over until he wanted nothing more than to put his hands over his ears. Nika raised an eyebrow, but he grimaced, shaking his head.

"West, no!"

That was loud enough to capture both their attentions. Corwin lowered his blaster, the crazy and totally inappropriate thought jumping into his head that while there *had* been occasions when he'd been tempted to shoot West, this was hardly the best time.

"Don't you fucking dare." Gavin's hands were braced on either side of West's face, fingers resting behind West's ears. Corwin didn't need to glance to the side to know that Nika was watching as Gavin's fingers tightened, voice dropping to that careful, inflectionless tone they'd heard on Bodum. "Westley, eat the cosmic egg."

Nothing happened. There was no boneless slump, no indication that the deeply ingrained fail-safe phrase had been heard at all. Gavin repeated it twice, with the same lack of success.

He looked up, the fear in his voice overriding the anger, gaze jumping around the room until he caught Corwin's. "He went in too deep."

"What do you mean, too deep?" Corwin was already dropping shields he'd held rigidly in place since setting foot on the ship, reaching out for West. Nothing. Not the nothing of coming up against the carefully constructed walls he'd tried to teach West how to build. Just . . . nothing.

Gavin glared up at him from his crouch in front of West, and West slumped forward against Gavin's shoulder. "Too deep, as in he followed D'lane down to where I can't reach him. He's unconscious. I can't Ground him when he's unconscious. The fail-safe phrase only works if he can hear it." Gavin pushed West back onto the couch, voice betraying little of his visible panic.

Corwin knelt next to them, automatically reaching for West's neck, fingers against the pulse point. Rapid but steady, and he leaned back on his heels, relieved. "Isn't there something else you're trained for? Some other way to get him out?"

"He's trained to seek me as an anchor. There are phrases I can use to control and guide him, while he's still able to recognize the world outside his Read. If he's under so far that he can't hear me, the only thing that will bring him out is the end of the Read, or another Active connecting with him and pulling him back."

Corwin moved from the floor to the couch, and pressed his leg against West's, using the physical contact to strengthen his reach. Before, the sense of nothing had been worrisome, but now Gavin's fear made more sense, and his own grew. The closest analogy he could find for this void was his voice echoing in an empty room. West wasn't shielded. West was *gone*.

"What now?" he asked, forcing his voice to stay even.

Gavin's hands twisted restlessly in the fabric of West's shirt, eyes following the movement. "The last time this happened, he spent months in a PsyAc medical facility, in a coma."

Corwin exhaled explosively. West had hinted at it, but he hadn't wanted to put all the pieces together. "Right. And since that's not an acceptable solution, what are our other options?"

"I don't know. He's not supposed to do this. We're not supposed to be hunting murderers through their own heads, but West can never just back down. They didn't cover this at the academy, at least not in my classes." Gavin snarled, one hand moving from West's shirt to his hand, thumb rubbing over the palm. "I can toss out guesses, but none of them are gonna help." He shrugged, shoulders sagging. "I need another Active."

"The nearest team is a full cycle away." Corwin's lips felt numb, the words dragged out of him. "And there's no guarantee they have a psy agent." A particularly loud shriek from D'lane made him flinch. In contrast, West was silent, face slack and expressionless. Corwin didn't enjoy watching West during Reads, but this was much worse.

Gavin nodded, staring somewhere over his shoulder. "Yeah. I know. I could try to stop his heart, but—"

"He could die," Corwin finished. The silence dragged for several long seconds; even D'lane's mutterings faded. Corwin didn't remember planning to speak, had no idea what he was going to say until he was saying it. "I'll try." Gavin's head jerked up, and he could feel Nika's gaze boring a hole in his back, but he kept going. "I'm not making any promises, but I'll try to get him back."

"How— No. You're not a trained Active. If it's knocked West this badly, you can't possibly handle it, especially if you're just a low-level receiver. You've got no Ground to guide you, no way to get out, and no guarantee you'll even be able to recognize your own thoughts once you get sucked in. No."

D'lane's voice fell to a soft patter, and Corwin glanced sideways again, to the empty shell that could barely contain West on a normal day. When he looked back to Gavin, he made sure their eyes met, that his voice was steady. "We don't have time for me to prove my credentials, so I'm asking you to believe me. I spent a decade of my life learning my Talent, and how to keep myself safe with and from it. I can find West."

It turned out that his secrets were easier to give up than he'd ever imagined. Gavin stared hard at him for too long, seconds tripping by with West still gone, maybe even losing ground while they waited. He was surprised when Gavin finally nodded.

"I trust you. I don't need to know. Doesn't matter how small the chance is. If you think you have one, do it." Gavin's gaze never left West. "Please. I'll help you if you think I can."

Corwin shook his head. "You can't." It was easier to tune out Gavin than it was to push that repetitious voice into the background, and he half considered asking Nika to gag D'lane. Instead, he drew in a deep breath, held it, and let it out slowly, centering himself as he drew upon every bit of training he'd so resolutely hidden away over the years. The wall went back up. He couldn't take a chance on being distracted by any joy Disby was getting out of this fucked-up debacle when he went hunting, so this time, he built the wall wider, pulling in memories of West. The annoying, the intriguing, the painful, and most of all the joyful. Anything that meant West. Training, societal norms, everything he'd grown up with and rejected had required that any psy contact be between bonded couples for this very reason. Only a bond truly allowed someone to accept the whole person, or so the rhetoric went.

"For what should be fairly obvious reasons, I'm going to follow West and not D'lane," he said aloud, as much for his own benefit as Gavin's and Nika's. "I know you can't act as a Ground for me, but if you could keep an eye on my vitals, I'd appreciate it."

"And if you quit breathing? Or your heart happens to stop?"

He smiled. "You hadn't heard, Agent Hale? I don't have one." He was still smiling when he leaned over to kiss West, projecting every bit of happiness they'd ever shared into the warm brush of lips. The jolt of pleasure was half-real, half-remembered, and he closed his eyes, letting it pull him under. He'd never know if it was the physical touch or the flood of *happy* and *you* that he sent through the touch that found West, and later he wouldn't care. It was enough that it let him glimpse West's smiling face, feel the tug of a hand in his.

Down, so far down he didn't know if he was falling or climbing or flying until he hit bottom. There was nothing of the cheerful chaos he'd felt in West's mind the first time he'd been allowed in. Then again, this wasn't West's mind, not this dark, echoing hallway filled with locked doors. Things scrabbled and screamed behind him, sometimes the knobs rattled, sometimes the metal itself bowed under an unseen force. He stubbornly kept moving forward, one dragging step after another, sensing West somewhere ahead.

CHAPTER 24

When West turned around, he was in an anonymous room for rent, the bed shoved against a wall scarred with dings and scuff marks. He didn't want to touch the bed; it was for other people, and they left so much of themselves behind.

With the door gone, there was no way out of the room. The only other access was a wide window, smeared with fingerprints and the stars knew what else. The walls looked too solid to break through, and for a second, the ceiling was made of tiles, ten by ten. He choked back a desperate cry, closed his eyes, and when he looked again, the tiles had been replaced by smoke-stained plaster, and he could breathe.

The window was his only option, but he didn't have anything to break it with. There was nothing in the room but the bed, bolted to the floor. Looking down, he realized it didn't matter. He was at least twelve floors up, and there was no balcony. Behind him, in the place where the door had been, he heard something tiny and scrabbling strike the wall from the other side. Outside the window, far down below, birds swarmed, swirling up in lazy spirals over a park.

In the middle of the park, glittering gold under light that couldn't have been a sun, someone had drawn the imperial seal in shifting piles of coins. West cupped his hands around his eyes, trying to get a better look. No, not coins, seeds. Seeds, and they were drifting, blown here and there by the fluttering wings of a hundred sparrows. They were eating his way out, and he had no way to get to them.

He turned away from the window, reaching into his pocket again, fingers closing around the cool glass ball. He'd always loved the Jacquard Towers, gleaming and impossibly tall in the Imperial City on Ylendria. His parents had taken him there as a child—the last family vacation before he had to go to PsyAc, because eight-year-olds weren't supposed to have active Talents. Eight-year-olds weren't supposed to know that their parents were afraid of them. He could remember racing to the top of the towers, the elevator going so fast it made his stomach swoop, and being buffeted back inside by the wind when the doors opened. Looking down, he'd seen the imperial palace in the distance, and then a cloud drifted by, below the observation platform. He hadn't meant to climb up on the railing, but he hadn't been tall enough to see over all of it, and being taller than the clouds wasn't something he wanted to miss. For a second, before his father's hand closed around the neck of his shirt and pulled him back, he'd wondered if the clouds would hold him. If he could fly. Instead, he'd been given a snow globe, where only the Jacquard Towers flew.

The little snow globe, swirling with an impressive amount of glitter, looked forlorn when he set it down on the bed. He'd have to remember this spot. This was a bad one, a place he'd get lost in on the way back. The miniature towers inside the glass weren't surrounded by clouds, but at least there weren't any birds in there, either. Before he could think better of it, he bit his lip and turned, making a full run at the window with his arms up over his face. He'd expected to bounce back, but instead he slipped right through, and it only took him a second to recover and throw his arms wide to embrace the wind.

He wasn't flying, but he wasn't falling, either; not until the first bird struck him, and then he was falling so fast he didn't think even the ground would stop him. He tried to angle himself some way that it wouldn't hurt, but he knew better. First contact always hurt, and this hurt worse than most. He grunted and rolled, coming up with a mouth full of dirt and trying to swat the birds away from his face.

They were eating the seal, pecking it away to hide the evidence, and while a few of them scattered as he limped into the center of it, they returned within seconds. There was no door to be found, and the hotel was gone too. West swallowed around a lump in his throat, fear and the feeling of being watched creeping along his shoulders until he squared them and looked down at his feet. This was the way, he knew it, and the birds knew it, and he had to beat them to the end. He was afraid of falling farther down, and there was no way he was going to make it out before Gavin started to worry, but he was even more afraid of being trapped here forever.

His tongue ached as he scratched the ground, a phantom remembrance, and next to nothing compared to the broken bones he could feel after his landing, even if they weren't real. They were real enough right now, and they throbbed along to the beat of someone else's heart.

It didn't take long for the birds to figure out what he was doing, and when they rose in a flapping, screeching cloud, he scratched harder, trying to make his broken body respond. He thought he'd had the right of it, *IEC* spread across the ground like a guilty billboard, but the birds were still circling, and nothing else had changed. There was no door.

West turned over, staring up at the featureless sky: bright, bright blue and empty of clues. The sky should have been safe. The sky *had* saved him, he remembered, when it had been caught up in Corwin's eyes. But the sky was an afterthought now, nothing more than a place to put the birds. One by one they folded their tiny wings, and he flipped back over, curling his hands into fists and pounding on the ground in the center of the seal. A handful of sharp beaks pierced his skin, then more and more, until all he could do was roll into a tight ball and stare at the dirt under his nose. Blood dripped down the side of his face as the sparrows attacked his ears, and when it hit the ground, the first ray of bright light shot up through it like a beacon.

So D'lane wanted blood? He could spare a little blood. Into his pocket again, but this time his fingers closed too tightly around one of the shards of glass from the hotel room. He hesitated for a second before slashing it down the length of his arm. The blood that welled up was sluggish, far less than it should have been, but it was enough. As the birds rallied for a second strike, he bled for them, and as the first one hit the back of his head, the ground opened up and swallowed him whole.

Bad transitions during a Read were normal, but this wasn't a normal Read, and he hated that it took him minutes—ages—he didn't know how long—to realize that he wasn't actually standing in a comic book store. West was standing in the middle of Christeven Disby's head, the same calling card impression he'd shown West back on Corve. Uninjured, clean, and lacking in feathered friends, granted, but he shouldn't be here, and there was something so wrong about it that he couldn't contain a cry of frustration.

When the covers on the shelf started to move, he caught it out of the corner of his eye. Of course, that was what covers did, moving as soon as someone walked near to play out scenes from the book. These were more garish than the standard comic, bright primary colors interspersed with the black and white line art from the interior. He picked a couple up, thumbing through the sample copies, and found nothing but stories he already knew. Villains with clear motives, heroes who knew what to do, insurmountable odds overcome with teamwork. His smile twitched for a second, before he remembered that he was alone here, and those odds weren't going to improve if he wasted time.

Like the hotel room, like the park, there was no visible way out. There had been a door in Disby's impression, because a person came inside to meet someone, and left again when he was done. This wasn't an impression, though, it was a trap. The covers all flickered to life again as he acknowledged that he was stuck. They weren't birds, but he was being watched all the same.

There weren't birds.

He spun back toward the racks, racing up and down the rows to inspect titles. There had to be birds here somewhere. The birds were the only constant in all the Reads, and all the places he'd been on his downward spiral into—

Hidden in the bottom corner of a rack, he saw a bird flutter, trying to escape the screen. West reached for the book, and came back with stinging fingers, almost like he'd been pecked. Ignoring it the second time, he examined the cover: A sparrow with spread wings, darting to and fro around the title. *Anajin: The Little Sparrow*. He got his fingers slashed at again as he opened the book, flipping through the pages and trying to make sense of a story he'd thought he already understood.

She wasn't little at all, Anajin, but tall and striking, even in black and white. She held a gun and kept Disby safe as they found themselves in adventures that seemed more of the "duck and run" variety than any of his and Gavin's recent cases. She was smart and a little evil, her cutting words rarely held back. He had a flash of Corwin, but Corwin couldn't be here, shouldn't be here, so he pushed that away. This was about Anajin and Disby, and how they fought the puzzle-piece man who searched for the missing heart of himself by carving it out of other people.

In the panels on his screen, the puzzle-piece man turned his blade on Anajin, and the first bloom of color spread across the page, bright red and unforgivable. She said something, but the speech bubbles above her head were empty, the words missing even when he reloaded the page. The story was there, but something was missing, and the next panel was nothing but feathers as the knife arced down again, and she burst into a flock of birds.

The entire room was something Disby had wanted him to see. Everything in it was a creation, a representation of something that Disby considered important, where everything else he'd seen so far had been murder and blood. There was no reason to be here. Except if D'lane was controlling all of this, maybe West had found himself here because Disby was trying to protect him.

He flipped back to the previous page, and in the last panel, there were now words in the speech bubble. D'lane's words, the confession Disby had told him to demand. *I killed Anajin Tsan.* The bubble didn't belong to anyone, not the puzzle-piece man, not Anajin herself, and West smudged the screen, running his thumb over them. He should have known all along, Disby'd said, but he'd thought it was a warning that D'lane needed to die. Now, he wasn't sure *what* he was supposed to know. It was all spare parts, none of them coming together, and everything felt the same.

He nearly dropped the book, but caught it tight in his hand at the last second as he stumbled back from the display racks. Everything felt the same. Everything, all the places he'd been since he'd dropped into D'lane's mind, including the comic book store he was standing in now. The store that was Disby's creation, every line of it drawn and colored by Disby's mind and memory. A place that, no matter what, D'lane never would have been able to re-create, and it felt the same to him as every Read he'd done since the first accidental brush with a dead woman on Ethris.

I killed Anajin Tsan, said the bubble on the page, and the man on his hands and knees in the panel, his face tipped up and filling the tiny rectangle. Even distorted by the crimson that dripped down from the knife in his hand, Disby's face was easy to recognize.

With shaking fingers, West turned the page again, and the birds were nowhere to be found, but Anders D'lane was kneeling in the middle of the room. He held a scalpel in one hand, blood obscuring what was left of the other. Disby stood over him, serene as he pushed his glasses up his nose. "Say it again."

"I killed Anajin Tsan."

"No, he didn't." West had kept mostly silent the whole time; PsyAc drilled it into them that they didn't want to attract attention in someone else's head, not when they were going into a hostile situation. Not when the birds might see. Disby looked up out of the screen, and West knew it wasn't a comic book anymore, not even a vid he couldn't stand to watch. It was the door he'd been looking for, and before he could think better of it, he reached into his pocket and yanked out the small stuffed hedgehog he'd slept with since he was twelve. He dropped it on the floor, not terribly surprised when it skittered away.

"You're wrong. He killed her. I *know* he killed her." Disby was paying more attention to West now, but D'lane didn't make a move to get up, his lips moving in a familiar pattern as he kept repeating his new mantra.

West shook his head, trying to beat back the fury he could feel homing in on him. "You know who killed her, Disby, and it wasn't D'lane."

"Yes it *was*." The screen of the book in West's hand cracked, but he held steady even as Disby's words battered against him. "He Pushed and Pushed, and I couldn't fight him, and . . ."

"And you hurt her." The floor under him rocked, cracking down the middle like the screen, and he pushed against it, digging in and trying to get through to the center of the maze. "You killed her."

Corwin almost ran into the wall that appeared out of nowhere, right in front of him, forcing him to choose left or right. Both directions faded into darkness no matter how hard he strained his eyes, a featureless uniform gray until it disappeared. He reached out for any sense of West, and came up blank.

At first he thought the smell of coffee was a hallucination, but there, just past the T intersection, a mug was suddenly sitting in the center of the left-hand corridor. Corwin cautiously reached for it. Filled to the brim, still warm, and when he turned it in his hands, the words *Best Psychic in the 'Verse* jumped out in a flash of neon pink.

"Only you, Tavera," he muttered, an unwilling smile tugging at his mouth. Carefully setting it back down exactly where he'd found it, he started down the left-hand corridor.

He wasn't sure when the walls began to rise, soaring over his head in a graceful arch. Soon after, the windows appeared. The first looked out on a garden, meticulously landscaped. The garden gave way to a beach, and then a cityscape and then a casino and then it was one continuous window full of images that met and fell together and apart like pieces of shattered glass in a kaleidoscope. Corwin wasn't surprised this time when the window corridor came to a three-way intersection completely made of glass. All the windows switched at once to a vision of blood—thick gobs of it spattered against the glass, dripping slowly down into a solid sheet of crimson.

When he forced himself to look away, there it was: A translucent ball rolling in a slow circle at the edge of the farthest left corridor. Inside, a miniature Jacquard Towers was surrounded by swirls and eddies of snow. It was icy to the touch, and where his fingertips met the glass, the snow melted in tiny rivulets. It wasn't the cold that made him set it back down so quickly, though. More the fear that his touch was unintentionally changing something that shouldn't be changed.

Four or five steps into the new corridor and he found himself smiling. The walls were tall, then taller, rising up into an impossibly blue expanse. The beige industrial carpet had big, cheerful swaths of color, and even as he watched, the color gained depth, became grass, green and yellow, dotted with flowers. He could feel West's presence in the riotous landscape, could almost hear West's voice in the breeze sighing through the grass, and he moved faster, scanning the pseudo-meadow anxiously.

Disappointment at the emptiness hit hard and heavy. There was no fighting the feeling that time was running short, that West was continuing to dance just out of reach and farther into danger, and he was as helpless as when he'd first started.

The five identical doors standing in a line across his path were no surprise. What *was* a surprise was the lack of a clue. He backtracked and approached the doors again, gaze locked on the ground. Nothing. He groaned, rubbing at the growing ache behind his eyes, but a faint noise made him drop his hands. At first he thought the rustling was the wind, but then it got closer. A little louder, a little closer, and when the tiny brown nose poked into view, he found himself holding his breath.

With a soft grumbling sort of growl, a hedgehog, no bigger than his outspread hand, trundled into view. Bright black eyes stared up with sharp curiosity, and Corwin swore that it grinned at him, a flash of sharp white teeth, before it continued to the second door on the right. It waited until he started to follow, watching over one prickly shoulder before disappearing into a key-shaped hole in the bottom of the door.

"A hedgehog. Not sure which of us that's meant to represent, but I intend to ask when I finally catch up with you." He grabbed the white doorknob, painted with delicate blue flowers, and pulled.

He had no expectations about what would pop up next, because really, trying to anticipate the unknowable was an exercise in futility. Having said that, opening the door and finding West's quarters on the other side caught him by surprise. More surprising still, West was sitting cross-legged in the center of the bed, hair standing up in its usual crazy tufts as he bent intently over the notebook in his lap.

"West?"

West's head jerked up, shock and pleasure forming a startling hybrid expression on his face. "What are you doing here?"

"Looking for you. Gavin can't Ground you, so I'm here to pull you out." He stepped closer to the bed, holding out a hand. "You went in too deep."

West shook his head, fingers gripping the notebook tighter. "I can't leave yet. This isn't finished."

"Then we need to finish it some other way." Both Disby and D'lane dying would hardly be the worst thing that could happen, but some superstitious twinge kept him from saying that out loud, not when he didn't know whose mind might overhear. He perched on the edge of the bed, wrapping his hand around West's bare foot, comforted by the feel of solid, warm skin. "I need you to come back with me. Please."

The crooked grin was familiar. "Do you know how hard it is to say no to you when you ask like that?"

"Then don't."

West's gaze flicked back to the notebook, and Corwin felt the tension spring into West's body. When he looked back up, a shadow of fear lurked behind the perpetual grin. "Inspector Menivie, you know it's not that easy. We can't walk away from the play before the final act."

Annoyance warred with a growing feeling of dread. "Don't play word games," he snapped. He received no response, as West's attention was focused on the screen again. Corwin leaned over, curious to see what was more fascinating than getting them both out of this nightmare dreamscape.

West jerked away with a startled grunt, dropping his hand to cover the screen and scrambling backward. Corwin barely saved himself from pitching face-first onto the bed, but in the flurry of movement, he knocked the notebook out of West's grasp, and they both froze.

A maelstrom of birds, brown feathers and blood-red eyes, swirling like a living cyclone, filled the entire screen. He couldn't look away, swallowing convulsively over the hot bile rising in his throat. No mere image, no picture of *birds*, should be able to invoke that much terror.

West recovered first, shoving the notebook under the blanket. "Time isn't time, and places aren't places, but you need to stay here and be safe, and I need to leave now," he said quietly. "For what it's worth, I'm sorry I can't go back with you. I really want to."

"Then let me come with you. We'll finish whatever it is you need to do together." He couldn't acknowledge the refusal in West's eyes, and instead he grabbed West's arm and pulled them together. The kiss was a last-ditch effort, half emotional blackmail, half invoking the link that ran between them here like an invisible rope.

The connection flared blue, an actual physical thing in this in-between place, and suddenly it was like he was staring down a tunnel. At the end, West lay on the ground in a crumpled heap as birds swooped too near.

"*I'm sorry.*"

Corwin closed his eyes, still hoping, but when he opened them again, he was alone on the bed.

"Damn it, West!" He stumbled to the door and slammed his palm against the lock, but nothing happened. Groaning, he popped the panel and punched in the override code. By the fifth attempt, he was forced to conclude that he wasn't escaping that way.

There had to be a way out. He was just afraid that his mind wasn't flexible enough to find it. He scanned the room, pivoting slowly and comparing it against the one in his memory. The furniture was all in the same place. The trick was going to be the shelves stacked with bits and pieces of West's life. No rhyme or reason to their placement, but he'd noticed that the first time he'd seen them.

Shelves one through three were exactly the same. Shelf four had an obvious mug-shaped hole in the dust, and Corwin grinned. Shelf five, predictably enough, was missing a cheap souvenir snow globe of the Jacquard Towers. Shelves six and seven were unchanged, and that took him to the desk.

More clothes, and he made a face. There had been clothes before, but he honestly hadn't paid enough attention to know if these were the same. That, and it just wasn't right to carelessly toss even clean underwear on a desk. That's why there were cabinets in all the crew quarters.

Working from right to left, he realized the stuffed hedgehog was gone. An old notebook still occupied the top corner, innards scattered around it where West had attempted to perform some sort of aborted repair work. Pictures of what he'd assumed were family members. Ah, there, right next to the picture of a gap-toothed little girl.

Corwin laughed softly. *The Heights of Inzerna*. His first novel, the one that still made him wince when he saw it on a store shelf. Of course West would find that one first. Picking it up, he thumbed idly through, stopping when he got to the first action scene: a shoot-out that ranged across an entire city, finally ending in an abandoned warehouse, where the hero managed to take out the crime lord and rescue his partner, all without getting a single scratch. It read as awkwardly as he remembered, and he couldn't imagine why West had chosen to keep it here, in this strange mental safe house.

He set it back down, then grabbed for the edge of the desk when a wave of dizziness swept over him. He missed the desk, hand landing heavily on the book instead, and suddenly he was falling forward in a long, sickening swoop.

CHAPTER 25

West lost his footing as the crack in the store became a chasm, but managed to keep his hold on the book. He hit the floor hard, wincing away from a damp patch he didn't think was water. Disby was on him in a second, and all he could throw out to protect himself was the truth he held in the palm of his hand.

He turned the book around, the pages reflected in Disby's glasses as they flipped by, horror after horror being stripped of the illusions Disby had caged them in. Disby recoiled, and West scrambled to the corner, backing into it and holding the book like a shield.

"What about all the others? Don't they matter?" Disby pushed closer to him, staring into the book screen, voice laced with desperation. "He killed those people, and we tried to stop him, but there was money, money enough to pay everyone off. I tried to, but his voice was so strong, and I wasn't expecting it." His hand trembled, hovering over the book when he looked up at West. "He killed them. He killed her. I *know*."

"Turn the page." Not sure what else he could do, he shoved the book at Disby again. If he could create enough distraction, he might be able to get D'lane out, but he wasn't going to be able to fight Disby at full strength. The raw power that surged and bent around the three of them was well beyond anything he'd ever dealt with before, and he couldn't think straight enough to formulate a plan if Disby was paying attention.

The page turned, and Disby seemed to disappear into it for a long time, until his head lowered, eyes falling shut. "He made me kill Anaj. But afterward, the rest of them . . . I could still hear his voice, but it wasn't him, was it? It wasn't D'lane. And they weren't her, and they didn't need to be her, but I made them be her."

Edging out of the corner, West glanced between Disby and D'lane. They were both victims, they were both killers, and it was his duty to keep them both safe long enough to bring them to trial. He had to get D'lane out before he could do anything for Disby.

"Can you let me go? I'll come back for you." It wasn't hard to be sincere. He couldn't leave Disby here alone, couldn't consign another person to pacing the space defined by their failures and guilt. "I won't leave you here, I promise."

Disby nodded, eyes never opening, knees hitting the floor as West slipped past. The room seemed smaller now, the walls closing in, and something pushed through one side. Disby didn't notice, but it was easy to see where the lights had dimmed around them, eaten up by the black cloud that misted out of nowhere and clung like a second skin, flickering in time with Disby's slow rocking.

D'lane's movements were eerily similar, but where Disby was just falling prey to the twisted things waiting in the dark, D'lane was already devoured by them. He barely moved when West gripped one shoulder, and the whispered, forced confession carried on. West managed to pull D'lane up, but if they were going to make it out before Disby stopped them, they had to be able to run. Disby had promised *him* safe passage—not him and D'lane.

The door was hidden in the book Disby was holding, but there was another door on the wall, and he thought he might be able to turn it into an exit if he pushed hard enough. He couldn't get the lock to turn, and the second time he tried, something smashed into it from the other side. He braced his hands against the door and shoved back. Nobody else could come in right now. He couldn't keep anyone else safe, and Disby was going to notice if the racket got any louder. He tried the door again, hoping he'd at least cleared the way, only to fall back into the shell of D'lane when something (*Some*one, *go away, please, I'm sorry.*) hit the wood, and it splintered a little.

"No, he has to stay. You're trying to let him get away with it." Exactly what he hadn't wanted. Disby's expression held only betrayal as he shuffled toward them. Before West could deny anything, even think up an explanation, Disby waved a hand, the tiny motion almost lost.

Power smashed into him with the kind of force he'd never really thought possible, crushing out the memory of a life without pain. He couldn't breathe, but that was almost a blessing, since it meant less of him was moving. D'lane was frozen, half-buried under him and muttering. Even though it was in all ways agony, West shifted himself over as best he could, trying to protect D'lane from anything else that might be thrown at them.

He heard the birds before they came, wings and feathers and displaced air in a rush that burned like acid over the expanse of his body. Disby had scoured him of his shields, crushing his walls and blowing holes in his filters. Wide open to everything, he risked the pain and clamped his arms over his ears, as though it would keep anything out. The tiny claws raking across his back felt like razor blades, and the impact of the flock, backed by Disby's unseen hand, was enough to drive him down, his forehead scraping against the bloody stone floor.

Corwin's first awareness was of gravel digging into his hands and knees; the second was the blaster jabbing his ribs. He blinked slowly, eased into a crouch, then stood up. At the end of a dark alley, windowless brick walls rose up on three sides. A quick inventory revealed skinned palms and a headache, but nothing obviously life threatening, and he settled for wiping his hands against his pants in an attempt to get the worst of the dirt off.

Lights from an occasional flyer washed across the end of the alley, illuminating a sidewalk piled high with trash, and Corwin hugged the wall as he cautiously made his way to the street. Overhead, the sky was a flat midnight blue, no suns, no moons, no stars, and when he looked up, it made him think of the inside of a closed box.

The sidewalk proved empty as well; nothing but boarded-up storefronts as far as he could see. He'd never been here before, but there was some niggling sense of familiarity that he couldn't ignore.

He was unprepared for the attack when it came, and he threw his hands over his head as the bird swooped down. Its claws brushed his hair before it swerved, and then there were at least a dozen, then two dozen, and they covered the fake sky like a sentient cloud. He closed his eyes as the feathers began to rain down, sharp pricks against his face and arms. It stopped as suddenly as it had started, the birds circling up into the otherwise empty sky like they had some other target in mind.

Stretching down the street in their wake was a path of black feathers.

He started walking, the feathers drifting up knee-high as he stepped on and over them. The trail wound unerringly on, with no change in either the width of the path or the depth of the feathers. Sometimes it ran in the street, sometimes on the sidewalk, turning corners so often that memorizing the steps was getting tricky, even for him.

Since leaving the alley, he'd seen no more flyers. No signs of life at all, now that the birds had disappeared. Even so, the gun was a comforting weight, riding at his hip. Not his IEC-issued weapon; this one looked newer, more substantial. He knew what it was, of course. Anybody who knew blast guns would recognize the bulked-up power of a Cougler, and anybody who'd wasted their time on his first book would know it was the weapon favored by the main character. Corwin double-checked the charge, and thumbed the safety lock off. He even spared a moment to be thankful he hadn't written in something useless, like a sword or an energy whip.

Time began to lose meaning, and while there was no sensation of being physically tired, he was starting to get bored. He tried slowing down a little, just to vary the monotony, but an immediate smothering feel of urgency forced him into a stumbling run until he'd made up whatever time he'd lost.

Ten more turns, and the urgency returned with a vengeance, except this time it was West, and he realized he'd never experienced someone else's fear, wasn't certain he'd truly known what fear was before this. What he'd thought was fear had been a touch of discomfort at most, maybe a bit of uneasiness, but nothing like this crushing dread. Hours (Days? Months?) ago, his and West's link had manifested visually; this time it was a physical sensation. Not quite pain, at least not pain as he would normally define it. This felt like something was being torn out of him—a long, continuous tug drawing him toward West.

A gust of wind dispersed the feather path, lifting them up into a cloud that thickened and coalesced into a flock of birds that in turn swirled back down, circling his head with shrieking cries. He ducked away until he realized they weren't actually touching him, each swoop merely raising a breeze that ruffled his hair.

With that worry gone, he focused on the link, letting it guide his feet as he pounded down block after block. His breath coming harder with each step, he was afraid he wouldn't be able to keep running, but he knew that if he didn't, the fear would completely overwhelm everything else. If he didn't keep running, he wouldn't be able to save West.

The staircase appeared so suddenly that he fell down the first three or four steps before catching himself on the rusty railing with a pained gasp. West was there, fear pulsing out from behind the door at the bottom of the stairwell in a steady flow. Corwin took the last steps in a staggering leap, and flung himself against the door shoulder first, once, twice, eyes closed as it splintered under him.

The door splintered inward, and the birds kept coming, the sound of them almost as terrible as the damage they were doing. West was afraid to look up, afraid they'd go for his eyes, his throat, fill his mouth with feathers and someone else's words like they had with D'lane. He ducked lower and tried to hold on.

Someone was calling his name, and he would have answered, but he was too busy being Disby, and D'lane, and Corwin. Corwin, who shouldn't have been there, Corwin, who he'd tried to leave safe on his bed because thinking about him here would only put him in danger. Corwin, who didn't fight with his Talent, only fucked and felt things. The birds were pecking him apart at the seams, and he missed Gavin, who always sewed him back together, patchwork and tiny stitches, so that only they knew.

"West!" Corwin was frantic for him, and that was sweet, but he didn't want the birds looking elsewhere. He felt their attention shift, Disby's interest wandering, and he couldn't have that at all, because it was his duty to keep people safe. The birds were still hitting him, but he pushed himself up anyway, kneeling over D'lane's pliant form and raising his voice to be heard over the whistles and cries.

"I'm going to tell everyone what you did to them. To all those people, and to Anajin."

Disby's attention snapped back to him, and the birds Corwin was batting away froze, like a faulty program hung up in processing. Disby's mouth moved, but the words came a second later. "You can't do that. I didn't do anything, it wasn't me."

"It was you. It's you who's hurting us now." If he was crafty, if he was clever and willing to risk spinning out like he'd done before, he thought he could pull it off. Disby wouldn't expect it. No PsyAc-trained Active would, and that brought him back to Corwin, who had to *leave*. Swallowing blood, he lifted a finger to point and stepped over D'lane, putting himself between Disby and the other two occupants of the room. "You hurt her for no reason, and I'm going to make sure everyone knows that you killed the birds. All the little sparrows, *squish squish squish* in your hands."

Cruelty personified, it worked better than he'd been expecting. The birds around Corwin disappeared, amassing like an army behind Disby. West looked over his shoulder, straight at Corwin, and whispered the three words he'd rather have yelled:

"Run, you idiot."

Disby didn't particularly need the second of inattention, but West was certain it helped. When he turned back, the birds were coming at him in formation, the great, sweeping wing of them seemingly endless. They shouldn't have fit in the room, but such was the nature of the mind. Free-form, expandable, and always able to surprise.

He held off as long as he could, waiting through an onslaught of fear so thick it felt like water. When they were too close, he took everything he had and pushed back, bricking up a wall so hard and fast that he could actually see it shimmer in the air between them. The birds shattered on impact, but they kept coming. He was going to lose, and whatever was left of D'lane's mind was going to die here, but he thought that maybe, if he tried hard enough, he could burn Disby out fighting him. At least he could keep everyone on the outside of this mess safe.

Something moved in the corner of his vision again, enough to distract him and let a bird through. It went for his face, and he let it, waiting until he could smack it aside with the back of his hand. He couldn't risk anything else when his heart was sinking and Corwin was moving up to stand next to him.

A blast gun was a relatively quiet affair, so the shot shouldn't have echoed the way it did, the sound rolling through like thunder. The birds scattered, some of them winking out of existence altogether. In a creeper-crawl that made no sense, the bright beam of light sliced through the flock and struck Disby in the throat. The second bolt took him between the eyes, and whatever was left of Christeven Disby after so long, after so much pain, was dead before he hit the ground.

Corwin half expected the room to disappear as Disby crumpled to the floor, expected *something* to change, and when it didn't, he turned to West. "Why are we still here?" he demanded as he shoved the gun back into the holster.

West swayed, the only color in his face the vivid streaks of blood. "He . . . Disby, he killed them, not D'lane." West's voice was broken, as if it had been screamed away, and Corwin had to grit his teeth and force that thought into the background for now. West grabbed his arm and shook it, almost knocking him off his feet. "It was Disby, all of them." West's gaze wandered before it jerked back to Corwin. "No, not . . . not all. Anajin, the others, the second ones. Not all the sparrows were his, but he was trying to keep the flock safe."

Corwin pried West's hand off his arm, but left their fingers linked together. "West, listen to me. We need to get out of here. Why are we still in Disby's head?"

"Because he killed them. No. No, wait." West shook his head, eyes clearing for a second. "He's not dead, not really, so the trap is still set. We have to follow the path back. I left bread crumbs, but I'm scared the birds got them."

The adrenaline rush was wearing off, leaving dread in its place—a terror that was gobbling up his ability to think rationally in huge, greedy mouthfuls. Whether he was ready to admit it or not, most of it was being fueled by the thought of losing West to this nightmare. West was slipping, and what he was saying wasn't always sane. Corwin gentled his voice. "What sort of path? Can you help me find it?"

"You were in my room. I wasn't really there, just a tiny part of me, but I wanted you to stay there. I wanted you to be there, with all the things I keep for myself," West said, as if that explained everything. "My head really hurts. I want to go home."

Realization flashed as bright as the blaster bolt, leaving the same afterimage behind his eyes. "Okay, we're going to go now. Can you walk?" D'lane still lay sprawled on the floor, blessedly silent now. If D'lane and West had to be carried out, he knew he wouldn't be able to handle them both. There was no doubt in his mind which of them he would sacrifice.

"Yeah, I can make it." West smiled, and while it was shaky around the edges, it seemed real. "I want a shower and some clean clothes."

"I think that can be arranged." He disentangled their fingers, waiting to make sure West wasn't going to fall over. "I need to get D'lane. Don't move, okay?"

He saw West's attention drift to Disby's body and then jerk back, focusing in on him with unnerving intensity. "Her name meant sparrow, and PsyAc teaches us how to find home no matter what, but they never teach us what to do when home isn't there anymore. I told you that Disby killed Anajin, right?"

"You told me." He kept his answer short, not wanting to delve into the reasons right now, and hoping West would hold on to enough of them to make sense once they were outside whoever's head they were still trapped in.

West laughed, the sound small and pained. "I'm scared I'll hurt Gav again someday. That's why I feel—felt—sorry for Disby. What if I'm no better than him?"

It was hardly the time to be comforting, and it wasn't a skill Corwin even possessed, but he grabbed West's shoulders and shook. "Don't be stupid. If you can't see the difference, I'll . . ." Words, of course, failed him, and he scowled.

"Never fuck me again?" West supplied helpfully, coherent for a moment. "Because that's a threat that would work."

"Right, okay, that."

D'lane was mobile, if uncommunicative, and he followed West when Corwin sent them both through the remains of the splintered door. Ducking out himself, he found them standing at the top of the stairwell, West staring apprehensively up at the sky.

"I'm pretty sure I'd be happy never seeing another bird."

He didn't bother replying, too busy reaching back into his memory. The feather path was gone as if it had never existed, and the only option left was retracing his steps from the map in his mind. If he missed a turn . . . He shook his head, pushing the thought away.

When he started walking, it felt like following the steps of a dance painted on a floor. Right, right, left, circle around, West and D'lane silent shadows at his back. He was so busy watching his feet that he didn't notice when the buildings started thinning out, fading first into vacant lots, then fields. Two more steps and the buildings disappeared completely, and they were walking through a meadow of knee-high grass.

Feeling safe to look up, he stretched out the kink in his neck. Above them, the sky expanded, losing the flat gray of the city and taking on the deep blue of a summer's day. There was a sun now as well, warm on his face.

West made a small, pleased sound, the first since the stairs. When Corwin turned to look, West's face was tipped skyward, eyes closed. "It's safe here. No birds."

"This is you, isn't it?" He already knew the answer. To be invited here wasn't the same as passing through on a quest, and he wanted confirmation that the warmth was real.

West nodded. "We can't stay. It's still a trap, just a nicer one." Expression guarded, West looked at him, then away to the summer landscape. "I'll get distracted here, trying to make things nice for us when I should be trying to get out."

The grass grew taller as they walked, brushing against his waist now with a quiet shushing sound. So continuous, so hypnotic that he almost missed the squeaky growl right under his feet. West laughed, pushing past him to kneel down and scoop up the hedgehog. When his hand closed around the tiny animal, a window slid open in front of him, rising smoothly in its wooden sash.

Corwin shrugged, calculating their options. "I guess we're climbing in." He stood back, waiting while West tucked the hedgehog into a pocket before hopping easily onto the window ledge, then swinging through to the other side and dropping out of sight.

D'lane required a push to get started, and then hesitated halfway through, body suddenly rigid. There was no time for niceties, and Corwin shoved hard, sending D'lane over the ledge, arms cartwheeling.

The shriek from the other side of the window froze him in the process of hoisting himself up, but then instinct sent him vaulting over, and he stumbled and hit his knees on the ground as he landed. He scrambled back to his feet, looking around and marking for threats, exits, and causalities. West was standing in the middle of the glass hallway, hands clenched and eyes wide with shock. Corwin followed his gaze and felt his stomach lurch.

D'lane was gone, but window after window held his face, a rictus mask of abject horror, mouth open in a scream locked behind the glass.

"He's home now. The birds came home to roost. Even though they were Anajin's birds, Disby made them a cage here." West's voice was barely audible, the shaking anger still easy to hear. "I should try to save him. It's my duty." Guilt made him look less like a strung-out version of himself, if only for a moment. "I can't do it, though. I didn't save enough of myself, and now I can't get in there. I was going to put them right in their heads, but one of us has to come out, and I'm the only one without a cage. We . . . we need to keep going. We're too far in, and the only way out is through."

It made sense to grab West's hand, squeezing tight as they inched their way up the middle of the hall, staring steadfastly at the floor. That's what he told himself, lying by sheer stubborn will as he pulled West away from the windows. Even so, D'lane's face still caught the corner of his eye if he let his attention slip even the slightest bit.

Eyes downcast, he almost stepped into the branching corridor before he realized it. The snow globe rolled under his feet, and he stopped abruptly, West running into his shoulder.

The snowstorm inside the globe raged, the towers almost completely obscured, cold seeping into his foot where the glass sphere rested against it. He released West's hand and stooped to pick it up. Tiny slivers of ice cut into his fingertips, and he hesitated when West held out a hand.

"Please?"

He nodded silently and dropped it into West's outstretched palm. Seemingly oblivious to the cold, West held it for a second or two. "The only way out is through," West repeated, and then, with no warning, threw the globe straight at the nearest window.

The glass exploded in a rain of razor-sharp shards, but worse than that, it released D'lane's cries. The scream was deafening, and as it rose, the other windows began to shatter, one after the other.

"Run!" Unable to tell if his voice carried over the combined cacophony of D'lane and breaking glass, he settled for dragging West to the corridor the snow globe had created beyond the broken window.

The sudden silence was nearly as deafening as the noise had been, and he swallowed hard over the ringing in his ears. The silence wasn't the only thing different this time. The doors were all open now, some splintered like the one to the basement room, some ripped entirely off their hinges. Whatever things had been inside the first time he'd passed through, howling and scratching to escape, were gone now. The rooms stood dark and empty, but he still flinched as they passed each one.

West sighed, the sound small and exhausted. "Disby killed them, but they're not sparrows anymore. They're people now, and he can't blame D'lane. He can't hide from them."

"They're not . . . they're not still here, are they?" The thought of stumbling into one of the murder victims was chilling.

West appeared to give the question some thought, head tipped to the side. Corwin had seen him like this before, this half-childlike fugue state, but always after a Read. During was unnerving. It took West a long time to decide, voice far away and almost singsong. "No. Disby had to turn the pages, and then they all broke free. Disby broke the birds, and you and the birds broke Disby." He reached down to pick up the shattered remains of a mug, *Psy* blazoned across the biggest piece in bright-pink letters. "It broke everything, though. It broke home, I can't feel it anymore. It broke everything."

Corwin refused to see the narrowing walls of their confinement, no matter how close they pressed. Disby might be gone, mind falling in on itself layer by layer, but he wouldn't leave West to that.

"Not everything." Fumbling for West's other hand, he aligned their fingers, wove them together, and thought of a *yet* they hadn't quite gotten to. "If you follow me, I'll take you home." West leaned against him, and shards of the real world cut tatters in the fabric of the illusion they were sharing. "Come home." His words echoed back to him as they fell, still hand in hand, still linked.

". . . two, three, four." Nika's voice sounded far away, sharp and frightened, and he knew he'd been hearing her for a while.

He wanted to tell her that everything was fine, not to be worried, but he was sliding into the familiar calm quiet of his own mind. It closed around him before he could find the voice to ask if he'd managed to get them both back or not.

CHAPTER 26

The picture frame on Ning's desk had cycled through three times before the chief inspector looked up from the completed case files and injury reports. Corwin was so focused on the smiling face of Ning's eldest child coming down a waterslide that he almost missed the quiet cough.

"Everything appears to be in order, other than your report, which I find perplexing. The words 'I was able to make contact with Agent Tavera and help him end the Read' come to mind, not so much because they fail to describe the situation in an observational manner, but because anyone who looks at both sides of this case file will immediately see that Agent Hale was unable to revive Agent Tavera. Even to the point that he couldn't trigger Agent Tavera's fail-safe phrase."

Corwin didn't shift in his seat, but only because as a rule, he didn't fidget. Ning was waiting for an answer, but to a question that hadn't been asked. He didn't really want to supply the right question, but he wasn't keen on answering the wrong one. "Agent Hale, being null . . ." He trailed off, not liking the way Ning's mouth was set.

"Agent Hale is trained to control and direct Agent Tavera, even in cases of extreme duress during a Read. Agent Tavera is trained to seek his partner out above all else if he finds himself in distress. They've spent two decades bailing each other out of trouble. You've known Agent Tavera for a grand total of two months. While I appreciate that you've grown to rely on one another as teammates, I need you to explain to me how it is that you were able to bring him out of a Read so deep that . . ." Ning dragged a finger down the screen, finding the relevant line before continuing. "Yes. A psychic episode so involved that Agent Hale was required to administer rescue breathing."

He'd spent four days not thinking about that, a model of avoidance the entire time. Coming back to find West still gone, Gavin pushing breath into his lungs between Nika's measured counts, was a feeling he hadn't been prepared for, and didn't ever want to try on for size again. Some of it must have shown in his face, because Ning's tone softened, features blending out into her female aspect as she spoke. "After what happened with the D'lane interview, I need your honesty on this. You have my discretion for the moment, but in return, I expect the truth. I can't have you in the field if you're in danger because you refuse to deal with a psy ability, Corwin."

He pushed himself out of the chair in front of her desk and poured himself a glass of water. "You're aware that I wasn't born an imperial citizen. I'm sure that if you've heard anything about Kaleia, it was something to do with the isolationist government." No matter what his ident papers said now, no matter how sincerely he'd meant his oaths to the Empire, he was born and bred Kaleian, and revealing himself would never feel right. "I'm sorry, I know you've granted me leeway, but I have to ask for more."

He turned back to the desk, unsurprised to find Ning returned to a neutral guise. "How much more are we talking about, Inspector? If you've broken the law in the name of your birthplace, I can't offer you immunity. As I'm sure you're aware, relations between the Empire and the Kaleian settlements are strained at best."

He raised an eyebrow, almost smiling. "Possibly because the Empire persists in referring to Kaleia as a settlement, despite five hundred years of independence." He set the glass down on the corner of Ning's desk, carefully aligned on a coaster, just to avoid saying anything for another few seconds. "I'm not a spy, if that's what you're worried about. But I have— Kaleia was a joint colony, Human and Akeloa. It was one of the last places the Akeloan plague hit, because of the isolation policies. And that blood is still present in the majority of Kaleian citizens. Most of them manifest some Talent for telepathy."

When Ning was angry, there was no escaping the feeling. It filled the room, thanks to Trakoran projection, but Ning's voice was without inflection. "Are you telling me that I've been sending an untrained telepath into the field? Please say that's not what you're telling me."

"Easy enough. I'm not untrained. I spent a decade in a highly regimented psy program, one every Kaleian enters as soon as they become Active. Until D'lane hit a particular trigger point, I'll swear on the imperial seal that it never once affected me or my duty to the IEC."

Ning sniffed something like a laugh. "But you're not Ylendrian."

"Yes I am, now. I left Kaleia. That means I don't get to go back. I chose the Empire, I chose my duty to the empress and to her citizens. I passed every IEC background check, and I know my communications were monitored for years. Ask Investigative Services if I've spoken to anyone from Kaleia since I took my imperial oaths. I got a card from the ambassador's office five months ago with three words on it: 'Mother is dead.' I'm surprised anyone bothered to tell me at all, since she made it clear I was no longer her son before I even left the planet."

Ning had every right to question him because of his background. Because he'd lied by omission for the entirety of his career. Every right, even though the IEC was his home, and he'd given everything he had to fit the mold carved for him by the life he'd chosen.

Though projection was a quirk a majority of Trakorans shared, most of them weren't terribly receptive, and Ning was no exception. When Corwin glanced up again to find Ning's features softening, he didn't bother to hide his glare.

"I'm not questioning your loyalty as a citizen, Corwin. I'm asking why you didn't trust us enough to tell us you're a psy."

He didn't want her affection, her pity, and the longer he glared, the further it faded, until only Ning's neutral guise remained, and the person he'd disappointed was his commanding officer. "Because my family disowned *me*, not the other way around. I don't want them hurt because I broke ranks. If a Kaleian overheard this conversation, I'd be considered guilty of treason, and my family would suffer for it. I'm trusting you with what amounts to a state secret; I'm trained in an entirely different method than someone at PsyAc would be. You can have Agent Tavera verify that, if you need to. You know how strong he is, and he thought I was as null as Agent Hale. Nothing about my physiology is a detriment to my work."

Ning seemed on more stable footing now. "You mentioned yourself that D'lane was able to exploit a vulnerability created by your Talent. You have yet to explain how it ties in with the discrepancies in your reporting."

Corwin winced, willing to bet that the phrasing meant Ning was well aware of the omissions on the report from the D'lane interview. "If I were still on Kaleia, I would most likely have formed a bond with another psy. It's one of the basic ideals of our—their—society, and through whatever accident of birth or breeding—" There wasn't enough water in the 'verse to cool his face down, but he drank the whole glass anyway before settling on a more succinct answer. "I've developed something like that bond with Agent Tavera. My abilities are entirely blocked on a day-to-day basis, but the creation of a bond necessitates a more open connection between the two people involved. It wasn't anything I had ever considered relevant, since I didn't work with psy teams, and I certainly didn't—"

Ning smiled at him, fingers steepled over the notebook between them. "I believe I understand. There's no need to elaborate on that particular topic. Unless— If it were you and Inspector Santivan, there would be something of an issue with your differing ranks, but the fraternization policy between IEC officers and PsyAc agents has always been of a more lenient nature. Did you want your medical and pension paperwork updated?"

Alarm coursed through him like ice in his veins, and he shook his head quickly. "Agent Tavera is not aware of the particulars. I'd rather this conversation, this *entire* conversation, remain as private as possible."

Ning nodded, scanning through the report again. Corwin appreciated the chance to pull himself together. Without looking back up, Ning prodded him on. "And this bond allowed you to reach Agent Tavera during his contact with Disby and D'lane?"

"Yes. It gave us a starting point that he and Agent Hale didn't have."

"I realize that some of this is embarrassing to you, but how much of it is truly confidential information?"

He took a seat again, curling his hands over the arms of the chair. "What have you ever heard about Kaleia, except that nobody is allowed to cross into planetary space without the express permission of the government? I'm sure you can imagine how much damage could be done to an entire planet of Readers if the information were made public. I'm not exaggerating my case to save my own secrets, Ning."

The silence while Ning stared at him was unnerving, but he didn't mind waiting it out. Eventually the chief inspector seemed to come to a conclusion. "You'll have to rewrite this, obviously. After speaking with you about your deep religious convictions, and their ties to the Kaleian isolation laws, I'm prepared to accept an amended statement that does not compromise your personal privacy or imperial diplomatic relations. I'll expect it tomorrow."

His mouth had gone dry again, so he nodded while trying to find his voice. "Certainly."

"Now, your involvement with Christeven Disby is another matter entirely. All four of you are quite clear in your personal statements that you knowingly broke regs to meet with him. And all four of you are lucky that this case is going to ground. It doesn't look good for anyone. It's messy. Command doesn't like that the D'lane family so obviously bought their way out of trouble. PsyAc doesn't like that Disby was a time bomb, and that somewhere out there, there's a lab still synthesizing Pezazuria. Neither of them like that there are at least twenty confirmed victims between the two, but they're both willing to take credit for *their* officers bringing down a dangerous killer."

"Who gets the blame, then? They were both killers."

Ning shrugged—not dismissive, but clearly as stumped as he was. "I honestly think they're hoping all of it will blow over before they have to acknowledge that. Typical, but not satisfying. Did you see the toxicology report on Disby?"

Ning held out the notebook, showing him the medical results, and he couldn't help a low whistle. "West said the drugs made his Talent stronger. That it was a common side effect of Pezazuria before it was banned. According to this report, that was the only drug in Disby's system at all. How did he manage that?"

Ning's nonplussed expression and the arch tone only cemented the feeling that he'd stepped in it. "I imagine a person can come into possession of just about any substance they want on Corve. Was that your impression, Inspector Menivie?"

"Had I traveled there recently, I might concur with that, yes." Why in the hell he'd finished his water, he wasn't sure. The urge to cough had to be a tickle in his throat, rather than the desire to give himself away.

"From the impressions Agent Tavera has been able to give us, it seems likely that Disby knew about the effects of the drug, and had been taking abnormally large doses for several months. While it can increase an Active's psionic ability, it also causes hallucinations and severe delusional episodes, and it's known to lower inhibitions."

"Right. Ill-advised sex with strangers." Giving up on the appearance of aloof, professional composure, he dropped his face into his hands and rubbed his temples. "So essentially, Disby went looking for a way to overpower D'lane and avenge his Ground, and managed to experience the perfect combination of side effects to send him completely over the edge."

"I have no idea what kind of sex he was having, but I'd agree with your theory on the rest. Agent Tavera seems to think the psychotic break occurred before Disby ever pharmed out, but he's not having any luck pressuring PsyAc into releasing those records. Like everything else from the first D'lane case, they've been sealed." Ning watched him, but he held still under the scrutiny, keeping rein on his emotions.

"You said they were going to separate facilities, right?" He couldn't imagine that the pension for PsyAc burnouts covered anything so grand as the secured psychiatric hospital the D'lane family could afford, but he also couldn't imagine there were many places willing to take uncontrolled psionic murderers as patients.

"Anders D'lane's family has requested that he be placed as close to Vimto as possible, while Disby will be sent to the PsyAc hospital on Windling. Further testing will be done to monitor both of them, but it's been deemed highly unlikely that either will ever recover enough to be tried for their crimes."

He'd worked cases that had ended in psychiatric convictions before, some rightly so. But it rankled him this time, when he thought of the deflection, the trail of taunting evidence laid out in blood and bodies halfway across the 'verse. "Disby created an entire case against D'lane. He profiled victims who matched D'lane's original patterns, who already existed on the fringes of society. When that didn't work, he managed to break into one of the most secure facilities in the Empire, steal DNA samples that reflect part of the imperial genetics patent, and completely change his methodology to convince us that D'lane was killing again."

He paused to draw a breath, the tight knot in his gut forcing him to accept how hard the case had hit him. "Disby's crimes made sense to him—at first because I think he wanted to believe someone would care about the kinds of people D'lane targeted. When he saw the case falling apart... I think he lost what little faith he had that the IEC was capable of providing justice for his 'sparrows,' and he chose to mimic D'lane so he could plant the evidence. Those may not be *sane* actions, but they aren't the actions of someone unaware of what he's doing."

West could sympathize with Disby, but Corwin couldn't stomach letting it pass. "If Christeven Disby ever crawls out of the pit he dug for himself, he needs to spend the rest of his life in a lockdown room."

"From what West has told me, that's where he *is* spending the rest of it, even if he doesn't recover." One long, triple-jointed finger tapped the back of the notebook. "Not that it matters, but Disby hired someone to break into Slipstream Labs for him. An Elisha Saporza, but that's a known alias for Cassilia Rheingild, who's been off the grid entirely since the day after the break-in. It's another point in favor of him being highly functional. I suppose he may have killed her, but given how public he made the other murders, chances are good she's alive."

Corwin snorted. "Wonderful. So *if* he's ever accountable for his crimes, we'll have a character witness. I hope we're able to dig up someone as exciting for D'lane. Maybe Agent Tsan can tell us her version of events via séance. While we've got her on the line, maybe she can explain Disby's sparrow fetish."

Ning's trill of amusement was unexpected. "I'm sure she could, since 'Anajin' means 'sparrow' in Trakoran."

"I knew I should have picked up a third language. I suppose I'll have plenty of time to take a class during my suspension."

The tension returned full force, and he immediately regretted his sarcastic quip when Ning's lips pursed. "I don't like what you did, any of you, but I understand that the corruption surrounding the previous case with D'lane left you very few options." The tempo of the tapping against the notebook increased, betraying agitation until Ning set it facedown on the desk. "I want to make it clear to all of you that in the future, I expect you to choose options that comply with IEC policy. I'm disappointed that what should be a triumph for this department, and your team, has devolved into something best kicked under a rug and forgotten about."

As dressing-downs went, it was so mild it barely registered, but Corwin took it in and knew that the disappointment wasn't just for show. The officer he'd been two months ago would never have stepped outside those lines, and in all honesty, the officer he'd become since then didn't enjoy it either. The man he'd discovered below the officer, though, couldn't be content without making a point of order. "I'm sorry, Chief Inspector. None of us were thinking much past stopping the deaths of imperial citizens."

"Which is why I'm going to edit your reports, let you get away with saying that, and shove you back into the sky. At least you're only a remote pain in my ass that way." Ning stood, and he followed suit, bowing because Ning had always respected his desire not to shake hands. "Your medical leave ends in two days, Inspector. I'll have a list of cases waiting for you when you return."

The corridor was nearly empty when he slipped out the door of Ning's office, and as always, the planetary light on Rogena seemed far too bright, even filtered through the bars over the dirty polyglass windows. He didn't do anything as dramatic as collapse against the wall, but he would have allowed himself a second to catch his breath, if not for his companion waiting in the hall.

He and West didn't touch as they walked out of the IEC building, and neither of them said anything much until West spotted a pastry cart and left Corwin's side. He returned a few minutes later with a couple of fruit-filled pies, and waited until Corwin took a bite before asking him anything.

"So? Did Ning go with the whole 'I have a secret psychic bond in progress' thing?"

Corwin nodded, carefully walled off. "Yes. And I can't believe I let you talk me into lying to our commanding officer about one of the cornerstones of my former society."

West gave him an odd look, making it painfully obvious that he had something to say that discretion had caged in. The moment passed, and apparently West's better judgment with it. "I can't believe you think I don't know you were almost telling the truth."

"I have better things to do than build an emotional sand castle with you, Tavera." Like getting another pie, or styling his hair by sticking his head out of an airlock.

West turned and started wandering down the sidewalk, regrettably in the opposite direction of the pastry cart. Heaving the put-upon sigh that seemed well on its way to becoming West's nickname, Corwin followed.

"Thank you for coming in after me." West didn't even bother to turn around to say it, like it was something anyone might casually mention on a street corner. "I wouldn't have made it back out, if you hadn't."

Nika's counting had been hitting him at the strangest moments for the past few days, the memory of her voice marking off the time between the breaths West should have been taking. It was probably because it was the first thing he'd heard as he'd come back to himself, but that didn't stop him from grabbing West's arm now.

"Look, if you really want another pastry—"

He knew he wouldn't get the words right if he tried, so he solved the problem by kissing West. Right there on the sidewalk, people shuffling past and West's dry lips soft against his. He held on until he was sure, until their heartbeats seemed to match and their minds buzzed pleasantly against walls neither of them wanted to let down in the middle of a busy city avenue. He kissed West until the breath against his lips was coming just a little too fast, and he felt safe enough to back a half step away, still at a loss for words.

West's smile was full of misplaced understanding, and he filled the silence for them. "I was just teasing. You don't have to say—"

Corwin cupped his cheek, relaxing just enough to cut him off. *"'Yet' was the second your eyes closed on that ship. I needed you back with me. That's all. It's fine if you don't feel—"*

West rolled his eyes, grabbing the front of Corwin's shirt and yanking him closer. "I don't love you, either," he said, but his kiss was demanding, and his mind was open to Corwin's, and full of joy.

It was the best lie Corwin had ever heard.

Explore more of the *Ylendrian Empire* universe:
riptidepublishing.com/titles/discretion-ylendrian-empire-novella

Dear Reader,

Thank you for reading Reesa Herberth and Michelle Moore's *Peripheral People*!

We know your time is precious and you have many, many entertainment options, so it means a lot that you've chosen to spend your time reading. We really hope you enjoyed it.

We'd be honored if you'd consider posting a review—good or bad—on sites like **Amazon, Barnes & Noble, Kobo, Goodreads, Twitter, Facebook, Tumblr,** and your blog or website. We'd also be honored if you told your friends and family about this book. Word of mouth is a book's lifeblood!

For more information on upcoming releases, author interviews, blog tours, contests, giveaways, and more, please sign up for our weekly, spam-free newsletter and visit us around the web:

Newsletter: tinyurl.com/RiptideSignup
Twitter: twitter.com/RiptideBooks
Facebook: facebook.com/RiptidePublishing
Goodreads: tinyurl.com/RiptideOnGoodreads
Tumblr: riptidepublishing.tumblr.com

Thank you so much for Reading the Rainbow!

RiptidePublishing.com

ACKNOWLEDGMENTS

Special thanks to Tammy and Shan, for beta reading and cheerleading.

No Disbys were harmed in the making of this book.

MORE STORIES FROM THE
YLENDRIAN EMPIRE
BY REESA HERBERTH & MICHELLE MOORE

The Balance of Silence
The Slipstream Con

ALSO BY
REESA HERBERTH

In Discretion (A Ylendrian Empire Novella)

ALSO BY
MICHELLE MOORE

If Wishes Were Coffee
Beach Patrol

ABOUT THE AUTHORS

MICHELLE MOORE has a well-documented obsession with travel, television, frappuccinos, and flamingos. These, however, come in a distant second to her love of writing. Most evenings she can be found huddled over her laptop at the local coffee shop, dividing her time between actually writing and pretending to be a barista. While Michelle would like to claim child prodigy status, the truth is that she's only been scribbling words on paper since she was six. However, she's moved beyond those initial Dick and Jane story knockoffs to slightly more adult topics (but not necessarily more mature characters).

Michelle has discovered that romance, her genre of choice, just so happens to do that peanut-butter-n-chocolate thing with such varied flavors as science fiction, magical realism, and historicals. No matter which mishmash she chooses, though, her style tends toward the sweet end of the spectrum. You can email her at MichelleMooreWrites@gmail.com.

REESA HERBERTH grew up in Hawaii, tried Arizona for a few years, and eventually settled in the DC area, where they have trees and rain.

She's held a variety of crazy writer jobs, including book and video store manager for a defunct chain of music shops, office goddess for an artisan ice-cream maker, cheese-cup scrubber at an organic goat dairy, high school secretary, and dye-stained proprietress of a small yarn and fiber business.

When not writing, she can usually be found reading, gardening, cooking, or spinning yarns of another sort entirely. She often resents her need for sleep. She welcomes your email at YlendrianEmpire@gmail.com.

Connect with Reesa and Michelle:

Reesa on Twitter: @reesah

Michelle on Twitter: @MarigotC

Facebook: facebook.com/pages/The-Ylendrian-Empire

Websites: michelleandreesawrite.com and ylendrianempire.com

Enjoy more stories like *Peripheral People* at RiptidePublishing.com!

The Tide of War
ISBN: 978-1-62649-265-3

Lucky Strike
ISBN: 978-1-62649-195-3

Earn Bonus Bucks!

Earn 1 Bonus Buck for each dollar you spend. Find out how at RiptidePublishing.com/news/bonus-bucks.

Win Free Ebooks for a Year!

Pre-order coming soon titles directly through our site and you'll receive one entry into a drawing to win free books for a year! Get the details at RiptidePublishing.com/contests.